Cape Seduction

By

Anne Carter

Beacon Street Books

Contemporary Romantic Suspense

Beacon
Street
Books

CAPE SEDUCTION
by Anne Carter

Beacon Point Romance – Book Two

All rights reserved.

Copyright © 2014, 2019 by Pamela Ripling
Cover © by Pamela Ripling

Print ISBN 978-0-692-25064-8

Previously Published under ISBN: 978-1-59080-678-4

Published In the United States Of America

November, 2019

Beacon Street Books
Santa Clarita, CA 91355-2026
http://www.beaconstreetbooks.com

Cape Seduction:

"Romance, a lighthouse, suspense, a California setting; a double story, the golden years of Hollywood, and ghosts...this book has everything. The author does a fantastic job of keeping the suspense going and both stories mutually interesting. The ending is satisfying for both romance and mystery readers.

"I love the way the author has researched her topic and brings in lots of references to old movies and lighthouses. It is clear that she knows her subject and has a talent for weaving it into a very interesting story. Anne Carter's first lighthouse mystery, Point Surrender was great, so I was really looking forward to Cape Seduction and I was not disappointed!"

Angel's Gate:

"This is the third in the series, and while they each revolve around different lighthouses, they have overlapping characters. Her books are insanely easy to read, and always have an element of mystery, romance, history and a touch of supernatural. I believe that this installment may be her best.

"This story pulls together quite a few characters from past books, plus a couple of new ones...a young Hopi Indian man and an absolutely adorable young South American woman... I appreciated this truly pure, uncomplicated love story between these two new characters. No drama, no cheating, no games, no lying, just two people who are loyal to each other and their friends. Like a breath of fresh air. I also love that the author has incorporated so much cultural diversity here.

"This book is an excellent, historical mystery. One that I read in record time, one where I felt GOOD when I finished it."

Cape Seduction - Excerpt

A metal staircase clung to the wall on her left, and she started up it with some trepidation, encountering a series of small rooms as she climbed. Stone steps led up into the tower. After passing a rudimentary laundry room, Rebecca carefully made her way up to the galley where the sink had been ripped from the wall, and tattered, rotted curtains blew into the room through a small, broken window. Cabinet doors stood open, with various bits of debris evident on the shelves. Rebecca snapped away, shooting the scene while holding her breath.

"Okay. Pretty worthless so far." She continued on up the stairs inside the tower, which remained much the same, she thought, as they must have been for the past one hundred years. Although dirty and cracked, the risers proved solid if noisy. She passed two levels of sleeping quarters. Again she felt winded as she reached the lantern room.

"Whoa. Now *here's* my shot." Rebecca took pictures from every angle of the gallery, even zooming in on Bill as he sat on the landing staring out at the sea. She shot the stairwell, the glass, the empty hole where the lighthouse's lens once turned. Carcasses of two dead birds lay at her feet. Looking back at the shore, she shot off a round of photos encompassing the Del Norte coastline.

She sought the bedrooms next. As in the other parts of the house she'd explored, decay was prevalent. In the lower room, a bed frame, its mattress bare, pushed forlornly into one corner. Rebecca marveled at its former beauty: solid brass with an ornate, filigreed headboard. A boudoir table, with a French beaded lamp, stood beside the bed, its elegant mirrors cracked and in pieces. And junk. Everywhere. Unpleasant and uninteresting.

Rebecca sighed, disappointed. She didn't know what she'd expected to find. She started to retreat from the room when something in the corner caught her eye. A small, wooden piece of furniture, buried beneath rotting blankets. With pinching thumb and forefinger, she carefully peeled back the cloths to reveal a stunningly beautiful baby cradle.

"Hel-lo. This is cool. This is very cool." Rebecca squatted, leveling her camera, but the darkness precluded a good shot. She dug the flashlight out of her pocket and propped it onto the discarded pile of bedclothes, then looked through the lens again. Long a proponent of available light photography, she turned the focus ring until the poorly lit cradle became clear. She rocked forward, readjusted the lens. *No, a little closer. The cradle should be framed just so...* She edged nearer, moving the wide-beamed flashlight to get more light onto the subject. Again she lifted the camera and peered through the viewfinder.

Her breath caught in her throat. What she saw forced a small cry from her lips and she almost dropped her camera. A baby, lying very still, peered through the wooden slats on the side of the tiny bed. Her wits only momentarily derailed, Rebecca snapped the shutter three times in quick succession, then grabbed the flashlight and rushed forward to peer into the cradle.

Empty.

Rebecca's jaw dropped. She'd seen the infant, a real, living baby, inside that cradle, its tiny hand raised in a baby-tight fist, its large eyes staring, its bow-like mouth working. Now, feeling around in the bed, Rebecca found only a badly tarnished silver rattle. She stood and looked around, as if someone might be watching her incredible encounter.

"I saw it." She pulled the baseball cap from her head and ran her shirt sleeve across her forehead, moist with perspiration. Swallowing hard, she stared down at the cradle, then brought the camera back to eye level. No baby. Empty bed. Silver rattle.

Rebecca pocketed the rattle and issued a shuddering sigh.

It was real. A real baby.

Dedications

John Gibbons
U.S. Coast Guard, Retired, and Former Keeper at
St. George Reef Lighthouse.
*Thank you, Gibby, for the interview, the stories,
the photographs and all your kindness.*

Dennis M. Powers
Author, *Sentinel of the Seas: Life and Death at the Most
Dangerous Lighthouse Ever Built.*
For your time and for finding Gibby for me!

Sue Ramage and Laura May
First readers extraordinaire
*Your interest and confidence
really buoyed this project.*

Bob and Sandra Shanklin
"The Lighthouse People," photographers.
*How could you have known how
perfect this photo would be?*

Karen Syed
Echelon Press, LLC
*Brave soul, mentor, and passionate publisher.
Your faith is so appreciated!*

St. George Reef Lighthouse Preservation Society
Crescent City, CA
*Keep up the good work!
Hold that next helicopter for me!*

To the late
Huell Howser
California's Gold (PBS)
For my first glimpse inside this charming relic!

To the late
Alice White
Hollywood Actress
*If only you could be here to star
in the role you inspired!*

and

**Tina Fumarolo, Alyssa Montgomery,
and Cheryl Norman**
My supporters and editors
Surely couldn't have done this without you!

One

P ea soup.

Rebecca Burke squinted at the road ahead, hoping to make out the taillights of the car in front of her.

Fog is nothing like soup. Not green, not hot, not tasting like some disgusting pureed legume.

The eerie silence unnerved her. She snapped on the radio and twisted the knob in search of something other than talk or rap. Settled on Garth Brooks.

Coast Highway ran only two lanes in either direction, and Rebecca kept to the right, nervously alternating between gas pedal and brake. She wasn't used to this thick, cottony mist. Dense fog almost never occurred back in Phoenix. She focused her attention on the white abyss before her. Surely it would burn off soon.

Was anyone behind her? Quick glances into the rearview mirror revealed nothing but retreating gray. *Perhaps I've entered the Twilight Zone,* she thought, trying to conjure a chuckle.

As the roadway swept around the base of a steep cliff, Garth's warble turned to noisy static. Rebecca reached for the tuner, intending to search for a stronger signal. Out of nowhere, a car charged past her on the left, churning up a brief clearing before being swallowed by the whiteness ahead. Startled, Rebecca's heart quickened, and she took tighter control of the steering wheel. She considered pulling over, but since she couldn't see the roadway to the side, she hesitated, slowed her speed even more. But what if a faster motorist hit her from behind?

The radio static grew. Rebecca again attempted to tune in something more agreeable, pausing when she discerned traces of a

1

female voice behind the noise. Just a word, here and there. "Time has come...find me..." Rebecca frowned, concentrating as she listened.

Again she checked her mirror. Seeing nothing, she started to pull her eyes back to the road when something appeared. A face, a woman's face, stared at her from the backseat.

A shockwave bolted through Rebecca's body at the sight. Grasping the steering wheel, she hit the brake, pulled the Volkswagen off the highway, and came to a skidding stop. She quickly twisted around, stared hard at the empty seat, the floor, the back window, and the fog.

I must be losing it.

Fortunately, there was a wide, flat shoulder where she'd left the highway. She looked to her left where the occasional car rushed by, traveling south. To the right, the fog lay heavy over the Pacific Ocean. Garth had resumed his mournful tale of unrequited love.

Rebecca smacked the *off* button on the radio, leaned back in her seat, closed her eyes. Clearly, her anxiety had caused a hallucination. There was no one in the car with her. She could barely recall the details of the woman's face, so brief was the vision. For a moment, she wondered if she'd seen her late mother's face; she'd dreamed about Mom just the night before. Heart still pounding, she opened her eyes and peeked into the rearview mirror. Nothing obstructed her view of the back window and the menacing fog beyond.

At 9:00 a.m. the sun hung somewhere overhead, lamely trying to burn through the clouds. The VW died; she twisted the key in the ignition, without result. No starter, only the futile clicking that usually foretold a dead battery. Eyeing the instrument panel in disgust, she thumped the steering wheel with the heel of her hand. The check engine light glared back at her, so there had to be some juice left.

Rebecca tried again to re-start the car to no avail. With a sigh, she reached for her wallet and cell phone, dialed, and peered again into the rearview mirror while waiting for an answer. This time, only her hazel eyes stared back. She shoved her bangs back off her forehead just as the tow service came on the line.

"I'm not exactly sure where I am. Somewhere near Crescent City. I know I passed an RV campground a few miles back. No, I don't have PGS or GSP or whatever it is." *Like I really want some satellite keeping track of me.*

The tow service dispatcher had more patience than she did, but Rebecca found it hard to be friendly, especially after hearing it might be an hour before someone would be by. "Well that's just grand," she muttered, slapping the cell phone closed before tossing it into her backpack on the passenger seat.

I can't just sit here. Reaching behind her to the rear floor, Rebecca grabbed her black camera bag and stepped out of the car, quickly walking around to the passenger side. Cars whizzed past, their drivers oblivious to her plight. She dug her digital SLR camera out of the bag, draped the woven strap around her neck and then popped open the trunk and dropped the empty camera bag in.

Carefully, she perused her surroundings, her photographer's eye searching for a subject. She hated the waste of time. There had to be something worth shooting. She didn't mind the grayness– she'd shot some of her best work in black and white–but there still had to be subject matter.

A lone gull sat atop a nearby trash can. Tentatively spreading its wings, the bird begged for attention.

"Forget it, pal. I've already got your mom, dad, and cousins on film."

Rebecca walked unhurriedly through the mist in the direction of the surf, still wishing she'd happen upon an interesting angle or unusual sight. There was nothing, and why should there be? Nothing else had gone right today, from the power outage in her hotel, which caused her to be late and almost cost her the job, to the breakdown of her car and the wait for the driver. Not to mention the ridiculous hallucination that had driven her off the road in the first place. Now here she stood, wasting valuable travel time walking on Nowhere Beach, California, USA.

She finally found a log big enough to sit on. Not comfortable but a tolerable perch while she waited. The fog lifted while the clouds thinned in response to the sun's persistence. Rebecca glanced back at the highway. Her car had recently been serviced and had received a clean bill of health, damn it! Yet it quit running when she pulled off the road. Died. No illness, no accidental cause of death. She huffed out a sarcastic chuckle. What next? A tsunami?

Shaking her head slowly, Rebecca could see the oncoming waves now. She imagined them to be like a string of small white animals, all rushing toward her before losing their collective nerve and retreating quickly back to the safety of the ocean.

Forced relaxation. She closed her eyes, tried for that calm, centering peace her yoga instructor always raved about. *I need a vision. Something soothing. Something–*

Rebecca's eyes fluttered open, and she felt the sting of threatening tears. The vision rising before her mind's eye did not offer tranquility. The face of the woman in the rearview mirror returned, and while she still couldn't be sure the image was her mother, fresh grief inexplicably washed over her.

"I don't need this," she murmured. "I don't need this at all."

Rebecca unlaced and took off her sneakers and socks, neatly stacking them on the log. *This water will be freezing.* She edged toward the wet sand, camera swaying below her chest. "Freezing," she repeated aloud as the first small rush of foam-crested seawater lapped at her feet. Still, she stood grounded, mesmerized by the thinning fog. There were rocks, some boulder-sized, in the waters before her, becoming visible as the waves crashed against them. The odd beam of sunlight, here and there, painted the individual rocks with an ethereal glow, intriguing her as the water sprayed up with each pounding wave.

Transfixed upon one huge rock miles out, Rebecca slowly brought her camera to her face, peered through the viewer as she focused on the rock, which, through the telephoto lens, turned out to be a small island with some sort of structure on it. Shrouded by remnants of mist clinging to its sides stood a building, as gray as the fog surrounding it, built on an islet barely large enough to support it.

Snap. Snap. Snap. The shutter worked its magic, stealing moments of time, freezing the waves, the spray, the birds, the rocks and the odd little structure on her micro memory card. The haze rapidly dissolved as Rebecca snapped away, and she moved closer as she filmed. Suddenly, the sun broke cleanly through the sparse clouds, evaporating the remaining fog, giving Rebecca a clear view of the island and its lone structure. She smiled as she lowered the camera, squinted into the sunlight, making sure the image spied through the lens wasn't some new mirage. No; her eyes, unaided by lens and filters, looked directly upon a lighthouse.

Maybe her luck was changing.

"Just sign here."

"Even though you didn't do anything?"

The tow truck driver shrugged. "Hey. I drove down here from Crescent City. I did something. Not my problem there's nothing wrong with your car, lady. You should be glad."

Rebecca frowned and took the pen he offered. "Know where I could get a decent motel room?" she asked, scribbling "I.M. Stupid" illegibly on the form.

"Straight ahead about two miles there's a Best Western. Clean. Got a coffee shop."

"Thanks," Rebecca said, handing the clipboard back.

"You're not from around here," he said, noting the time on his watch and jotting it onto the form.

"Nope." *Duh.* Could the Arizona license plates have clued him in? Phoenix seemed like a million miles away. Digging into the hip pocket of her jeans, she pulled out some ones and handed them to the driver. "You know anything about that lighthouse out there?"

The driver pocketed the tip and looked up. "No," he said, staring straight into Rebecca's eyes. "Nothing." He turned to go.

"Is it still in use?" Rebecca asked, following the man to his truck.

"No. It's not occupied anymore. *Es vacante. Abandonado.* "

"Is there any way to get out there?"

"Not many guys are willing to take a boat out there. Killer rocks." He hesitated. "There is one guy. He's in town," he said, motioning over his shoulder toward Crescent City. "He might. Ask at the bait shop."

"Thanks," Rebecca murmured and stood back to watch as the tow truck merged into traffic. She paused, looking from the VW back to the lighthouse, then to the road and the southbound traffic. She had time to kill. Her rescheduled appointment wasn't until late afternoon, and she now felt compelled to stay on the beach for a while.

From the trunk she dug out her father's binoculars and her aluminum accessory case. She selected a telephoto lens from the case, swiftly exchanging it onto the camera body, then grabbed the binoculars before heading back to the driftwood log. Bracing her elbows on her knees, she leveled the camera before her eye and snapped a few frames before turning the camera sideways, framing the lighthouse vertically.

Something was different now. The water line rose higher on the rocks, the tide rolling in.

"I wonder how far it is," she said, tilting her head and trying to figure the distance between the beach and the island.

Perhaps her client would know. He might even be able to see the lighthouse on a clear day, as his home perched on a bluff not too far north of where she sat.

Soon, she rested her camera in her lap and lifted the binoculars to her eyes. The lighthouse looked old, gray and beaten. Tall, a squarish tower rising from the center of an immense oval base. Rebecca's mind searched for a word. Forlorn. Cold. *Forgotten.*

The waves crashed, relentless in their attack on the small rock, almost as if the sea was trying to reclaim it, to destroy the man-made structure and return the islet to its natural state. Build–crash–retreat: the water glistened over the rocky island base as it trickled back into the sea. Rebecca wondered what the lighthouse looked like inside. *Who had lived there? Was it scary, being surrounded by water, all alone out there? Who owned it now, and why did they allow it to fall into such disrepair?*

There were answers, Rebecca was sure. Adjusting the focus, she made one more perusal of the island. Moving slowly in order to take in the smallest detail, Rebecca noticed something she'd not seen before. Something red, a small figure, perhaps, at the top of an external stairway on the base below the lighthouse. She strained to hold the binoculars steady, squinting her eyes.

A woman.

Taken aback, Rebecca started, her focus lost. She struggled to locate the same spot, and when she did, the stairway was empty.

"How strange," she murmured, re-examining every section of the stairway and its surrounding structures. No signs of life. Could the woman have gone inside?

At noon, she reluctantly packed her equipment, put her shoes and socks back on, and returned to her car, hoping to find the motel with the coffee shop close by. She sighed with relief when the VW started and she eased out onto Coast Highway.

The laptop grabbed the Wi-Fi signal right away. Rebecca took a large bite out of the apple she'd brought back from the convenience store, then placed her fingers on the keyboard, carefully typing in the name her client gave her: *Dragon Rock Lighthouse*. She chose the most informative looking link and clicked. Her eyes raced over the words, unable to pause for even a moment. She had to know everything about the lighthouse, and fast.

"Abandoned in 1947...failed attempt by local preservation society to gain ownership in 1988...shown in backdrop for *The Keytooth Affair*, Sandstone Productions, 1996..." She read aloud to herself, nibbling on the apple as she reviewed site after site. "Ownership is private...identity veiled by corporate documents...no plans to restore the property at this time."

She found photos, of course, many of them from a time when the lighthouse was young and in good condition. Rebecca leaned close to her screen, poring over each picture. "Just over six miles offshore. Built in 1891...also seen in the film *Cape Seduction*, MGM, 1948."

Cape Seduction. Her father was an old movie buff. She picked up her cell.

"Dad? It's me. Yeah, still in Northern California. My shoot went off great when I finally got there. He has a '34 Packard, Eleventh Series Eight Convertible. Yeah, pristine. I shot it in a kind of *film noir* look. Hey, speaking of films, did you ever see a movie called *Cape Seduction*?"

He paused and with a mumble, her father reached into his memory. "Let me see. Seduction. Hmm."

Rebecca found herself drumming fingernails on the desk. "It might have had a lighthouse in it..."

"Lighthouse. Oh, yeah! Hell, that must've been...1938..."

"Forty-eight."

"Yep. Errol Flynn was the hero, I believe. Is he even still alive? Oh, what a Casanova, let me tell you. Friends with Doug Fairbanks, Olivier, you know, that whole gang. The woman was a new actress, back then, anyway. Can't remember her name right off. Young, real pretty, dark hair."

"Did she make any other films you can remember?"

"Nope. Now that I think on it, I don't think we ever saw her again. Your mother, God love her, she...she really liked that picture."

Her father went silent as they both thought about Rebecca's mother, dead for over fifteen years. Jebediah Burke still grieved. Rebecca flushed at the memory of her surreal experience in the car that morning, and her thoughts about her mother. *Shake it off, Bec.*

"Thanks, Daddy. I saw this lighthouse today, and for some reason, I just got crazed to know all about it. So. How's the weather there?"

"You know what they say. In Phoenix we have two temps, hot and hotter. It's only hot right now."

Rebecca chuckled. "Hey, I'll be home in a week. I have about ten more cars to shoot for the magazine. Love you."

She tossed in bed, her sleep broken into short, fitful naps. As she twisted restlessly beneath the sheets, visions of a nameless face appeared in settings, familiar and yet out of place. A woman sat behind the wheel of a 1944 Packard. *A Brown Bomber,* her father said, nodding in approval. The woman smiled from behind dark glasses. Smiled, yet Rebecca shuddered at the appearance of a single tear sliding down the fading cheek of the driver. *Wait,* she called out, wanting badly to remove the sunglasses from the woman's face. The car drove away. Her father bowed his head.

Rebecca awoke fatigued but determined to get moving on her plan. At 8:00 a.m. she phoned Pat, her boss, hoping he'd had his first cup of coffee. Even two.

"Okay, I have this excellent idea for a photo story. You ready? Lighthouses."

"Lighthouses? And why would our readers care about lighthouses? Isn't that a bit too cozy-romantic-sappy for our jet-setting subscribers?"

"How about mystery, intrigue, weird history?"

"What sort of weird history?"

"Well, I don't know yet. But I will. There must be thousands of lighthouses around the U.S., and they all have stories, right? There's even one right here, not more than ten miles from where I'm staying." She decided not to share her sighting of the woman in red.

"Where you *were* staying. You have to be in Sacramento by 5:00 p.m., right?"

Rebecca groaned inwardly. What a stick-in-the-mud. She tried again.

"Our readers are wealthy travelers with a variety of interests. Lighthouses have an aura...they're different, out of the ordinary, unique places of history where people risked their lives every day to protect our coasts." Paraphrasing the website still on her screen, Rebecca rolled her eyes at the trite words.

"Let me think about it. You just get those cars digitized for September."

"But I'm here *now*. Why would you want to go to the expense of sending me back?" A risky question. She hoped Pat wouldn't use it against her.

"Rebecca. What are you asking for? More time? Money?"

"Can we set the car shoots back a few days...give me time to see if I can get on the island and film the inside of this lighthouse before I have to move on? It'll be worth it, Pat. I guarantee it. And I never guarantee anything."

She pictured her boss chewing on his fake cigar.

"Okay. Look. I'll bump Sacramento and San Jose to the end, so that'll give you three days before you have to hit that kid in Monterey with the 1930 Pierce-Arrow ragtop. Got it?"

Rebecca smiled, danced her fingers lightly across the top of her laptop. "You won't be sorry," she said honestly. "You're gonna like this."

"I hope so."

"If there are no tours, how do I get out there?" Rebecca asked. The clerk behind the counter of the Del Norte Visitor's Bureau smiled.

"You can get there by helicopter but not without the owner's permission."

"And the owner would be..."

"It's called the St. Paul Foundation. But honestly, no one around here really knows who they are."

"They must have an address somewhere. What if...what if something happened out there, an emergency or something?"

"Their address is in care of an attorney in Beverly Hills. That's about all I can tell you." The woman, a nice looking senior, wore pearls the same color as her up-do hair.

Rebecca lifted her chin, took in a deep breath, considered the clerk. "I, uh, understand they filmed *Cape Seduction* out there."

"Oh, yes. Our local claim to fame in the '40s. Jordan Kent became all the rage, and that Darla Foster..."

"The leading actress?"

"Yes. When she went missing, it brought all sorts of notoriety to our little town. It was the only movie she ever made, you now."

"She went missing? Like, disappeared?"

"Mm-hmm. About a month after the picture came out. It debuted at Grauman's Chinese Theatre, you know. In Hollywood. Oh! What a fabulous night."

"You were there?"

"Well, no, only in spirit. They did a radio broadcast, and my girlfriends and I, we sat up all night chatting about it."

"What about Douglas Fairbanks. He played the hero, right?"

"No, no, definitely Jordan Kent. Douglas Fairbanks wasn't in the film."

"You wouldn't happen to know if your video store has a copy, would you?"

The older woman's eyes fairly twinkled, Rebecca thought, as she gazed back at Rebecca with a knowing smile.

"Yes, it does. It just came out on DVD, too. Part of MGM's anniversary celebration. You going to rent it?"

"I think I will. Say," Rebecca ventured on, sensing the clerk's enjoyment of their conversation. "Is Jordan Kent still around?"

"They say he's reclusive. He's in his late 80s, you know."

Rebecca nodded, filing the information away for later. She got directions to the video store and bid the clerk goodbye.

She smiled as she left the video store with a copy of *It Happened One Night* in her hand, along with a rain check for the already-checked-out *Cape Seduction*. Tonight, it would be room service and a good, old-fashioned romance. She giggled aloud at her own foolish thoughts and at the realization that *Cape Seduction* was drawing her in.

Two

Hollywood, California
March 20, 1948

Before Cecelia Kent brought the cigarette to her lips, the two men sitting in her midst thrust their lighters forward. One of them, her husband, the charming and much lauded film star, Jordan Kent. With his crystal blue eyes and slicked back, rich sienna hair, his face had launched many a teenaged heartbreak. The other man, her powerful, movie mogul father, Harvey Bregman, flicked a flame first and lit the Chesterfield. Batting her eyelashes as the gray smoke swirled about her face, Cecelia wore a bored expression as she panned the restaurant around her. A waitress appeared, filled their water glasses.

"Well, it's a shame about Rosalind. Everyone in town swore she'd be taking home Best Actress," Cecelia lamented, tapping her cigarette on the ashtray before her. "They're saying *Variety* already had the headline typeset. 'Rosalind Russell wins the gold for her stunning portrayal of Lavinia in *Mourning Becomes Electra!*'"

"Did you see March's face when he opened the damned envelope? He was shocked as hell. You could tell," Jordan agreed, taking a quick puff off his own smoke before snuffing it out.

"*Frederic* was shocked? Poor Ros had already begun to rise out of her chair to accept. But what did she do? She went right into a standing ovation."

"Yeah, she's a class act all the way." Jordan glanced at Harvey Bregman, who'd kept quiet during the exchange with Cecelia. "So. Harv. What do you say?"

Bregman shrugged, reached for his scotch. "Loretta deserved the Oscar."

Before anyone could comment further on Loretta Young's surprising upset, another couple hurried up to the table. The woman, Jordan noticed, couldn't have been more than twenty-one years old. Her full-length, faux fur coat matched her dark brown hair, cut into a bob years out-of-date but which gave her dark eyes and fair skin a sort of pixie look.

"Sorry we're so late! The traffic on Sunset was just *awful*," she gushed, hanging onto the arm of her date a little too tightly. "Russell, honey, could you get this animal off my back?"

"Sure, doll." Russell Harrington made a great show of sliding the coat off the woman's shoulders, then flagged a waitress to remove it to the coat room.

"It's freezing out there! Can you believe the wind? Where shall I sit? Are we boy-girl?"

Cecelia looked up through lowered lashes at the woman, her expression one of distaste and arrogance. She said nothing, letting the smoke from her cigarette create a fog around her. Jordan, however, grinned.

"Damned cold, yes. Did you see Reagan's hair when he came into the Shrine? Ha!"

"Ronnie always looks perfect to me." Cecelia uttered her comment toward her husband but did not look him in the eye.

"He looked okay when he did Best Picture. Anybody surprised?" Russell asked, leaning down to help himself to a bit of caviar from the plate on the table.

"I thought *Possessed* should have won," the brunette said, finally settling into the open seat beside Jordan. Russell sat on her other side. "Joan Crawford–"

"Darla, sweetie, *Possessed* wasn't even nominated," Russell corrected. "I put my money on *Body and Soul*."

"Joan *was* a smash. Jordan Kent, by the way," Jordan said, holding his hand out to Darla. "And you are?"

"Darla Foster. Pleased to meet you." Darla smiled sweetly, shook Jordan's hand, then subtly jabbed Russell with her elbow.

"Sorry, Jordie boy. Forgot you hadn't met Darla. She's new in town. Darla, Cecelia. Jordie's little woman. And Harvey Bregman."

"Hi," Darla said, offering a little wave as Cecelia gave a curt nod while puffing away.

Harvey Bregman lifted halfway out of his chair, leaning across the table to take Darla's hand. "Welcome to Hollywood, Miss Foster. Gateway to mayhem and madness."

"How do you do?" Darla replied, taking Bregman's hand briefly.

"What's a guy gotta do to get a drink around here?" Russell waved down another cocktail waitress. "Martini. Dry. So, Mr. Bregman, wha'ja think about *Gentleman's Agreement*? You think it deserved Best Film?"

Bregman swirled his drink, squinting his eyes in thought. "Peck actually did a remarkable job. I was one of the skeptics. Didn't think he could pull off playing a Jew."

"Well, isn't that the gist of the film? A gentile pretending to be Jewish so's he can report firsthand on anti-Semitism?" Russell asked.

The filmmaker nodded, plumping out his lower lip in surprised respect. "Yeah. That's the idea. Film's already made back the two million it cost to make. Took Kazan twelve weeks to make his picture."

"I thought it was worth half a buck to see. Dorothy McGuire ain't too hard to look at, neither."

Darla turned to her date with a pout. "She's no Joan Crawford."

On her other side, Jordan laughed. "No, but she *is* sitting at the next table, Miss Foster."

"Oh!" Darla briefly clapped a small hand over her red-painted lips. "I didn't realize—"

"Yes, it will be all over the *Hollywood Reporter*. 'Starlet Slams Seasoned Scene Stealer at Brown Derby.'" All of the men at the table chuckled, and Jordan patted the back of Darla's hand. "They'll probably let you off this time. First offense."

The blush went from Darla's hairline down to the modest cleavage shown off by her lacy black cocktail dress.

"Indeed. So, Miss Foster, how is it you came to be here tonight?" Bregman asked, causing Cecelia to turn toward him with a sneer. "You an actress?"

"You bet she's an actress. Damned fine one, too," Russell answered.

"Russell, please. I'm quite capable of answering on my own. Yes, Mr. Bregman, I do act. I just finished a production of *Streetcar* in Pasadena."

"Stage. Done any film? You got pictures?"

"Yes, no, and yes. You have to have pictures in this town, right?" Darla asked, smiling broadly to reveal an enviable set of teeth and apple cheeks reminiscent of Shirley Temple. No one said another word as the waitress distributed drinks around the table. Finally, Jordan broke the silence.

"So, what's in production?"

Bregman took a swig, put his glass down. "DeHavilland is doing *The Snake Pit* for Fox. Olivier's signed on for *Hamlet*. Warner's got Lew Ayres and Jane Wyman doing *Johnny Belinda*."

"But what about you, Harv? Aren't you working with MGM on something?"

"*Cape Seduction*. We're in pre-production. Lookin' at locations. Gotta find a lighthouse we can shoot inside and out."

"A lighthouse? Ooh, sounds romantic." Darla clasped her hands eagerly.

"Sounds melodramatic. You're better than that, Daddy," Cecelia stated, reaching for a glass of champagne. "I think you should do a picture with Bette Davis."

"She's with Warner, Cec."

"They'll loan her out. They loaned her to RKO, remember?"

"*The Little Foxes*. Yeah. But I don't work well with Bette. I'm looking for someone...fresh."

Jordan tilted his head. "You could shoot the interior on sound stages and maybe use some file film or fly-bys for the exterior."

"I want to get a real lighthouse. There's a feel in this story. It needs authenticity."

"How about Old Point Loma in San Diego?" Russell asked, scraping up the last of the caviar with a cracker.

"Nope. Too clean looking. I want something a little spookier."

"Is it a ghost story?" Darla asked, her eyes wide. "I love scary stuff."

"Not exactly." Bregman opened a menu. "It's a suspense. My illustrious son-in-law will play the lead."

"News to me," Jordan murmured, lifting his glass.

Ignoring the comment, Bregman continued. "Looking for a best actress contender."

Russell, too, opened up his menu. "I hear Lana Turner is looking."

"She's mad at MGM over that *Three Musketeers* disaster." Bregman closed his menu. "Don't know why I look. I always get the New York steak."

"Ingrid Bergman?" Darla asked, her eyes darting from the producer to the actor. "I just love her accent."

"Nope. She's doing *Joan of Arc* with Victor Fleming. They got their own company now. *Good luck.*" Bregman finished his scotch.

"I'll take the prime rib. Darling?" Jordan turned to his wife, who merely shrugged.

"Petit filet," she finally muttered, leaning back in her chair.

Jordan sighed. He didn't know what bugged Cecelia, nor did he care. She'd been sullen and antagonistic for weeks. Maybe months. He'd given up trying to please her. He turned to Darla, who frowned at her open menu.

"Maybe I'll have the chicken." She looked around then, obvious in her hope for approval. Cecelia rolled her eyes. Jordan took the menu from Darla's hands and snapped it closed on top of his own.

"Great choice. It's settled, then. How 'bout you, Russ? You still like swordfish?"

"Naw. I'll go for the New York. At least it's completely *American.* Don't know who might be listening, right?"

Russell's reference to proponents of the "red purge" gave Jordan pause. None of them needed a link to Communism.

"Don't look at *me*," Jordan said, running a nervous hand over his hair. "John Wayne is my favorite cowboy."

"And Mickey Mouse your favorite cartoon buddy. I gotcha," Russell agreed. "Hey what do you think about what they're saying about TV? You really think it means anything?"

"What? That television will kill the movies? Malarkey. The studios would never let it happen. They aren't letting the networks show their films or use their stages. They'll kill TV." Jordan wasn't as certain as his words would indicate, however. He took a gulp of champagne and looked around the room.

Russell shook his head. "I dunno. They got a lot of power, those TV guys."

17

"I think we need to be very, very careful," Bregman spoke up. "Yeah, there's only a million TV sets in America, but I heard it'll quadruple by next year. Why should 90 million people pay forty or fifty cents a pop to go see a film when they can get sports, Milton Berle and game shows for free? And don't forget some independent studios are making pictures for the tube."

"What? *Howdy Doody* beat out *It's a Wonderful Life*? I don't think so," Jordan argued.

"CBS is planning to put news on TV this year. What'll that do to the papers?" Russell challenged. Before Jordan could respond, Darla sat forward.

"My uncle works for CBS. Says people are getting away from newspapers. He says a human being reading the news to the public on TV will be the greatest thing to ever happen to people. He says–"

"The papers will always be around." Cecelia reached for her cigarette case. "This television thing is just a passing fancy. Movies are the mainstay of entertainment. I think you're all wrong."

Quiet ensued while each thought about Cecelia's comment.

"Well, I want to hear more about your lighthouse movie," Darla announced, directing her question to Bregman with a sunny smile. "I once got to go inside of the one at Point Fermin. It was so...exciting. I wanted to stay all day there, just absorbing all the history and stuff. Can you believe how those lighthouse keepers used to live? All alone, with all the storms and such? Does your picture have lighthouse keepers, Mr. Bregman?"

Bregman pondered a moment, fingering a book of matches on the tablecloth. He tilted his head, peered at Darla across the table. "Would you like a copy of the screenplay, Miss Foster?" he said at last, his gaze intent on her face.

The smile froze on Darla's lips, and her fingers went to her throat, as if to toy with a necklace not worn tonight. "I–I, gee whiz, I'd love that! Wow, is it okay? I mean, do you have an extra?"

The girl's exuberance and naiveté charmed the men at the table, especially Jordan, who threw an arm around her shoulder for a quick squeeze. Again blushing, Darla turned her face up to him.

"I'm pretty green, aren't I?" she murmured, and he chuckled.

18

"You are merely refreshing, my dear. Take the gentleman up on his offer and then thank him."

Bregman watched them closely. Taking a pen and a business card from the inside pocket of his dinner jacket, he began to write on the back of the card. "What's your number, doll face?"

Three

Crescent City, California
May

The boat captain looked skeptical but took Rebecca's money and pocketed it. "You got permission, right?"

"It's okay. I promise. I have the key, see? Why would I have this if it wasn't okay?" Holding up the key to her father's storage barn, Rebecca forced her best white-lie smile.

The captain grunted and reached out to grasp Rebecca's hand as she stepped off the small dock. "Okay," he muttered gruffly as she climbed onto his skiff. "If it's too rough out there, we're turnin' back. And I ain't gettin' in no trouble over this, hear?"

"Of course you won't get into trouble. Do you think *Travel One Magazine* would send me out here if–"

"Okay, I get it. Just...sit down and put on a life vest. It's rough water between here n' that rock." He coiled up the rope he'd just unhooked from the dock and moved to sit near the engine. "Name's Bill."

"Burke," Rebecca returned, tugging down her Diamondbacks cap by way of a greeting. Her escort wasn't the type to make eye contact, she noticed. He was seventy, if a day. "How do you do?"

Bill nodded and fired up the motor. "You a photographer, you say?"

"Yup. We're doing a story on old lighthouses with interesting pasts. We think this one might have a good tale behind it."

"You might not want to be knowin' the tale behind Dragon Rock."

Rebecca opened her mouth to ask why just as the small craft lurched forward, its motor screaming for maintenance.

It took only minutes, dodging the rocks surrounding it, to reach the small atoll. Rebecca hadn't seen the tiny, jury-rigged landing from shore. Bill struggled to get the boat close enough to the dock to tie up without being dashed on the surrounding reef.

"Wow," Rebecca muttered, staring at the switch-back of rotted wooden steps leading up the rock to the elliptical caisson beneath the lighthouse. "You coming?"

"Nope. I stay right here. Can't stay too long, either. Tide's too rough. You'll have to make it quick up those steps before the next wave washes you right off!"

"Gotcha. Well. Here I go!"

Heavy camera bag slung over her shoulder, Rebecca began the climb, gingerly stepping around gaping holes in the decaying risers, crabs and other crawly things she didn't want to squish. Harboring her progress, a small sea lion lay squarely in her path, one of several lounging on the rocks around her.

"Shoo! Out of the way, bud! I don't have time to play." With a gentle nudge from her toe, the sea lion grumbled and climbed off the riser. Rebecca wished she could take time to photograph the animal. "Maybe next time, pal."

Though she considered herself to be in good shape, she found herself panting by the time she reached the top. She turned to look back down but couldn't see Bill or his skiff due to the angle of the jutting rock.

At the base of the caisson, another rusted iron stairway snaked around and upward, hugging the side of the elliptical base. These steps, where she'd seen the woman in red, proved even more treacherous than the rocks below. Rebecca crept along, grasping the rough stone exterior for support until she reached the door near the top.

The door was bolted shut. Rebecca took a deep breath and pulled a tiny set of files from her pocket. It didn't take long for her to pick the aged, corroded lock. *Daddy would be proud*, she thought, pocketing her tools. Most fathers didn't teach their daughters such skills.

"Whew. *That* was fun." She regained her bag and pulled out a small flashlight, shining it around what appeared to be an engine room. Her beam illuminated an immense, cavern-like space with high ceilings. The smell of rotted wood, mold and fuel overpowered as she viewed old generators, compressors and other huge pieces of equipment she associated with the electricity and foghorn.

Rebecca shivered. Aside from the offending odors, something ominous, something very disturbing pervaded. Her analytical mind buzzed, filtering thoughts and images until she came to one that tripped her imagination. The woman in red, standing on the very steps Rebecca had just climbed.

"No way," she muttered, again training her light on the ancient machines, the dank and pitch-dark expanse. "She couldn't have been here."

A metal staircase clung to the wall on her left, and she started up it with some trepidation, encountering a series of small rooms as she climbed. The sparse furniture lay in shambles. Broken chairs, shredded upholstery and decomposing rugs lay heaped around the first room. Rebecca shuddered. Remembering Bill's warning, she got out her camera and started taking pictures.

Stone steps led up into the tower. After passing a rudimentary laundry room, Rebecca carefully made her way up to the galley where the sink had been ripped from the wall, and tattered, rotted curtains blew into the room through a small, broken window. Cabinet doors stood open, with various bits of debris evident on the shelves. Rebecca snapped away, shooting the scene while holding her breath.

"Okay. Pretty worthless so far." She continued on up the stairs inside the tower, which remained much the same, she thought, as they must have been for the past one hundred years. Although dirty and cracked, the risers proved solid if noisy. She passed two levels of sleeping quarters. Again she felt winded as she reached the lantern room.

"Whoa. Now *here's* my shot." Rebecca took pictures from every angle of the gallery, even zooming in on Bill as he sat on the landing staring out at the sea. She shot the stairwell, the glass, the empty hole where the lighthouse's lens once turned. Carcasses of two dead birds lay at her feet. Looking back at the shore, she shot off a round of photos encompassing the Del Norte coastline.

She lingered as long as she dared, breathing in the salt air and enjoying the immenseness of the setting. "I could stay up here awhile," she murmured, letting the wind pull her hair away from her face. Again remembering her boat taxi driver, she returned to the stairwell and descended.

She sought the bedrooms next. As in the other parts of the house she'd explored, decay was prevalent. In the lower room, a bed frame, its mattress bare, pushed forlornly into one corner. Rebecca marveled at its former beauty: solid brass with an ornate, filigreed headboard. A boudoir table, with a French beaded lamp, stood beside the bed, its elegant mirrors cracked and in pieces. And junk. Everywhere. Unpleasant and uninteresting.

Rebecca sighed, disappointed. She didn't know what she'd expected to find. She started to retreat from the room when something in the corner caught her eye. A small, wooden piece of furniture, buried beneath rotting blankets. With pinching thumb and forefinger, she carefully peeled back the cloths to reveal a stunningly beautiful baby cradle.

"Hel-lo. This is cool. This is very cool." Rebecca squatted, leveling her camera, but the darkness precluded a good shot. She dug the flashlight out of her pocket and propped it onto the discarded pile of bedclothes, then looked through the lens again. Long a proponent of available light photography, she turned the focus ring until the poorly lit cradle became clear. She rocked forward, readjusted the lens. *No, a little closer. The cradle should be framed just so...* She edged nearer, moving the wide-beamed flashlight to get more light onto the subject. Again, she lifted the camera and peered through the viewfinder.

Her breath caught in her throat. What she saw forced a small cry from her lips and she almost dropped her camera. A baby, lying very still, peered through the wooden slats on the side of the tiny bed. Her wits only momentarily derailed, Rebecca snapped the shutter three times in quick succession, then grabbed the flashlight and rushed forward to peer into the cradle.

Empty.

Rebecca's jaw dropped. She'd seen the infant, a real, living baby, inside that cradle, its tiny hand raised in a baby-tight fist, its large eyes staring, its bow-like mouth working. Now, feeling around in the bed, Rebecca found only a badly tarnished silver rattle. She stood and looked around, as if someone might be watching her incredible encounter.

24

"I saw it." She pulled the baseball cap from her head and ran her shirt sleeve across her forehead, moist with perspiration. Swallowing hard, she stared down at the cradle, then brought the camera back to eye level. No baby. Empty bed. Silver rattle.

Rebecca pocketed the rattle and issued a shuddering sigh.

It was real. A real baby.

Reluctant to leave, she looked around the room again, committing to memory the shape and layout. Some things a camera couldn't capture.

Finally, she decided to return to the boat. No sense in aggravating the boat captain.

"'Bout to leave without you," Bill complained. He didn't look at her as he busied himself with launching the boat. "Thought maybe you'd done yourself in."

"No. No. I'm fine," Rebecca answered, definitely not fine. Pragmatic, reasonable, rational Rebecca Burke wasn't given to hallucinations, nor did she believe in ghosts. She trusted herself implicitly, never second-guessed what she saw or heard. Yet inside of twenty-eight hours, she'd seen an apparition in her backseat, a phantom on the steps outside the lighthouse, and now, a non-existent baby. She couldn't come up with a rational explanation for what had occurred.

"What did you mean earlier...what might I not want to know about this lighthouse?" she asked.

Bill stared straight ahead, expertly steering around the rocks jutting from the surf.

"Nothin'."

Where have I heard that before? This guy been talking to the tow truck driver?

Rebecca adjusted her cap. "You meant something," she said boldly, not caring if she pressed too hard. She got paid to be nosy. She needed information, right?

"Nothin' much. Got a few skeletons in the closet, you might say. Coupla' guys was killed building the damned thing. Took 'em ten years to build it, cost more'n any other lighthouse ever. Then they abandoned it."

"What about the movies they filmed out here?"

25

"Yep. They did that. Then after the film folks pulled outta town, coupla' of 'em stayed on out there."

"Really." Rebecca turned around in her seat to look back at the shrinking silhouette of the lighthouse. "There wasn't much left in the house now. A bed frame, some broken chairs...a baby cradle." She watched carefully for Bill's reaction to her words. If he had one, she missed it. "Do you think there was actually a baby out there?"

Bill waited to respond. Whether for effect or just out of habit, Rebecca didn't know, but she fidgeted while waiting. Finally, he spit into the water and turned toward her. "Story is, a gal lived out there for a while. Local kid took groceries out a few times. Don't think he ever saw the woman; he always just left the stuff for her. Once he thought he heard a baby crying."

A chill shivered across Rebecca's back and arms. "When?"

"Oh, 'round... 1949, I'd say."

"Is the boy–the man–still around? The one who delivered the groceries?"

"Nope. He's dead. Freak thing. Rogue wave hit his boat...ploughed into a rock right over yonder." He pointed a short distance to the south. Rebecca's eyes grew wide.

"He told you about the woman himself?"

"He was a friend."

"Oh...I'm sorry. When did he die?"

"1949."

Rebecca suddenly felt she had to swallow. She needed a notepad, a telephone and access to Google. It wasn't until an hour later, as she collapsed onto her motel room bed, that she remembered the photos she'd taken. The photos of the baby in the lighthouse.

Four

Burbank, California
June 1948

"I promise, Mom. I'll call when I get there."

"It's a long ways. Cold up there."

"Yeah, it's farther than San Francisco. It's somewhere up by Oregon. I have plenty of warm clothes, don't worry. I'll call. I *promise.*" Darla gently nudged her mother from the room and went back to her suitcase, nearly over-full with clothing and necessities. She pondered for a moment, thinking about how far away she would be from home. Except for the short run of a play in San Francisco, she'd never strayed more than a few miles from her parents' house in Burbank.

But this was different. She would star in a big Hollywood picture. Star with Jordan Kent! Who would have thought it possible for a small-time, two-bit actress to meet and impress the big famous producer, Harvey Bregman?

All because of Russell. Dear, crazy Russell, whom she'd met at the dry cleaners while haggling over charges. They'd hit it off right away. Russell's lop-sided smile, jet black hair and disturbing ebony eyes had intrigued her. But then, nearly all the actors she met intrigued Darla.

Now, as she hurried to leave for her mind-boggling trip to Crescent City, she felt a pang of guilt. Russell, of course, would be staying behind. He wasn't a part of *Cape Seduction*, despite the numerous hints dropped and the constant whining about how much he would miss her. Darla sighed, forced her bulging suitcase closed. She couldn't worry about him right now. She'd done her best to make him feel better, done more than she should have, to be sure. No, this was her big break. At some lonely, mysterious lighthouse off the coast of Northern California, she would become a star.

Western Airlines Flight 408 taxied for takeoff from Los Angeles Municipal Airport with the entire cast of *Cape Seduction* aboard. Jordan Kent sat in a window seat, periodically rubbing his chin. He didn't enjoy flying, even in the giant, four-motored DC-6. The most luxurious plane ever, with a cruising speed of 300 miles per hour. He turned to his companion.

"Comfy?"

Darla Foster squirmed in her seat. "It's heavenly. Do we really get a glass of champagne?"

"You can't be old enough to drink," he teased with a brief, nervous smile.

"As of last January, I am."

Darla looked around the aircraft cabin. "This is my first time. I never thought they were so big inside. So rich!"

The plane, now aligned on the runway, began to build speed. Jordan glanced out the window at the spinning propellers on the wings. "Yup. Rich."

"Did you hear about the plane that crashed last November? The one in Utah? My mother said it was the same kind as this one. Nobody survived."

"Yes, well, we don't need to talk about that right now, do we? Have you studied your script?"

The vibration built, the plane shuddered and bounced. Jordan grasped the arm rests, his left hand coming into contact with Darla's. "Oh! So sorry." He pulled his hand away, not knowing quite where to rest it.

"No, it's all right. We can share!" Her giggle both charmed and annoyed him; he closed his eyes and leaned back against the seat.

At last, the big craft was airborne, and the tremors diminished somewhat. Jordan began to relax. Darla seemed wired, barely restrained by her seatbelt. "I'm so excited I could just pop!"

"Yeah, well, wait until you see this place. It's a real hoot."

"The lighthouse?"

"Yup. Way the hell out in the water, surrounding by jagged rocks, big waves...really isolated. A person could go bonkers out there like that. Gives me the willies."

"Ooh...sounds like my kind of place!" Darla clasped her hands together in apparent joy, and Jordan couldn't help but laugh. Her exuberance stimulated.

"Like I said, wait 'til you see it."

The flight was long and tiring, the subsequent bus ride tedious, but the weary travelers from Hollywood were met with a smattering of small-town fanfare. Even the mayor turned out to greet Bregman and his troupe of movie talent. Ever the promoter, Jordan smiled, waved and signed autographs for the two dozen or so fans gathered at the bus station in Crescent City, while Darla seemed more like a devotee herself than a celebrity. In awe of all she saw, she happily shook hands and exchanged words with the fans.

She couldn't wait to see the lighthouse, but evening fog had already settled on the tiny coastal town by the time the crowd dissipated. They walked the two blocks to their beachfront motel and were efficiently checked in by the wide-eyed clerk.

"I guess they don't have a bar," Jordan commented, glancing around the meager motel lobby.

"This ain't exactly the Ritz, Kent," Bregman responded.

"There's a liquor store on the corner, Mr. Kent." The clerk gestured toward the door. "They're open 'til two."

Jordan turned to Darla, who'd been admiring the area photographs on the lobby wall. "What do you say we get a half-pint, kinda celebrate this big adventure?"

Darla whirled. "Oh, I don't know. I think I'll just turn in for tonight. I'm pretty exhausted."

Jordan grinned. "Your loss, then."

"Yeah. My loss." Darla gazed at Jordan for a few moments, a soft smile turning the corners of her mouth.

The look wasn't lost on Bregman. "I'll take you up on that offer, Kent."

"My pleasure, Harv."

"Catch me if you can," Darla shouted over her shoulder with a laugh as she hurried up the wooden stairway toward the base of Dragon Rock Lighthouse. With precariously perched cameras rolling below, her liveliness seemed contagious as Jordan gave chase behind her. It felt more like a real-life frolic than a scene from an adventure film, with Jordan charging up the steps in hot pursuit. He caught up with her at the door, per the script they'd rehearsed, and he pulled her into a passionate embrace. The camera at the top zoomed in for the best movie-kiss Jordan had ever performed.

He turned serious.

"What are you trying to do to me, Mary? Don't you see you're killing me with this senselessness?"

"It's not my choice, Reginald. We'll never be free, never be together, not as long as...as long as..."

"I know. It's Myrna again, isn't it? Always my step-mother."

"She holds our future in the palm of her hand, Reggie. We both know it."

Harvey Bregman squinted from behind his dark glasses. "Cut it there! This is good. This is better than good." Concentration hardened his features as he pointed up at Darla. "Stay right there. Henry! Move up about six feet. Kent? Pick it up with that last line."

Animated, he paced on the small pier below them, thoughtful, focused and so unconcerned with his own surroundings that he failed to see the rogue wave approaching his vantage point. With his arms flailing about his short, rotund body, the surf swept Bregman below the dock in the blink of an eye. The nearest crew members were halfway up the haphazard stairway, manning the second camera.

"Jesus! Harv's overboard!" The two men put the camera down and raced back to where Bregman had disappeared beneath the surface. One of them quickly pulled off his shoes and launched himself into the water.

"Damn! Did you see that?" Jordan asked, his eyes wide with alarm. "Harv just pitched right into the damned water!"

Darla's hands flew to her mouth. "Oh, no! Oh my God! He could be dead!"

But Jordan was already racing down the steps. "He can't swim! He can't swim! Get him out, quick!" After what seemed an eternity, Jordan reached the dock and also dove into the swirling, turbulent waters.

Darla remained frozen to her spot at the top of the stairs, watching with horror as Jordan and the other man repeatedly came up for air. Finally, Bregman's head appeared as the three men struggled to hoist the heavy director onto the planks. Gasping, sputtering, choking, Bregman spewed water as he writhed on the small dock while his rescuers dragged themselves from the drink.

The stunned crew stood by while they loaded Bregman into one of the waiting boats and took him back to shore. Still panting, Jordan waived to the men on the stairs and above.

"Pack it up! We're done for today."

Darla said nothing as they waited for the transports to return. The whole incident unnerved her, and she was relieved to be back on the beach when it came their turn to be ferried. She then followed Jordan through the motel lobby and out to the street.

The corner liquor store had become Jordan's routine stop, but today the clerk saw him earlier than usual. "Bourbon, Mr. Kent?"

"A good bottle of port."

"You got it, sir."

"And glasses."

"Yes, sir. Comin' right up."

The motel had a picnic table on the waterside of the building, and Darla waited for him there.

"That was so scary. He coulda died," Darla said, her eyes round with emotion. She took a gulp of the heavy wine, licked her lips. "You saved his life, Jordie. You absolutely saved his life."

"He's my father-in-law."

"No matter. You would have saved a stranger."

"A stranger who has my future in the palm…"

"In the palm of his hand. Yeah. Where have I heard that before?" Darla asked with a giggle. "Are you serious?"

Jordan refilled his wine glass. "Yup. Why do you think I stay married to his loathsome daughter?"

"You can't mean that."

31

"No, I guess I can't," Jordan murmured, staring out at the flaming sunset as he brought the wine glass to his lips. "But I do."

Darla remained quiet while she considered his comment. Jordan had been a flirt from the very night she'd met him, but she thought it common with actors of his notoriety. He didn't mean anything by it, she was certain. But now, hearing his disdainful words about Cecilia, she wondered. She'd kept her distance, at least emotionally, from the unthinkably handsome megastar, made light of his innuendoes and sideways glances. She'd even rationalized away the depth of his kiss today on the set. Now, a new light was cast.

Darla held out her glass. "A bit more, please?"

"As you wish, my dear." Jordan poured, sighed. "I thought we'd lost him for sure. The rocks, the waves–it was hellacious down there. I've got a gash on my leg resembling a shark bite. Couldn't find him at first in all that murky water. Then, I saw him, spinning, sort of…his eyes wide open, panicked, you know…it *was* scary. I thought for a moment we couldn't do it, but we brought him up. Damned hard getting him out."

Darla nodded solemnly, trying to imagine what it must have been like under the surface. At five feet tall and 105 pounds, she would be hard-pressed to rescue a puppy, let alone a 250-pound man. "Well, I sure hope he appreciates what you did."

Jordan took a sip of wine, lifted his chin, and stretched his neck. "Me, too," he muttered in agreement.

"Let's not talk about today. Let's talk about the picture. It's going to be a hit, right, Jordie?"

"Oh, you bet it is, darling. Jordan Kent and Darla Foster will be the toast of Hollywood! Personal appearances, premieres, spotlights–the works. You'll see. You will be tinsel town's newest sweetheart."

"Oh, I hope so," Darla said with a sigh. "It's what I've wanted my whole life. To be a star. Nothing else."

"*Cape Seduction* will put you there, mark my words. In fact, let's make a date here and now. I'm taking you to the Academy Awards next year."

"Oh, are you sure? Me? But what about Cecelia?"

Jordan pulled a pack of cigarettes from his shirt pocket, took one out and lit it. He blew the smoke away from Darla's face, then turned back with a grin. "Cecelia who?"

Darla giggled. "Now, Jordie, you just said Mr. Bregman was your future. You mustn't be mean to his daughter. How about I go with Russell and we all sit together?"

"Of course, you're right. I'd forgotten about dear Russ. Have you called him?"

"Once."

"We've been up here three weeks, and you've only called him once? The guy's probably bonkers by now. Do be kind and give the old boy a ring tomorrow, won't you?"

"If you insist. I really hate to encourage him, though."

"How do you mean?"

"He's just more serious about things than I am. We never really said we were committed, you know. He sort of assumes things. But I think we need to cool things off a bit. I'm up here, he's down there...you know."

Jordan picked up his wine glass, peered at the dying sun through its deep red hue. "I guess I do know. That's kind of how it is, right? We're up here, they're way down there. We're in the moment, here. You and I. Together."

Darla didn't respond. His words confused her, but she liked the sound of his voice. Liked hearing him talk about them being together, even if she was unsure of his meaning. It was mysterious and romantic. She swallowed the rest of the port in her glass.

"That's good stuff in there. What's it called again?"

"It's port wine. This one is from Spain. More?"

"Just a teeny bit, please."

He poured her another glass, then topped off his own. "A woman after my own heart. I knew when we met that night at the Derby, you were different."

"Different, how?"

"Refreshingly honest. Unspoiled by Hollywood. Virginal."

"I beg your pardon!" Darla put her glass down a little too forcefully, outrage on her face. "I think that word offends me."

Jordan quickly placed his hand on her bare arm, running his fingers smoothly down the length of it. "Meant in the purest sense, my dear. I'm sorry if I set you off. I only suggest that you're fresh and alive and new. Not soured by the business, not beaten down by the rogues. You are a breath of spring in a smoky room."

Darla relaxed as quickly as she'd become vexed. Her smile returned, and she tilted an admiring gaze in Jordan's direction. "Oh."

She became heavy-lidded, and Jordan stood, picked up his glass. "Let me see you safely to your room, Darla. You must be worn out from today's events."

She nodded lazily, taking her time to rise from the bench, glass in hand.

"I might need to be tucked in," she slurred, punctuating her words with a small burp. "Oops! Gosh, I'm sharry, uh sorry…"

"No matter, my dear. I'll take care of everything."

Five

Grogan's Head, Northern California
June

"I'm not sure, but I think these are the wrong faucets. You didn't order brass, did you?"

"Hell, no. We ordered chrome. Don't tell me we got brass." Matt Farralone tossed his clipboard onto his already buried desk and turned to his co-worker. "Damn."

Case McKenna shrugged out of his denim jacket and draped it across the back of a dust-laden chair. He looked across the tiny construction office at Matt and pulled a packing list from his pocket. "They'll replace them."

"Yeah, right. In two weeks. Maybe three. We're already behind on this. I need them now."

"Okay, so we'll get the chrome ones now, get the refund later. No big deal."

Matt sighed, walked to the small trailer window and gazed out at the new clubhouse under construction. "You're right. It'll all work out." He turned back to his friend with a smile. "Lunch time yet?"

Case returned the grin. "You are a bottomless pit, man. Yeah. I could eat. I'll ask Jack to keep an eye out."

The weather in Grogan's Head was better than usual. Sunny, with just enough warmth to encourage short sleeves. The men settled at a table on the deck behind The Salty Pine. The waitress nodded that she'd be with them shortly.

"Done much work on your house?" Case asked, cranking open the table umbrella as he spoke.

"Nope. The clubhouse is taking everything right now. If it's not done soon, the summer will be gone. The kids'll have to wait another year."

"It'll be done by the end of September. We've got great weather, lots of help..."

"Broken window glass, the wrong faucets..."

Case grinned. "Ever the optimist, eh?"

"You get that way in my business. There's always the downside. Always the risk, the negative."

"You miss the courtroom?"

"Like I would miss herpes. Nope, I'm not going back anytime soon. When the Boys and Girls Club is finished, I'm gonna work on completing my house."

"Then?"

"Something will come up. It always does."

The waitress appeared with their usual soft drinks. "Burgers, guys?"

"Sure," Case answered. "And give us a heap of those greasy, cholesterol-laden onion rings."

"No cheese on–" Matt began, but the waitress had already turned.

"No cheese. I already know that, Matt, honey," she called over her shoulder.

Case jabbed his friend in the arm. "You been hittin' on Donna, you rascal?"

"Donna? Her?" Matt asked, referring to the retreating waitress just disappearing inside the restaurant. "Naw. She's just friendly, that's all. Got a son who belongs to the Club."

Case nodded. "Thought maybe she was after your dough."

"That would be sad, since I'm almost broke."

"Like hell. You must have a cool million or two in the bank."

Matt grinned, took a slug of cola. "Not quite. I did make a pretty decent fee off my last case. Not sure it was worth it, though."

"Murder can be murder?"

"It almost came to that. Nickols was a bad ass, and he had lots of friends. But I–" His beeping cell phone cut short his recollection. He peered at the screen, touched the proper icon, and pressed it to his ear. "Farralone."

"Didn't think I'd reach you," a man's voice, crusty with age, said. "What's going on?"

36

Matt cleared his throat, looked out at the glistening sea. "I'm up north. Working on a construction project. It's a charity thing."

"How far north?"

"If I threw a rock real hard, it would land in Oregon. What's up with you? You okay?"

"I'm well. I have something I need you to take care of."

Matt inhaled, sighed out the breath, and licked his lips. "Not a case, I hope."

"No. Nothing like that. It's about Dragon Rock."

His interest piqued, Matt leaned back in his deck chair and looked toward Case. "What about it?"

"We have a problem."

Rebecca tossed her garment bag onto the bed and kept walking on into the bathroom, where she flipped on the shower. She turned to the mirror, examined her travel-weary face.

"What a trip. What a hellacious trip," she muttered, leaning close to the mirror to inspect her budding crow's feet. She gently pushed the tiny lines away with her fingertips, inadvertently poking herself in the eye. "Ouch! Damn."

Quickly stripping down, she stepped into the steaming spray and leaned back. She remained motionless for a time, letting the hot water wash away the stress of the long, desert drive, the sleepless nights and desperate fast-food binging. Eyes closed, she lathered her hair, reluctant to wash the soothing suds from her head as she massaged the tension from her scalp.

Her eye still smarting, she reacted, momentarily forgetting the shampoo on her fingers as she rubbed at her eye.

"Dammit! Oh, crap!" Rebecca turned her face into the shower's stream in an attempt to wash the soap from her burning eye.

She'd also forgotten to bring in a fresh bath towel. With more cursing, she reached for the hand towel and proceeded to dry herself as the phone began to ring.

"Holy Toledo," she complained, hurrying from the bathroom holding the tiny terry to her chest. "Hello?"

"Thought you'd call when you got in."

"Hi, Daddy. I'm sorry. I just couldn't wait to get in the shower. Can I give you a buzz in a bit? I need to unfold a little."

"No problem, Bec. Talk to you later."

Rebecca hung up the phone and went in search of her bathrobe and a new towel.

She ended up on the balcony of her second-floor townhouse, sipping iced tea and staring out at a desert sea of *saguaro, cholla* and *ocotillo*. An occasional jack rabbit scampered by, and even a couple of roadrunners made an appearance before darting off toward the horizon.

But Rebecca wasn't watching the Arizona flora and fauna below. Her mind insisted upon reliving the events of the week before, specifically the visit to the lighthouse and the aftermath in her hotel room.

An eternity had passed before her laptop booted. The tiny display on the back of her camera revealed nothing out of the ordinary, so she anxiously enlarged the photos on the memory card to full screen. She was barely breathing as the photos slowly displayed, one by one. The lighthouse, the rocks, the boat…the stairs, the entry room, the kitchen…finally the bedroom. The brass bed. The cradle.

The cradle.

Eyes wide, Rebecca stared hard at the pictures, looking for evidence of the baby. And saw none. The flashlight beam clearly centered on the baby bed, illuminating the slatted front side and behind it, the back side. There was nothing between. No baby. No mysterious shadow. No nothing.

Now, back at home in Scottsdale, Rebecca sighed. She couldn't make sense of the visions she'd had. Couldn't reconcile the memory of the infant, its unblinking eyes wide in wonder, its little hand raised in determination. Wracking her brain for details, she tried to remember more about what she'd seen. *What was the baby wearing? Did it have hair? What color were its eyes? Was its mouth open, did it have teeth yet?*

Rebecca closed her eyes and recreated the scene once again. A blanket wrapped the baby, a white blanket with some small pattern…rabbits. Yes, pink rabbits. Pink! Perhaps the baby was a girl.

And a small patch of dark hair tufted on the top of her head. No memory of eye color or teeth–perhaps the mouth was closed. The hand fisted, not much movement, but the baby lived. Staring, as if–

The phone rang again. The memory vanished. Rebecca rubbed her eyes and reached for the cordless. It would be Daddy. She took in a breath, forced a smile.

Matt stared at the phone number on the sheet of paper just emerging from his fax machine. The address above the number confirmed the party resided in Arizona. He folded the paper and slid it into his desk drawer. The old man was likely over-reacting. People often inquired about the lighthouse, most of them never following up.

He left the office and locked the trailer door behind him. On a whim, he wandered through the empty construction site, admiring the workmanship, lamenting at the forced shortcuts. The kids would be happy here. He could almost hear their boisterous laughter as they ran through the halls.

A place to play and be safe. That's all it had to be. Staffed by caring, nurturing volunteers who made it their lot in life to help kids. With a satisfied nod, Matt left the building and walked to his Jeep.

Soon he unlocked another trailer, this one his temporary home at the edge of the forest. After depositing his knapsack in the corner, he opened a beer, turned on the television and sat down at the tiny kitchen table. He watched for a few minutes, unable to concentrate. He picked up the remote, idly seeking something of interest.

A black cat with white paws soon joined him, jumping into his lap and demanding to be petted.

"Hey, Lucas. What's up, cat?"

Lucas responded with a very vocal purr, rubbing his head against Matt's massaging fingers before settling down on his lap.

Remembering he'd dropped today's mail in his knapsack, Matt reached for the bag and retrieved five or six envelopes. He opened them one by one, making *save* and *recycle* piles on the table. He paused at the last one, a small, pink, hand-written envelope. No return address, but he'd know the handwriting anywhere. Chelsea.

He took a long draught of the beer before unfolding the letter. His too-long, wavy hair hung down his forehead, and he hastily swept it to the side, suddenly annoyed. Chelsea could do that to him. In an instant. Destroy him, silently, from hundreds of miles away.

But not this time. He wouldn't let whatever she had to say bother him. Licking his lips, he began to read aloud.

"Dear Matthew. I hope this letter finds you well. I am fine...role in a new play...joined a tennis club...blah blah blah...*hell*."

He reached for his beer, continued reading. "Would really like to get rid of your piano. Any chance you can move it this month? I'm sure you can find room for it. Here are the dates I'll be available to let you in..." *Of course, she had the locks changed.*

"I also still have your hockey gear. Makes it hard to get the Hummer in the garage, so I'll put it with the piano when you come. Let me know, you have the number. Love, Chels."

Love. Yeah, right. She loves me like she loves a new zit on her perfect little chin.

Hockey gear. How long since he'd played? A lifetime ago. A lifetime since he'd been with Chelsea Garfield.

Another gulp of beer. The letter, now formed into the shape of a paper ball, launched through the air, landing squarely in the small sink.

Where the hell could he put a grand piano? He'd keep his hockey stuff; his buddy Jack had been talking about getting a game together for months now. But the piano was huge. He loved the piece and wasn't about to sell it. His new house, months away from completion, would have plenty of room for it. His home in Hollywood didn't really have the space.

Damn Chelsea. Why'd she have to fall out of love with him anyway?

Rebecca watched Pat chew on the plastic cigar as he carefully reviewed the proofs she'd placed on his desk.

40

"Good. These are very good. Excellent. Although I can't figure people dropping so much cash on cars." He punched a key on the intercom. "Janie, come get Bec's pictures." He looked up. "Is there a reason you didn't just upload these? Is there a disk here somewhere?"

"In the envelope. There. The, uh, wi-fi was down."

Pat dumped out the manila envelope she indicated, picked up the small zipped sandwich bag with the disk inside and handed the stack to the woman now standing beside his desk. He turned back to Rebecca. "Is there something else?"

Rebecca handed him a second envelope from her lap. "Just these."

Pat pulled out a group of photos and began laying them out. "Wow. I'm impressed. Same trip?"

"Yeah. You like them?"

Her boss took his time answering, examining the six pictures in order. Finally, he looked up. "Can you get more?"

"Lighthouses? You bet. You think it's worth a story?"

"Don't know yet. I particularly like this one." He gestured toward the lighthouse perched on the rock. "This is the one you first told me about, correct? With the woman and the kid with the groceries?"

"Yes. Dragon Rock. The others, in order, are Point Montara, Point Surrender, Big Sur, Point Pinos and Trinidad Head. They all have stories."

"This one," Pat repeated. "It's got something. Weird."

"You don't know the half of it," Rebecca mumbled.

"Got interior?"

"I have some, but I didn't have the proper lights. I only had a few minutes. This kinda creepy old sea captain took me out there. He didn't seem to want to get near the place. It's dangerous. There are jagged rocks, lots of surf–"

"Dangerous? All the better. Hows about we get a real crew to go with you? Maybe we do some video we can hand off to Platinum Pictures?"

Rebecca's heart leaped. Pat was getting behind the story! And Platinum Pictures? She'd always wanted to work with their sister film company.

41

"Whatever you think, Boss. I'm in."

"Do what you have to do to get us inside. Permits, contracts, whatever they want. They'll want waivers; that's okay, we got good insurance. Find a decent boat guy to haul us out there."

Rebecca grabbed a Post-it pad from Pat's desk and scribbled down his commands as he spewed them. "I've already left a message for someone who is supposed to be in charge."

"Block out a few days in late June. In the meantime, call back up there and see who has the story. Maybe that old coot with the dinghy has some more to his. Find friends of friends who remember. And get me a copy of that movie!"

Six

Del Norte County, California
July 1948

Jordan Kent woke with a start to someone knocking hard on his motel room door.

"Kent! Are you awake? Time is money!"

He sat up, shook his head. Beside him, Darla stirred, a soft smile twitching on her lips. Her ivory-white arm slid from the covers, bent at the elbow above her head. She sighed. Whatever her bliss, Jordan wished he had it, too.

He had a headache.

"Kent! Dammit, open the door!"

Harvey Bregman wasn't one to wait.

"Be there in a sec! Go on down without me. I'll catch up," Jordan called, hoping the boss would do as requested and leave the hallway. He couldn't afford to be found, by his father-in-law, with Darla.

"Don't disappoint me, Kent," Bregman huffed, his voice trailing as he thumped heavily down the hall.

Jordan blew a breath from pursed lips. "That was close. Darla, my love. Time to get up. You must get back to your room." He paused to give her cheek a caress. She was so simple. So naïve. So insatiable! He chuckled to himself, stood, and caught a glimpse of himself in the dresser mirror. Quickly he sucked in the beginnings of a spare tire and turned a profile.

"Jor-die," Darla sang. "Come back to bed. Surely we've got a few more minutes…"

He turned and looked back. She *did* invite, this one. Soft fingers, beckoning, even as she pulled the sheet up to her chin. Modest breasts, pushing against the sheet, begging to be touched. One knee lifting as he watched, smoothly sliding upward, suggesting he would be a fool not to heed her request. His headache, and his future, momentarily forgotten, Jordan lowered himself back onto the bed and nested his lips in the hollow of Darla's throat.

His headache returned, tenfold, at the site of Bregman's reddened face as the two men met at the pier.

"Do we have a problem here, Kent?" the older man asked, his fisted hands pressed against his waist. "Maybe you don't wanna do this picture?"

"Of course I do, Harv. Just nursing a hangover. You know how it is."

Bregman grunted and looked past Jordan's shoulder, where Darla seemed to virtually float along the sand on her way to the dock. His frown softened.

"Good morning, Miss Foster. Sleep well?"

"Heavenly, Mr. Bregman. Just heavenly. Are we back at the lighthouse today?" she asked sweetly, blinking in the bright sunlight.

"No. Today we're here, on the beach. Hence the cameras there." He gestured to the crew, already set for the first scene.

Jordan looked down, rubbed the back of his neck. It was going to be a long day.

"Wonderful," Darla responded, spontaneously kicking off her flats and running down the beach toward the cameras, dancing in circles as she ran.

Bregman turned to Jordan, who stood staring after Darla in wonder.

"She's a nut! A certifiable nut! But she's got the look. Okay, let's get started. We're doing the murder sequence today. You ready?"

"As ready as I'll ever be," Jordan muttered.

The two men followed Darla down the beach. The cast and crew came to life after having spent the best part of the morning waiting. Camera angles were adjusted, boom microphones lowered. Darla plopped herself down amidst them all, spreading her red and white chiffon dress about her.

"I'm ready. Let's go!"

Jordan sat beside her. He took a moment, closing his eyes, breathing deep. He needed to become Reginald Wilsey. *Reginald.*

In love with Mary Triton...but no! Mary wasn't his true love after all. She'd betrayed him. He'd loved her until he'd found her with another man. The lighthouse keeper. *Yeah, right. What a cockamamie story this is, anyway.*

"Quiet on the set! We'll pick up where we left off yesterday. Darla, you're still upset. Jordan has just accused you of seeing another man."

"Yes, Mr. Bregman. I have it."

"Cameras rolling."

"Action!"

The scene began. On cue, Darla began to cry.

"It wasn't what you think, Reggie. I swear. He–he made me do it. He threatened me! Yes, that's what it was. He said he'd kill me if I didn't...if I didn't–"

"What kind of fool do you take me for? I heard you laughing, singing, and swooning for that guy. A penniless no 'count hermit. Gotta be somethin' wrong with a man who holes up in a God-forsaken lighthouse in the middle of the ocean!"

Darla jumped to her feet, kicking sand onto Jordan's lap.

"How dare you talk about Franklin like that! He's a noble man and a courageous man!"

"So, you *do* love him!" Now Jordan got to his feet, fire in his eyes.

Her hands fisted at her sides, Darla leaned forward, a tiny dynamo of pure rage. "At least he isn't tied to his stepmother's apron strings," she shouted, then turned away. Jordan reached out, grasped her by the forearm.

"Where do you think you're going? No way are you getting out of this. No woman betrays Reginald Wilsey and then turns her back!"

The camera came in close as the two tussled back to the ground, Darla on her back with Jordan's hands at her throat. "Stop! Stop it! You're choking me! I–I can't breathe!"

"You deserve worse than death, you vixen!"

Darla's screams carried down the sand, causing the few beach goers to stop and stare. Still they struggled, Darla convincingly trying to loosen Jordan's hold on her neck. Jordan's expression became a murderous glare.

45

At last she stopped thrashing about. Slowly, as though the life had trickled out of her, she let her hands slide free and drop to the sand. Mary Triton was dead.

"And that's it. Cut it there." Bregman pulled a wrinkled handkerchief from his pocket and mopped his brow. Jordan sat back on the sand, stretched his arms out and opened his hands wide.

"Almost got a cramp," he quipped, and several people chuckled. Darla, however, remained motionless.

"Darla, it's time to get up. Did you not get enough sleep last night, dear heart?" Jordan asked, then stood and brushed sand from his trousers. "C'mon, be a good girl and get up."

"What's wrong with her?" Bregman asked, looking Jordan in the eyes. "She's not getting up."

Jordan fell to his knees and grasped Darla by the shoulders. "Come on, darling. No time for jokes. Open your eyes!" He began to shake her, gently at first, and then with more force as she failed to respond. "Oh, God. I didn't–I didn't do anything. She must have fainted. I didn't really–"

Lifting her wrist, he tried to feel a pulse, then turned to the many who'd crowded closer. "Anybody know how to do this?" Without waiting for an answer, Jordan leaned down into her face, turning his ear to her nose and mouth.

"Is she breathing?" someone asked.

"I can't tell. It's too windy!" He tried again, pressing his ear to her parted lips, at which moment Darla bit him on the lobe.

"Ouch! Good God-*dammit*!" Jordan pulled away, pressing a hand to his ear as Darla erupted into fits of giggles.

The company all shared a hearty laugh, and Jordan turned a pained smile back to them. "I'm sure I deserved that, somehow," he declared, as Darla continued her hysteria. But he frowned when he looked again in her direction.

The clerk in the lobby stopped her as Darla walked by on her way to her room. "There's a telephone message from a Mr. Harrington in Los Angeles. He said it was urgent that you call him."

"Oh, okay. May I?"

46

"There's a pay telephone across the lobby," the clerk advised her with a timid smile.

"Well...I'm afraid I'm fresh out of dimes. Could I just maybe please, just this one little time, use yours?"

The clerk reddened, then turned the desk phone around. "Just don't talk too long, or I'll lose my job. Here's the number."

Darla gave him a sunny smile. "You will for sure go to Heaven, now..." she glanced at his badge. "...*James*." She dialed the telephone and waited. Russell answered on the third ring.

"Oh, baby, Jeez, where are you? I've been trying to reach you for weeks!"

"I'm still here, Russell. In Crescent City, California. At the same motel as when I called you before. Nothing's changed."

"Something's changed, all right. I miss you like crazy, doll. This ain't fair, you bein' gone so long. I'm a mess."

"I'm sorry to hear that. Maybe you need a...hobby or something. Get out a bit. Go for a drive. You can go—"

"A hobby? Are you kidding? Aw, come on home, Darla. Just for a while. I need you here."

Darla sighed and felt a small crease pinch up her forehead. She caught the clerk watching her, and she lifted her chin, smiled.

"I'll be back when I'm done, Brother Russell. It was kind of you to contact me. Bless you, too."

"What the hell are you talking—"

Her smile pure goodness and light, Darla hung up the phone and very carefully turned it back toward the blushing clerk. "If the good pastor calls again, tell him I've gone to bed for the evening. Good night, James."

"Good night, Miss Foster. Sweet dreams!"

Darla nodded and sashayed down the hall to her room.

Jordan lay on his back in his motel room, a bottle of rum in one hand and an envelope in the other. He looked from one, the *cause*, to the other, the *effect*. He raised his head slightly and took a slug of the effect.

The cause was a message from Cecelia. On her way to Crescent City, she would arrive in the morning. The walls began to swing, as if he were lying in a room-sized hammock swaying in the breeze. Only it didn't feel good, like a hammock would. It felt sickening. He had, in fact, felt sick from the time he'd read the telegram.

He groaned. Darla would be coming to his door at any moment. He would turn her away, with regret. As much as she annoyed him by day, she enthralled him by night. She wasn't nearly old enough to have learned the things she knew how to do. Such talent. Such drive. Such madness!

She said she was twenty-one. At twenty-eight, Jordan thought he'd seen it all. Most of what he'd learned in the bedroom had been taught by thirty-something ladies who'd taken his cash for their teachings. And Darla put most of them to shame.

Shame. He squeezed his eyes tightly closed. Here he lay, thinking about the sexual prowess of a young starlet when his own wife sat on a bus en route to warm his bed. A bed still warm, he realized, from the body of said young starlet.

Cecelia would kill him if she found out. Or have her father do it. At the very least, Harv would see to it he never worked in Hollywood, or elsewhere, again. In which case, he might as well be dead.

Perhaps the notion of his own murder caused his leap from the bed when Darla knocked. He nearly became ill as he walked to the door.

"Hey, Mr. Handsome Big Shot Actor," she said, leaning against the doorjamb. "What say we take a little moonlight stroll?"

"Can't tonight, Darla. I'm a bit under the weather."

"Aw, I can fix that, poor baby."

"You don't understand. I just…can't. There's a complication."

Darla moved closer, put her hand against his chest. "What could possibly be so complicated, big boy?"

"Cec. She'll be here in the morning."

Darla stared at him for an uncomfortable length of time, as if reading the implication in his eyes.

"Cecelia. Your wife."

"Yes. One and the same. She can't know about us, Darla. It would ruin me. The picture. Everything."

"What do you mean, *us*, Jordan? What is there to know?" Her level stare did not flinch. She dropped her gaze to his bare chest, where she lifted her hand slightly and dragged her fingernails down to his stomach. She turned to go. "See you on the beach."

He didn't sleep well. When he did sleep, he did so fitfully, fraught with unpleasant dreams. He felt dragged out and disoriented when he finally climbed out of bed at 6:00 a.m.

Cecelia waited for him in the lobby, a cup of black coffee on the table beside her. Her peach suit and wide brimmed hat looked more Beverly Hills than Del Norte Beach, and her matching pumps would be useless on the sand. Yet she emanated a class he admired and respected. And had never gained himself.

"Jordan. You look like hell."

"Good morning to you, too, darling." He bent, and she turned a cheek his way. Her rebuff wasn't lost on him, but it didn't matter much. "You look smashing, as usual. Have you seen Harv?"

"He's down arguing with some surly boat captain. I understand we are going to the lighthouse today."

"We are? You are...going with us?"

Cecelia stood. "Get my bag, will you? I'll need to change in your room. That stuffy bus was such a bore."

Jordan complied without a word, leading his wife down the hall to his room. Despite the fact that he'd already scoured the room for any evidence of his nighttime activities, he swept it once more with his eyes in search of any trace of Darla Foster's presence. He swallowed.

"Here we are, darling. Take your time, of course. I'm going to run down to the rec room—your father has commandeered it for our use. There's probably a pot of coffee going, and I could use about a gallon."

"I'll meet you down there."

In the make-shift commissary, Jordan tried to hold his coffee cup steady while taking a sip of the scalding liquid. Bregman eyed him suspiciously.

"Tie one on again, did you? Better straighten up, son. My daughter is coming up today."

"She's already here," Jordan muttered miserably. "She's getting changed."

Bregman nodded, and for the first time, Jordan briefly felt as if his father-in-law might be as dismayed at the prospect as him.

"Today we have a tough shoot. We'll be inside the tower. Sound is terrible, it's dark and small. We're taking a minimum of equipment since it's damned hard to get out there. Can't afford too many goofs. Got it?"

"Yeah, yeah, yeah. I got it." Jordan took another burning gulp. "Just you stay clear of the rocks this time," he added, unable to resist his own admonition.

"I'll take care of myself."

Jordan nodded. *Sure you will, Tubby.*

Seven

Crescent City, California
June

"Is this Mr. Farralone?"

Matt sighed, then single-handedly buried his axe into a tree stump in front of his house, holding his phone in the other.

"Yeah, this is Farralone."

"My name is Rebecca Burke. I'm calling about Dragon Rock Lighthouse."

Matt paused, took a breath. "What would you like to know, Miss Burke?"

"My magazine would like to do a photo shoot inside and around the outside of the lighthouse. I understand you are the person to talk to."

"I would be, if there was anything to talk about. However, the lighthouse is not open to the public."

"We are not the public, Mr. Farralone. *We* are *Travel One Magazine*, and our readers would like to know about Dragon Rock."

"I'd be happy to supply you with an informational packet on the lighthouse. It contains the history, photos, folklore, that sort of thing. And you are welcome to photograph the outside to your heart's content, if you can get any boat to sit still enough out there. You might be able to hire a helicopter–"

"I don't think you understand, Mr. Farralone. We want to do a *feature*. We don't want rehashed facts and figures. I already have that information. It's all readily available online. What I need is the real story, the *feel* of what happened there. We need live film with commentary. Inside."

Matt stretched his neck, walked to his Jeep and slid into the driver's seat. He looked back to the frame of his house, the fieldstone fireplace already standing, the beginnings of the roof. He huffed out a breath.

"I'm sorry. I just can't help you. The lighthouse is closed to everyone."

He could hear the woman bubbling with irritation.

"Why?"

"Why what?"

"Why is it closed? What's the big deal? You could be there, give us a quick tour, and we'll be gone."

"It's unsafe, for one thing. The whole thing is in disrepair. There is no longer a working light, no electricity, it's dank, it's moldy..." What was he thinking? She didn't need to know that much. "At any rate, the answer is simply no. If you don't need any additional information about the lighthouse, I need to get going."

"Surely there are remnants of belongings from the last keepers?"

"No. Nothing. It's empty."

"No furniture? A bed, perhaps?"

"Miss Burke. I don't know where you are getting your information, but I can tell you–"

"Have you been inside?"

Her question sounded more like an accusation than an inquiry, and Matt was taken aback. "I'm sorry, but I can't answer any more questions. Good luck, Miss Burke." He snapped the cell phone shut and dropped it onto the passenger seat. *What a nervy bitch!* He straightened his back, ran a hand through his hair. Hopefully, that would be the end of it.

Something told him it wouldn't be.

Scottsdale, Arizona

Rebecca put down her phone, fuming. *What a liar!* She'd seen the inside, the pieces of the past. Yes, in disrepair; yes, probably moldy. But not particularly unsafe. The more Farralone argued, the more determined she felt to get inside. Inside, *again.*

To distract herself, she turned on her television and DVD player, then she sat down on the couch. The MGM lion roared, and opening credits began to paint across the screen. Thoughtful,

Rebecca reached for her steno pad and pen. She turned to a fresh page and began a new list.

Jordan Kent. Darla Foster. Jeannette Yarber. Stephen Sisco. Harvey Bregman. Stuart Feinstein.

Copyright MCMXLVIII.

She put the tablet down on the coffee table and stretched out on the couch. The film intrigued her, and although she'd watched it twice already, she couldn't turn it off.

The handsome man on the screen chased a young woman up the rough stairway at the rocky base of the lighthouse. Rebecca squinted, leaned forward to look closer. The lighthouse appeared to be in much better condition in the film. Of course, it had been sixty years. Sixty years ago, her father was ten years old. She smiled, thinking about Daddy sitting in a movie theater watching first a newsreel, a cartoon and a serialized Western, all before the main feature. The last film Rebecca saw in a theater came to the screen only after twenty minutes of commercials and fifteen minutes of ear-blasting trailers. And she'd paid twenty-four times the ticket price of *Cape Seduction*.

Remote in hand, Rebecca paused the action as the camera closed in on the hero's face. Jordan Kent was nothing if not slick, good-looking and smooth. Darla Foster looked every bit the innocent Hollywood newcomer she was. They seemed to have what critics today tagged chemistry.

But what did she know of chemistry? Surely she'd never experienced it with any man. Nothing close to what she imagined it to be, anyway. And most likely, she never would.

She resumed the film, watched as the lovers laughed their way through the door to the lighthouse. Reginald picked Mary up, carried her across the main room as the cameras followed, then preceded, them up the stairs into the bedroom. Reginald dumped Mary playfully on the bed, then sat down beside her.

Rebecca shook her head slowly as she watched, wondering about their antics and whether or not they continued off-camera. Suddenly alert, she again pressed the *pause* button on the remote, then the *slow rewind*. Something had caught her eye, something missed before.

The bed. Behind Darla Foster's head stood the curving brass headboard remaining today at Dragon Rock Lighthouse. Shiny and new, feminine and ornate. *Uncharacteristic for a lighthouse,* Rebecca thought. She picked up her pen and made another note.

Leaving the couch, she went to the kitchen for a glass of iced tea. Her frustration returned. She had to find a way to get back into the lighthouse. A way that did not include Mr. Matthew Farralone. And just who was this guy, anyway?

She went to her laptop and typed his name into the browser, surprised when more than three pages of entries appeared. It only took a moment to realize most of them referred to high-profile court cases. She picked one at random.

"Judge Hector Groff issued a warning to the defendant's counsel, Matt Farralone, for reportedly leading a witness during Wednesday afternoon's hearing…"

"At the preliminary hearing on Monday in Los Angeles…Matthew Farralone, Esq., will be representing Mrs. Bernice Turner, accused of murdering her husband, real estate financier Thomas Turner…"

"Attorney Farralone has announced a hiatus from his practice in Beverly Hills. Mr. Farralone, a long-time supporter of the Boys and Girls Club, will be working alongside other philanthropists in Northern California to build a new facility for the Club."

"Hmm." Rebecca made more notes on her steno pad. "So he's a lawyer. Figures."

Next, she clicked on *Images,* after which a screen full of thumbnail photos appeared. She selected one.

"Damn. Where are my glasses?"

She found them on the coffee table, then hurried back to the computer.

Light brown hair, slightly curly; keen, dark eyes. Youthful haircut. Clean shaven. Suit.

Next photo. Sunglasses, courthouse steps. Lots of reporters.

Next. Standing at microphone, gesturing with hands. Intelligent face.

"Well."

Rebecca bookmarked a few sites then left the computer. The day was getting away from her, and her father expected her for dinner in an hour.

"Put it in the new rec room." Case stood up from where he'd knelt at the indoor pool, watching the young sea otter swim away. He grabbed a towel to dry his arms. "That room is almost done."

Matt shook his head. "The kids will ruin it. This is a really nice piano."

Case smiled, clapped his friend on the shoulder. "We'll figure something out. Where is it, again?"

"Brentwood."

"As in, next-door-to-Beverly Hills? You can't fit it into your house down there?"

"I probably could if I could do without a couch. That house is one of those old Spanish haciendas, has a pretty small living room. This piano is like…like Elton John's. I can put it in there until my house up here is done. I was just hoping I wouldn't have to move it twice."

"I could store it at Hastings House, for a while. I could move the small piano…" Case grew thoughtful. "I think there's room. I'll ask Amy."

"Naw, don't worry about it." Matt looked back to the otter, which swam around the perimeter of the pool. "Looks like he feels better already. You still like being a vet?" he asked, as the two men walked into Case's nearby lab.

"Most of the time. Been here at the Institute fifteen years. When I inherited the inn, I cut back to consulting here. That way I can divide my time between here and Hastings House. It's quite a drive down to Newburg."

Matt nodded. "Which reminds me. When I am going to meet the lovely Miss Amy?"

"Soon enough. She might come up this weekend. If so, we'll get together with Jack and Maddie."

"Oh, sure. I'm odd-man-out again."

Case grinned. "There's always Donna from the diner…"

"Unfortunately, not my type." Matt watched as Case picked a file from a drawer and opened it on a nearby desk. "That for the otter?"

"Yeah. I have to note whenever he gets medication." Case answered, carefully jotting information into the file before replacing it in the drawer.

"An otter with a personal physician. I like it."

Case's blue eyes crinkled with merriment. "Nothing but the best. I'm done here. You want to get some dinner, or go back to the site?"

Matt considered, then nodded. "Both. I want to check out the packages Jack said we received today. Maybe it's the faucets."

"You and those damned faucets," Case said with a chuckle. "I'll drive."

The sun would set soon, and the sky was picture-perfect clear. Coast Highway seemed less busy than usual. They were southbound and perhaps two miles from the new clubhouse site when a loud popping sound shot out and the green Triumph roadster swerved. Case fought to gain control of the sports car, maneuvering it to the side of the road.

"What the hell was that?" Matt cried, looking around the small car as traffic passed by them.

"Blowout," Case muttered, getting out of the car. "Dammit."

"Flat tire? It sounded like a gunshot!"

"Always does. Just got these blasted tires, too. Must've run over something back there."

The men squatted beside the right rear wheel. The tire was ruined.

"You do have a spare, right?"

"Yeah, I do. I hate changing tires."

This time Matt grinned. "I got real good at it when I was a kid. Where's your jack?"

After Matt had the car up on the jack, Case started removing the lugs from the wheel. Matt wandered a short distance onto the beach, watching the sun as it dipped lower in the sky. The high surf crashing against the ragged rocks captured his attention, but his gaze shifted to the lighthouse just south of where they'd stopped.

Soon, Case joined him. "It's done. Piece of crap tire. I doubt I'll get anything on the warranty, either. Whatcha lookin' at?"

"Nothing much."

"There's that old lighthouse out there. It's supposedly abandoned. A wonder they don't tear it down."

"They should." Matt spoke softly, his thoughts diluted by recent events. "Would cost a fortune."

"You okay, dude?"

"Yeah. I'm fine."

They returned to the Triumph and resumed their ride, Matt reflecting on their coincidental stop within view of the problematic lighthouse. He thought about the Burke woman ragging on him to let her inside, and the old man's demands that no one be permitted entry. The piano he had to move, and the faucets he had to replace when the plumber had already finished and left for Canada. The woman who had walked away.

"Screw it," he said at last. "Let's just get dinner. I could really use a beer."

Jebediah Burke placed a steaming plate of spaghetti down on the kitchen table while Rebecca poured them each a glass of deep red wine. The tossed salad waited, and heat radiated from the foiled-wrapped garlic bread.

"Smells so good," Rebecca pronounced. "I'm starved."

Jeb grinned. "Good to have you home, Bec. Did you bring me copies of the photos?"

"Of the cars? You bet. You're going to love the Phaeton. The car was just...yummy. I could see you behind the wheel, Dad."

"Only if I could still keep my little Chevy."

Rebecca smiled. The "little Chevy", her father's most prized possession, lounged out in the garage. So clean, he always said, you could eat off the engine block. Every year, just after the Independence Day Parade over in Winnoja, he spent days cleaning every inch of the car all over again. Rebecca delighted in her father's hobby.

"Yessir, that '57 Bel Air is worth something. Not like these cars today, what's the new square one called? It's an abomination, that's what it is."

57

Rebecca served up the salad while her father unwrapped the garlic bread.

"No question."

"Now, take that little Mustang of yours. A classic, too."

"Oh yeah. Um-hmm. You'd have to pry the keys from my cold, dead fingers to get it away from me," Rebecca said with a laugh. "You can't get a '65 Mustang in that condition anymore. Especially with the leather seats and the horses."

The Mustang shared the garage with the Chevy. Her father politely refrained from criticizing her Volkswagen, which had run letter perfect since the day it had quit on her at the beach.

After dinner, she laid out the copies of the photos for her father. The last one, brought by mistake, was a picture of Dragon Rock Lighthouse.

"What's this?" her father asked, lifting the photograph up to eye level.

"Oh, just a lighthouse I saw. Didn't mean to bring that one."

"Kinda derelict, isn't it?"

"Yes. It's been abandoned for a long, long time. I'm trying to get permission to do a story on it. It's the lighthouse from *Cape Seduction*, you know."

"It is? Oh. I see." Her father put the photo down. "So, you'll be going back to the coast?"

"'Fraid so, Daddy. But not for long. Just a day or two, as soon as I can get inside with a camera crew. We're going to shoot video, too."

"Video? Wow. That's new for you, isn't it?"

"Yeah. I really want to do this, too. And there's this cranky guy standing in the way. He's going to be a tough obstacle. But I'll figure out a way in."

"You always do," her father agreed. "Just watch out. I don't want to be worrying about you. I promised your mom."

Rebecca looked down. He didn't often mention her mother, so when he did, she was unprepared. "Well, I got a feeling she's looking after both of us."

Her mother had been dead for fifteen years, and Rebecca still had questions. Questions about the accident, her mother's last hours, her last words. Where had she been going that night? Why wasn't the driver ever prosecuted?

The questions grew as Rebecca grew; a ten-year-old's knowledge of vehicular manslaughter didn't amount to much, but at twenty-five, Rebecca was more curious than ever. Yet reluctant to bring pain to her father's eyes, she inevitably postponed her questions each time they arose.

Tonight was different, for some reason.

"Can I ask a question, Daddy?"

"You're entitled."

"The night Mom...Mom had the accident; did you know where she was going?"

Her father paused, and Rebecca could see him reeling in the memories. He didn't seem particularly uncomfortable, so she ventured on.

"Was she upset when she left?"

"She'd received a phone call. Something to do with some research she'd been doing. A man had some information for her, and she went to meet him at the library. About her genealogy stuff. All seemed perfectly legit, safe, I wasn't worried. Said she'd call me afterward on that first cellular phone we bought."

"And the guy who hit her, he was drunk?"

Her father shrugged, a look of despair beginning to cloud his face. "She was crossing the street. They called it a hit-and-run. Cops presumed he was drunk. That's what they said."

"And he just...just got away with it?"

"There was a witness. A man standing on the corner."

Rebecca could feel years of hidden anger welling up inside. "So, did he tell them anything?"

"No. Whatever he saw, well, it didn't matter." Jeb looked to the side, not meeting his daughter's intense stare. "Because he died."

"He died?" An unexpected twist. "When?"

"During the night. He was supposed to go for questioning the next morning. But he never woke up."

"Was he hurt in the crash?"

"Nope. He was just a-standing on the corner. They said he had a bad heart, though. That's why he died. A heart attack, I guess."

Rebecca took a moment to process this new information.

"What about the man at the library? Did anyone contact him?"

"No. No point in that. There's an article from the paper. It's in the trunk upstairs. You might as well read it." Jebediah was done talking about her mother. Rebecca picked up the lighthouse photo and quietly tucked it away.

Eight

Del Norte County, California
August 1948

"How can I be in this scene? I'm already dead," Darla exclaimed, arms akimbo.

Bregman blew out a breath. He wasn't quite sure this dame was worth it. "We sometimes film scenes out of order, Miss. Foster. Did you review the screenplay? Today we are shooting the scene where your boyfriend finds you with your lighthouse keeper. Remember? He hasn't killed you yet." He turned, shook his head and muttered under his breath. "Okay. Sisco. You're over here. Kent, you'll enter from the door. Miss Foster...Miss Foster?"

Darla had started up the tower steps. Bregman hollered into the stairwell. "Please, Miss Foster! We need you down here, in the bedroom! Now. Let's get this show on the road. I may only have twenty years left."

Returning to the bedroom, Darla flashed her dimples and struck a pose beside Stephen Sisco, the actor playing the lighthouse keeper. "Here, Mr. Bregman?"

"That's about right." He turned and motioned for his cameras. "Can you get...can you get it so the door is in the background?"

The cameramen shuffled about, and Jordan Kent made his exit in preparation for the scene. Bregman made a full circle turn, checking every detail and angle. "Okay. This is it. Action."

Despite her earlier confusion, Darla went immediately into character and played her role with perfection and flare. Bregman nodded slowly in approval, forgetting his annoyance and thanking his lucky stars for the chance meeting with the young starlet.

"Oh, Franklin...you know I won't be seeing Reginald again. He's such a fool, and he'll never escape from greed. You...you're nothing like him. Your life is simple, pure, dignified–"

The bedroom door opened, and Jordan stormed in, as if he already knew what he would find. He stopped at the foot of the bed, stared hard at the couple who stood facing each other below the small window.

"What's going on here?" he demanded, looking from Darla's face to Sisco's, then back.

"Why, Reggie, this is Franklin. He's the keeper here. He's just returned, and we–we were just discussing the history of the lighthouse."

Fists tightened, Jordan took a step forward, squinted at Sisco. "Franklin, you say? *Franklin?*"

Sisco swallowed hard, extended his hand. "Franklin Webster. And yes, I am the keeper here. Have been for ten years."

Jordan ignored his offer of a handshake, reached for Darla instead. "C'mon, Mary. We have to go."

Darla frowned at Jordan, turned back to Sisco. "I enjoyed our conversation. Quite a pleasure," she said, taking his still outstretched hand. "I hope to take you up on the offer of a full tour one day."

"The pleasure was all mine, Miss Triton."

With another frown directed at Jordan, Darla strode heavily past him and out the door. Jordan glared at Sisco, his jaw working. After playing out a meaningful, silent moment, he turned and followed his co-star out the door. The cameras, now trained on Sisco, followed his movement as first he exhaled, then moved to the bed and slowly sat down. The sound of the engine room door opening gave him pause, and he turned to see Darla hurrying up the steps and back to the bedroom.

"What happened? Why did you come back?" he asked, his voice a rough whisper.

"I told him I forgot something. I'll meet you tomorrow at 6:00 p.m. on the shore. I'll have the car. Don't be late. It's our only chance to get away." She kissed him briefly, then fled back down the steps and out the door.

Sisco looked as if he'd been punched. Pushing the hair back from his forehead, he slumped against the headboard and closed his eyes.

"Cut! Beautiful. Simply divine," Bregman called.

"It's really very sad," Darla said, between bites of linguini. "She really loved Franklin. Umm. Not fair that she gets killed before they can be together."

"Doesn't matter that she's cheating?" Jordan asked, filling his wife's wine glass.

"She was just afraid to break up with him. Afraid it would ruin her life somehow. And she was right, wasn't she? He *did* kill her."

Cecelia looked up from her salad. "Adultery. She deserved to be killed. You can't cheat like that and get away with it."

"Oh, I don't know. It happens every day. Or so I hear," Darla returned, winding another forkful against her spoon. "Sometimes couples just aren't compatible, and one of them falls for someone else. But they don't have the guts to call it off with their husband." She stuffed the noodles into her mouth, chewed a bit, then cocked her head. Swallowing the load of it, she directed her most innocent smile at her nemesis. "Or their *wife*, of course."

Cecelia's eyes blazed, and her fork skidded across her plate as she jabbed at a cherry tomato.

Jordan tugged at the collar of his Hawaiian shirt, loosening an imaginary tie. "How's that lasagna, Harv?"

"It's good. Not like Mario's, but good."

"Aw, nobody makes it like Mario. It's unfair to compare," Sisco added.

"Who's Mario?" Darla asked.

"Only the best Italian chef in Hollywood. I'll...we'll have to take you there sometime. Uh, perhaps we'll have the wrap party there. What do you think?" Jordan directed the question to his father-in-law, who merely nodded, his mouth full of lasagna.

"I can't wait," Darla cooed, her eyes fixed on Jordan's. Jordan took a gulp of wine, then another. He turned to his wife.

"I think we'll turn in early tonight, if that's all right with you."

"If this restaurant is the extent of the local nightlife, we might as well."

Darla ignored their comments and brightened. "Isn't there another scene between Franklin and Mary? Don't they at least *do it* once before she dies?"

Cecelia uttered a subtle sound of disgust and picked up her napkin.

Bregman seemed unaffected by her uninhibited tact. "Yes, you are correct. There's a scene in the boathouse. They *do it*, as you say, and Reginald sees them leaving the lighthouse from a distance. He goes ballistic. It's right before the scene we shot the other day on the sand. Where Mary bites the big one."

"Oh, goodie! Another love scene. But we don't really do it, do we? I mean, we can't do that stuff on camera, right?"

Cecelia grinned, shook her head. "This conversation is way over *my* head. I think I need to powder my nose." She stood, and Jordan got rapidly to his feet, saw her away, then returned to his seat.

"To answer your question, Miss Foster, no. We merely intimate…suggest…sex is occurring off-camera." Bregman ripped an Italian roll in half. "Does that set your mind at ease?"

Darla's eyebrows rose, and she turned an innocent expression his way. "I'd like to think I'm not the kind of girl who would sleep with her leading man unless directed to," she said easily. "I mean, not that Jordie and Stevie aren't just the cutest two boys to ever walk this earth…"

Stephen Sisco laughed out loud, and Jordan smiled through a blush, silently thanking the powers-that-be for Cecelia's shiny nose; she'd missed Darla's comment.

Darla surprised them all by standing abruptly. "I think I shall also powder my nose," she announced, snatching up her handbag and walking casually toward the ladies' restroom.

Jordan felt himself beginning to sweat. The imaginary tie now choked him.

"She's quite a piece of work," Sisco said, still chuckling. "I wouldn't mind a bit of that hellfire in my bed."

Jordan tried to laugh, but only a gurgling sound came from his throat. He couldn't take much more of the dramatics.

Bregman snorted. "I wish you *would* bed the girl. Maybe it would keep her from sniffing around Kent so much."

"Is that so?" Sisco asked, his interest obviously piqued. "I never would have guessed. Oh, except for the way she walks a little too close, talks a little too sweet, laughs at all your jokes…"

"You can stop any time, Stevie-boy. I've seen her rub up against you once or twice." Jordan tried to maintain calm, to move the spotlight onto his co-star. He couldn't wait for Cecelia to return so he could escape the nightmare.

"Is it *Chanel*?"

"I beg your pardon?" Cecelia asked, leaning close to the mirror to re-apply her lipstick.

"Your perfume. I'll bet it's *Chanel*." Darla stared at the other woman in the mirror, then dug into her handbag. "It's nice."

"I don't know what it is. I didn't bother to look. It might be *Chanel*."

"Wow. To have so many you don't know what it is. That's rich." She paused, looked herself in the eye. "Like that airplane we flew on. I told Jordie, it felt so *richish*. Like we were royalty or something."

Cecelia carefully replaced the lipstick in its case, dropped it into her purse. She turned to Darla, her chin held high. "Let me give you a piece of advice, Miss Foster. Jordan Kent is mine. Always has been, always will be. He'll never leave me, not for you or any other fresh skirt anxious to drop her panties for a starring role. So just put yours back on and leave him alone."

Darla's eyes narrowed just slightly, and she moistened her lips. "I have no idea what you're talking about." *Come on. I'm ready.*

"Oh, I'm quite sure you do know what I'm talking about. And if you think this is not serious business, just keep right on with your little charade. Have you forgotten that you are working for my father? Cross me, and I'll see to it you never get another role or even a crumb from anyone in Hollywood. Am I quite clear?"

Darla stared levelly at Cecelia. "You really don't get it, do you? No, you can't lose Jordan because you never really had him in the first place. I would much rather be the mistress of a man who loved me than the wife of a man who kept me because of my fat father's power. I'm not afraid of you or your father. Because I know enough about all of you to blow your reputations right out of the water. About how you all took advantage of a sweet young girl with no experience and forced her to do things she didn't want to do...about how you and Jordan haven't slept together in

65

months…or is it years? And how about the time your father made a pass at me? Christ, I'm barely twenty-one, and he's grabbing my behind in the dressing room."

Cecelia's lips partly slightly in surprise. "You're lying. You're a lying little slut and not worth the breath to even speak to. You can collect your things and get on the next bus back to your tawdry, menial life in the Valley."

"Oh, I don't think so. In case you've forgotten, my uncle is an executive at CBS. He doesn't just know the media; he *is* the media. And anyway, I don't think you have to guts to call my bluff. You really want to put the choice to Jordan? I wouldn't if I were you, because you'd lose." Darla turned to go, then looked over her shoulder. "And don't worry about my panties. I don't wear them when I'm with your husband."

Inordinate quiet prevailed on the way back to the motel. Jordan didn't know whether to be relieved or not. The silence continued as Cecelia prepared for bed. Jordan poured them both a short scotch, called to her through the bathroom door.

"Enjoy dinner, sweetheart?"

"It was tolerable." She emerged then, and Jordan's next thought dissipated into the air between them. She wore a lacy, red baby doll, not unlike the garment she'd worn on their honeymoon six years before.

"Oh, my, my," he murmured, handing her the scotch. "What's the occasion?"

"Does there have to be an occasion?" she said softly, taking a slug of the bourbon and putting it on the dressing table. "Can't I just seduce my husband for seduction's sake?"

"Anytime," Jordan responded, smoothly divesting himself of his shirt as his wife worked on the buckle of his trousers. "It's just a pleasant surprise."

As soon as he'd freed himself from his pants, Cecelia pushed Jordan onto the bed. He wasn't quite sure *seduction* properly defined her attack; wanton desperation fueled her kiss, furious determination controlled her touch. Even as she drove him to the brink of insanity, Jordan sensed something missing. Her kisses, while deep and intimate, lacked affection. The passion burned hot but empty. He discarded his reservations as inconsequential–after all, she was screwing his brains out. It wasn't until later, as he lay watching her restless sleep, that he recognized the sense of foreboding growing within him.

He called her a cab in the morning. Her odd goodbye, a rare, misty-eyed adieu, caused him to wonder if her regret was connected somehow to the unprecedented encounter of the night before. Again quiet, Cecelia seemed uncharacteristically humble as she waved goodbye from the taxi. Jordan, more confused than ever, wandered back to his motel room and fell into bed.

From her window, Darla watched the cab speed away, a satisfied smile curling her lips.

Nine

Beverly Hills, California
July 1

"Ever wonder what this place was like back in the day?" Matt asked, flipping on his right signal at Sunset Boulevard.

"The *day*?" Jack asked, peering out the passenger window at a particularly ostentatious home. "You mean, the 'hey' day? Hollywood's *golden era*? My uncle was a screenwriter back then. I remember lots of whispers in the kitchen. Gramma wanted him to ditch the business and buy a delicatessen in the Midwest. She was scared."

"Of what?"

"Two words: Joseph McCarthy. Some of those writers–the Hollywood Ten–they were pals of my grandfather's."

Matt glanced at Jack, then returned his attention to the road ahead. "Did anything ever happen? Did he get fingered?"

"His compromise was television. He took a job writing for Milton Berle on Texaco Star Theatre. It seemed like a safe place to land."

"Those must have been grim days. I'm talking about the glitz– the parties, the glam, you know."

"It's still there. We just see it through different eyes."

Matt nodded, navigating unhurriedly through the streets en route to his destination. He hoped the piano movers had already parked at Chelsea's; he didn't mind paying them to wait a bit as long as they got there first and precluded any kind of confrontation. Jack's presence would help, too.

I've become such a wimp. This isn't like me. Worrying about seeing Chelsea again.

His fears were founded. The driveway leading up to the estate was empty, save for Chelsea's BMW roadster in the far corner.

"Damn," he muttered, pulling his Porsche Cayenne alongside the curb across the street. The two men got out of the luxury SUV, and Jack stretched, then looked up at the mansion.

"Jeez-Louise! Does she own this place? You lived here with her?" Jack asked in astonishment.

"We met three years ago at a party. I'd just started my remodel. We started hanging out, I stayed over...one thing led to another."

"So, she already lived here. How does she afford it, if I may ask?"

"Her family is loaded. Her father invented some kind of medical widget used in hospitals, and he sold the patent and invested the money. She's done some modeling but is basically unskilled."

Jack smiled. "I'll reckon she has some skills, my man. You lived with her for how long?" He gave Matt a light punch. "Looks like no one's here yet. I just hate being the first one at a party."

"Me, too. Let's find the bar first." Matt took a deep breath and blew it out through pursed lips. "Okay."

Chelsea answered the door, a Boston terrier cradled in her arms. "Oh! Matt! Is it today?"

Matt suppressed the urge to roll his eyes. "You set the date, Chels. This is my friend, Jack." Matt moved passed the surprised woman and into the elegant entryway of the Tudor mansion.

"Hi," Jack offered, holding out his hand. The platinum blonde disentangled her right hand from the dog and shook Jack's, her gray eyes curious.

"Nice to meet you, Jack. Can I get you guys something to drink? A beer or something?"

"No." Matt turned back, crossed his arms. "None for me. The movers should be here any time now."

"I wouldn't mind. What've you got?" Jack said.

"Corona?"

"Fine."

Chelsea dropped the dog into a child's playpen in the corner of the living room and headed for the bar, where she took two bottles of beer from the refrigerator. "Glass?"

"Bottle's fine." Jack shook his hair from his forehead. "Nice. It's getting toasty out there."

"I was just going to lie by the pool when you arrived. Would you guys like to join me?"

"Shouldn't someone wait for the movers?" Matt asked, wishing he'd asked for a beer but too stubborn to say so.

"Of course, we can hear the bell out there. You know—"

Before she could finish her thought, the doorbell did in fact ring, and Matt stepped forward. "There. There they are."

"Well, fine. The piano is right where you left it. You might want to collect your sheet music while you're here. And the hockey stuff is in bags, in the garage."

"Right. The hockey stuff. Jack, could you..."

"Got it. Keys?"

Matt tossed him the keys to the Cayenne, and Jack followed Chelsea's pointing finger to the door leading out to the garage. Matt answered the front door.

"We're here for a grand piano," the first man said. "S'posed to be on the ground floor."

"Yes, it is. Right this way," Matt said, directing the two men to follow him through the luxurious house. Just as promised, the beautiful, ebony black Yamaha stood in the generous family room at the rear. Matt ran a hand over the lid covering the keys. It felt good. It felt good to be moving the piano away from this bad place.

He turned to the piano bench as the movers began working on the piano. He opened the hinged lid to remove a few sheets of music he'd left inside, then noticed something amiss with one of the legs. Near the bottom of the leg nearest his own, the bench had been chewed down to the raw wood inside. It didn't take much thinking to determine the culprit.

"This isn't good," he murmured, turning to peer at Chelsea, who stood in the doorway watching. "You know about this?"

"About what?"

"Your mutt using my five-hundred-dollar bench as a chew toy?"

Her eyes belying the truth, Chelsea shrugged. "Don't know anything about it. I thought it was like that when you moved in. Didn't you have some kind of stray mongrel when we met?"

"Molly? Are you kidding? She wouldn't deface property like this...and anyway, you might recall Molly died–on your watch–the week before I got the piano. In this house. I didn't have the piano when I moved in here, Chels."

Chelsea turned away, clearly finished with the conversation. She picked up a beach towel from the back of the couch, along with a paperback book. Lifting a pair of sunglasses from a side table, she started for the back door.

"I'll be outside. Lock the front door on your way out."

Matt watched her go, and while he'd been clearly incensed about the piano leg, seeing Chelsea walk away was somehow cathartic. Her callous words about his beloved dog were only the icing on the cake; he'd been down this road with her before. The quiet in the room brought him around to the realization that the movers were standing by.

"Can we open up the double doors, sir?"

"Of course. Do you need anything from me?"

"Your signature once we have it loaded."

"Sure. I'll stick around."

Jack held one of Matt's hockey gloves, turning it slowing in his hands. "RBK. Not too shabby."

"What do you use?" Matt asked, feeling relaxed for the first time in days as he unloaded the Porsche, backed halfway into his garage.

"CCM. Bauer. I have a mish-mash of stuff."

"Me too. Hey, just toss it in the corner there. Are you in a hurry? I just need to check on a few things."

Jack chuckled. "Me? In a hurry? You gotta be kidding. Take your time." Dropping the gloves and pads as directed, Jack followed Matt into the house.

"Great place you got here," he commented, looking around the long, narrow living room of Matt's restored Hollywood Hills home. "Spanish architecture is sure popular around here."

"Didn't you live near here once?"

72

"On the Valley side. In a condo. It wasn't my favorite place to live." Jack wandered to the broad, arched window facing the street. "Did you do the work yourself?"

Matt sat on the rugged leather couch, a pile of mail on his lap. "This stuff never ends...uh, yes and no. It was in process. They built the place in the '20s, and it's been through various changes over the years. The upstairs is done, the back, well..."

"Back?"

"Yeah, it looks like a single level from the front, but the back of the lot slopes down and the bedrooms are down there. And the pool. And the view."

"Ah. Cool. Maybe I'll look around, if you don't mind."

"Go ahead. No skeletons in my closets, at least none I know of. I haven't been here much the past six months, you know."

Most of the mail consisted of junk. He was almost to the bottom when the house phone rang, a sound so foreign, Matt had to put conscious thought into finding the device.

"My name is Denise. Denise Murray. Linda Chandler referred me. Do you have a moment?"

"If this is about representation, I'm sorry but I'm not taking any new clients at this time. My partner, Jason Abberley, will be glad to schedule you an appointment."

"Oh, no...it's not like that. It's about the Boys and Girls Club. I'm interested in information about the facilities you are working on."

"Oh! In that case, forgive me. What... how can I help you?"

"Well, our group grants a substantial donation to one deserving non-profit organization each year. This year, we voted to consider three charities, one being the Boys and Girls Club. However, when we discovered the new clubhouse facilities you're building, we were especially intrigued."

Matt grinned, sat. "Wow, that's very cool."

"The donors have asked me to review the project and report back. Possibly even tour the site? Do you think it would be possible?"

"Of course. Where are you calling from? I could meet you there day after tomorrow."

"I'm in Los Angeles at the moment. Would you care to meet in advance, to maybe go over the terms of the grant to see if it would meet your requirements?"

My requirements? For money?

"How about lunch tomorrow? I could meet you at, say, 11:30? Uh, where in L.A. are you?"

Quiet ensued as the caller hesitated. "I'm in Burbank. 11:30 would work fine."

"Hmm. How about we meet in Studio City? There's a great little café on Ventura Boulevard near, uh...Laurel."

"Super. I'll see you there."

"How will I know you?" Matt asked quickly, before she could hang up.

"Don't worry. I'll know you."

Jack returned just as Matt hung up the phone.

"How odd."

"This place is awesome! What a view!" Jack went to the back of the room and pulled open the wooden shutters. "What's odd?"

"That call. Just wondering how she got my number. Weird that I just happened to be here when she called. I'm never here."

"Somebody Chelsea put up to calling?"

"Naw. She has no motivation to do something like that. No, this girl...woman...sounded legit. It's just...strange. She mentioned Linda Chandler. I haven't seen Linda in ages. She used to be one of my paralegals."

"So, what did this chick want?"

"She has some money to grant to our cause, if she likes it."

"What's not to like? Hey, when will the piano get here?"

"Any minute." Matt said, looking out the front window. "Man, it's going to be tight in here. Help me move this couch."

The two men pushed all of the furniture to one end of the room, finishing just as the big moving van appeared in the driveway.

"Let's get your gear re-packed and go slap some pucks as soon as they finish," Jack said, propping open the front doors.

"Okay, but remember I'm not the all-out, end-all jock you are, man. I haven't played in...let's just say not in recent lifetimes."

Jack grinned. "Hey, it's just like riding a bike."

Phone wedged between her ear and shoulder, Rebecca reached up to pull her overnighter from the closet shelf. "Daddy? It's me. Yeah, I take off at one. Only a few days. What's that? Oh, it's the lighthouse story. No, L.A. this time. Flying into Burbank. Rental car? Let's see…what should it be?"

She tossed the small suitcase onto the bed and headed for the dresser. "How about a '57 Corvette? I think Jackson just got one. If not, I'll get the '72 we rented from him last time you went with me." Pawing through her lingerie, she flung underwear into the case. "I'll call you later. Love you!"

Back in her small office, she picked up a few sheets of paper from the desk, glanced over them one last time. The masthead at the top looked pretty good, as did the phony letter she'd typed below. "Not bad, if I say so myself," she murmured, tucking the paper into a folder and then into her carry-on. "Mr. Farralone, meet Ms. Murray, who will charm the keys to the lighthouse right out of your proverbial pocket."

ANNE CARTER

76

Ten

Del Norte County, California
August 1948

D arla closed her motel room door and leaned back against it. She stretched, then wrapped the silk dressing gown tighter and walked back to the bed. Jordan had lasted exactly forty-eight hours after Cecelia left Northern California for Los Angeles. Just two days, and he'd come back to Darla's bed, riding her like he hadn't been laid in years. She lay down, cupped her breasts in memory of Jordan's incredible hands. Smiled.

"Ah, Jordie, Jordie, Jordie...you'll be mine one of these days. You'll see who it is that truly loves you. It was meant to be. Yes." Filming was nearly over. Just yesterday, Bregman announced it: they would be home within the week.

Her smile dimmed as she thought about poor Russell, who would undoubtedly suffocate her from the moment she'd step off the plane. Something had to be done about that one. He expected way too much from her. Worse, he offered nothing in return. Nothing important.

Too bad she couldn't pawn him off on Cecelia. Dear Cecelia, who'd backed off so fast she'd nearly stumbled over her own lame feet. *I showed her, I did! She even believed the cockamamie story about my uncle.* Darla giggled. Uncle Charles did work at CBS. As the janitor for Cosmopolitan Beauty Salon, he got to sweep up the tresses of some of the best heads in Hollywood.

Jordan didn't often walk on the beach. The weather was too damp, too cold for his liking. He longed for Santa Monica, the tanned bodies and snow cones of his youth. Soon, he'd be back there. So why did he feel so down?

He shoved his hands into his trouser pockets, wandered along the sand in an aimless search for an answer. It wasn't hard to figure out, really. Darla Foster had complicated his life, big time. It might have all worked out, too, if Cec hadn't suddenly come on to him like a blooming cactus. Now he struggled, clouded and uncertain.

Who was he kidding, anyway? Whether he liked it or not, Cecelia remained powerful, the daughter of *the man*. The man who would put him on the map to stars' homes. He couldn't leave her if he wanted to. And right now, he wasn't sure he wanted to anyway. What if she was still crazy about him? What if she jumped his bones again when he got home? Could it have been a fluke, that little motel orgy she'd conducted before leaving him?

But there was still Darla. Beautiful, nutcase Darla. Loony, greenhorn actress by day, insatiable nympho by night. How would he see her in Los Angeles? Cec would have him strung up by the balls.

Jordan shook his head, as if he could shake away the image of Cecelia and Darla squaring off. A scary thought, that. No, as hard as it was to admit, he would have to let Darla Foster go. Tell her goodbye, now, before they left Crescent City.

He grimaced. They were set to leave tomorrow.

"Come on. Please? Just one more time? We can do it."

"No, Darla. It's not safe. I'm not good at that stuff."

"You can't row a damned boat? Aw, c'mon. For me? I want to go back to the lighthouse just once more before we go. We'll never get another chance. We could be alone in there, Jordie." Darla stood on tiptoe, whispered close to his ear. "We've never done it in there. Why do you think they call it *Cape Seduction*?"

"That's just the name in the film, dear heart. And unlike you, I have no burning desire to brave those killer rocks and waves. It's dangerous."

Darla pushed out her lower lip. "I didn't know you were such a coward." She paused, pouted. "You know it's going to be different when we get home."

Jordan turned toward her at the comment. Maybe she understood. Maybe this was his chance. "I do know, Darla. I've wanted to talk to you about that. When I get home, I'll be with–you know."

"Shh! Don't say it. Don't hurt me. Just give me this. Take me out to the lighthouse and love me. Love me to death. One more time."

She looked so pitiful, begging. Jordan looked around. The beach, and the nearby dinghy, were empty. He rubbed his hand across his mouth, looked out across the surf to where the lighthouse stood, its rocky base standing solid against the crashing waves. Looking back at Darla, her sweet, yet challenging, eyes fixed on his, he made his decision. He knew he would forever regret not granting her wish.

"Okay. Let's go. We don't have a lot of time, so we need to be brief."

"You got it, Skipper! Let's sail!" She saluted him in her eccentric way, the offshore breeze fluttering her short brown hair. She looked childlike, and Jordan got a funny sort of arousal out of the image of making love to a girl. He quickly dashed the thought and proceeded to launch the skiff.

The bedsprings squeaked and groaned. Darla grasped the brass headboard tightly as Jordan slammed against her, into her, in a prolonged ritual of carnal joy. She let herself go, let herself abandon, for one time only, her careful and calculating ways. This was purity, intimate love with Jordan, and he belonged to her. Despite what she'd told him, it was only the beginning. Because she would not stop, would not rest, would not go away until she had him all to herself. The small victory of persuading him to make the treacherous trip in the dinghy was evidence enough that she had a chance.

She whispered obscenities as he pumped, because she knew he liked it. Cecelia, she suspected, was too big a prude to ever get dirty enough for a man like Jordan.

"Ooh, yeah. Oh, yeah, baby. Come on. Come on." Jordan quivered, and Darla met his rhythm, stroke for stroke. She let go of the headboard and wrapped her arms around him, nipping his earlobe, sucking on his neck, panting in a bigger passion than she'd ever known.

"Ah, Darla, Darla…God damn…I can't…I can't…"

"Don't hold back, Jordie! Come, you nasty boy! Come hard!"

If Jordan heard her, Darla couldn't tell. They were lost in each other, lost in the moment, lost in time.

Cold air, damp and still, surrounded them. The only sounds were those of the waves splashing against the rocks below the lighthouse, the occasional squeal of a gull, the distant clanging of a buoy. Darla lay curled against Jordan, their sweat-slicked bodies cooling now in the aftermath of their bliss.

Jordan wondered how he could let her go. There had to be some way he could see her after they returned home. Perhaps a schedule, a weekly obligation he could cook up. A club, perhaps? He snickered to himself. He could fairly see Cecelia waiting beside the door, rolling pin poised in her folded arms, foot tapping. Rolling pin? More like a tire iron.

Darla said this would be the last time. Could she really be done with him? After the sex they'd just enjoyed, after they'd nearly torched the sheets on the movie prop bed, could she just turn away?

"Dar?"

"Hmm?"

"What are your plans after we get back? Maybe I could come by sometime, you know…"

"Jordan. Surely you don't think I could bear to share you with another woman. I mean, this is fun and all. Really it is. But it's hard for me to think about you going home to…her."

"You know I don't love her."

Darla was quiet. She ran her foot slowly up the side of Jordan's shin and back down. "So you say."

"No, really. I'm only with her because of Harv. You know that. You saw through us right away. Once I make it big, once I'm good on my own, I can walk away from them both."

"Mm-hmm. Right. And in the meantime? I don't know. I think I'll be better off going my way. You can look me up when you're free."

Jordan held back a sigh. He hadn't expected this at all. It only served to make him want her more. Before he could think of what to say next, she sat up on the bed.

"Come on. I want to go into the tower."

"Now?"

"Yeah, now. Come on!" She bounded from the bed and dashed from the room.

"Darla, wait! Let me get something on."

"No!" She turned back, grabbed him by the hand and pulled. "Come *on*." She dragged him from the bed and led him to the stairs, where she scampered ahead of him in the darkened tower. Laughing, youthful, joyous sounds echoed back down to him. Reluctantly, he followed her up the steps, finally emerging in the lantern room.

"Look! Look at me! I'm naked as a jaybird," she shouted. "Here. I'm going out."

Jordan tried to pull her back, but Darla remained intent on going out onto the gallery.

"Look! Naked!" She spread her arms wide, closed her eyes as the wind tore at her hair. Jordan watched from inside the lantern room, shivering but safe behind the glass, wondering if he was in love or just in awe.

The next morning, she'd changed.

I am a different woman. I can be whatever I want to be, different every day. After all, I am an actress.

Gone, the playful, spunky, child-woman with attitude; in her place, a quiet, almost dignified young woman, politely waiting for their bus.

Darla knew the others noticed. Jordan seemed at a loss for words. Harv merely enjoyed the silence. Sisco persisted in engaging her, but she remained softly demure all the way to Los Angeles Municipal Airport, where she hailed a cab with the last of her spending money.

Her mother hugged her when she walked in. Darla let her hold on for a moment, squeezed her back, then pulled away.

"How was it all, Darla? Great?" her mother asked, looking much like one of the women who'd met their arriving bus in Crescent City.

"The cat's meow, Mom. Now I have to go to bed. We'll talk tomorrow."

"Wait, honey. You might want to take those upstairs." Her mother gestured to the sideboard in the small dining area, its top littered with letters and small packages.

"From my many fans, I suppose," Darla muttered, picking up one of the letters.

"From a certain fan, actually. That Russell Harrington fella has been calling non-stop."

Darla dropped the letter back onto the pile and walked on to her bedroom.

Eleven

Studio City, California
July 2

Rebecca arrived purposely late. She had an advantage being able to identify the attorney, him not knowing her from Eve. Along with the keys, she handed the valet a ten spot. "Take care of her," she warned, then sighed as the driver took the wheel of the light green, 1957 Corvette convertible. *Wouldn't that look great in Daddy's garage?*

Despite her height, she chose heels today. She barely recognized herself in the hotel room mirror; she'd all but forgotten what her own legs looked like below the hem of skirt. Still, she was playing a role. The shapely legs and stylish clothes belonged to Denise Murray.

The small restaurant had charm and just the right aroma. Matt Farralone sat alone, the only lone diner in the place, and after a subtle breath, Rebecca walked purposefully up to his table.

"Mr. Farralone. Denise Murray." She thrust out her hand as Matt got quickly to his feet.

"A pleasure, Ms. Murray. I just got here myself." Despite the intense July heat, her lunch date wore a crisp, sky blue shirt and power tie. She wasn't surprised.

Rebecca slid gracefully into the booth across from him. "Water. Great. I'm parched!"

"It's a warm one out there. Do you live here in Southern California?"

"Umm. No," she replied, swallowing a gulp of water. "I'm from Seattle. Not used to this kind of heat." *Ha! Might as well play it big.* She'd gone to school in Washington State, so she wasn't entirely out of her realm.

"Staying here in the Valley?"

"Holiday Inn." Rebecca picked up the menu, quickly selected a salad.

After they'd ordered, she opened her portfolio. "I took the liberty of bringing some of the information about our group." She handed the faux documents to Matt, sat back.

"Hey, that's great." Matt took a moment to read through the three pages, then handed them back. "So, what do I need to do to qualify? I don't mind telling you, the project has been largely funded, so far, by my own funds. I do need the write-off," he paused, smiled, "but there are things I just can't afford that would really enhance the facility. For instance, the playground is pretty bare. My goal is to get the kids away from electronic garbage as often as possible. They need playground equipment more than they need video games, for example. I'd almost rather not put in all that gaming stuff–" Matt stopped abruptly, grinned. "Sorry."

Rebecca stared intently, however, absorbing every word. "Don't stop," she said, folding her hands and leaning forward. "Do go on. I love hearing your ideas."

"You'll have to bear with me. I tend to get a little zealous. It's just the kids–if you knew them..." He sat back, adjusted the napkin on his lap. "You have any kids, Miss Murray?"

"Please, call me Denise. No, not yet. Maybe one day. So. Playground equipment. Like swings? Sandboxes?"

"Basketball courts. Handball. Tetherball. Soccer nets. Roller skates. Maybe even a tennis court. Whatever. Whatever will get them outside and pumping up their hearts instead of exercising their thumbs, if you know what I mean."

"Of course. It's all great. I'm impressed. I'm sure the committee will be, too."

Matt uttered a short sigh. "Hope so. I can use all the help I can get. So, do you do this sort of thing for a living? Or do you normally work at something else?"

Rebecca hesitated, took a sip of water. "I, uh, restore automobiles. With my father. We have a business."

"In Seattle?"

"Um, yeah. Lake Washington."

"Wow. That's different. Classic cars? Muscle cars? Foreign cars?"

"Mostly American classics. Some of them are muscle, yeah. How about you? Did I read somewhere you're in law?"

"Sadly, yes. I'm an attorney. Dead tired of it, too. Burned out at twenty-nine. But my grandfather put me through school, so I have to stay with it awhile, at least. Hey, I used to have a '66 Mustang years ago. Could kill myself for letting it go."

"I can understand that." Rebecca nodded. "Those early ponies are priceless. That 289 engine has never been rivaled, in my opinion. A little low to the ground, they wash out easily in high water. Had to replace the tie-rods on a '65 just last year. What a job! Of course, the brakes were bad, too, and–"

Now it was her turn to curb her enthusiasm. Blushing, she picked up her fork and loaded it with lettuce from the salad that had just arrived.

Matt seemed intrigued. He considered his sandwich, picked it up. "You really do know about cars. My tie-rods went bad, too. I have a friend with an old Triumph roadster. Obviously not American, but what a great car. Just last week we were cruising down Coast Highway and had a blow-out. We felt it, too. It was all Case could do to get the car to the roadside."

Rebecca hurriedly swallowed the salad in her mouth. "Coast Highway? Whereabouts?"

"Oh, up by the project. Not too far from Crescent City. And he hates to change tires. So, I–"

"You changed it for him. What a guy. Yeah, I like those old Triumphs, too. It's Daddy who's the all-American. He's ex-union, so, you know."

"Sounds like you're very close."

"We are. We're pretty much all each other's got right now."

"I know the feeling. Just have my mom and my grandfather, and he's older than dirt. And a stray uncle, too. I haven't seen them much lately, spending all my time up north."

Rebecca nodded. "I like that area up there. It's nice, more unspoiled. Why, I'll bet where you had your flat tire, there was nothing around, right? Just beach and water."

"Gee, how did you know? Well, there was actually this one seagull...there's a lot of gulls and water birds around there, because of the reef. It's deadly. It's like the equivalent of road-kill."

"Reef? Roadkill? Explain." Rebecca picked up her water, took a gulp. She knew that gull.

"Dragon Rock Reef. There's this massive bunch of rocks just offshore. Really deadly, rough surf, and there always seems to be a lot of wildlife casualties–fish, birds, whatever, so the gulls and even some birds of prey hang out around the lighthouse there. It's not really a very pretty site."

Rebecca tried not to choke on the water. Hiding a sputter with her napkin, her eyebrows went up. "Lighthouse?" she managed.

"Yeah. They built a lighthouse on the largest rock, they called it the Dragon, about 120 years ago. It's closed now, no longer in service. It's an eyesore."

Rebecca, now composed, smiled. "Hard to imagine any lighthouse being an eyesore. I wonder if it's the same one Daddy and I saw. We toured that area a few years ago, and I remember we pulled over to see a lighthouse out in the water. It was squarish, not round, perched on a big oval base."

"Yep. That's the one. In fact," Matt continued, reaching for his cola. "One of my clients owns the damned thing."

"How interesting. I didn't know private individuals could own lighthouses."

"Sure, they can. The Coast Guard used to own or be in charge of most of them, but over the years, they've divested themselves. Sold them off. Anyway. It's a pain in the butt."

Rebecca smiled. "If you say so. So back to our project."

"Our project? I like the sound of that."

"*The* project. When might I tour it? I'd like to get moving on this as soon as possible."

"Say when. We could leave today."

Matt inhaled deeply and stepped from the elevator. The floor was quiet. He'd timed his visit well–medications had just been dispensed. As he walked down the familiar, antiseptic hallway, he thought about his offer to accompany Denise Murray to Crescent City in the morning. Was he nuts?

He'd flown down, so leaving a car wasn't a problem; she said she'd drive. But thirteen hours could be a long time in the car with a total stranger, albeit a lovely one. Aw, what could go wrong? Traveling with a sharp, witty woman whom he found both attractive and interesting would be fun.

As he reached the corner room, he paused outside the door. He hoped it was a good day. Licking his lips, he moved forward and opened the door.

The old man sat in his chair, staring out the window. He didn't turn when Matt entered the room, so Matt moved to stand beside him.

"Gonna be a hot one today," he said. He placed a hand on the man's shoulder, prompting him to look up.

"It's always cold in here. They don't let me go outside."

"Sure they do. You go outside every day. You just can't stay out too long. It's not good...too hot." Matt sat on the end of the bed. "You have everything you need? Got new movies to watch?"

"Hmph. Can't stomach most of the crap they dish out. Those pansy-asses don't know how to act. Hmph. Call them movies. It all stinks."

"Yeah. You know, you're right. They sure don't make 'em like they used to, do they, Unc? Say, I'll try to bring you some better stuff next time I come. I'll pick up some old classics for you, okay? You like, uh, Errol Flynn? Or, uh, Gary Cooper? Or maybe a Western. John Wayne."

His uncle shuddered. "Wayne was a spy. Him 'n the others. Pointin' fingers at honest workin' folks. Callin' us all Commies. They were the ones who shoulda been on trial, rattin' out their friends for no good reason! They oughta be the ones now who— who—"

"Whoa, whoa, settle down there, pal. No need to get all stirred up about stuff now. Hey, a friend of mine, his granddad worked as a writer back then. Said he went into television comedy to steer clear of the witch hunt."

The man calmed somewhat, turned to look at Matt. "Some did, you know. Some did. Those were tough times."

Matt stayed another fifteen minutes and bid his uncle adieu. He shook his head as he retraced his steps to the elevator. It had been close; his uncle had been known to need restraints when he became agitated. Sighing, he made a mental note to pick up a copy of *Sunset Boulevard*. A film about a crazy old actress...for a crazy old actor.

Rebecca checked out of the hotel just before 7:00 a.m. She questioned the wisdom of offering to drive Matt Farralone all the way to Crescent City. He was a stranger, after all. Handsome, witty, charming, but a stranger, nonetheless.

He liked cars. He liked Mustangs. And Jackson had given her permission to take the 'Vette to Northern California. "Cars are for driving, not sitting," he'd assured her. "Have fun."

It would take them all day, but what better way to endear her subject to the enticing Miss Murray?

He walked up as she headed out of the lobby. Blue jeans, white tee, duffle bag. Rebecca sucked back a sigh. "Hey," she managed.

"Good morning! Sure you don't want me to drive?"

"You can help drive, but we'll take my car. I've already asked the valet to bring it around."

Matt nodded, then dropped his jaw as the immaculate, vintage, Chevy sports car came around the corner. "Whoa. *That's* your car?"

"For the next few days it is, yeah." Rebecca grinned, opened the trunk. "Good thing your bag isn't too big."

Matt wasn't ready to get in just yet. Walking around the perimeter of the car, he dropped his bag into the back and blew out a low whistle. "I've never seen one this color. This is...incredible."

"Cascade green. One of 550. The coves are 'shoreline beige'." Rebecca slammed the trunk lid and slid behind the wheel of the classic two-seater. "You coming?"

Matt hurried into the passenger seat, still agog. "Horsepower?"

"Uh, 270. Dual quads."

"Man. Very cool."

Rebecca revved the engine, let out the clutch. "Wish it was really mine."

"Whose is it?"

"Belongs to a friend of my dad. If I could afford it, I'd buy it for him. For Dad."

Matt stretched, hunted for the seat belt. "What do you do, anyway? You must do something besides restore cars."

"Oh, nothing important. Dabble at writing. Some administrative work."

Matt ran a hand over the dashboard. "So how much is it?"

"The car? Way more than I'll ever make, that's for sure."

Matt watched her smoothly downshift as she entered the freeway on-ramp. Her long legs looked as fetching in jeans as they did the day before, bare. He caught himself staring, pulled his gaze back up to her head. Her honey-colored hair fluttered in the wind, her eyes guarded by dark glasses. She had a lot of something, this one. He turned his eyes back to the road ahead. It was going to be an interesting trip.

ANNE CARTER

Twelve

Hollywood, California
September 1948

Cecelia carefully tugged at Jordan's collar, untwisting it behind his neck.

"You look smashing, darling. I'm so glad you didn't wear that tacky print shirt."

"It's my favorite one, Cec."

"Nonetheless, you need to look a little more sophisticated."

"For a wrap party? I don't think so. It's supposed to be casual."

Cecelia smiled. "All the more reason to look better than everyone else. You are the director's son-in-law, and the leading man. You have a responsibility to look perfect."

"Yeah, yeah, yeah. Fine." Jordan slipped on his blue blazer. "You look lovely, by the way."

"Why, thank you. It's an Edith Head."

"Harv buy it for you?"

"Daddy buys most of my gowns. You know that."

"Yep. I do."

The Beverly Hills Hotel had opened up the poolside patio for the event. Hedda Hopper held court in one corner, her flamboyant headgear upstaging all those around her. Jordan seated Cecelia, then wandered toward the bar to get them drinks. He gave a wide berth to the gossip queen; he wasn't in the mood to be entrapped by Hedda's political hogwash. Her plumed bonnet was an unwelcome sight to Hollywood's liberals, who feared Hopper's nose for anti-Americanism might sniff them out in error.

"Tom Collins. And, uh, give me a Manhattan."

"You got it, Mr. Kent," the bartender said. It impressed Jordan every time someone recognized him. He dropped a couple of bills into the tip bowl before taking the two drinks in hand, then slowly made his way through the throngs of people in the general direction of the table where he'd deposited his wife. He was, perhaps, halfway back when a petite brunette stepped from the crowd and planted herself before him.

"Why, Darla. I was hoping you'd be here."

"And why would I miss it, dear Jordie? Ooh, thank you!" She took the mixed drink from his hand and immediately sipped. "Oh, yum. Is it a Collins? How *did* you know?"

"Well I didn't, actually...I got it for Cecelia. Of course, it's yours, now, darling. Here, walk back to the bar with me."

She trotted alongside him as he returned to replace his wife's drink. "I haven't heard from you for a couple of weeks. What's going on in your life?" he asked, signaling the bartender for another Collins.

"Oh, the usual, you know. Reading for parts, dancing at the club..."

"Dancing, eh?"

"Yes. It's good for me. Calms my nerves. What about your handsome self? What are you up to?"

"Glad this picture is over, for one thing. Ready for something new. I think I'm already bored."

Darla looked up through silken lashes. "I know what you need, big boy," she said, just loud enough for him to hear.

Jordan stared down at her for the time it took the bartender to finish mixing Cecelia's drink. The plunging neckline of her sparkling, crimson dress boasted a mouth-watering cleavage. Her face held a knowing, candid expression, an invitation to resume things between them. She ran her fingertips lightly down his arm. "There's this wonderful place on Sunset. They have rooms there, and nobody knows or says anything. I've heard it's where Tracy and Hepburn sometimes go."

The bartender put the drink on the counter. Jordan snapped to attention, dropping another bill into the tip jar. He looked around, fearing others might be listening. "Well, well. That's something to consider, isn't it? What do you say we keep in touch? I'll give you a call next week. Maybe we can arrange something?"

Darla maintained a level stare, refusing to let Jordan move away. A rosy flush began to creep up his neck. "What it is, Dar? What do you want from me?" he urged, his voice quiet but determined.

"You know what I want. What we both want. Call me, Jordie. I know you have the number."

He didn't remember walking back to the table. He sat down, restrained the desire to run a hand through his hair. Cecelia swirled her glass, gazed across the patio to where her father stood engaged in an animated conversation with Mrs. Hopper, whose ostrich feathers bobbed and flicked as she spoke. Not taking her eyes off of Harv, Cecelia spoke in soft tones to her husband, who stared down at the cocktail he held.

"I'd advise you to keep your hands to yourself."

"What?"

"And remember you're a married man. Don't take the bait, Jordan. She'll end up a shameful embarrassment for all of us."

"I don't know what you're talking about, darling."

"Why, I'm talking about the sleazy, if childishly charming, Miss Foster. She wants to ruin you. Ruin us. I know her kind. She's a user."

Jordan turned in his seat to face his wife. "I think I've just about had it with that kind of talk. What is it with you, anyway? I haven't even seen Darla for weeks. I say hello to her at the bar, and you're giving me the business." He stood up.

"Where are you going?"

"For a walk. Why don't you go talk to that Hopper woman? I'll bet you two have a lot in common."

Grasping his drink, he marched away, hoping to lose himself in the crowd. He felt hot and murderous. At the next empty table, he shrugged out of his blazer, removed his tie, and flung them both over the back of a chair. He took a moment to polish off his cocktail before heading toward the hotel lobby.

Damn women. Who needs them anyway?

Jordan sat down at the bar adjacent to the lobby, rolled his shoulders, felt his breast shirt pocket for his cigarettes but didn't find them. He looked around for a machine, but his attention was diverted to a scene transpiring at the entrance to the pool. Two men argued. Unless Jordan mistook the scene, the larger man was a bouncer. The shorter one, Russell Harrington.

"Look, Bub, I'm the leading lady's main man, okay? Just go ask her if you don't believe me. I'm *supposed* to be out there."

The bouncer quietly folded his prize-fighter hands and smiled. "I'm sorry, Mr. Harrington. I can't be disturbing Ms. Foster at this time. I'm sure you're acquainted, but she didn't leave an invitation for you."

"It's okay, my friend. Mr. Harrington is my guest," Jordan said, clapping Russell on the back with a grin. "I told Miss Foster I would leave word at the door, and it slipped my mind." He turned to Russell and started to lead him back to the lobby bar. "You don't happen to have a cig, do you?"

Russell seemed uncertain about accompanying Jordan, glancing nervously back to the party entrance. "Uh, no, I'm quitting. Hey, did she really mention me?"

"Who, Darla? Why of course, your name always comes up. Let me buy you a drink. Dry martini, right?" Jordan slid back onto his stool, and Russell reluctantly joined him.

"Yeah, sure. Hey, there's the dame with the cigarettes." Russell waived the girl over.

"What'll it be, boys? Cigars or cigarettes?"

"Gimme a pack of Luckies," Russell directed, reaching into his dinner jacket for his wallet.

"Lucky Strike? I thought you quit. I'll take the Regents," Jordan said, also opening his wallet. "I'll get them, Russ."

Frowning, Russell put away his wallet and took the cigarette package, carefully picking the tear strip from the corner. "Thanks."

"Don't mention it."

The air around them grew hazy with smoke. The sounds of the party wafted across the lobby, with the occasional shriek of laughter bursting through the clinking of silverware and drink glasses. The bartender brought their cocktails, but Russell remained edgy, repeatedly turning his head toward the door.

Jordan stared at his reflection in the mirror behind the bar. "We're quite a pair, aren't we?" he said at last, lifting his drink with the same hand that held the cigarette pinched between his fingers. "Here's to the ladies."

"Broads. Ain't worth the trouble. They think because they got a great set of gams, they can walk all over a guy."

"Taking you for a ride, is she?" Jordan asked, turning his glass on the bar, examining its frosted sides. "She doesn't mean you harm, you know."

"She's a real Sheba, and I'm a sap. She's knows I'm carryin' a torch. She don't care. Only cares about gettin' parts." Russell tilted his glass, drank down the martini. "Now, Cecelia, she's a class act. You got it made."

"Oh, yes. I've got it made." Jordan downed the last of his Manhattan, then stood. "C'mon. Let's go find that little Sheba."

In her shimmering, red sequined gown, Darla wasn't hard to find. The deep scarlet dress created a stark contrast against her pale porcelain skin and dark hair. Blood-red lipstick completed her China doll look. Her laughter came easy and naturally, and men flocked about her like bears after honey. No mind that the hive could be full of bees.

Russell straightened his shoulders, and Jordan gave him a gentle nudge against his back. "Go on. Be the Sheik."

Taking a deep breath, Russell moved forward, purposefully, into the trove of Darla's admirers, quickly throwing a possessive arm around her before she could protest. "There's my girl. Darla, sweetheart, I'm sorry I'm so late."

"Russell! How…kind of you to stop by. I was just telling these nice gentlemen about the simply marvelous beaches we filmed. It's really a shame you didn't get to come."

Some of the men exchanged looks; Russell tightened his hold, and Darla narrowed her eyes in a veiled threat. She allowed Russell to lead her away, suggesting they talk at the far end of the pool.

"What do you think you're doing?" she hissed, when they'd moved beyond earshot of the other party goers.

"Just stealing my best girl away, that's all. How's about we go see that new Bogie picture? Uh…*Key Largo*. That's it. With Bacall. It's at the Egyptian."

"Are you *nuts*?"

"Okay then, we could see *The Pirate*. Judy Garland. I think it's still at The El Capitan…"

"You just don't get it, do you? You barge in here, man-handle me in front of my friends, and you think I want to go to the show with you?" Darla backed away, hands on hips, all but stomping her size five pump at the bewildered man before her. "You're a nutcase! Whatever you think was between us, which really wasn't anything, is now officially over! How'd you even get in here, anyway?"

She checked her voice and turned her head toward the softly lapping pool water, catching her breath. Looking back at Russell's stunned expression, Darla softened her tone. "Look. I'm sorry things didn't turn out the way you wanted. But I've got a life, now, Russ. For the first time in my life I *am* somebody. I have a chance to really make it big. And that means I can't be connected with you, or anybody else. Especially since you have…connections with…those people." She paused, hesitant to say more aloud. "Anyway, girls who have a guy on the side, well, they just don't make it."

"I get it. I'm not good enough for you and your highbrow friends. It ain't got nothin' to do with who I know or what I do. Well, the joke's on you, sister. 'Cuz you ain't good enough, either. And they'll find out. You'll see." Red faced, Russell spat the words, his eyes bright with unshed tears.

Darla stepped forward, placed a hand on Russell's arm, rethinking her harsh words. "I didn't mean that. I didn't mean you weren't good enough. It's just not the right time–"

"I don't need your sympathy!" Russell tore his arm away from her as if burned by the touch. "I don't need it, I don't need you, I don't need anything!" He turned from her, walked a few steps, and adjusted his dinner jacket. Without looking back, he lifted his chin and strode straight to the exit doors back into the hotel.

A sigh escaped, a breath Darla didn't know she'd been holding. She replaced it, filling her lungs once or twice before straightening her own posture and walking back toward the crowded bar.

Thirteen

Northern California
July

Rebecca stood at the cash register of Trudy's Café in Santa Cruz. She arched her back, leaning left and right to stretch it out. Matt, just returning from the restroom, joined her.

"I'll drive from here," he said, digging his wallet from his hip pocket. "Man, that was good. I was starved."

"Me, too. Now I'll get sleepy."

"It's okay. Feel free to take a nap. I promise to stay off the sidewalks."

Rebecca gave him a sideways glance, trying with all her might not to let his boyish grin charm her. He's the enemy, she reminded herself. Her goal included access to the lighthouse, nothing more.

"Sure I won't wake up in Mexico?" she teased, pushing the heavy glass door open as they exited the restaurant.

"Can't promise. I'm a great driver...not so good with directions."

"I'll take my chances."

They did consult their map before leaving the parking lot. "Didn't realized I'd become so dependent on the nav," Matt said.

"Maps are so passé," Rebecca responded in jest. "Had to buy this one in an antique store."

After a few moments of discussion, they had their route. Rebecca re-tied back her hair, folded the map smaller and buckled up. "Let's ride."

Matt was in heaven. The vintage Corvette handled well as they coursed through Highway 17, hugged by redwoods on either side. The sun, the wind, the car–and the beautiful woman beside him– seemed to make his world right for the first time in six months.

Since the day Chelsea had changed the locks. But even the thought of his obviously misguided ex couldn't dampen this day.

"I can't believe this! What a car," he called against the headwind created by their speed. "First time I've driven a 'Vette!"

"Oh, I didn't know you were a virgin!"

Matt flashed a quick smile. "I hide it well." *She's funny. Where has this woman been all my life?* "So, how do you like Seattle? Does it really rain all the time?" he asked.

"It's cloudy and threatening most of the time. Let's just say I save a lot on sunglasses."

"Ah. I don't know if I could live there. I'm a hot-weather kind of guy. I don't even like to stay up north all that long. It can get pretty dreary there, too. I'm actually thinking about getting a place in Palm Springs."

"That's hot. I have a good friend who lives in Phoenix. Now that's an inferno."

"I went to Phoenix once. Rained like a sonuvabitch the whole time I was there. Summertime, too." Matt shook his head. "Nasty. Water over the curbs."

"Monsoons."

"I'm sorry? What was that?"

"Monsoons. Big, wet, summer storms. It's common around there. Best to just stay inside." His companion looked away, then back. "But Palm Springs. What's it like? What's the draw?"

"Do you play golf?"

"I have, but it's not my strength. They do have a lot of golf courses there, right?"

"Like a patchwork quilt. I play sometimes but not a big fan either. I do like the ambiance. It's just relaxing there. Maybe it's just because I don't bring my obligations with me. I like to swim, go out for a good meal, see a film. What about you?"

She pondered a moment. "You're asking what I do to relax. I read; I watch old movies. I swim a lot, too. Bike ride. Walk. Sight-see."

"Sight-see? You mean around Seattle or elsewhere?"

"You can never see enough, even in your own hometown. There's always a museum, a special event, an antique store, a collection I haven't shot—"

"Shot? As in, photographed?"

"Just for fun," she answered quickly. "My dad bought me one of those little pocket digital cameras for Christmas last year. It's a bear to figure out. Most of the time my pictures are upside down, peoples' heads are cut off...I just don't have any smarts about that stuff. But you oughta taste my apple pie!"

Was she actually blushing? It was hard to tell with the sunlight flickering across her face from the canopy of treetops above.

"Apple pie? Really? Now you've done it. You won't hear the end of it until you bake one for me. It's my favorite. My *all-time* favorite. *Á la mode.*"

Rebecca closed her eyes, letting the wind rush across her face. She'd almost blown it and would have to be more careful. Hopefully, her lame explanation about the camera had been enough. Now, the pie comment was a whole 'nuther thing. She wouldn't worry about it because she'd never have to bake that pie.

Pie crust. Something her mother would have taught her.

"Where does your mother live?" she asked, making conversation.

"Los Angeles. She's still pretty good. Plays tennis, does the bridge thing."

"And your father is deceased?"

"Yep. Heart attack. Dropped dead at his desk five years ago."

"That must have been tough. I'm sorry." Rebecca thought of her own dad, his up and down health.

"How about *your* mother?"

"Hit and run in a crosswalk. I was ten."

Matt stole a glance. "That's *really* tough. Any sibs?"

"Nope."

"Did they catch the guy?"

Rebecca shook her head.

Matt thumped the heel of his hand against the steering wheel. "I'm sorry. It just pisses me off when stuff like that happens. I see it all the time in my business. There's no way to reconcile it."

Rebecca looked down. How right he was. It still bothered her about the eyewitness, dead in his own bed the next morning. There was just something so wrong about the whole thing.

"You said you have a grandfather," she said at last.

"Oh, yeah. My grandfather. He's a piece of work."

"Is he your mother's or your father's?"

"Mom's dad. Crotchety old dude. Still sharp as a tack. Bucks up. Lives in the Hollywood hills."

Rebecca smiled. "I don't have any grandparents. I mean, they're all dead. My dad's parents lived in the east, died when I was little. I never got to meet them. My mother's parents are both gone, too. Gramma and Grampa. They both got food poisoning while traveling. Talk about weird."

"Food poisoning? Really?"

"E. Coli. Salmonella. So I've been told. My mom was really close to them. It just devastated her to lose them both at the same time," Rebecca explained. "I have a few pictures of them...hoping to restore." There she went with the photos again. She bit her lip.

"Wow. Your family has had more than its share of grief. This was awhile back, I assume?"

"In the mid '80s, I think. They were touring with a group. It happened in Canada, too, not like some depressed Third World country with rotting food. And the strange part is, no one else on the tour got sick."

Her driver merely shook his head as he carefully maneuvered the curves in the road. "I think if that happened today, there would be an investigation," he said at last. "Look at what a big deal it is if people get sick on a cruise ship."

"I don't know. Mom didn't like to talk about it. I was just a little girl, anyway. Maybe if she were here now, she'd tell me a lot more."

"True. To this day, I wish I'd talked more to my dad. To get the stories, the background about his life before I knew him. I remember him always working. Incredibly long hours. That's why I vowed not to do that. I work hard for a while, stock up some dough, take time off. Go back to work when I need to."

Rebecca regarded Matt as he drove. The fact that he wasn't married astounded her. Of course, he could be attached, but for some reason, she didn't think so. His wavy light brown hair bounced a little in the wind, tanned face belying his love of the sun,

100

brown eyes smiling behind his sunglasses. Strong, bare arms expertly manipulating the steering wheel.

"What are you looking at, Denise Murray?" he asked, interrupting her appraisal.

"Just wondering what your wife was doing, letting you gallivant about the country like this."

"She's home baking apple pie," he said with a grin.

San Francisco delayed them. Late afternoon traffic was crippling, but Matt didn't let it get to him as he waited at red light after red light. "People either love this town or hate it," he commented.

"I guess you're right. I like it, but I wouldn't live here."

"Too dry, eh?"

"I'm not really a rain person, either. I like sun as much as the next guy," she said.

"Obviously. I've been wondering how you manage that terrific tan living in the shade all year."

"I'm just...just naturally dark. Not tan. But *you've* clearly been working outside," she said, gesturing to his arm.

"On the clubhouse, yeah. I work with the guys. No sense in sitting in an office all day."

"How many people are participating?"

"Oh, we have a crew of about fifteen guys. Then Case and Jack, my two friends, they help weekends and some evenings. They're working stiffs."

"I see. Do they have children?"

"Jack does. Kind of a blended family. One stepson, two sons, one daughter. He's quite the family man. Case isn't married, but he's working on it."

"Working on it. He has someone in mind, I take it."

"Oh, yeah. I hear she's a sweetheart. He's a marine veterinarian and she's a schoolteacher turned innkeeper. They live in Newburg part time, and Grogan's Head the rest of the time."

"Sounds complicated. And they aren't even married."

"I think marriage in general is complicated. Like trying to merge two worlds into one."

"I agree. I've always thought it takes a really special person to stay married for long."

Matt nodded. His grandparents had fought like cats and dogs, and his parents had seemed to merely co-exist. One couple passionate in their discontent, the other coldly aloof. "Really special," he agreed.

Two hours past sundown, the light green Chevy sports car rolled to a stop in Crescent City. The Bayview Inn had a reservation for Miss Denise Murray. She paid in cash.

"Well, I'll see you in the morning, then," Matt said, as Rebecca slung her bag over her shoulder. "Breakfast at eight?"

"Sounds good. Thanks for all the driving."

"It really was my pleasure. My Jeep is going to feel terribly awkward now."

"Sure I can't drop you off?"

"Nope. I think I see my ride now. Have a good night."

Rebecca locked her hotel room door behind her, dropped the bag on the floor beside the bed. Walking to the window, she pulled open the drapes and gazed out of the fog bank blanketing the bay.

"Some bay view," she mumbled, closed the drapes and reached back to pull the elastic band from her ponytail. A feeling of disquiet had settled.

In the bathroom, she washed up and thought about ordering a sandwich to be brought to her room. She was exhausted, and eight o'clock would come early. She turned on the TV and fell back against the bed pillows.

Barely able to concentrate, Rebecca flipped through the stations, deciding she would forego the meal and just go to sleep. She turned off the television and the lights and slipped beneath the covers. Still, she tossed, unable to clear her mind. Something bothered her.

The bed wasn't right. The room was too cold, the night too dark, her skin too dry. Maybe some lotion and some heat? She got out of bed, flipped on the bathroom light and turned up the heat. Retrieving her cosmetic bag, she slathered some moisturizer on her arms before sliding back between the sheets.

"This is crazy," she murmured, twisting around and bunching up the feather pillows. Try as she might to make excuses to the contrary, she knew in her heart the reason for her discomfort.

Matthew Farralone was a nice guy. Far too nice to be trusting a sneaky girl like Denise Murray.

Fourteen

Hollywood, California
October 1948

Jordan stood at the hotel window, peering down four stories through the sheer panel curtains at the oval hotel pool below. He wanted a cig. Everything was moving much too fast. With the debut just weeks away, Bregman had people working night and day on editing, sound mixing and foley.

Behind him, Darla lay curled on the bed like a sleeping kitten. He didn't think he could handle her much longer. She was an addiction, no less so than cocaine or heroin. She always knew when he was low, vulnerable, needy. When the world had bruised him, battered him, made him feel small and insignificant.

Like his father-in-law, for instance. Dangling that next plumb role just out of reach, making demands, sticking it to him so he'd beg for it. Cecelia, who, for the first time in all the years he'd known her, had become clingy and uncertain. When had she ever needed anyone but her father? And Russell. The poor schlub couldn't get a job to save his sorry life. They clawed at him like hungry dogs.

And that's when Darla would appear, soft, warm, building him up, making the world into a spinning whirlwind of lust and satisfaction. Taking, giving, creating a fantasy world for him that he was loathe to leave.

But leave he must. It became more and more difficult to traverse between the make-believe of their suite at Chateau Marmont and his "real" life. Cecelia asked questions about his absences, and Jordan was petrified someone at the hotel would recognize him.

Darla stirred, and he began buttoning his shirt. He could not, would not stay another hour. He would tell her it was over. For good this time. Yes, he would tell her.

Next Friday, for sure.

He found dinner on the table when he got home. Cecelia, wearing a long, velvet caftan to ward off the early fall chill, had prepared his favorite meal: veal chops and mashed potatoes, asparagus and dinner rolls. The aroma surrounding him as he made his way into the dining room was already helping to wash away the image of Darla, sitting up in the middle of the bed, her pouty lips and heartrending eyes accusing. He loosened his tie, came up behind his wife as she stood pouring wine into glasses at the candlelit table.

"Mmm...what's the occasion?" he said softly, wrapping his arms around her waist. He smelled a scent in her softly curling ochre hair, so bright against the black velvet. Perfume, perhaps.

"Something special," she murmured with a smile. "Go ahead and sit down. I'm hungry."

"You are always hungry, lately, my dear," Jordan said, pulling out his wife's chair. "I'm glad to see you're actually putting some meat on those delicate bones of yours."

He watched for her reaction, but Cecelia merely smiled and reached for her napkin. "Shall we toast?"

"Of course. To what? Shall we wish for a sell-out next week?"

"Wish? It's not a birthday cake, darling. Just a toast. How about something simple, like ourselves. Our future."

"Sounds good to me." Jordan made a show of clearing his throat, then raised his glass. "Here's to us. May we have a stellar future, despite this nasty town we attempt to survive in!"

Cecelia uttered a short laugh, then leaned her glass against his. "Here, here," she said, taking a generous sip of white wine. "Mmm. It is good, isn't it? Daddy recommended it."

"Daddy. Of course."

They ate in comfortable quiet for a time, each making an occasional comment about nothing in particular. Soon, Cecelia brought out a cherry pie.

106

"Oh, now, you must have done something very bad," Jordan quipped, eyeing the pie before him. "Did you spend all our money? Rob a bank?"

Cecelia stared at him, a soft smile lazing on her lips. "Why, nothing of the kind, darling. We're just celebrating, that's all."

"I love celebrations. As long as it doesn't involve your mother coming to stay with us."

"You may change your mind about that." Her murmured comment piqued his interest, put him on alert. He scooped up a forkful of pie, watched Cecelia delicately spear one cherry.

"Going to keep me in suspense, are you?" he asked, shoving the bite of pie into his mouth. The explosion of flavor and sweetness caused his eyes to flutter closed. If the reason for the celebration was half as good as the taste of the pie, it would be a fabulous party.

"Well, I'm not one to beat around the bush, so I'll just tell you straight. I'm pregnant. We're going to have a baby, Jordan."

Her words struck his ear at the same moment his molars came together against a cherry stone. He nearly choked. Reaching for his napkin, he carefully ejected the pit into the burgundy cloth with as much decorum as possible, feeling his face begin to flame. She couldn't have said what he thought he heard.

"I'm sorry, what did you say?" he asked, hoping against hope he'd heard wrong. "There was a pit in my pie."

"A baby. You heard me correctly. I'm pregnant. The doctor calculates three months, but I know it's closer to four. I know because it was while you were on location. When I came to visit you, darling, don't you remember?"

Jordan swallowed, tried to keep his eyes from bugging out. "Yes, but Cecelia, how can that be? You've–we've been very careful. We agreed, did we not, to wait awhile?"

"You can only be so careful, Jordan. Some things just can't be helped. You *are* delighted, aren't you?"

The look on Cecelia's face placed somewhere between sublime and murderous. It was Jordan's choice.

"Of course, I am, my love! This is fantastic news!" He got quickly to his feet and traveled around the table to give her a hug. "Wow-wee. Have you told Harv?"

"Why no, I waited. I wanted you to be first to know. First after Dr. Breyer, anyway. Oh darling, this baby will be just what we need. She'll be the best thing that ever happened to us! Beautiful, and talented, and smart, and—"

"Whoa, whoa, hang on there! Perhaps *he* will be talented, and smart, and handsome."

Cecelia giggled. "Oh, whatever! Oh, Jordan, I am so happy! I can't wait to tell Daddy." With those words she got up from the table and left the room, heading for the telephone in the parlor.

The smile felt frozen on Jordan's lips.

"A baby." *What the hell.* Cecelia was pregnant. After a moment of reflection, Jordan reloaded his fork with pie. His life had taken another turn, whether he liked it or not.

Surely now he could muster the nerve to tell Darla goodbye.

Russell Harrington sat at the counter in Schwab's, turning a toothpick in his fingers. He took a sip of coffee, signaled the waitress for a warm-up.

"Waitin' for someone, Russ?" she asked, tilting the glass pot over his thick porcelain mug.

"Yup! Waitin' for Miss Opportunity, doll. Anytime now she's gonna walk right through those front doors. And for once, I'll be in the right place at the right time."

"Sure, handsome. Sure you don't want something else? Pie, maybe? A donut?"

Russell shrugged. "Naw...It's okay, Nance. I got food at home."

Without another word, the waitress went to the pie case and withdrew a lemon meringue confection. She carefully sliced a piece, took it back to Russell.

"Here ya go." She leaned forward, eyes darting left and right, and whispered. "It's on the house. I know it's your favorite."

"Aw, Nancy, you're the greatest, you know that? And I'm gonna make it up to you. You'll see. I got some irons in the fire, you know. Gonna meet with Kazan later this week. Not to mention, DeMille's second-string assistant. Yeah, they're lookin' for guys like me."

Nancy leaned on the counter, her chin propped on her fist. "Of course, they are," she said softly, lowering her eyes. "And maybe you'll recommend me for a part, when you make it big, of course."

"Without a doubt, you're definitely in."

Russell ate the pie slowly, thinking about Kazan and DeMille and Jack Warner. What a joke. Not a one would even let him read for a part. He'd been thrown off the lot at Paramount, and unless he could disguise himself somehow, he wasn't welcome at MGM either. Get acting lessons, they said. Get an agent. But no agent in town would touch him.

He could call Jordan again...No! He wasn't no charity case, and besides, Jordan had somehow twisted Darla away from him. Taken sweet, innocent little Darla and made her into some kind of shrew. His face burned at the thought of the way she'd treated him at the party. *Little tramp.*

He should never have told her about the meetings he'd been to. He thought he could trust her. And anyway, it didn't mean nothin'. He'd been talked into going by a guy he met, a guy who said he could get Russell a lucky break. But the meetings had nothing to do with pictures, so he stopped going. Now, the Commies probably had his name on some list.

Newly angered, he scraped up the last of the lemon crème and stuffed it into his mouth. He fished around in his trouser pockets and came up with $1.12 in coins, which he slapped down on the counter. "See ya later," he called out to Nancy, then pushed his way out onto the street.

Harvey Bregman settled into a leather game table chair in the lobby at the Chateau Marmont. His meeting with Selznick had been canceled, but he'd managed to get Stanley Kramer to commit to talking about doing a picture at his new company, Screen Plays, Inc. Kramer was working with Kirk Douglas, but needed a property–and a director–as a follow up to Douglas' *Champion*. Bregman wanted in.

While waiting, Bregman amused himself by watching the people coming and going. Anyone who was anybody could be seen on any given day, either hamming it up for fans or hiding behind dark glasses and hats as they moved smoothly through the lobby on their way to secret trysts and clandestine meetings. In fact, wasn't that Bogie coming out of the elevator just now?

Bregman chuckled to himself as Bogart strutted into the lobby, straightening his lapels. Would Lauren Bacall be in the next carload? Only slightly miffed at his own classless interest, Bregman watched carefully as the elevator left, then returned minutes later. As the doors opened, his anticipation peaked. But instead of the sultry-faced starlet he expected, his son-in-law emerged from the elevator, buttoning his suit jacket and looking guilty as hell.

Jordan Kent exuded anxiety as he scanned the lobby, seeking someone who clearly wasn't present. Weighing the possible outcomes, Bregman waved him over. Jordan paled but advanced toward his beckoning father-in-law.

"What brings you here today, Dad?" he asked, still glancing about.

"Was just going to ask you the same question."

"You first. A meeting perhaps?"

"Actually, yes. I'm expecting Stan Kramer at any moment."

Jordan nodded, tugged at his cuffs. "Fabulous. Good news, I hope. Well I, I was just inquiring about getting a suite for Cec's birthday party. It's coming up, you know."

"Still three months away. Why the rush?"

"In case you haven't noticed, sir, she'll be rather ungainly at that time. She'd like to celebrate before she starts resembling a beach ball."

"Hmph. Well. Let me know if I can help you out. Spare no expense. This may be one of her last carefree parties. Kids do that to you, you know."

"So I've heard. Ah! I see Mr. Kramer now. I'll just take my leave."

"Stay out of trouble, Kent."

Jordan blew out a deep sigh. He dared not even think about what would have happened had Darla appeared in the lobby while in Harv's company. But where was she, anyway? She'd never missed one of their "dates." Hadn't left any kind of message. Wasn't answering her telephone at home.

He lingered near the hotel entrance, could see Stanley Kramer shaking hands with Harv. But no Darla.

Today, he'd planned to tell her goodbye. He thought about all the self-admonishment, the pep-talks and conscientious prodding he'd done, working himself up to the task. All for naught. And worse, now he was worried about her.

Fifteen

Del Norte County, California
July

"I don't know what to say. This is...fabulous." Rebecca stood in the middle of what would clearly become a very nice gymnasium.

"We have to do a lot of things inside because of the weather," Matt said. "Of course, they'll be outside as much as possible. But it never gets really warm here."

"Yeah, I get that," Rebecca muttered, letting her eyes drift across the shiny plank flooring. "I didn't think it would be this nice."

Matt fairly beamed at her. "Aw, shucks, ma'am." He started for the door. "I didn't show you the computer room."

"Computers, too? Can I come stay here?"

"Anytime you want. You could work with Amy. She's just agreed to be our director. I'm so excited."

"Amy. That would be...Case's girlfriend?"

"You're a quick study. Yeah. I may have mentioned, she's a schoolteacher. This will be perfect for her."

Rebecca followed Matt outside and across a small covered breezeway into another building. Inside, they found bundles of black cables and open wall outlets. "All being wired up now. We won't have the units for a while, I'm hoping by Christmas we'll be able to buy them." He squatted, inspecting one of the hanging cables. "'Course, it might be smarter to do this before the playground equipment, being's we are heading right into the cold weather soon...I don't know...but your donation is gonna go a long way, either way."

Rebecca smiled, tried to swallow the lump that had suddenly appeared in her throat. *My donation.* She turned away, looked out the window. "Yep. I'm sure it will."

Matt joined her, sharing a view of the pines. Placing his fingertips together, he sighed. "Well. You want to get lunch? I'd like you to meet the guys."

"Why not. I could use a cup of coffee."

It was a bit early for the lunch crowd, so Donna found them a table on the almost-sunny patio. Jack and Case, already seated, stood when Rebecca walked up.

"Case McKenna. Glad to meet you." Case took her hand.

"Denise Murray. And you must be Jack."

Jack, too, extended his hand. "Jack McKenzie."

Rebecca smiled. "McKenna, McKenzie. Right."

"Well, you know how it is with us romance novel heroes. Hasta be 'Mc' something-or-other," Jack said with a grin.

Taking her seat, Rebecca nodded. "I don't know, but my mother was a big fan of those books. I seem to recall there being a series of books on our shelf about some McKinleys or McDonnells or something."

Jack punched Case on the arm. "See? I told you."

"What about poor Mattie, here? He wants to be a hero, too," Case offered, opening his menu.

"Okay, he can be McFarralone."

Rebecca laughed. She liked these guys already. Over the top of her menu, she gave them each the once-over. Case, with his longish, dark chocolate hair, bright blue eyes and goatee, was easily romance hero material. Despite the humor, his expression remained solemn as he chose his meal. The serious type.

Jack, she suspected, with his wavy, sun-streaked hair and warm brown eyes would be hard-pressed to keep a smile from his face. The family man, she remembered, with four assorted kids. He looked happy.

"Miss?" The waitress stood beside her, pen poised over pad.

"Oh, give me a cheeseburger. No onion. And coffee. No, make it a vanilla shake. And fries would be great."

"A woman after my own heart," Matt proclaimed, closing his menu. "Denise's from the Seattle area," he told his friends. "So, she's used to this crappy weather."

Rebecca felt herself wince. All three of her lunch companions stared, as if waiting for a comment. "It's not so bad, really," she offered. "They have great coffee."

Jack grinned. "Now she's after *my* heart."

"Jack's a caffeine freak," Matt explained. "He can never be very far from a Starbuck's. He starts to get the shakes."

Rebecca giggled. "Okay. Good to know."

"So, did you work at the Institute today?" Matt asked, directing his question to Case. "You seem a bit...what's the word...pensive."

Case leaned back in his chair, shrugged, looked to the sea. "We lost the young otter today."

"No. I'm sorry. That's a shame," Matt responded, shaking his head. "That's the one I saw?"

"Yeah. Can't quite figure it out." Case stroked his goatee thoughtfully. "We think it may have had some kind of allergic reaction to the antibiotics we were giving it."

Even Jack's normally cheerful face reflected gloom. "We raised its mother. She had a damaged tail and couldn't be set free. She was the first animal I ever got involved with at the Institute, when I first came up here."

Rebecca wet her lips. *Great. Compassionate lugs, too.* "I'm sorry to hear about that. It must be terrible to work with animals, get to know them, then see them go."

Case sighed, straightened. "Loss is a part of life, unfortunately. But you're right. It's hard when you get to know them. Impossible not to get to know them."

Matt shifted in his seat. "So, Miss Denise here likes the clubhouse."

"Like I said before, what's not to like?" Jack said with a grin, clearly happy about the change in subject. "It's a no-brainer, right?"

Rebecca smiled, nodded, took a sip of water. "Yup. No-brainer."

Case sat forward. "So, what, or who, exactly, do you represent again? The name didn't sound familiar." He flashed a tight smile. "Google didn't find it."

Damn. She didn't expect this. "Oh, it's a fairly new organization. There's probably not much public information yet. But it's a great group of investors. The, uh, corporate papers are just being filed now."

"501 (c) (3)?" Case questioned.

"Uh, yeah, I think so. I'm just sort of the messenger, you know?"

"Well, that's an important bit of info." Case unfolded his paper napkin and spread it across one thigh.

"Aw, leave her alone. I reviewed the papers already. I'm the lawyer, remember?" Matt interjected.

Jack laughed. "Like we should trust you! You're the one who can't shake off that nagging photographer lady."

"I did shake her, thank you very much. She hasn't called back."

Rebecca tilted her head, gave her best "somewhat quizzical" look. "Someone harassing you?"

"Naw, it's nothing."

"Nothing! This chick had him stewed up for days," Jack said.

Rebecca crossed her legs, leaned back. "I find that hard to believe, Mr. Cool, Calm and Collected."

As Matt smiled and shook his head, Jack continued. "Come on, admit it, she got to you. All over some decrepit lighthouse."

Case looked up, and Rebecca went on alert.

"What about it?" Case asked, appearing more interested than amused.

"Okay, I got a call from some woman who wanted access to the inside. She's a photojournalist. Wouldn't take no for an answer. That's all."

"What's the problem?" Case frowned slightly in question. "She can't go inside?"

"Nope. Strict orders. No one gets in to see the wizard, not nobody, not no how."

Rebecca could hold her tongue no longer. "Sounds mysterious. Do you know why?"

Matt turned to look Rebecca in the eye, and her throat swelled again. But before Matt opened his mouth, Case continued.

"Seems kinda harsh."

"Not my decision. My client has his reasons. Besides, it's a mess inside. It's been derelict for something like fifty years."

"Have you seen it?" Jack asked, much to Rebecca's relief.

"A few years ago, I had to go over. Some vandals had broken in. My–my client insisted I go see if there'd been any damage inside. It's dark, and dank, and there's still some old furniture tossed about. Moldy. Actually, pretty creepy."

Case nodded. "Lighthouses can be pretty creepy. It takes a passionate soul to run one, and passionate people do crazy things. Sometimes."

Jack leaned forward, reached out with ghoulish hands. "Woo...I am the ghost of keepers past..."

Case flashed a quick grin. "Hey. I know about these things."

"Oh yeah, Point Surrender is haunted, right?" Jack asked.

"Not anymore."

Rebecca regretted the turn in the conversation. She wondered how to get back on Dragon Rock.

"I'm curious. When you went out there, how did you know it had been vandalized?"

Matt paused, rubbed at his chin. "Somebody reported it. I think some fishermen–they saw people on the rock."

"When you went there, did you find anything? Did they steal any of the props?"

All three men turned eyes on her, and Rebecca's face grew warm.

"Props?" Jack asked. Matt, in particular, stared hard at her. She cleared her throat, mind racing.

"Yeah, I mean, I would assume there are still some movie props there, right? I–I talked to the hotel manager this morning about the area, and she told me about a movie they filmed here back in the '40s. She said they used that lighthouse. It's the one you're talking about, right?"

Matt nodded.

117

"I've been thinking, there are so many movie nuts out there, my dad is one...and someone might get the bright idea of stealing something out of there and putting it on eBay."

"Wow. What a great idea. Why didn't I think of that?" Jack said, his chuckle breaking the chill of the moment. "Maybe that's what the lady wanted to do. Steal something. You think?"

"She was no lady," Matt muttered, redirecting his attention to the hamburgers being distributed.

That's for sure. Rebecca picked up her own cheeseburger and jammed it into her lying mouth.

She didn't complain when Matt insisted on taking her sightseeing after lunch. His Jeep was better suited than the Corvette, he explained, for touring the back roads through the redwoods, so Rebecca climbed in and buckled up.

"I swear, I have never seen such enormous trees," she exclaimed in wonder, as they drove through the forested landscape. She thought about how, at home, they remarked at the "tall" saguaro cactuses. Tall? *They* hadn't seen nuthin'! "This is phenomenal. I would have missed all this...beauty."

Matt smiled. "You have big trees in Washington."

"Yes, but...not like these."

"There's a small museum in town I'd like to show you. And no tour would be complete without a look at the lighthouse."

Rebecca pulled her eyes away from the scenery and glanced at Matt in question.

"Battery Point. It's really awesome. When the tide is down, you can walk right in."

"Tide is down? You mean, it's like across the water?"

"It's only about 200 feet. But it's a must-see. I belong to the Historical Society, so it's free. It's been restored. Privately operated. You a lighthouse fan?"

Rebecca looked away, through the windshield at the road ahead. "No more so than anyone else, I guess."

"Just wondered. You seemed interested during our talk about Dragon Rock."

118

"Well, that one intrigues me, yeah. It's so far out there. One can't help but wonder what it's like inside. Especially after all these years, you know?"

"It's a pit, believe me. If it was up to me, they'd tear it down. It doesn't serve any purpose out there. It's kinda sad, in a way."

"Sad, how?" Rebecca looked back at Matt as he navigated through the forest.

"It reminds me of a dying animal. The lens has been removed. It's trashed inside. The waves batter the damned thing incessantly. At the risk of sounding maudlin, it just seems so wrong. It used to be an engineering marvel, a proud symbol. I mean, men died out there protecting the coast. It had purpose. Now, it's just a rusting, broken shell."

"So...why *don't* they tear it down?"

"I know the owner pretty well. He's a client. I manage his affairs. I think it's just too much for him to deal with. First off, it would cost a fortune because you can't just dump the remains into the ocean. Most of it would probably have to be hauled back to shore and put somewhere, like a landfill, I guess. Those stones making up the caisson, you know the big elliptical base under the tower? They weigh tons. Each one. There are engines, generators, diesel fuel...took them ten years to build that damned thing. Could take years to dismantle it."

Rebecca nodded, felt herself blushing with emotion. "Um, has anyone thought about restoring it instead? Like Battery Point?"

Matt paused, thinking over her question. The road they traveled suddenly brought them back to daylight and civilization.

"We've been approached by a couple of groups over the years. They do want to get in there and restore it. But there are big problems. First of all, it's treacherous even going out there. The landing is unsafe. You know, a hundred years ago, there was a boom, and they literally lifted boats out of the water and plopped them down on the boat deck. When it came out of use, people used to take small launches out there, but it's incredibly dangerous. The rocks are pretty unforgiving. Nowadays, we use a helicopter to get out there. Nobody would be fool enough to take a skiff."

"Really."

"Helicopter rides aren't cheap. To move workers, materials, and equipment back and forth–would cost a fortune. But even if someone was that determined, and that rich, the old man wouldn't go for it."

"The old man?"

"My client. He's established a foundation that actually owns the lighthouse, and it would practically take an act of Congress to make any changes. He's pretty stubborn about the whole thing."

"How old is he? I mean, is he in good health?"

"Are you thinking about what will happen when he dies?" Matt chuckled. "He's pretty healthy. He'll be around for a while. After that, well, there are successor trustees to be empowered with decision-making."

Rebecca nodded. "And how long has it been since you ventured out there?"

"Oh, a couple of years or so. No plans to go back anytime soon, either. I only went because of those vandals I told you about."

"Oh, right." Rebecca paused, wondering just how far she could take the conversation without arousing suspicion. She decided she had nothing to lose. "The lady I talked to really rambled on about the movie they filmed out there. That's why I wondered about the props the studio used. Did they leave stuff out there, do you know?"

"Yeah, I suppose they did. Have you seen the flick?"

"Actually, I have. My dad and I are old movie buffs. I didn't realize it was the same lighthouse until yesterday. In the movie, the place is furnished like a home. It's about a lighthouse keeper and a woman, and they fall in love and have an affair there."

"Oh, I've seen it. A few times. In reality, women were never in residence. They deemed it too dangerous for the wickies to have wives or children out there."

Rebecca adjusted the heater vent in front of her, feeling a chill in the car. "No children. Not even if one of the wives had a baby or something?"

Matt smiled, shook his head. "Especially no babies."

Sixteen

Hollywood, California
October 1948

Darla stood at the edge of the Colorado Street Bridge, crying hysterically.

"If you come any closer, I'll jump! I swear I will! Just go away…" she cried, turning away from Jordan who reached out to her from the roadway.

"Darla, please come down! I'm sorry, truly I am! We can work something out, I'm sure, dear one. Only please, don't jump. That won't solve anything!"

"It's no use, Jordie. Everything is ru-hu-huined…" Darla sobbed, looking out at the blurred city lights of Los Angeles twinkling in the distance.

Jordan ventured a look over the side at the black abyss of the Arroyo Seco, where countless people had ended their lives since the bridge was built near the turn of the century. He couldn't let Darla become one of them.

"I'll figure something out! I will! I promise," he called.

"Oh, yeah, you fixed everything real good. How c-could you get your wife pregnant! All the while you were m-m-making love to me! We can't figure that out, Jordan Kent!"

Jordan's shoulders slumped. He'd known her reaction wouldn't be good, but he didn't expect her to head straight for Suicide Bridge. This was awful. What if someone came by and stopped? It would be in the *Herald* in the morning. Harv would kill him.

"Darla, sweetheart, come back down, and let's talk this through. You know how much I…I care about you. You're important, very important to me! Come on, now, be a good girl and–"

Darla spun around and stepped off the ledge, stamping her foot in front of him. "I'm *not* a good girl, and we both know it. If I was, I wouldn't be in this spot, would I? I'd be married, that's what. I'd be legit, like Cecelia. But you know what? I don't want to be like Cecelia, because look at her life. She's married to a two-timing bastard!"

"Darla—"

"But not me, no sirree. I'm not married to the two-timing bastard; I'm just carrying his illegitimate baby. Yeah, you heard me. Me 'n Cec have got more in common than just our bad taste in men. We both have his buns in our ovens!" After quickly smearing the tears from her face, Darla turned on her heel and stomped to Jordan's car, where she got into the front passenger seat and slammed the door.

Jordan smoked five cigarettes in the next hour, sitting across from Darla in the small Burbank diner near her home. Darla was shoveling in chocolate cake.

He considered the fact that he could very well be in shock. His mind was numb, his stomach on fire. Darla waved at the waitress.

"Could you please bring me another glass of milk?"

Jordan looked at his watch. He'd have to call home soon or risk Cecelia calling the cops out to look for him. He rubbed his forehead, closed his eyes.

"You really should try this, Jordie. It's ex-quellent."

"It looks great. So, let's go over this again, okay? You are how far along?"

Darla's chewing slowed; she sat perfectly still. Eventually, she put down her fork, took a gulp of milk and turned to Jordan.

"You're doubting me."

"No, not at all. I'm just trying to get it all straight in my mind."

"I've been pregnant since maybe late June. So, the baby's due in March."

March. Cecelia was due in May. This wasn't looking good. He pulled his cigarette box from his breast pocket.

"You've already got one burning up over here," Darla said, gesturing to the ashtray. "And smoking up a storm isn't going to make this go away. We have to do something. *You* have to do something because this is your fault."

Jordan tossed the cigarette box onto the table, smoothed back his hair. Truth be told, it *was* his fault, and he could fix it. If Darla agreed.

"You know, darling, there are places...doctors...who can help with this sort of thing. We can take care of it tomorrow. Of course, I'll pay for the costs..."

Darla's mouth dropped open, and she fisted both hands. "An abortion?! You want me to have an abortion? Are you nuts?" Her voice rang out, reverberating off the diner's low ceiling.

Jordan leaned forward, his hands outstretched as if he could contain her outburst. "It's okay. Calm down, I was only trying to suggest–"

"This baby is already a baby, Jordan. Four months already. No. I won't do it. I can't kill our baby. And I hate that you would even suggest it." Darla's cheeks blazed and her chest heaved with emotion.

Jordan sat back, drew in a breath. She was right, of course. But if Cecelia or her father got wind of this bit of unlucky news, his life would be over. He'd have to join Russell on a lonely stool at Schwab's. Or worse, clean their tables.

He looked at his watch. "Darla, dear heart, I have to go soon. Give me–give me a couple of days to sort this out. You have to realize what a shock this all is. I want to do what's best for all of us, without any bloodshed. I'll drop you off. We'll get together later this week, and I'll have some sort of plan by then."

Out came the bottom lip, but Darla put on her sweater and slid out of the booth.

Cecelia turned a critical eye on the painters wielding their brushes against the guest room walls. She wasn't sure of the color. It might be a tad too bright for a baby's room. Looking down, she tugged to straighten the new maternity blouse. She wasn't "showing" yet but couldn't resist using the Broadway gift certificate her parents had sent her following the announcement. Jordan thought it was cute.

Wandering over to the window, she decided to let in some fresh air to dispel the paint odor gathering in the upstairs room. She hesitated; Jordan hated the look of window screens and had removed all of them from the front of the house. She parted the curtains, pushed up the heavy sash window and leaned slightly out. *What a gloriously sunny fall day.*

Being pregnant could be the best thing to ever happen to her. While she'd been terribly sick the first two months, she felt better now. *We should have done this a long time ago,* she thought happily, perusing the street below, where a woman pushed a stroller while walking her Yorkie. *Maybe we'll get a dog, too.*

Shifting, she gazed in the other direction, toward the foothills, and noticed an older model car parked across the street. A brunette woman, wearing a hat and sunglasses, sat low in the seat behind the wheel. The dark bobbed hair gave her away.

Darla Foster! What is she doing?

Behind her, the phone rang, and Cecelia turned away. When she returned to the window a short time later, the car had gone.

She didn't know whether to tell Jordan or not. Everything was going so well. He came home for dinner most nights, became attentive and interested in her again. He made no mention of Darla, and, except for one night in particular the week before, seemed optimistic about their future. She didn't want to rock the boat. Perhaps she'd just forget what she'd seen, ignore the incident. Unless it happened again.

Darla didn't care whether the almighty Cecelia Kent had seen her or not. She held her chin high as she drove back to Burbank. Jordan had better call her soon, or she'd knock next time.

Once home, she parked her mother's car on the street and went inside. Ravenous, she was raiding the refrigerator for leftovers when her mother caught her with a drumstick in hand.

"Dinner will be ready in an hour. Do you really want to eat twice?"

"I'm hungry now."

"Yes, but you really should be watching closer what you eat. I didn't want to say anything, honey, but you're putting on weight. Especially since you got back."

Darla shrugged. "Nerves. I eat when I'm nervous. You know that."

"What do you have to be nervous about?" Her mother closed the fridge door and turned toward Darla, arms crossed.

"Everything. The picture will be out soon, the holidays are coming, there's this other picture I might get, but I might not, in which case I gotta start reading for parts pronto. All kinds of stuff."

"Maybe you don't need to do another movie so soon. Maybe you should just take a break. Or get some classes. They have night classes at the high school."

"I need the money, Mom. I want the work. I love the work. I want to do another picture now, while I still can."

Her mother shook her head and went to the stew pot on the stove. "Dinner will be ready at six."

In her bedroom, Darla pulled open her small closet door and began sliding hangers on the rod, looking for something to wear. Something that didn't feel like a girdle. Stripping down to her underwear, she stood before her dresser mirror, turned sideways, tried to suck in the bump.

"Oh, Lord. Just look at that," she said with a sigh. She went back to the closet, pushed hangers in the opposite direction, eventually choosing a pair of pleated trousers. They'd always been too big, but she'd had to have them after seeing Katharine Hepburn sporting a pair on the big screen. Now, they served to disguise her impending motherhood.

The pants hung too long, especially with her loafers. She snickered. "I look like Charlie Chaplin." *But who cares? Not me. It can be my Halloween costume.*

Grabbing her handbag off the dresser, Darla clattered down the stairs and lifted her overcoat from the hook by the door. "Goin' out," she called.

Her mother leaned out of the kitchen doorway. "What? I made stew!"

"Not hungry now. Gotta go!"

Her mother followed her to the door, called after her.

"Don't take my car! I might need it to pick up your father!"

The day had chilled, and Darla wrapped her coat tightly around her. She didn't mind walking the five blocks to the Pacific

Electric Red Car station. She made the trip frequently, as the Lankershim station was just a few blocks from her favorite movie house. The La Reina Theatre had the best darned popcorn in Los Angeles.

At the box office, she dug into her handbag for the admission, coming up with three quarters. The woman in the cage pushed two dimes and four pennies back through the slot. With the three nickels in the bottom of her purse, she could buy the popcorn and a soda. *Great!*

"Better hurry. The cartoon's just started," the woman said.

Darla grinned. "Long as I don't miss Lana," she explained. "I can do without the other stuff." She took her time to admire the movie poster for *The Three Musketeers*, lingering to examine Gene Kelly's smiling likeness beside Lana Turner's.

"Van Heflin, too," she murmured. "And June."

Within minutes, she sat happily munching her heavily buttered popcorn, giggling over Donald Duck's unsuccessful efforts to get his three nephews bathed.

The newsreel bored her; she spent the time looking around at other movie goers, despite the dark. She enjoyed the Western, then settled back to immerse herself in the swashbuckling story of Porthos, Athos and D'Artagnan. Darla shivered at the first close up of Kelly and her eyes widened at Turner's portrayal of the evil Lady De Winter.

I could be her. I could do that role, I'm good. Mr. Bregman said so.

Except now. The realization that her life had taken a serious turn was interrupted by a feeling in her abdomen, like a cluster of bubbles popping. Not quite a tingle, certainly not uncomfortable...but something she'd never felt before. With startling clarity of thought, Darla quickly pressed a hand to her tummy, upsetting her near-empty popcorn box. All notions about leading roles and big pictures dissolved.

The baby had moved.

Seventeen

Grogan's Head, California
July

McAfee's was probably the nicest restaurant in town, the only one with votive candles on the tables. Matt ordered scampi, and his guest opted for salmon Provençal.

"I really appreciate the tour today. I actually learned a lot about this area."

"My pleasure. You can do the same for me when I come to Seattle. I've always wanted a look around Bainbridge Island." Matt tilted his head, watched Denise as she lifted her wine glass to her lips. "So, you've mentioned your dad. Is he the only man in your life right now?"

"Pretty much. I'm not really dating. I'm kind of a stick-in-the-mud."

"What's your favorite thing to do on a Friday night?"

"Flannel jammies, mint chocolate chip ice cream, old movie."

"Sports?"

"Used to. Rock climbing, water skiing, went parasailing in Mexico once...did some river-rafting. Lately I just watch tennis on TV."

"What happened? Injury, work or laziness?"

Denise laughed. "Guess I'll have to own up to number three. Maybe two, also."

"We'll have to work on that, then." Matt took a swallow of wine, put his glass down. "Tell me about your father."

"Hmm. Well, he's sixty-five. He's a retired mechanic. He loves old movies, old cars...he's really into nostalgic things. We have dinner together once a week."

"He lives near you?"

"About a mile away. I can practically see his house from my balcony."

"That's good. You know, I keep thinking about what happened to your mother."

Denise shifted in her seat. "I think about it a lot, too. What a wonderful, sweet person." A veil clouded her eyes, and Matt could see she suffered after fifteen years. "It seemed so unfair."

"Have you ever tried to...dig into what happened?"

"No point. Oh, I've thought about it, thought about trying to find the family of the man who witnessed the accident...but I can't really see any benefit now."

"A witness?"

"Apparently. A man standing on the corner." Denise's eyes again glazed over as she recalled the past. "My mother was crossing the street in the intersection, with a green light. A car came out of nowhere, ran her down. The car never stopped. When the police arrived, the car was long gone. The witness told the cop he saw a man behind the wheel."

"So, what happened to the witness?"

"He died in his sleep the same night. Before he could be formally interviewed."

Matt shook his head. "That's really strange. Why wouldn't they take his statement right away? What about the cop he talked to? Did he consider the man's account credible?"

"I only know what little my dad has told me, which isn't much, and the story in the *Phoenix Gazette*."

"Phoenix? Is that where it happened?"

Denise broke from her trance. "Oh, yes. She, uh, was there meeting a fellow genealogist."

"I don't suppose the witness got any part of the license plate?"

His companion looked up, and Matt thought the sadness in her eyes would break his heart.

"No. As far as I know, he only reported the color of the car. A black sedan. That's it."

Matt said nothing for a time, thinking about the details and wondering. Finally, he ventured on. "Do you happen to have the name of the man who witnessed the accident?"

"Actually, yes. It's in the news clipping. But I don't think–"

"Was he from Phoenix?"

"Yes."

"Do you remember the date? I'm just curious."

"August 4, 1993. And since you're probably going to ask me, no, I don't know the person she planned to meet. A man, I guess, who had some information for her about her ancestors. She was big on all that genealogy stuff."

Matt smiled. "What about you? Are you interested in your past? Your relatives' pasts?"

"Not really."

"So, she went all the way from Seattle to Phoenix to meet a man for info about her relatives. Sounds pretty important. They had email in 1993, so why the in-person meeting? Doesn't that seem strange to you?"

Denise looked uncomfortable.

"I'm sorry. I'm an attorney, remember? I can't let anything rest. I'll shut up now."

"No, it's okay. Just...a bad time. Mom was pretty independent. She liked to travel. She knew other people in Phoenix, she went to school there, so it she made it a combination trip, I think."

"Okay. No big mystery."

Despite the cold, they went for a walk after dinner. From their vantage point at the pier, they could see the beam from Battery Point lighthouse. Matt slid a tentative arm around Denise's shoulders.

"I'm glad you looked me up. This has been a fun couple of days. Forced me to get away from work," Matt said.

"Me, too. I need to get back soon, though."

"I understand. You'll be in touch?"

"About the grant? Of course."

"Not just about the grant."

Denise turned and looked into Matt's eyes. Was it regret he saw there? Before he could delve deeper, she moved away from him. He wasn't to be dissuaded.

"I guess what I'm trying to say is, I'd like to see you again. Aside from the grant. I'd love to come up to Seattle. I've never seen Lake Washington. Think you could whip up one of your famous apple pies?"

Denise cleared her throat. "I don't know, Matt. I'm–I'm not really looking for anything right now. But hey–" she added, giving him a playful punch in the ribs. "If I was, you'd be the guy."

Matt smoothed back his hair, tried to determine why he felt she was lying. The parking lot lights picked up a glisten in her eyes. Tears?

"So…okay. That's cool." He looked around, took a deep breath. "Look, don't let my…forwardness scare you. I'm just a regular guy. Not a stalker, not a slug. You get in touch when you're ready to move on this. Maybe you'll change your mind about the other."

Denise nodded, looked away briefly. "Thanks. Like I said, if I was in the market–"

"I get it." He put his arm back around her anyway, gave her a light squeeze. "Trumped by flannels and ice cream again. When will it end?"

She giggled then, and he laughed. He laughed because he knew he'd find a way into her heart. He just didn't know how yet.

"No. I haven't gotten the okay yet. And I'm not sure I'm going to get it." Rebecca hung her head as she sat, cross-legged, on her bed, cell phone pressed to her ear. *Why didn't I just let it go to voicemail?*

"You talked me into this. Now you're saying you can't even get inside the damned place? Look, I bumped Chad's piece on the new ultra-light gliders so we could do your lighthouse thing."

Rebecca rubbed her eyes. "I know, I know. I just didn't dream it would be this hard. We can do the story on Point Surrender, just down the coast, it's open to the–"

"We agreed on Dragon Rock. That was the deal. Crap." Pat went quiet now, and Rebecca felt like she could throw up at any moment.

"I'll explain more when I get home."

"Yeah, you do that."

Rebecca slowly closed her cell phone. She hadn't felt this dreadful in…ever. What was she doing here, anyway? Deception wasn't her game. Lying, impersonation, possibly fraud! All because of her obsession, her need to find out what had happened inside

Dragon Rock Lighthouse sixty years ago. It wasn't about the article, or Pat, or even Matt. She couldn't explain it even to herself. Something had taken over, a force more powerful than her own will. Bizarre, untenable thoughts came out of nowhere, spurring actions she'd never have dreamed of in the past. It was as if she were no longer in control.

The shower nearly scalded her, but she didn't care. Didn't care about wasting precious Northern California water, or that the room had filled with so much steam she could barely breathe. She washed her hair, let the spray rinse the suds down the drain and wished all the badness would rinse away, too.

What else could she possibly do?

The oversized bath towel felt good against her skin. She huddled inside it, reluctant to leave the warmth of the bathroom for the chill of her hotel room. Standing before the mirror, she flipped on the exhaust fan to suck out at least some of the steam, hoping to see herself well enough to dry her hair. She pulled the hair dryer from its rack and endeavored to turn it on, only to discover it was unplugged.

"Is nothing easy anymore?" she murmured aloud, plugging the dryer in and picking up her hairbrush. Turning back to the mirror, Rebecca slowly put down the dryer. There, finger-written into the fog on the mirror, she saw the words.

DON'T GIVE UP!

"Oh...my...God." Rebecca stepped backward, pressed herself against the opposite wall. Instinctively wrapping the towel tighter, she gulped air as she read the words again. She wasn't sure what upset her more, the fact that someone had been inside the bathroom while she showered or that they knew her most intimate dilemma. Stunned, she rushed out of the room, checked the locks on her hotel room door. All, including the safety bar, remained in place. No one had come through the door since she'd locked herself in when returning from dinner with Matt.

Icy fear replaced the nausea. She wandered back into the bathroom and carefully placed her hairbrush on the sink counter. Almost afraid to look, she slowly brought her eyes back to the message on the glass, only to be further shocked by the addition of more words below the first.

WE CAN DO IT.

Rebecca sank to the floor and sat, watching the fog, and the words, fade from the mirror.

If she dreamed, she did not remember, and no new messages waited when she awoke. Unsure of her next move, she decided to do nothing until after breakfast. She selected a corner booth in the mostly empty coffee shop.

"More?" the waitress asked after taking Rebecca's order. Rebecca nodded gratefully, slid her cup forward then reached for a folded newspaper on the opposite side of the table.

"Oh, here. I'll take that. Sorry. That last young lady must've left it."

"Oh, it's okay. I could use something to read. Thanks."

Rebecca opened the newspaper and perused, sipping the coffee, trying to feel normal after the troubling events of the night before. The mayor proposed a new curfew. The school district reported improved scores. A young thief snatched a woman's purse from her grocery basket. Rebecca stifled a yawn, turned another page.

A frown wrinkled her brow as she passed over a surprising headline. "Dragon Rock Lighthouse Subject of Vandalism." Her eyes raced over the words describing the report of vandals breaking into the lighthouse and the owner's representative reporting little damage.

> *"Seems they were kids looking for a place to drink beer," commented Matthew Farralone, legal counsel for the St. Paul Foundation.*

When did this happen? Rebecca couldn't believe she hadn't been told. Her eyes searched the corners of the paper for a date. Her lips parted in surprise when she found it: May 17, 2006. Shuffling furiously, she turned back to the front page of the paper, confirming the date below the masthead.

"Miss? Miss," she called out when she saw the waitress emerge from the kitchen. "I'm sorry. You said the last patron left this newspaper here?"

"Why, I presume so. I did see her reading a paper, yes. It must be hers."

"What did she look like?"

"I barely got a look at her. Joan's last customer; I'd just come on duty. Uh...short dark hair, very fair skin. Young. Why? Is there something wrong?"

Rebecca drew in a controlled breath, exhaled quietly. "No. Not really."

She looked back at the article, the hazy newsprint photo of Dragon Rock in the two-year-old paper. The owner had sent him out, Matt told her, to inspect after the vandalism. The owner was concerned about the vandals. Matt followed his orders.

WE CAN DO IT.

Rebecca picked her phone out of her knapsack. "Pat? It's me. Can you give me two more days?"

Finding prospective vandals proved easier than she'd thought it would be. It took every ounce of courage and a bit of desperation to approach the three young men who gathered around a billiards table in the bar adjacent to the tattoo parlor. She made it clear they should not to do any actual damage, just make sure they got seen and then got away. A practical joke on a friend, she told the men, who turned out to be college fraternity brothers. They would happily oblige in return for free beer and ice hockey tickets.

Now all she had to do was wait and make sure she was with Matt when the call came in. They'd set a time window for tomorrow morning.

Matt sat at his desk inside the small construction office trailer, trying to organize the various piles of paperwork associated with the project. With a sigh born of boredom, he moved one stack onto the adjacent filing cabinet, then went back to the rest.

Invoices. Time sheets. Materials lists. Permit applications. Where did it end? Where was his secretary? He smiled, envisioning Rhonda, typing away at her lavish marble workstation in Beverly Hills. Here he sat at a battered, thirty-year-old Steelcase covered with as many years of grime.

Armed with a fresh box of file folders, he slotted the piles into the folders and carefully printed titles on the tabs. Only a few sheets of paper remained. Denise's paperwork.

Putting aside the newly created files, he picked up the top sheet and re-read it.

"The September Society is a national organization dedicated to providing physically and environmentally safe havens for children of all races, religions and genders...the foundation offers grant opportunities twice a year to other non-profits..." Matt murmured the words as he scanned through the document, recalling that he'd not yet read the fine print. After his cavalier behavior at lunch the day before, he thought it might be prudent to actually examine the grant restrictions.

It was all pretty much standard legalese. He stood, reading as he crossed the trailer to the coffee pot and poured his morning stimulant. He stopped, cup midway to his lips, as he read to the bottom of the page. In even smaller printed italics, it read:

The September Society has provided 1,300 Bingo game sets to a variety of senior centers throughout Arizona. As an approved vendor for AARP, the Society hopes to reach more seniors in   than in previous years with its new, customizable personal convenience packs.

What the hell?

He looked again at the top. Something odd about the type, he now noticed. Wherever the organization's name appeared, the font didn't quite match. Denise had said the group was new. It wasn't uncommon for non-profs to put together their own documents; enough of them had come to his attention in the courtroom. Brows knitted, he returned to his seat at the desk. What did this mean? Did the September Society deal with seniors *and* children? Were they two separate entities?

A ringing phone cut short his time to ponder. While answering, he carefully restacked the papers and set them in the center of his desk.

"Oh, hell. Not again. How many were there?" Matt listened while the Coast Guard ensign described the scene at Dragon Rock.

"Yeah, I probably should go out there. No, it was locked up tight last time I went. Thanks for the head's up." He ended the call, then dialed the airport. After a few brief words, he confirmed the chopper would be waiting. He grabbed his keys and left the trailer, then headed for the Jeep. No sooner had he started the engine than he saw the familiar light green Corvette in his rear-view mirror. He smiled, turned the engine off.

"Well, well! What brings you out here today?" he asked, walking up to the driver's door of the Chevy. Denise offered a sunny grin.

"Just out for a ride. Looking for something fun to do on my last day here. What are you up to?"

"Oh, just work and more work. But I'm free for an early supper if you're going to be around."

Denise tilted her head, considered. "I'd hoped we could do something this morning. It's such a beautiful day, and I'm sure there are sights you haven't shown me yet."

Matt nodded, rubbed his chin. "You could be right, m'lady. I just have something pressing that can't wait. A little job I have to do."

She looked crestfallen. Matt lifted her chin with his finger, admiring the hurt look in her intelligent eyes. She intentionally pushed his buttons, and he was flattered. "Tell you what. Why don't you tag along, then we'll do something more fun afterward?"

"Really? That would be great!"

"Follow me. I don't want you leaving your car out here. I'll meet you at the airport." He turned to walk back to the Jeep.

"The airport? Are we going somewhere?"

Matt only chuckled and re-started his car.

Eighteen

Hollywood, California
November 1948

S earch lights shone toward the heavens, sweeping across the night sky in celebration as limousines lined Hollywood Boulevard. Unconsciously, Darla reached for Russell's hand as their limo neared the red-carpet before Grauman's Chinese Theater.

"Don't be nervous, doll. This is your night. Enjoy it! Look at 'em, all packed along the street there. All to see you." Russell gestured with his free hand at the droves of fans lining the block.

"More likely to see Jordie," Darla murmured, eyes darting from the fans to the limo ahead of them, just now stopping at the curb. Her teeth began to grind as Jordan stepped out, then turned to assist Cecelia from the back seat.

"Will ya look at that? What an odd sorta dress," Russell proclaimed, eyeing Cecilia through narrowed eyes.

"Maternity," Darla snarled. "It's a maternity dress. As if she even needs one yet. What a show-off."

Russell grinned. "What? You're jealous of her gettin' knocked up? It ain't pretty, doll. I seen my cousin Pearl when she was p-g. Downright sickening. She got them veiny mark things all over her gut. Like a damned road map. You don't wanna look like that. Too bad for Cec."

"Yeah, too bad." Darla let go of Russell's hand and smoothed her taffeta gown across her abdomen. The girdle she'd stolen from her mother's drawer cinched her so tight she could barely breathe.

Enormous posters displayed her and Jordan's likenesses above the blazing title, *CAPE SEDUCTION*, with the lighthouse in the background. While she'd seen a small rendition, the full-sized ad for the movie completely overwhelmed. *I'd want to see that film,* she thought happily.

When their turn came to climb out of the limousine, Russell dutifully took her hand as she stepped onto the carpet. Flash bulbs showered them with quick, intense bursts of light, and Darla couldn't help but squint. Fans on either side of the velvet ropes stretched out their hands to touch, and hopefully shake hands with, the starlet creating all the latest talk in Hollywood. Darla did her best to suck in her tummy and walk bravely through the theater's famous forecourt. She wished desperately to stop and look for Jimmy Stewart's handprints, just imprinted in February. Or Gary Cooper's, or Margaret O'Brien's... *But tonight is for me*, she reminded herself. Holding her head high, she graced the crowd with a queen's smile.

Once inside the theater, they were shown to seats beside Jordan and Cecelia. Darla couldn't believe her bad luck at being seated next to Jordan's wife. She couldn't even steal a glance at Jordan without having to look across her archrival's velvet, tent-like dress.

Darla rested a hand on her tummy. *I'll bet her baby isn't even kicking yet. If she even really has a baby. She could be lying. She probably is.* Consoling herself with the fantasy that Cecelia was faking her pregnancy, Darla turned her attention to the beautiful interior of the theater.

"It's like being in a Chinese palace," she whispered to Russell, who nodded slowly, his eyes fixed on the enormous round brass lantern chandelier above them. "It even smells like Chinese flowers in here. Did you see those gigantic dogs outside? They must be straight from Hong Kong or Shanghai or someplace like that. Look! Look at the dragons on the floor!"

"Do you *mind?*" Cecelia hissed, glowering in Darla's direction.

Darla now turned toward her nemesis. "Do I mind what? Sitting beside you? If that's the question, then yes. *I do.*" Darla returned her attention to Russell. "Change with me. Change seats," she insisted in his ear.

Russell shifted uncomfortably. "I can't do that. We're already seated. It wouldn't look good. People would notice. Just stick it out. The picture's gonna start soon anyway."

Darla folded her arms across her middle and stared straight ahead. But try as she might, she couldn't ignore the incredible scenery inside the theater. Her eyes drifted upward and trailed around, forcing her to twist in her seat. "Look, Russ, that's Mr. Grauman's private box up there! By the projection room. I read about it in a magazine."

Russell, too, stared in awe. "Those columns are something else. They must weigh a ton."

"I heard it cost two million to build this place. Two million dollars! How can anyone have so much money?"

"That Pickford dame and her husband. They can."

"Mary Pickford is no *dame*, Russell. She's a lady. And Douglas Fairbanks is a real hero, not just a husband."

"Aw, sure."

"You just don't understand Hollywood people. That's your problem." Darla refolded her arms and looked back at the velvet drapes covering the screen. Maybe she'd made a mistake by asking Russell to escort her to the premiere. Stephen Sisco had arrived solo, but Darla hadn't the nerve to ask him. Besides, in spite of her annoyance with Russ, he was *safe*. She resigned herself not to speak again until after the movie ended. She would have made good her resignation had the baby not given her a startlingly hard jab.

"Oh! Oh, my. That was a big one." She blinked, not sure what to make of the sudden kick.

"What's big? What are you babbling about now?" Russell asked as the lights began to go down.

"Never mind. You wouldn't understand. It's a woman thing."

Russell rolled his eyes. "Yeah, that's what they all say. Like guys are idiots. Guys don't know squat about dames. Got it all figured out, do you?"

"You couldn't possibly know what a woman feels when she's...when she's going through what she must go through, sometimes. After all, women are different than men. They're built differently. Their bodies can create a baby, for example, and–" Darla could feel Cecelia's eyes burning into the side of her face. Annoyed, she turned to scowl at Jordan's wife. "What are *you* looking at?"

"In case you didn't notice while you chattered away, the lights have dimmed."

"Well that's good, isn't it? Now we don't have to see each other so well. We can pretend to be strangers."

Cecelia gave her a hard look, then turned back toward the screen, now revealed by the parting drapes. The projector came to life, and the premiere of *Cape Seduction* began to unfold.

As Darla lost herself in the screening of her first starring role, Jordan could barely keep track of the plot. Fidgeting in the ornate red, gold and black seat, he shifted his position repeatedly and winced during the love scenes, stealing glances at his heavy-lidded wife beside him. Despite the ludicrous size of her evening gown, Jordan had complimented Cecelia and made certain she was comfortably seated. Their relationship still tenuous, his entire future hung in the balance.

A plan began to materialize in his head. Triggered by the remark he'd overheard just before the curtains parted, it wasn't a happy sort of thought, but one growing infinitely more necessary. The word uttered by Darla and heard by both he and Cecelia was *baby*. Now, an hour into the film, the echo remained. Darla had nearly slipped. She couldn't hide the tell-tale bulge at her waist much longer. Something had to be done, and soon.

He went through the various plots he'd devised again, but none seemed feasible.

Darla could admit the pregnancy and blame some unknown suitor. It would ruin her, but it would keep himself out of the picture. He couldn't see her agreeing to it, nonetheless.

She'd already ruled out an abortion.

She could go away for six months, return alone and back to normal. It would be easy to adopt out the child. Clearly the best option, if he could get her to go. Go, and keep her mouth shut. He knew a woman in Canada, a former actress...but Darla was stubborn, and her loose lips couldn't be trusted.

No, if she went away to have the baby, it would have to be someplace remote. Someplace where there would be no danger of her being recognized, with no one to talk to. But where did such isolation exist?

Jordan sighed and tried to focus on the screen. Here was Darla-as-Mary, inside the lighthouse, running up the stairs. In his mind's eye, he saw her padding up those stone steps, stark naked. Bursting out of the lantern room in a fit of giggles, standing at the gallery rail with her arms outstretched. He smiled involuntarily as he recalled her impish, crazy ways.

The camera pulled back, giving a wide, panoramic shot of Dragon Rock. The smile on Jordan's face diminished as the answer to his dilemma presented itself right before his eyes.

"This isn't the way we came in," Darla worried, as Russell pulled her along. The tunnel wasn't too wide or well-lit, but Jordan, Cecelia and several others hurried along behind them. "Where does it go?"

"The Roosevelt Hotel. Across the street. So's we don't get stampeded by all those gawkers out there. They'll even follow you home and camp on your lawn. Your mama wouldn't like that, now would she?" Russell explained.

"Oh, no, I guess not. I didn't know about this. How wonderfully smart of them!"

"Yeah, some of those guys have something on the ball."

They neared the end of the tunnel and the doorway leading to the hotel stairs as Jordan and Cecelia brushed past them. Cecelia seemed to be in a hurry and kept on walking after landing the heel of her pump squarely on the center of Darla's velvet-slippered foot.

"Ow! Dammit! Oh, Christ that hurts!" Darla stumbled to the ground, grasping her foot with one hand and instinctively protecting her abdomen with the other. "Why the hell'd you do that?" she demanded, as Cecelia and Jordan turned back at the sound of her cry.

Russell dropped immediately to her side. "Darla, sugar, I'm sure it was an accident. Right, Cec? She wouldn't do that on purpose," he consoled. "You okay? Is your stomach hurting?"

Darla caressed her belly and gave Jordan a bruised look. "It's okay, I think. I hope. I did bump it on the ground." Her aching foot forgotten, she turned angry eyes on Cecelia's cold stare. "Getting a little clumsy with your big stomach there, Cecelia? Must be hard to manage, being so huge already."

Russell huffed out a sigh and helped Darla to her feet. Neither Jordan nor Cecelia commented but stood aside as Darla limped past them with Russell's help.

Jordan turned to Cecelia, who looked away. Any remaining doubt in his mind evaporated. His plan was set.

Nineteen

Newburg, California
July

Rebecca's adrenaline level flew off the chart as the helicopter centered to land on the top of the great caisson base at Dragon Rock Lighthouse. Her fingers shook as she tried to unhook her seatbelt. She was finally going to get back inside, and although she had no camera crew, she did have her small Sony Digicam. Surely Matt wouldn't object to a few minutes of film. But before she could negotiation the latch on the belt, Matt covered her hand with his own.

"You need to stay in the chopper. I'll only be a few minutes," he nearly shouted, competing with the helicopter's loud whir.

"What? I can't go in with you?" she yelled back in surprise. "But–"

"Nope. Not this time. Sorry." He pulled a high-powered flashlight from behind the seat. "Just sit tight. I won't be long." He started away.

"Wait! I want to go with you! I really do," Rebecca pleaded, flipping open the latch and grabbing her shoulder bag. "I won't touch a thing, I promise!"

Matt returned and planted himself in her path as she stepped from the cockpit. "No. No good. Please, just get back in. I have to insist."

They locked eyes for several moments. Rebecca felt hers welling with tears, and she made an abrupt about-face before Matt could see. She climbed back into the chopper to wait.

I was so close. I am so close. She's counting on me, and I'm failing. Again.

They didn't speak until they landed back in the airport.

"Look, Denise, I'm sorry about what happened back there. I have strict orders. You have to understand."

"It's fine. I just didn't know, that's all. I'm the one who should apologize," Rebecca said quietly. "Sorry I made a scene."

"No, I should have warned you. He—my client—he's a stickler. The pilot is on his payroll."

"And he would have busted you. I get it. Let's just forget about it, okay?"

"Sounds great. And didn't I promise you something fun now?"

Rebecca swallowed hard and smiled. "It better be good," she forced out.

The afternoon with Matt proved more depressing than fun but only because Rebecca found herself more and more enamored. His wit and subtle affection wore on her, in a way she would normally grasp with both hands, never to let go. As they toured local sights, tramped through the museum and even the oceanography institute where Case showed them around, Matt seemed more a companion than an acquaintance.

She nearly broke down when he dropped her off, knowing his heart was there for the taking while her own was breaking.

"This has been a wonderful trip," she told him in the motel parking lot. "I'll never forget it. Thanks for all the trouble you've gone to."

"Trouble? Oh, sure. Yeah, you're trouble, all right." He ran his fingers over a lock of her hair. "You've already given me the brush, so I figure I have nothing to lose." Leaning down, Matt pressed his lips to the corner of her mouth. "You take care, Denise Murray. You know where to find me."

Friday morning, Rebecca tossed clothes into her soft-sided bag in the middle of the hotel room floor. She had no reason to stay longer, having failed her one chance to get Matthew Farralone to offer her a look at the lighthouse. It was a long shot, a dumb idea to begin with. She'd only succeeded in compromising her integrity with lies and deceit. The sooner she got away, the better.

She thought she'd covered her own tracks pretty well. She could see no way that Matt could trace Denise Murray back to herself. She hoped.

From the dresser, she scooped up some coins and dropped them into her pocket, then collected the various pieces of paper haphazardly lying about. She paused at the sight of three business cards beside the lamp. Dr. Case McKenna, Marine Biologist, Olsen Oceanography Institute of California, Grogan's Head, California; Jack McKenzie, Independent Set Designer, Hollywood, California; Matthew H. Farralone, Esquire, Beverly Hills, California. Another card, cast aside, was the bank depository information for the Boys and Girls Club.

Rebecca's face burned. Gathering the cards, she started to drop them into the wastebasket. Instead, she shoved them into the back pocket of her jeans.

Squatting beside her bag, she zipped it up and stood, hoisting it to her shoulder. With one last look around, she left the hotel room.

It was too far to make it home in one day. She planned on stopping somewhere near San Francisco for the night, then drive on to Burbank tomorrow. She'd return the 'Vette, fly back to Phoenix, cancel her plans to shoot the lighthouse. It was that simple. Right?

It would have been all right, she insisted to herself, if it wasn't for Matt.

Matt, the baby, and the dark-haired ghost.

Rebecca dug into her jacket pockets as she strolled along the B Street Pier. The early morning fog still clung, the air damp and biting. Around her, fishermen busied themselves with buckets, nets and lures. She was in no hurry to reach the end of the long, narrow pier, for once there, she would just turn around and return to the car.

She wasn't quite ready to leave Crescent City, either. Her failure to gain access to the lighthouse weighed heavily, a huge disappointment. Made worse, of course, by her deceit. Matt wasn't a half-bad guy. Had they met under different circumstances, things would certainly be different.

Rebecca turned, leaned against the wooden railing. Below her, the surf restlessly tumbled onto the rocks, only to reluctantly retreat back into the sea. Gulls soared above and below the pier, anxiously seeking the odd tidbit cast off by the waves.

145

The rocky shoreline was deserted, except for a lone figure a half mile or so down the coast. For want of anything more interesting to look at, Rebecca watched as what appeared to be a young woman meandered along close to the water line. She was slight of build, with short, dark hair and sunglasses. Rebecca might have looked away had she not been surprised by the woman's attire. The sundress would be a great beach compliment–in Santa Monica or Venice. But here in the 42-degree morning, the sleeveless cotton frock invited pneumonia, at best.

Clearly unconcerned about the possibility that she wasn't alone, the woman twirled now and again, causing the yellow-flowered dress to flare out. Incredulous, Rebecca squinted, her mouth open in surprise as she caught sight of the woman's bare feet splashing in the icy foam. She grew closer now, close enough for Rebecca to hear her giggle.

"What a nutcase," Rebecca murmured, transfixed. "I wonder where she escaped from?"

As if she heard Rebecca's words, the young woman stopped dancing, thrust her hands into the deep patch pockets on her dress and stared up at the pier. Rebecca wanted to look away but found she couldn't avert her eyes, as if the woman immobilized her, restrained her movements with her gaze. The workaday sounds of the pier dissolved into quiet.

The two women remained so locked for some time when at last the beach dweller slowly removed one hand from her pocket and placed her fingertips against her lips. Before Rebecca's astonished eyes, the woman blew her a kiss, then turned around and walked back the way she came.

The sounds returned. Beside her, a fisherman assembled his rod and reel.

"That was weird," Rebecca said, turning to the man with an uneasy smile.

"What's weird?"

"That woman down there. She–she–"

The fisherman followed Rebecca's gaze back to the empty beach below. "What woman?"

Rebecca stared at the dark, rocky sand, the foamy surf, the gulls. The beach, clearly visible for miles, showed no sign of any activity, let alone a bizarre, dancing woman.

"Why–" Rebecca looked back at the man, who'd returned his attention to his lures. "How long have you been standing here?"

"Oh, five minutes, give or take. Before you."

"And you didn't see a woman down there on the beach?"

"I kinda wondered what you was lookin' at. Nope, didn't see anybody myself."

Rebecca nodded. "Okay. Right."

On her way back to the car, she opted for a detour and wandered out onto the beach, retracing the path she thought the woman had made along the waterline. She stared hard down the coast, straining to see any evidence, any fleck of color that might be a young woman's sundress fluttering in the ocean breeze. Turning around, she estimated the spot where the woman stood, then looked up at the pier herself. The fisherman touched the brim of his cap and nodded.

Rebecca nodded back, looked around once more, then walked slowly back toward the path leading to the pier. She glanced behind her, again hoping to see her visitor in the distance. With a heavy sigh, she went back to the car.

Behind the wheel of the Corvette, Rebecca took Pebble Beach Drive to the end and turned left, ending up in the parking lot at the Dragon Rock Lookout. She got out of the car and stood facing the wind, her eyes narrowed as she stared out across the waters between the point and the lighthouse. What was happening here? Why did it pull on her? It wasn't even a pretty beacon. Dark, rusty, damaged...punished by the raw, pounding surf, chided and belittled by the reef it was supposed to be guarding against.

There was no sense to it, no documented reason why, but Rebecca felt some strong *ju ju* going on. Although her mission did not come off as planned, she knew it wasn't over. She would return to Dragon Rock Lighthouse and discover its secrets, and maybe a few of her own.

Rebecca rubbed at her eyes, took another sip of the hot coffee before her. Dusk loomed, and she was tired of driving. Tired of thinking. She'd pulled off the highway in search of a caffeine jolt and decided she couldn't possibly go any farther tonight.

The waiter approached, coffee pot in hand. "Sure I can't get you somethin' to eat? You look like a gal who could appreciate a good rack of ribs."

Rebecca looked up at the man, who now refilled her mug. "Yeah. Maybe so. That sounds good. And do you happen to know where I could get a room for the night?"

"Only place near here is Hastings House. Back the road a piece. Bed and breakfast. They might have a room, beings it's midweek. You want cole slaw or potatas?"

"What the heck. Bring on the carbs. And whatever light beer you have. In a bottle."

"You got it. Name's Riley, by the way. You on vacation?"

Rebecca smiled. "Nice to meet you, Riley. I'm Rebecca. And yes, I'm just touring around, on my way back down to So Cal."

Riley nodded, moved a quarter turn and paused. "The lighthouse has a couple rooms they sometimes let. If Hastings is full."

"Thanks. I'll remember that." *Another lighthouse. Interesting.*

Unable to stifle a yawn, Rebecca stretched in the booth and glanced out the window at the growing darkness. At least she'd gotten past San Francisco and its confusing traffic patterns.

She nearly put her head down. The Corvette, while charming to drive, murdered her hips and she'd be achy tomorrow. She welcomed the beer Riley placed before her.

"Suppose you wanna retire this coffee," he said, reaching for her mug. "No reason to ruin a good buzz."

Rebecca felt a giggle bubble up. "Got that right. I wasn't originally planning to stay here tonight. I wanted to try to make Monterey or Carmel, but I'm just running on empty."

"I got the wife givin' Hastings a call for ya. She'll find out what rooms they have open tonight."

"Why, thank you! What a nice thing to do. I was just wondering how I could manage this."

"You been driving awhile, I take it."

"From Crescent City. I got a late start, or I would've driven straight through."

"Straight through to where?"

"L.A.; Burbank, actually. I have a plane to catch tomorrow."

Riley nodded, and motioned toward the kitchen. "I'll check on those ribs."

When he returned with her dinner, Riley sat down in the booth opposite her. "Hastings has rooms. I asked her to reserve you one, hope you don't mind. It's pretty economical weeknights."

"Mind? You've just saved me from figuring out what to do. And that might have taken my last few brain cells. Thanks so much. You'll have to give me directions."

Riley took a blank meal check from his pad and turned it over, drawing out a small map. "As you drive along here, you'll see an unmarked dirt road on your left. That's the entrance to Point Surrender. But you just keep on driving, and pretty soon you'll pass the hospital, and then a few more blocks and make a left. Hastings House is on the corner of High Street. You can't miss it. It's the only three-story building in Newburg. The lady there is Amy Winslow. She'll check you in. Real nice girl. Usta work here, 'while back."

"I think I've got it. I really can't thank you enough."

"Aw, don't mention it."

"Hey, about this lighthouse. Where is it, exactly?"

"The dirt road. Point Surrender is the lighthouse. It's off the road, can't see it from the highway. Amy's brother owns it, but he lives in the city most of the time. He 'n Judy have twins, and it's just too cramped to live there. In the lighthouse, I mean. So, they rent it out from time to time."

Rebecca nodded politely, unable to take in much more information. She *was* curious about the lighthouse, and maybe she'd do a bit of exploring before she left town tomorrow. But right now, she needed to get into a bed and crash.

As promised, Amy Winslow was a friendly young proprietress, who showed her to "Jacelyn's Room," a suite both feminine and comfortable. Rebecca, however, would have rented "Hell's Kitchen" for a bed and a bathtub. Now, as she settled into the deep, downy soft mattress, she eased out a sigh. This felt good, and right. *Good think I didn't try to drive farther.*

Rebecca closed her eyes, hoping to drift off to sleep without troubling thoughts. She needed a good night's sleep. Tomorrow would be a long, difficult day. Yet a vision came to her, a vision of a young woman in a flowered dress. Closer now, not twenty yards away but face-to-face with Rebecca. The woman removed the sunglasses and peered with dark brown eyes into Rebecca's hazel ones.

Her face seemed familiar: a small mouth, her lips full. Rebecca immediately thought of Betty Boop and her heart-shaped kisses. Questioning eyes, expectant–fearful, perhaps. Instead of feeling scared herself, Rebecca felt a wave of compassion and sorrow. As the sadness grew within her, she became uncomfortable with the vision and forced her eyes open, willing away her imaginary visitor.

Rebecca sat up in bed and blinked several times. Yet the woman's cheerless expression remained before her for several seconds before fading away into the darkness of her room.

"Sleep well?" Amy Winslow asked, pouring orange juice into a tumbler before Rebecca at the breakfast table.

"When I finally got to sleep, yes," Rebecca answered. She scooped up a forkful of apple strudel and savored it on her tongue. "Mmm."

"I'm sorry, I hope the bed was okay."

"Heavenly. I just...had trouble unwinding at first. Tell me something. Is this house considered haunted?"

Amy paused, looked at Rebecca thoughtfully. "Not that I know of," she said quietly. "Why do you ask?"

"Just curious. Sometimes these old houses...you know."

"Were you visited?"

Rebecca smiled. "I don't know. There's this woman. I saw her yesterday morning on the beach at Crescent City. I kept seeing her face last night."

"A memory, perhaps?"

"Yes, and no. In my vision, I could see her eyes. On the beach, she wore sunglasses. It's all too weird for me."

"We had a ghost or two at Point Surrender," Amy offered, now filling Rebecca's coffee cup.

"Surrender? The lighthouse? How creepy."

"Why? I think a lot of lighthouses are haunted, or so I hear."

"I guess...it's just weird because, I have this strange feeling the woman I saw is somehow connected to the lighthouse up there. Don't ask me why, it's just...a feeling."

Amy put the coffee pot on the table and sat down. "We knew who our ghost was."

"Is he...is he gone now?"

Amy looked away, her smile wistful. "Yes. Once he got what he wanted, or needed, he just went away."

"Who was he?"

"The former owner of this house. My fiancé's father." Amy gestured to a large, black and white photograph on the dining room wall. A man and a boy, with a white cylindrical lighthouse behind them. "That's him, with Point Surrender in the background. The boy is Case."

Rebecca nearly choked on her orange juice. "Case, did you say? He's your fiancé?"

"It's actually Casey, but he goes by Case. Case McKenna."

"Oh! Interesting. Is he about?"

"Not right now. He works up north, not far from where you said you came from. Grogan's Head is just up the road a bit from Crescent City."

"I see." Rebecca nodded. "That's quite a commute, isn't it? Well. I guess I'd better get checked out. I have a long drive ahead of me. This has been great." She glanced at the empty breakfast plates around her. "Lovely food. Thank you."

On Coast Highway, Rebecca sped right past the turnoff to Point Surrender. She no longer had any desire to poke around there. Her brain was already on overload, what with the visions of the strange little woman and the discovery of the innkeeper's connection to Case McKenna—and Matt Farralone.

Stopping only for a drive-thru burger and bathroom breaks, Rebecca drove through to Burbank, arriving with plenty of time to return the 'Vette and check in at Bob Hope Airport. She boarded, pushed back her seat and closed her eyes as the jet taxied for takeoff. Within moments, the woman's face reappeared in her mind's eye, only this time the vision was clearly just a memory.

151

Calmer now, Rebecca took a moment to absorb the woman's features. The sad, ebony eyes, the porcelain complexion, the cute, helmet haircut.

Rebecca's eyes shot open with a startling revelation. The woman's face seemed familiar because it was. How many times had Rebecca paused the action on the DVD player to study the lighthearted, teasing expression on Darla Foster's charismatic face?

Twenty

Burbank, California
November 1948

Helen Foster dabbed at her eyes, watched as her daughter went about packing the oversized, tan and brown plaid suitcase spread open on the bed.

"Mom. Please. It's just like last time. I'll be back before you know it." Darla pulled open another drawer in her dresser, scooping up a stack of neatly arranged undergarments and placing them into the suitcase. "I'll write you. The phone rates are terrible from over there."

"I can't believe you're going so far away. I didn't know they filmed movies in France."

"Oui-oui, maman. Jordan says it's the latest. Even Lana Turner might be going."

She didn't like to lie to her mother. Sometimes it was just necessary. Like now. "How about making me a little sandwich. Could you do that, Mom?"

Her mother straightened, sniffed. "Sure, I can." Her mother seemed glad for something to do and rushed away.

Darla sighed, sat on the edge of her bed and folded her hands in her lap. The cab would be here in twenty. She hadn't allowed herself to think about the future, about the truth. About where she was really going. Jordan had handled it all, and she trusted him. She trusted him completely. Right?

"It'll go by quickly, you'll see," he'd told her. "I'll be there every two weeks. You'll have everything you need, delivered each week. Books, magazines, how about chocolates? There's a good girl."

"I might get scared, Jordie. I've never been all alone like that before. Especially out there. What if I get the creeps?"

"You won't, dear heart. Quite the contrary! It will be relaxing, what with the sound of the ocean waves, the sea birds calling. Or you could turn on the radio if you want a little Nat King Cole...or maybe The Andrews Sisters. Hey! I can arrange for you to have a record machine, too. I'll get you a copy of *On a Slow Boat to China* by Kay Kyser if you'd like."

Darla punched out her now infamous lower lip, avoiding his eyes. "It won't be the same there without you. What if there's a storm? Will it fall over?"

"No, Darla. That lighthouse is built to take the harshest weather. It's been there for nearly sixty years. It's not going to fall over. Say, what about a set of oil paints and canvasses? Think of the scenes you can create."

"I'm no good at painting."

"But you could–"

"I don't wanna talk about it anymore. I'll go. But you'd better show up every other week, Jordan Kent. Don't leave me out there alone. Promise me you'll come."

Jordan had bent to embrace her tenderly. "Of course I will, Darla dear. Like clockwork."

Now, she stood, slammed the suitcase shut and snapped its fasteners. Her mother was calling from the kitchen.

Jordan checked his watch. Another hour, he figured, before the train stopped in San Francisco. The bus would be waiting. His plans were in place, as long as the people he'd hired followed through. The swaying of the train car made him drowsy. Beside him, Darla alternately napped and read magazines.

He marveled at the brilliance of his idea. The production company had taken out use permits for the filming of *Cape Seduction*. He'd merely extended them with a phone call and a check by mail. It shouldn't be difficult to find a kid in town willing to deliver groceries and necessities. When the time grew nearer, Jordan would find a doctor to pay a visit to Dragon Rock, to see to the reclusive "heiress" residing there in secrecy. Money would insure that secrecy.

He felt remorse, certainly. Remorse over Darla's reluctance to go, regret that she'd become pregnant in the first place. Wonder that he'd fathered two children simultaneously. Jordan felt the slightest smile tug at his lips, then dashed the thought. This was no time for self-congratulations. With the baby due in March, plans needed to be made. Thanksgiving had already passed. With Darla's tiny, petite frame, she'd already begun to bump out. It wouldn't be good to wait any longer, possibly arousing suspicion. All he'd need would be for Russell to catch on, or worse, Harv. That nightmarish premiere had cemented his worries.

No, the path was clear. Especially since Darla had so vehemently vetoed abortion. He wasn't too fond of the idea himself, since he'd given it more thought. Still, the baby would have to be given away. A black-market adoption might be the best idea. Three couples already waited to hear back from him.

Darla, of course, planned for her mother to raise the child. He'd deal with that issue when the time came.

The pout hadn't left Darla's face for ten days. If anything, it grew worse now that she and Jordan had reached Dragon Rock Lighthouse.

"It's freezing in here! Where is the heater?" Darla complained, dropping the smaller of her two bags onto the living room rug. "Don't tell me there's no heater. Because I can't live in the cold, Jordie. If you know anything about me, it's that I like it hot. So, where's the damned heater!?"

"It's down below, my sweet. We just have to light it up. We'll get it nice and toasty in here for you. I'll show you how to operate it."

Damn. The heater should have been lit. Jordan put down Darla's other suitcase and proceeded on to the galley, where an assortment of food items had been stowed. He grunted in subdued approval and beckoned to Darla. "Here are the chocolates I promised you, love!"

"Jordan! The light switches don't work," Darla called from the bedroom.

Jordan soon joined her, the box of candy in hand. "Dearest one, the electricity is off. We just need to go downstairs and get the generators running. The stove takes fuel, too. Just like the heater. It will be fine. You'll see. Rather adventurous, don't you think?"

155

Darla lifted her eyebrows but did not comment.

They shared a simple dinner of canned spaghetti and salad. Jordan stayed the night, trying to ignore the nagging guilt growing within as Darla snuggled against him in the brass bed.

"Stay one more day, Jordie. Please? Pretty please?" she whined, tracing the outline of his lips with her finger. "It's going to be so long before you come back."

"I wish I could. It just isn't possible, angel. I have a big meeting Monday morning in Hollywood. I can't miss this one."

"When will you be back?"

"Two weeks. You have my word."

She made him repeat it when he got into the motorboat the next morning. The young man piloting the skiff looked the other way when she kissed Jordan goodbye.

"Don't forget me, Jordie. Don't forget about me."

"I could no more forget about you than I could forget my own mother, darling. You be careful. Very careful, you here? Take care on those stairs. Keep the windows closed. Don't go out on the gallery. Don't–"

"Yeah, yeah. We went over it all already. I'll be good. I promise."

"Okay, then. Till I return."

She watched until his boat became a tiny bump on the water, then turned and climbed the long, curving stairway that hugged the side of the caisson. She looked again before going inside the lighthouse but couldn't make out the boat as it neared the shore.

"Just like that? She left and didn't call me?" Russell could barely contain his astonished anger. Helen reached for her apron, tied it around her waist.

"I'm sorry, Mr. Harrington. It all happened quite fast. This part came up, she packed and left. I was upset myself. But it's only four months. She'll be back by Easter."

"Yeah, right. Jordan Kent behind this?"

"I believe Mr. Kent made the arrangements, yes. He's not actually in this movie, though. At least that's what Darla said. I'm just getting a brisket out of the oven. Would you like to stay to dinner, Mr. Harrington?"

Russell shook his head. *Damn that Jordan. Damn him!* "No, Mrs. Foster. I gotta look up an old friend. But thanks, just the same. I'm going to leave my number. If you hear from Darla, would you ask her to call me?"

"I will. Here, let me just cut you off a bit. Ted and I will never eat all this. I bought it before I knew Dar was going. She's got quite an appetite these days, that girl."

The delicious aroma coming from the oven nearly bowled him over. It had been weeks since he'd had a decent piece of meat. "Sure. That would be swell."

On his second night back, Jordan had a nightmare. He rowed in a small dinghy, in rough waters off the coast, heading for the lighthouse. He could see Darla quite plainly, standing at the top on the gallery, a baby in her arms. She waved wildly with a handkerchief in her free hand. But the boat wouldn't move forward, no matter how he opened the throttle. Frustrated, he turned to look back at her. To his horror, he watched helplessly as a seventy-foot wall of water rose up behind the lighthouse, curling satanically in preparation for slamming down on Dragon Rock Reef. Jordan's heart pounded frantically as he witnessed the impossible: the lighthouse began to tilt forward, the great wave pushing it over like a chess pawn. Darla's stricken expression tore at his soul, the baby thrust from her arms into the sea. Its mother soon followed, the toppled lighthouse close behind her.

Jordan awoke with a start. He'd certainly had nightmares before, but never so vivid, so chilling. He slipped from the bed, leaving Cecelia sleeping, and went to the living room bar. He poured himself a shot of bourbon and swallowed it in a single gulp.

In the bathroom, he grabbed a hand towel and dragged it across his forehead. He stared into the mirror, wondering briefly if he'd done the right thing by leaving Darla alone in the lighthouse. It could work. It *would* work. It had to. There was too much on the line for both of them.

As he dumped two aspirin into the palm of his hand, Jordan forced his thoughts away from Darla and onto his wife, sleeping in the next room. A flicker of anger crossed his mind. He shouldn't be in this position. After years of regretting his marriage, the strain of maintaining some semblance of normalcy, keeping Cecelia happy for his career's sake–she'd suddenly become a different woman. A woman who needed him, cared for him, carried his child. Things were finally right between them, and he'd gone and mucked it up by dallying with Darla Foster.

A cold wind rushed across the bedroom, seeking an exit at the high, cracked window above the bed. Darla pulled the bedspread up to her ear as she lay shivering in the dark. Despite the pre-dawn hour, her pillow still lay damp from the tears she'd shed during the night.

How could this be happening? She turned onto her other side and drew up her knees. Every spot on the bed she'd not lain upon felt like ice against her skin. She half expected the sheets to crack when she touched them. In the darkness, she reached over and felt for the matches on her nightstand. She didn't trust the foul-smelling generator or the crusty electrical wiring. Reassured the matches were still there, she quickly withdrew her hand and curled it against her chest beneath the covers.

Jordan is home in his snug bed with his stupid, hateful wife. He's not cold. Darla let her anger build, knowing it defended her against another onslaught of tears. *Correction: his body is not cold. Just his heart.* But was it really? Darla frowned, wishing she knew. She'd trusted him. Sure, she'd been stupid, too. She knew well how babies were made and how to prevent them. Somehow, it didn't seem important, or dangerous, during those exciting nights with Jordan in her arms. She couldn't get enough of him, nor him, her. Conceiving a baby, or taking care not to, had been the farthest thing from her mind since that long-ago night at the Brown Derby.

Worse, he'd had the nerve, that night in the diner when they'd talked, to suggest she'd been the responsible one. *She* should know when it was "safe" to have sex. She certainly had plenty of experience, he'd said.

Yeah. She had. Hadn't she lost her virginity at fifteen with Bobby Walker at the Pickwick Drive-In Theater? She didn't really enjoy it all that much, only the part about how excited it made Bobby to be with her. That was the best. Making boys, and then men, happy with sex. She went to great pains to keep her parents from knowing; it would break their hearts. And Darla had been careful–she'd studied the "rhythm method" and had even tried to explain it to Russell. Yet she needed men to like her, to love her, to use what she had. She learned from them, discovered what they liked and what she liked. But only one man had ever thrilled her. Only one had aroused her to the point of satisfaction. To madness.

Jordan Kent.

Twenty-One

Beverly Hills, California
August

He couldn't sleep. Downstairs, the grandfather clock chimed 2:00 a.m. With a heavy sigh, he threw back the covers and carefully swung his legs over the side of the bed, then reached for the cane he kept against his nightstand. He wasn't convinced he needed the damned thing to walk, but it offered comfort when standing from his bed. He put on the black satin robe draped across the footboard.

It took him awhile to navigate the wide, sweeping staircase, but he eventually found his way to the bar in the back of the mansion. Careful not to wake Esme, for she would no doubt scold him. He just needed a bit of brandy to smooth out the night.

He carried the drink to the back windows and peered out at the estate grounds behind the house. The pool lights were still on; he'd have to speak with Esme about making certain the timer functioned properly.

So, it was August again. And he'd been dreaming, dreaming of *her*. Sixty years had gone by, and now, near the end of his life, he'd been almost clear of her. Almost made it. But she'd returned. What did it mean? Would he die soon?

"I'm sorry," he murmured, still staring out the window. "I'm so sorry."

As if conjured by his words, an image appeared, reflected by the glass. She stood beside him. While he was now palsied and gray, she looked exactly the same as she had. He stared at the reflection, knowing if he turned to look, she couldn't be there.

"I was too late," he whispered. He wondered if she would speak, could speak. Her lips, poised in that classic, jutting pout, were painted the color of the red silk Chinese cheongsam she wore.

"I'm so sorry, my love," he repeated. The figure in the glass shook her head slowly, her dark eyes filled with sorrow.

Matt hurried through the outer office, tossing down a small bouquet of summer flowers onto Rhonda's desk as he passed her. She looked up in surprise.

"Good morning–why, thank you, Mr. Farralone!"

"I missed you, Ronnie," Matt called as he sailed past into his office. *She has no idea.* "I might need you to take a letter in a few minutes. Is there coffee made?"

"Yes, a fresh pot. I'll get–"

"No, I'll get it myself. Anybody dying to hear from me?" Matt came back from his office with an empty mug and headed the other direction.

"Actually, you-know-who has been calling. Said your cell must be off."

Matt smiled as he headed for the coffee station. It figured. "I'll call him this morning. Anything else?"

"Mr. Abberley wants to meet with you at ten to go over your files. Mrs. Cannon would like to see you this week. That's it for the important stuff."

"Okay. Great." Matt paused at her desk and took a swig of coffee. "Ahh. Good. I'm going to be doing a bit of research, then I'll call you in for that letter."

After his computer booted, Matt logged on to his newspaper archive subscription service. Within a few keystrokes, he had the obituary on the screen for one Harry J. Costantino. Died of heart failure on August 4, 1993. Survived by his wife, Bella, and son David, aged 13. Matt printed the item and went on to search for the mention of the car accident claiming the life of a Seattle woman the night before. What he found had him scratching his head.

Mrs. Louise Burke, aged 44, died in a hit and run accident at Woodson Avenue and Park Drive. Mrs. Burke, a resident of Phoenix, leaves behind a husband, Jebediah, and ten-year-old daughter Rebecca. The driver of the car fled the scene and is wanted for questioning by the police.

Matt frowned. What was this? Burke. Jebediah, Rebecca. Phoenix? Automatically, he reached for his briefcase and dragged out a stack of papers. The papers Denise had left him. Re-reading the small print, he quickly found the passage he sought.

> *The September Society has provided 1,300 Bingo game sets to a variety of senior centers throughout Arizona.*

He looked back at the screen. The name Burke. He dug through the stack again, this time withdrawing a folded fax transmittal and opening it, re-reading the information on the rude photojournalist who'd stopped calling.

"I don't believe this. I don't freakin' believe this!" Denise Murray was really Rebecca Burke? He stood, reached for his cup, took another gulp of the scalding liquid and slammed it back down. *Lake Washington and apple pie, my ass.*

He'd been had.

Rebecca took the day off upon her return from California. She swam, slept, tried to read. She left a message for Pat, explaining her inability to produce the lighthouse story and offering to put in extra time to make up for the trip. She avoided her father.

There wasn't a magazine in her stack interesting enough to take her mind off of Matt Farralone and what she'd done to him. She recalled with vivid emotion the feel of his arm around her shoulders, the light hug he'd given her. The warm, hungry look in his eyes. He'd wanted to kiss her, she was certain.

And she'd wanted him to.

But she wanted him to want to kiss Rebecca, not Denise. As long as she masqueraded as Denise, nothing could ever happen between them. Chances were slim to none she'd ever see Matt again.

The idea depressed her. What had gotten into her in the first place? Trying to be a hot-shot reporter, lying, deceiving, putting on the whole shebang just to get the story. Matt was a real guy, a nice guy. She'd tried to hoodwink him. It shamed her now, and she blushed just recalling the words she'd said.

Was there any way to fix it? Could she possibly make it up to him somehow? Oh, she could be Denise and call him, and maybe find some words to explain what she'd done. If he hadn't discovered her identity yet, that is. But finding those words would be difficult. She was basically a coward at heart.

"I blew it, and life goes on," she muttered. *It won't be the first or the last time he's been...deceived.* She wandered to her desk, sat down, sighed. Started to open her laptop, then changed her mind and pulled a box of stationary from her bottom drawer. A brief smile crossed her lips; no one used stationary in anymore. This box had been her mother's. She found a ballpoint pen and poised herself to write.

"Dear Matt," she began aloud. "I don't know how to explain what I've done; I...only...know...I...have...to try." Her pen lifted, then resumed.

> *The story about the grant was a ruse. My real name is Rebecca Burke, one and the same as the irritating photographer who harassed you about the lighthouse. When you refused to give me my story, I–*

Rebecca paused, looked aside to find the words.

> *I went undercover to try to get you to like me well enough to change your mind. I went too far, and I'm deeply sorry for what I did. I don't expect forgiveness. That would be too much to ask. But I cannot go on without at least apologizing for my despicable behavior. It really isn't me. I guess I just wanted to play in the big leagues. I now know it isn't worth it. I didn't expect you to be such a nice guy.*

Tears stung her eyes as she re-read her letter. There wasn't much more to add. How could she explain about the ghost? About Darla Foster? It would only offend him more, her thinking him fool enough to believe such a story.

"Best of luck to you and your Club. Please know that if I were, in fact, who I said I was, I would be first in line to help out your cause. Best regards, Rebecca Burke (Denise Murray)"

Sniffing, she folded the page and took out an envelope. Where to send it? She looked for the business cards she'd brought home from Northern California and found them still in the pocket of her discarded jeans in the hamper. His Beverly Hills office? Or the Crescent City address hand scrawled on the back of the card?

Impatient to be done with her unhappy task, she chose the Crescent City post office box and addressed the envelope.

He drove recklessly, and he knew it. The Cayenne handled well in the canyon, and while it was no '57 Corvette, he enjoyed the road and the air rushing through the open windows. Matt turned up the radio and focused on his task at hand.

Esme answered the door, greeted him with a smile. "He's out back, getting some sun," she advised, stepping aside. "Can I bring you some lemonade?"

"How about a double Scotch whiskey?" he asked, breezing past her. To her surprised expression, he replied, "Just kidding. Lemonade would be great. He's not in the sun, is he?"

"Oh, no, no, I made him sit in the shade. He's perturbed about something. I'm glad you came today."

"Well so am I, and me, too. Thanks. Oh, did you get your check okay this month? I changed services and some things got messed up."

"I did, Mr. Farralone. Thanks for asking."

Matt continued on to the backyard. Spying the old man sitting under the patio cover, he pulled up a chair.

"So, how's Crescent City?" The question came before Matt was even seated.

"Still there," Matt answered. "How you doin'?"

The man grunted. "Sorry to point out, I'm still here, too."

"Sorry? You want to die, do you?"

"Some days more than others."

"And today?"

"Yes."

"Are you in pain?"

"Only here," he muttered, patting his chest.

"Heart burn or heartache?"

"Both."

They were quiet then until Esme brought their drinks. Matt took a big gulp, put down his glass. "Is there something you wanted to tell me?"

"Something's going on. You didn't let that photographer into my lighthouse, did you?"

Matt nearly choked on his anger. "I most certainly did not. What do you mean, something's going on?"

"I can't explain. Just a feeling. I need to be certain everything's secure."

"With the lighthouse? I do my best. The place is bolted up. Nobody goes out there. It's too dangerous for a boat, and I've got eyes watching the catch deck. Twenty-four-hour surveillance by radar. No copters land, no ships touch rock. That better be good enough because outside of moving into the damned thing, it's the best I can do."

"You're in a mood."

Matt picked up the lemonade, swirled it like a cocktail. "Yeah, I'm good n' pissed off."

"Client or woman?"

"Chick. I got taken. I'll get over it." He took a drink. "Just as soon as I sue her ass."

"Sue? Did you sustain a monetary loss?"

"No, fraud. And because you'll probably find out anyway, I might as well tell you it was that photojournalist."

His companion stood, stared down at him. "What kind of fraud?"

"She lied about her identity, got me to talk to her under the pretext that she represented a non-prof interested in supporting the Boys and Girls Club. She lied through her teeth."

"Hrmph. Let it go."

"What? Are you kidding? I've got documents she forged, fraudulent signatures, the works. She won't get away with this."

"Broke your heart, did she?"

Matt now wished he had the double scotch. He rubbed his lips, watched the old man walk away from him toward the pool. Eventually, he got up and followed.

They walked the perimeter of the oblong, Olympic-sized pool. "I'm still going to go after her. What she did was wrong, and she should pay for her actions. You can't just go around lying about contributions. What if I had relied on her offer?"

"Shame on you, then. You should know better. You trust facts, and facts only. Once your heart gets involved, it all goes out the window. Common sense, reason, responsibility—everything."

Matt considered, opted to change the subject. "Is there something I should know about the lighthouse? You're awfully focused on security. What are you hiding?"

"Nobody's business but mine, you got that? That's what I pay you for, to keep people away from my business. Once I'm gone—have the God-forsaken thing blown up. Till then, consider it a shrine not to be breeched."

"Interesting choice of words." Matt stopped walking, shoved his hands into the pockets of his jeans. "But you're right, of course. It's your place, my duty to keep it locked up."

"Thank you. And look. Don't sue that woman."

"Now you're treading on my turf. This is something I feel strongly about."

"Go find her, have it out with her. Clear the air. There are forces at work here you don't understand. Suing her won't solve anything."

"Forces? What are you—"

Esme's call from the back door of the house sidelined Matt's question. "Your broker is on the phone. Do you want to take the call out here, Mr. Kent?"

Twenty-Two

Dragon Rock Lighthouse
December 1948

D arla shuffled down the cold, stone steps from the bedroom to the galley, her chenille robe wrapped snugly around her middle, ready to commence the routine she'd painstakingly developed over the past week. Turn on the stove; put on the coffee pot; wind up the twenty-five-year-old Victrola. Today she selected a record by Doris Day.

"Wonder if the newspaper is here yet?" she joked aloud, peeking out one of the small side windows. "Hmm. The milkman is late again." While waiting for the water to heat, she returned to the bedroom for her hairbrush. She needed to look her best when Jordie arrived, and she had no idea what time to expect him. Still, today was the day. She hummed while brushing her short locks into place.

Just yesterday, she'd taken care to fill the generators in the engine room. The smell of the diesel made her sick, and she didn't want that smell clinging to her when Jordan arrived. She swore she was building muscle by lifting the fuel canisters every few days, but without the generators, there would be no electricity. She had to be careful, too, not to let the batteries run too low when the generators were turned off. Otherwise, they wouldn't start the next day. Keeping the lighthouse running made her feel incredibly smart and self-sufficient.

Back in the kitchen, she poured herself a cup of Maxwell House and sat down at the table. A letter to her mother lay unfinished, and she picked up her pen.

"It's even more beautiful than I ever thought. The Eiffel Tower is so big," she said as she wrote, then crossed out the word "big" and replaced it with "giant." She took a sip of coffee, pondered.

"The French policemen are sassy. They flirt with me every day. I think they are saying nasty things, but since I don't know French and can't be sure, I just smile." She smiled now, envisioning her imaginary policemen, all of them vague and faceless except one. Jordan would look dandy in a uniform. "I have been shopping in the most adorable little stores. Perfume is very expensive, so I mostly just sample it. The coffee is just the end." From a stack of magazines on the table, she pulled out a glossy, colored issue and thumbed through the dog-eared pages, selecting a story about Paris she'd read three times.

"Yesterday I walked to the Louver..." she wrote, staring hard at the words, then looking back at the magazine before penning a correction. "Louvre. I saw lots of famous paintings and statues. I even saw the original of that Jesus one we have hanging in the hallway at home, next to the coat rack. It's even better in person."

She couldn't think of anything else to say. She looked around the small kitchen area, imagining what her mother would say if she knew where Darla truly sat. "Every day I have to check the generators to make sure they are full of that nasty diesel stuff. Otherwise I might not have lights," she said aloud, as if she intended to write the words in her letter. "The baby is kicking a lot now. He's an active little bastard. Oh! I made a funny because he *is* a little bastard!" She giggled a little, then broke into laughter. "Little bastard," she murmured at last, her laughter subsiding as she rose to pour the last of the coffee into her cup.

At the window, she observed the sea. Restless, as usual. Churning. The sky was cloudy, not a good sign. In the two weeks since her arrival, there had been two quick storms. Nothing terrible, but cold. She couldn't seem to get warm, no matter how she cranked up the heater. The cistern, luckily, had stored up quite a bit of rainwater.

Her wristwatch read 11:35 a.m. Maybe Jordan would be here soon. Brightening at the thought, Darla quickly dressed, tugged on her overcoat and went for the door. Outside, the wind blew far stronger than she'd anticipated, and momentarily caught her off balance as she stood on the porch and peered toward the coast. Was there a boat? Squinting, she combed her hair back with her fingers. The waves pummeled the small islet on which Dragon Rock stood, creating a fog-like spray that rose from the base where the rock met the sea.

Could his boat already be down there, struggling against the roiling surf as it tried to dock? Darla imagined Jordan trying to make fast the small launch, toiling to secure the rope. *Maybe he needs help. If he's down there.* The size of the caisson made it impossible to see the rocks below, so Darla began a nervous descent down the open, damp stairs in hopes of finding Jordan at the bottom.

Halfway down, a gust of icy wind slammed her from the side, and she paused to brace her footing. She tightened her coat, hunched her shoulders and forced herself to continue down the treacherous steps.

At last she reached the point where she could see the small battered dock. It was empty. Darla stood stock still, eyes fixed on the spot where she'd last seen Jordan Kent. Lifting her chin, she turned to look back at the expanse of ocean that remained between Dragon Rock and the shoreline. He'd be here soon. She sat down.

By 2:00 p.m., the air had grown colder, the sky darker. Darla shivered now, wishing she had a heavier coat. She longed to be in her bed, with the blankets piled high. She swore she'd never again complain about the cold inside. This bone-chilling wind made her bones ache.

Countless times she thought she saw a boat. For each time, disappointment followed.

By 2:50 p.m., she decided she could no longer stand the cold, and she stood, once again bracing herself against the wind as she climbed back up to the lighthouse.

Darla waited a while before taking off her coat. She sat down at the table, pushed aside the unfinished letter to her mother. The only sounds were of the wind, the surf, and the hollow, moaning echo circling inside the tower.

He wasn't coming. *He would be here by now.* Darla filled her lungs, exhaled. She got to her feet and crossed to the small cabinet beside the stove, where she withdrew a near-empty pint of Scotch whiskey. Half-heartedly, she glanced around for a glass, then opted to put the bottle to her lips for a quick gulp.

"Look! Isn't this just the sweetest?" Cecelia cooed, holding up a tiny, pink knitted sweater she'd pulled from a circular rack. Jordan looked up, clearly distracted.

"What? Oh, yeah. The sweetest. Isn't it a bit soon to be buying baby clothes?"

"Never. She's going to need a whole collection, of course. You're no fun. I need to go shopping with Daddy. He's already asked me to help him pick out Christmas gifts for mother."

"Good idea. Let's find a payphone and call him right now."

Cecelia put the sweater back on the rack and turned, dismay coloring her features. "What's the matter with you, anyway? You usually love Christmas. Maybe you need to have a talk with Santa."

"He's got nothing in that brown bag for me," Jordan muttered, shoving his hands into the pockets of his overcoat.

"Oh, you're just being a big ol' Scrooge. Let's go get some lunch. You'll feel better."

Jordan looked at his watch, noting the sound of a distant clock striking noon. He wondered what *she* was doing right now. Eating lunch? Reading a magazine? Sick in bed? Something could have happened to her out there, and he wouldn't even know. No one would know because he'd covered their tracks so well.

"Jordan? Did you even hear me? I said, let's get lunch. I'm starved."

"Sure."

He should have been at the lighthouse yesterday. Instead, he waltzed Cecelia down Beverly Boulevard as she *ooh*ed and *ahh*ed over the lighted, prancing reindeer strung across the street. Darla was alone, holed up in a cold, dangerous place. Eccentric Darla, whose silly antics drew laughs but could get her killed.

They walked to the restaurant on the corner of Wilshire Boulevard and slid into a booth. Cecelia immediately opened her menu. Jordan lit a cigarette.

"I'm going up to San Francisco," he said suddenly, and Cecelia lowered the menu. "Tomorrow. Early. I have to see to some property my mother owns. She doesn't know what to do with it."

"Tomorrow? But that's when the baby's furniture is coming. Do you have to go tomorrow?"

"Afraid so, darling. But I'll only be gone two days."

"I didn't know your mother had property."

"It's just some ramshackle building near Petaluma. It's kind of a legal mess, and I've got to help her deal with it."

Cecelia went back to her lunch selection. "Fine. I can get Daddy to come over to meet the delivery people."

Daddy. Of course. At least she'd bought the story about his mother. Truth be told, Alice Kent didn't own a pot to pee in, much less property in California or anywhere else, for that matter.

"I'll have the tuna salad sandwich," Cecelia announced. "On white bread."

Jordan blew out a puff of smoke and stubbed out the cigarette, picked up his menu.

"I'll have the red herring," he murmured.

Although he detested flying, Jordan dipped into his private savings account and splurged on two flights, then caught the bus from coastal Arcata. The sense of urgency grew with each passing hour, and he found himself nearly running to the dock at Dragon Rock Lookout.

"Nobody around that can take you out there right now," the dock master advised. "Best I could do is rent you my launch over there. Ever pilot one of those?"

With mild embarrassment, Jordan recalled the day he and Darla had slipped away, alone, in the skiff. "Yes, I have. That would be great. What's the forecast?"

"Colder n' a witch's tit in January," the old man told him, taking the cash Jordan handed out. "But no storms. At least not for the next twenty-four."

"Great." Jordan turned, then rethought his decision. "Say, you got a minute?"

The dock master paused, looked wary. "I can't take you out there, if that's what you're thinkin'."

"No, nothing like that. I wonder, can you be...discreet?"

"Discreet? Like keep my mouth shut? What you got going on, son?"

Jordan looked away, toward the lighthouse, then to the ground. Finally, he spoke. "Listen. I'm going to be staying out…there…for a couple of months. I don't want to be bothered. I have permission, I've rented the place out. I'm working on…on a book, you see. What I need is, is someone to delivery groceries and necessities once a week or every ten days or so. You know. A kid maybe, good at getting back and forth and all that. I can pay well. Do you…do you know of anyone I can trust to do this?"

The old man eyed him for several moments. "You won't be coming off the island at all?"

"I may be, from time to time, but I'm not a good sailor. I don't plan to leave there much while I finish my project. So, if I just leave a list of what I'll need, and the cash, you could have someone deliver it out there to me and just leave it at the door. I really don't want to be disturbed."

"Well…I do know a kid. He's real good with boats, pretty dependable, too. He cleans up the bait shop twice a week. And he could use the money. I'll talk to him about it."

"That would be swell. I really appreciate it. It's very important it be done regularly, you see–"

"This ain't really about you, is it?" The man looked him straight in the eye and didn't flinch.

Jordan sighed, looked around. "I guess you're too sharp for me. No. It's not. There's this woman, you see. She's an heiress. She's very wealthy, and well, she's from New York. She was near a breakdown, and her doctor recommended some isolation. I can't be here to care for her all the time, but I need to be assured she'll get the food and necessities without fail. She's a stubborn person, doesn't want to see anybody while she's there."

"That's the place for it. Doesn't get much more isolated than Dragon Rock."

"I'll be coming around about every two or three weeks. I'll be back here tomorrow to finalize the plan, okay? You can have the kid here? I need to meet him."

"Yep. I'll have him here. She related to the Vanderbilts? The Rockefellers?"

Jordan raised his eyebrows, smiled. "You didn't hear it from me. Thanks a lot, old chap."

He was drenched by the time he made the six-mile crossing, the waves tossing the small launch like a toy boat in a child's tub.

The spray from the unrelenting sea as it battered the rocks in the reef around him rained down as he struggled to keep the craft on course. As sundown neared, he secured the tie ropes with icy, stiffened fingers before grabbing his knapsack and clamoring up the multitude of steps to the front door of the lighthouse. Locked.

"Darla! Let me in! It's Jordan," he called, thumping his reddened fist on the door. "Darla? Are you there?" He grasped the doorframe to steady himself against the wind.

She thought she was dreaming. Sitting up in bed, she rubbed her sleepy eyes and listened. "Jordan? Jordan!" Darla leapt from the bed, ran for the door and thrust it open.

"Oh, Jordie, Jordie, Jordie!" She slammed herself against him, wrapping her arms so tightly around his middle he could barely get a breath.

"Darla, I'm soaked! Here, love, step away, and let's get me a towel."

"I don't care if you're spouting rivers! Oh, Jordie, I thought you were never coming back…" The sadness of her own words made her cry, and she began sobbing into his already drenched shirt.

"I'm so sorry, pumpkin. So sorry. I just had trouble getting away. It takes so damned long to get up here, too. Are you all right? Is everything…okay?"

Darla nodded, sniffed, unable to keep the pout from her lips. "I waited outside all day on Wednesday. The day you were supposed to come. Yesterday I waited in the tower, watching, but it got too cold. Today I didn't get out of bed."

"Oh, Darla. My love. I wouldn't abandon you. Surely you know that. You must try to understand, my visits will be…estimated dates…it's impossible to know exactly when I'll get here. Okay?"

"You're here now. Nothing else matters. Nothing!"

His feet were freezing, the knuckles on his hands chafed and he thought his ears would crack from the cold; still, the greatest pain was the one growing deep in his heart.

Twenty-Three

Hollywood, California
August

Matt sat down at the piano, stretched his fingers, closed his eyes. The ivories felt nice beneath his fingertips as he began playing an old torch song from the Ella Fitzgerald songbook. The notes flowed from the piano as if someone else played them. He hummed along. Wished he could sing.

The scotch in his belly warmed him. The scotch in his head blurred out some of the pain. As he hummed, he saw Denise–Rebecca–standing under the parking lot lights. Looking every bit as intent on a kiss as he'd felt. Yet she'd shied away, and he now knew why.

He wondered if she would figure out her faux pas. Too much information had passed between them. Did she not realize what an info-geek he was? It took him all of forty-five seconds to uncover her deceit. Maybe she'd wanted him to find out.

How would he tell the guys? He stopped playing and reached for the glass on the coaster. He didn't need to tell them just yet. At least not until he'd filed the complaint.

With a stab to his aching heart, he remembered the advice he'd received. Why shouldn't he sue her? She'd willfully, purposefully lied, made an offer she never intended to carry to fruition. *The nerve.* She really had him fooled. So smart, warm, beautiful…and false. How could he have been so wrong about her?

The song became a dirge. Kent's words came sneaking into his brain, something about seeking Rebecca out and clearing the air. Like that would ever happen. Because if he did see her again, he wouldn't just be clearing the air.

The more he thought about it, the angrier the song became until he literally pounded on the keys. He didn't even hear the phone ringing until the last tones of Mozart's Requiem died away.

Too drunk to drive, Matt suggested Chelsea come to him. Her eyes were red from crying, but Matt, too busy watching her take off her clothes, barely noticed.

"He was downright cruel. Said I didn't have a chance at the promotion because I wasn't smart enough. Can you believe it? I want you to help me take him to court, Mattie. You will help me, won't you? For old time's sake?"

Matt fumbled with his buttons, so Chelsea came to rescue him. He dropped his hands to his sides and let her undress him, his eyes fixed on her breasts.

"Are those new?" he slurred, eyebrows lifted. "I don't sheem to recall..."

"Oh, Mattie, just get in bed. How did you get so shitfaced? Just my luck."

"I'm not so very drunk, Chels." Matt fell back onto the bed, eyes opened wide. "On sheckond thought, maybe I am."

"Who did this to you? You're not a drinker. Some girl, I presume?"

"Two girls, ackshually. Ruh-bec-ca-Duh-nese. She's the one."

"You said two."

"Why'd you come here? You dumped me, r 'member?"

Chelsea slid between the sheets, pulled Matt's head to her shoulder. "It was a mutual thing, babe. Don't worry about it right now. We'll talk in the morning."

But Matt was already unconscious.

He dreamed of Denise. The two of them climbing the steps at Dragon Rock. She laughed, he chased her. The sun shone; the sea glittered a brilliant blue. As they neared the door, they both stopped. From inside, they could hear the sound of a baby crying. Denise turned to him. "See? I told you." Told him what?

He puzzled over the dream the next morning as Chelsea poured him a cup of coffee on the patio. The dream concerned him more than the fact that his ex-girlfriend had shown up in the middle of the night and slept in his bed.

"Tell me again what this is all about? You want me to defend you against your boss?"

"Not defend me. I want to sue him for sexual harassment."

"Did he offend you sexually? Did he use your gender against you?"

"He called me a dumb blonde."

"Hmm. Did he use those exact words?"

Chelsea leaned across the table to reach the sugar, brushing Matt's cheek with her bosom. "Not those same words, but it's what he meant."

Matt tossed back his few curls, then combed through them with his fingers. "What, exactly, did he say?"

"It was about that stupid test I took. He said I wasn't smart enough."

"Was there a score you had to reach on the test in order to get the promotion?"

"It's a stupid test. The score shouldn't matter."

"You didn't reach the score."

"I told you, it was a really stupid test. I almost passed. I only needed ten more points."

Matt shook his head, splashed some milk into his coffee. "I'm sorry, sugar plum, but you *are* a dumb blonde."

Chelsea's eyes opened wider, but she didn't respond. She seemed to be regrouping.

Matt smiled. "No offense, Chels. When a company has certain criteria for different job levels, it's their prerogative to use that criterion. If you didn't pass, you didn't pass. You don't have a case."

"I didn't mean to hurt you, Mattie." Chelsea caressed the lapels on the white terrycloth robe she wore, her gift to him the Christmas before.

Matt looked up. "What are you talking about now?"

"I'm sorry it didn't work out between us. And I'm sorry my dog chewed your piano leg. You're a softy, you know that? Don't let girls hurt you. Nobody who would hurt you is worth it. I know I wasn't."

Matt didn't know how to respond. It sounded like Chelsea had come to Jesus since they'd split. "Apology accepted. I'm fine. It won't happen again, I promise you."

"Wanna go get breakfast somewhere downtown?"

To Chelsea, *downtown* meant Beverly Hills. Matt took a moment, then grinned. "Why the hell not?"

Jordan Kent stared into his bathroom mirror. Sixty years. Where had they gone? Sometimes when he peered at his reflection, he saw the man he was then. Dare he use the term dashing?

The rich, dark brown hair had been replaced by a shock of startling white locks. His eyes, however, remained a crystalline blue, sharp and discerning. He wasn't as wrinkled as he thought he should be at 88. He stayed remarkably healthy; a curse, he sometimes believed.

He rarely went out. He felt both disappointment and relief when people didn't recognize him. The autograph hounds had long since disappeared from his porch, but the occasional fan did turn up at odd times. He usually obliged them by signing on a paper napkin, a theater program, an envelope.

Jordan emerged from his bedroom and called down the stairs. "Esme? Is the car ready?"

"Yes, Mr. Kent. It's at the door. Do you need any assistance?"

"Of course not. I'll be right down." He tried to make his descent seem effortless while sliding his hand carefully down the banister. Esme watched. "Get me a bottle of water, please," he told her, hoping she would let him get to the car under his own steam.

"It's already in the drink holder. Do you need a hat?"

"No. I mean, yes. My brown one. It's in the study."

There. That would get rid of her. He picked up his pace, grabbed a cane from the holder by the door and walked outside to the Cadillac parked and waiting. His driver opened the backseat door. "Good morning, Mr. Kent."

"Hello, Wilson. Thanks for making yourself available today."

"No problem, Mr. Kent. Will Miss De Lauder be accompanying you today?"

"Yes. Although I certainly don't need any assistance. I think she just wants to get out of the house. Women, you know."

179

"Yes, I do know, sir."

Esme soon joined them, handing Jordan the hat he never intended to wear. She climbed into the front seat beside the driver. "You know how to get there," she murmured, and Wilson nodded.

The cemetery wasn't busy. Wilson drove through the beautifully manicured grounds, leisurely taking the winding road to the top of the hill before pulling to the side. Ignoring Esme's fussing about the proper procedure, he smoothly opened the back door and offered a hand to Jordan, who allowed the man to help him out of the car.

"I won't be long," Jordan told them, using his cane to walk a short distance further up the hill to a stone mausoleum.

He sat on the bench and leaned against his cane, staring at the three names on the small structure. Harvey Louis Bregman. Shirley Marlene Bregman. Cecelia Louise Bregman Kent.

Jordan drew in a deep breath. Cec would have been 87 today. How long had she been gone, now? He frowned, sorted through jumbled memories for one that would enlighten him. It'd been at least ten years. Yes, she was 77. He'd tried to get her to stop smoking when he did, but she refused. Ridiculed him for his concern.

Harv had gone in 1998, too. Tough old bastard. Who would have believed he'd outlive his daughter at 94 years old?

But Harv had been young when Cecelia was born. Jordan shook his head. His own daughter, Eleanor, arrived just after his own twenty-ninth birthday.

Eleanor. He felt someone beside him and turned with a start.

"Hello, Daddy. I thought I might see you here."

"I was just thinking about you, sweetheart."

She gave him a hug, and together they sat considering the grave.

"Esme says you're doing well this week. Wanna see a movie later?"

"You mean, go out to the theater? Why don't you just rent something, and we'll watch it at my house. I spent a pretty big wad on that projection room."

"Okay, whatever you say. Sounds like fun."

Matt tossed his keys onto the kitchen counter. He was spent. His body wasn't used to the booze; it had been a long time since his college days. He eyed the empty scotch bottle on the piano with disdain, then tossed it into the recycle can.

What to do next? His mind buzzed with disjointed thoughts, a sense of disquiet. Chelsea's surprise visit delivered a shock to the system. Jordan Kent's admonishment was unwelcome. But Rebecca's Oscar-worthy performance had cut him to the quick. He couldn't get her out of his mind.

He felt better about Chelsea. He could see clearly, now, how wrong they were for each other. With the pressure of being a couple off, they'd enjoyed their lunch and parted ways friends. Funny how the introduction of another woman could change everything.

Rebecca *had* changed everything. A part of him wanted to call her, confront her, ask her why she'd done it. A part wanted to lock her in jail and throw away the key. Still another scenario included him taking her in his arms and kissing the daylights out of her. He'd sensed all along that there was more to her than met the eye. She'd gone to great lengths to get the story she wanted. Yet in the end, she'd backed off. In retrospect, she hadn't tried very hard.

Matt struggled. He opened his wallet and dug out a slip of paper containing her cell phone number. She hadn't actually given it to him, but he'd stored it when she'd called him from the hotel in Crescent City. He hadn't noticed the Arizona area code then.

What would he say?

Dropping onto his recliner, he blew out a breath. She didn't know for certain she'd been found out. What if... what if he continued the game? Perhaps there was room for two in this contest. With a smile forming on his lips, he dialed.

Rebecca stared up at the nut on the bottom of the oil pan. It was clearly tweaked, probably nailed by a big rock jutting out of the road. The socket would no longer seat. She'd have to bend it back in order to change the oil on the old Ford her dad had just taken in. She smiled. *Taken in.* Like a stray cat.

She rolled out from under the car and went to the workbench for a hammer.

"Bec! Your phone's ringin'," her dad called from the kitchen. Wiping her hands on a rag, Rebecca took the cell phone he handed her from the doorway.

"Hello?"

"Denise? It's Matt."

Rebecca felt the blood drain from her face. "Oh, hi. How–how are you?"

"Just great. Hey, listen, I wasn't kidding about stopping by. Turns out I have to be in Seattle tomorrow for a deposition. The witness can't travel, and I want to personally interview him for a case. I thought we could get together; you could show me around Lake Washington?"

Rebecca stood stunned, braced a hand against the wall. "Where are you now?"

"Home. Hollywood. Back to work for a while. Gotta pay the bills. So, you on? Give me your address."

"I, uh, I'm not going to be around, Matt. I'm sorry. Dad and I are leaving...tonight...for a brief trip."

Her father looked up, and Rebecca turned and walked back to the garage.

"Really? Too bad. When will you be back? I can postpone my trip a few days, if that'll work."

"Um, it might...can I...can I get back to you? I need to check my calendar."

"Sure. Hey, I don't suppose you've had a chance to get an answer back from your people yet."

"No, actually. We haven't met yet. I'll, uh, let you know when we do."

"Great."

A bit of quiet ensued before Matt continued. Rebecca closed her eyes as he spoke.

"I also wanted to tell you what a great time I had at dinner. I needed a night out."

Rebecca nodded, felt her eyes tearing up. "Me, too," she said honestly. "It was fun. Thanks again for...for everything."

"No problem. We'll have to do it again. Oh, by the way, you might be interested in this–about the lighthouse? Dragon Rock? I talked to my client the other day, and he's had a change of heart.

He's going to allow me to give that photojournalist a tour. How about that? Wild, huh?"

Rebecca's jaw dropped. She couldn't believe his words. "Really? Wow. That's–that's really surprising. Have you–have you called her?"

"Not yet. There's just one condition. Only she can come. No other photographers, reporters, nobody. He's eccentric that way. So, I'll invite her, and if she shows, I'm authorized to take a chopper out there and give her the red carpet." He chuckled. "Wild."

Speechless, Rebecca felt sick to her stomach. She hadn't thought things could get any worse.

"I guess if she wants the story, she'll agree to your terms."

"Yup. We'll see. So…I'll wait to hear back from you about getting together up there. How's the weather, by the way?"

"Oh, same as always, you know…"

"Of course. Well, talk to you soon."

"Sure. Bye, Matt."

Rebecca ended the call and sank to sit on the dolly.

What will I do now?

Twenty-Four

Dragon Rock
December 1948

Darla snagged the last of the cherry cordials out of the box and sat down at the kitchen table, her favorite spot. She picked up a list and read it aloud, something she found herself doing quite frequently of late.

"Shampoo. Oranges. Real butter. Lots of Water! New *LIFE* Magazines." She automatically looked down at the March issue on her table, displaying "Sir Laurence Olivier in *Hamlet*" on the cover. March! Surely Jordan could do better than that. From beneath it, she pulled out a copy of *Motion Picture Magazine*. This one was even older, dated February 1948! But she loved this issue, all about Joan Crawford.

"She takes four showers a day. Can you imagine?" In the lighthouse, Darla had trouble getting the water hot enough for even one bath. The shopping list forgotten, she thumbed through the worn magazine. "'She has a closet for suits alone and another for furs.' *Imagine*! 'She is well-liked on the set and is very friendly. She calls everyone 'honey.'"

With a deep sigh, Darla reached to pull out a second chair on which to prop her slippered feet. "Thank you, honey. Oh, could you get that for me, please, honey? Yes, I'm quite comfortable now, honey." She giggled, motioning to an imaginary visitor as she spoke. "I'll be fine if I can just get in one more shower, *honey...*" Now she laughed out loud. "Oh, Jordie, you should be here! I'm so funny!"

Her laughter slowly ebbed, and she picked up her pencil. "Ivory Soap. Peanut butter." She stuck the eraser end into her mouth and nearly bit through it before she remembered not to. "And jelly. Grape jelly."

She was to leave the list in a corked bottle just outside the door to the caisson at the top of the stairs tomorrow. She could expect the items a few days later, weather permitting, Jordan had told her.

Weather permitting. As if she could see into the tower, her eyes went to the ceiling as she listened to the wind swirling and hissing above. It was raining again, and the sea thrashed the rocks around Dragon Rock, ominous and angry. Yes, she thought. *Angry.* Darla no longer looked out the window when waves pummeled the islet. The height of the surf scared her, made her dizzy and sick with fear.

"Okay, Baby, where's our music?" she said softly, getting to her feet and going to the Victrola. She perused the few records in her collection, chose a Glenn Miller opus and began to crank. "I-don't-know-why-I-can't-have... an-e-lec-tric-ma-chine," she complained with each turn of the handle. But the big band music soothed and lifted her spirits a bit. The baby always moved when the music started, and Darla decided she would be a dancer.

"Like Ginger Rogers," she said with a smile, launching into a brief soft shoe in the middle of the small galley. "Hell. I'll never be a hoofer," she muttered, sitting back down. She placed her hands on her swelling abdomen, cooed. "But you will. You will dance for the president one day, Lana."

Again propping up her legs, Darla kept time to the music with her feet, swaying them back and forth with the beat. She hummed along, closing her eyes, imagining what it would be like to be in a ballroom listening to Glenn Miller in person. Maybe the Andrews Sisters would be there, too. And Jordan. Always Jordan.

She wished she had something to drink. A bit of champagne, perhaps? Her eyes flew open and she reached for her list. *C-H-A-M-P-A-G-N-E* she printed neatly across the bottom. Why not? Jordan could afford it. With Cecelia's money, he could buy anything.

She was pondering the luxuries within Jordan's reach when the lights dimmed and then went out.

"Oh no. Oh no. Oh no." Like a crazy nightmare, the music continued to play in the dark. Darla stood up, walked in the direction of the counter and felt around for the flashlight she hoped was still there. She wasn't very good about putting things back where they belonged. Panicked, her fingers flew over the battered metal breadbox, a small stack of dirty dishes and a hand towel.

"Oh no. Dammit!" A knife. The flour canister, followed by one for sugar and the smallest, for coffee. "It's gotta be here. Come on, please..." The song ended, but the record continued to spin and the Victrola to broadcast scratchy noise as its motor wound down. "Oh Mary, mother of Jesus, I'm sorry, I'm sorry..." At last her hand closed over a box of matches. "Hallelujah! Oh, Lord, Jesus, thank you so much!"

She struck a match, held it up and looked around. On the wall, hanging from a hook, she found the black metal flashlight. Darla uttered a nervous giggle. "Well imagine that." She blew out the match, switched on the weak beam. Only now could she begin to question why her power had ceased.

"Did I?" she asked aloud. "Did I forget?"

The Victrola ended its noisy accompaniment to her ordeal. "Okay. Okay. Gotta get my shoes. Can't go down there without shoes."

She quickly climbed the stairs to her bedroom and put on her sneakers, then began her unhappy trek to the engine room. She wasn't quite sure when she'd last filled the generator.

"The days...the days all run together," she explained to no one. "It's not my fault. Everything is the same. I get up, it's cold, I eat, I drink coffee..." She picked up the pace, fearing her flashlight would give out before she got to the diesel holding tank.

She put the flashlight on the floor, felt her way to the tank and filled the vessel. Edged her way to the generator. She spilled a little as she poured. "Oh, Hell's bells! I hate this part!" Turning her head away from the fumes, she gagged. "Oh, Lord. Mama's sick. Oh, Lana, hold your baby nose, sweetie."

She thought she would retch but managed to grab her flashlight and hit the reset switch before running to the stairs. With a groan and a whirr, the big motors began to turn. She prayed the lights in the living quarters above had come on. As she ascended, she could see the glow of the galley ceiling fixture.

Darla went straight to her bedroom and fell onto her bed, not even taking time to remove her shoes.

"Please God," she whispered. "Please make this go faster. I don't like it here. I know what I did was wrong, and I'm sorry. I'm going to make it up to you, I promise. I'll be the best mama ever. Just get me out of here."

Darla rolled to her side, curled her knees to her chest and continued praying. The lighthouse shuddered as a ninety-foot wave struck the west side of the tower.

Russell lit another cigarette. Lakeside Drive was dark where he'd parked his car, and he watched the restaurant doors as patrons came and went from the popular Burbank eatery. What took them so long? The way he felt right now, he could devour a five-course meal in ten minutes. But Jordan and Cecelia had been inside The Smoke House for nearly an hour.

Across the street, the hateful Warner Brothers Studios sprawled. He couldn't bear to look. Stupid people.

His wait soon ended. A couple walked toward him, laughing as they made their way down the street. Russell got out of the car, tossed his cigarette to the ground. He walked forward, then leaned against Jordan's car.

Jordan stopped abruptly, his smile gone. "Why, Russell. Imagine meeting you here!"

"Yeah. Whaddya think about that. You two have a nice dinner, didja?"

"Delightful," Cecelia gushed, tightening her grip on Jordan's arm. "How are you, Russell, dear?"

"Peachy-keen, Cec. Couldn't be better. I got a few words to say to your old man, doll. Maybe you better just get in the car."

Uncertain, Cecelia hardened her gaze and looked to Jordan, who patted her hand. "Good idea. Here, let me get the door for you, darling." He retrieved the car keys from his pocket and bent to unlock the door. Cecelia cast an uneasy look at Russell, then got into the passenger seat. Jordan closed the door.

"So, what brings you to the neighborhood, Russ? Haven't seen you around lately." Jordan slipped his cigarette box from his pocket and withdrew a smoke, lit it. He held out the box to Russell.

"No thanks. Got my own. So, you wanna tell me what happened to Darla?"

"What do you mean, what happened to her? She's off on location or so I heard."

"So, you heard. Like you don't really know. C'mon, Jordan. You know good 'n well where she is. She don't make no moves widout tellin' you. You're like God to her. Although I can't think why."

Jordan took a long drag off the cigarette, walked a few steps away. Russell followed.

"You know, and you ain't tellin'."

"Why you think I have anything to do with Darla Foster is beyond me. Don't you see how things are with me and Cec now? We're having a baby, for Chrissakes. You think I would jeopardize our happiness for someone like...like Darla?"

"Hey, are you sayin' she's cheap or something? Because she's not. She's just had it rough, that's all. She's smart. A little too full of herself sometimes, but she's got it on the ball."

"Never said anything of the kind. I'm just saying I resent your insinuation that we have more than a professional relationship. Darla is a fine actress. I'm sure she'll go far. Word is, she's in Europe shooting for a French film company."

"So how comes she don't call or write? Huh? Tell me that!"

Jordan smiled. "I do believe you're in love, Mr. Harrington. I suspected it before but–"

His words were clipped short by Russell's fist to his jaw. Caught unaware, Jordan went down to the sidewalk. Behind them, Cecelia screamed and jumped out of the car.

"I'm sick of you changin' the subject! I'm sick of you lying all the time. You and Darla had a thing going up there, I know it, you know it, and everyone else knows it. She was ga-ga over you, then she suddenly disappears when your wife gets prego. Stinks like a carton of rotten eggs to me!"

Jordan sat up, rubbed his jaw. His eyes were on Cecelia's face, not Russell's, as he slowly gained his feet and stood.

"I don't know what you're talking about. I wouldn't make such unfounded accusations if I were you. You just might find yourself in court facing a slander suit."

"Slander, my ass. It's all true, and you know it."

Cecelia, who'd rushed to Jordan's side, now dropped her arms and narrowed her eyes. "Jordan. I think we'd better be going."

"I'd keep my eyes open if I were you, doll. Don't turn your back on this one. He's a slippery eel, he is. Lady's man. Always will be. I known him from way back, see. I *know*." Russell's eyes widened with anger and determination. "You'll see it one day. Mark my words."

Jordan's face was grim. "Get back in the car, Cecelia."

"Jordan, I–"

"*Get in the car.*"

Cecelia fairly hissed but did as she was told. Jordan turned back to Russell. "You will regret what just happened here. If you weren't such a crazy bastard...if I hadn't promised to look out for you–I'd lay you out right here!"

"Yeah, you look out for me real good. Steal my parts, steal my girl, make a fool outta me..."

"I got news for you, Russ. You do all that real well on your own. Go home and sleep it off. And stay away from me. Stay away from *us*. If anything happens to Cecelia's baby because of the stress you just laid on her, I'll beat you senseless. Now get the hell out of here."

Heart pounding, Jordan got behind the wheel and started the car. Beside him, Cecelia sat in stony silence.

Twenty-Five

Phoenix, Arizona
August

Rebecca tried not to pace but feared she'd wear her carpet thin. When the phone did ring, she uttered a little cry, put her hand on the phone, hesitant to answer.

It was Pat. "I don't usually bother with this, but I want you to know the car piece is excellent. Good job. Now, we need to talk about the next assignment."

"Thanks, Pat. I appreciate the news. Cars are my forte, second to cameras. I'd–"

"Whatever. Look. Our December issue is about alternative holiday locales. You know, folks are sick of the same old Christmas stuff. Traditions are getting tossed. I need five different places, events, settings, you get the picture. Like that place in Colorado where people can pretend they're in a damned Norman Rockwell painting. Or Hanukkah in Cabo. Whatever. I got Janie looking at some possibles. You look, too. Get started."

"Okay. Got it. But listen, about the lighthouse–"

"It's canned. History. Nothing lost. Forget it."

"But it might be–"

"Got another call."

Pat hung up, and Rebecca stared at the phone in her hand. *Damn him.* He was always abrupt and even rude. On the surface. She allowed herself a few moments to be frustrated with him, then put the phone down.

Holiday locales. *Wanna spend Christmas in a haunted lighthouse, Pat?*

This time she did not jump when the phone rang. Taking a deep breath, she put the phone back to her ear.

"Rebecca Burke?" Matt's voice. Her heart began to race. Again.

"Yes?"

"This is Matthew Farralone. We spoke a couple of weeks ago about the lighthouse. Dragon Rock."

"Oh, yes." Rebecca cleared her throat. "What–what can I do for you?" *Keep the quiver from your voice at all costs.* She hurried to the refrigerator, took out a carton of milk.

"I was wondering if you're still interested in a tour."

She poured the milk, took a sip. Swallowed. "Um. A tour?"

"You wanted to take photos inside. I'm asking if you'd still like to."

"Well, uh, yes, I would. However, I'm on another assignment now, since I couldn't gain access to Dragon Rock. We shelved that story for now." What if he recognized her voice?

"I see. I'm not sure how long the invitation will be good. The owner is rather eccentric. For some reason, he's granting you permission right now. I'm afraid it won't last forever."

Rebecca squeezed her eyes tightly shut, reopened them. What a nightmare. She really, really wanted to go back inside Dragon Rock. *Needed to.* She'd been thinking about it ever since Matt had called "Denise's" cell phone the day before. What did she have to lose? He'd find out who she was anyway, as soon as she read the letter that undoubtedly waited for him in Crescent City.

"I guess I could shoot the pictures and hold them until we can schedule the story..." she pretended to wonder aloud. "When would this...tour...be?"

"I'm going to be out of town for a couple of days, so next week would work. How about Monday? There's an airport in Crescent City, you can catch a commuter from San Francisco or Sacramento. Oh, and one more thing. You have to do this alone. Not to sound freaky or anything, but that's the stipulation. So, bring whatever equipment you need."

"Well, okay."

"I'll meet your plane. You can e-mail me your flight info."

"Sounds good. How will I know you?"

"Don't worry. I'll know you."

Rebecca pressed a hand against her forehead. *Yes, you will.*

"Ha!' Matt re-cradled his phone, leaned back in his executive office chair. He could almost see the alarm on Rebecca-Denise's face. So, she was ready for the showdown. He figured "Denise" wouldn't be calling him back about the Seattle trip. Why should she bother when the charade would all end on Monday anyway?

She must really want to get inside the lighthouse. *Tenacious chick.* She hadn't even balked about coming by herself. He thought she'd fight on that one. Unless she'd figured out the joke...

He pondered the possibility. The phone on his desk rang, interrupting his analysis. The Arizona area code displayed.

"Matt Farralone."

"Hi Matt. It's Denise. I'm calling because I'm not going to be able to meet you in Seattle. It's just not going to work out with my schedule. But hey, we can keep in touch, all right?"

Matt smiled, but the smile wasn't accompanied by any sort of joy. He heard sadness in her voice, a sadness he knew he'd caused.

"Of course. I'd like that. Is everything okay? Dad doing well?"

"Oh, sure, yeah. Everything's fine. I'm just a little behind, have a lot to catch up on. Feel like I might be coming down with a summer cold. You know how that is."

"I do. Well, we'll get together another time. You take care of yourself, you hear?" Matt flinched at the sincerity of his own words. "Don't get sick."

"Right. Bye."

No laugh of triumph punctuated the end of this call. Matt hung up the phone slowly, wondering if he'd done something incredibly stupid.

Worse, he hadn't expected her to call his bluff. He had no such permission to show her the lighthouse. In fact, Jordan had quite deliberately prohibited the tour. He'd have to play this one by ear.

Monday blazed hot in Phoenix as August came to a blistering close. Rebecca was glad to at least be getting away from the blast furnace the garage had become. As the commuter jet neared the Crescent City airfield, she fidgeted some. Oh, she'd come to grips with the probable repercussions of her actions. Was expecting to face anger, ridicule and, most likely, rescission of the tour offer. But for reasons she didn't understand, she knew she had to try.

As she walked across the tarmac between the jet and the terminal, she wondered if he watched her from inside. Wondered if he'd turn away and abandon her. Try as she might to control the flutter in her chest, she felt her pulse pick up and her face burn.

He leaned against the far wall. As their eyes met across the terminal, no surprise registered on his face. No outrage, shock or loathsome expression changed his placid features. Halting at first, she took a breath and headed toward him. He took her heavy carry-on.

"This all you have?" he asked.

"Two cameras, a toothbrush and an extra pair of jeans."

He turned toward the exit signs. "How was your flight?"

"I don't remember."

"Okay. I'm over here."

She followed him to the Jeep, got in without a word.

They drove in silence. Rebecca opened her mouth to speak, but each time, she closed it again, reluctant to say anything. He must have read the letter. Still, she expected some sort of reaction, fury, sarcasm...anything but this cool, business-like demeanor.

They hadn't gone far when Matt parked the car and got out.

"Where are we?"

"The copter's right over there. You are ready, aren't you? This is the best time of day, best light. We had some fog this morning. Later, the tide will be up, and you'll get some awesome shots."

Words jammed in her throat. Rebecca scrambled out of the car and followed as Matt led her to the waiting helicopter.

"You're lucky. It's a beautiful day."

Rebecca nodded. "I can carry that," she called, as Matt hustled her bag ahead of her. He ignored her comment and handed it to the pilot, who carefully stowed it. Matt climbed inside, then turned to assist Rebecca.

"Strap in, Miss Burke. You're in for the ride of your life."

Wide-eyed, Rebecca buckled the belts around her for the second time. She'd long given up on the possibility that she would actually get back into Dragon Rock Lighthouse.

It took only minutes to land on the catch deck. Matt watched Rebecca as she ogled the tower, then unpacked her bag and assembled her biggest camera. She took pictures of the lighthouse, the helicopter, the coast. Changed lenses, repeated the process. Matt stood in the shadows, his arms crossed. She worked as a professional, no doubt about that.

He'd unnerved her, to be sure. Had unnerved himself, too. His carefully thought out plan to tell her off at the airport and walk out had evaporated around 3:00 a.m., when another scenario had come to him.

Unable to sleep, he'd gotten up for water and tripped over the tape. How it got on the floor of his mobile home remained a mystery, when it normally resided on a shelf at home in Hollywood. A VHS copy of *Cape Seduction*. Without conscious thought, he put it into the VCR and turned on the television. Sat watching until 5:30 this morning.

Jordan appeared so young; the vivacious Darla Foster, so attractive in an odd-ball sort of way. Engrossed, Matt waited for the grisly scene near the end of the film, where the jealous husband strangles her. But this time as he watched the familiar scene unfold, the actress turned and looked into the camera. Perplexed, he didn't remember it that way, although he'd seen the film a half dozen times. He rewound, watched again as she looked straight into his eyes with terror and sorrow. Almost as if asking him, Matthew Farralone, for help. A chill passed over him, bringing with it a moment of instant clarity and absolute resolve. He knew he would ignore Kent's directive and escort Rebecca into the lighthouse.

Even now, standing on the top of the caisson, watching Rebecca laboring with great love, he knew he'd had to bring her here.

"Ready to go inside?" he called, and she nodded. Despite the bad blood between them, she was enraptured, her color high with the wind whipping her hair around her face. He felt something, too, an ominous sense of foreboding he wanted to ignore.

They covered their noses when entering the enormous, dark engine room. The smells of decades past, of diesel fuel, mold, rot and refuse assaulted them until they reached the main level and the laundry room. Rebecca knelt over her bag and withdrew a small video camera. "I'm going to do the motion stuff first, if that's all right," she told Matt.

"I won't get in your way. Just don't do any digging around, and don't get hurt. Shoot it as it is, okay?"

"Sure. Moving pictures aren't my usual gig, so I'm not the best," she uttered, adjusting the camera for low light.

They moved to the galley. Rebecca scanned the room, turning in a slow circle as she endeavored to take in all aspects of the small kitchen. She paused, lowered the camera. "Check this out," she said, motioning to the table, where a magazine lay open as if someone had just been reading.

Matt looked over her shoulder. "Gala Event Marred by Star's Disappearance." He reached around Rebecca and turned to the cover of the Hollywood gossip periodical. "February 1949. Hmm."

"Darla Foster," Rebecca murmured. "I heard she went missing. She never turned up, did she?"

"I wouldn't know," Matt answered, shaking off a shudder at the thought of Darla's face in the film he'd just watched. "Likely the last keepers left these here."

"No. They abandoned this lighthouse in 1947. The movie was filmed in 1948. This magazine came in here after that. So, someone lived here, after the movie people left."

Matt shrugged, but his mind buzzed with questions. Rebecca was right.

She started to open a cabinet door.

"Ah ah ah!" Matt shook his head. Rebecca frowned.

"Let's–let's move on. We have a finite amount of time, here," Matt said.

Rebecca gathered her gear and preceded him up the cold stone steps to the first bedroom. She went through the motions of filming the room, taking special care to document a small piece in one corner. Matt followed to investigate.

"Looks like a cradle," he muttered, squatting down. "That's weird."

"Um-hmm. Weird." Rebecca squatted on the ruined peg and groove floor and felt inside the cradle, sweeping each corner with her fingers. "Nothing there."

"Did you expect to find something?"

"Not really. It's just dark. Wanted to be sure."

"I asked you not to–"

"Yeah, I know. I'm sorry, okay?"

"A bit testy, Miss Murray?"

Rebecca froze for a moment, then continued shooting. Matt chastised himself for the comment; he'd planned to withhold all such references to Denise until later. But he was edgy and anxious. Drawn back to the cradle, he contemplated. He'd not seen it before but had never really looked at the furniture in this room. Rebecca returned.

"Would you mind if I take a closer look at the cradle? I want to see if there's a manufacturer's name anywhere."

He started to protest but acquiesced. Rebecca pulled the tiny bed away from the wall and into a narrow beam of light coming from one of the small windows. There was, indeed, a tiny bronze sticker on the end. "The Broadway, Fine Home Furnishings Department, Beverly Hills, California. That's interesting," Rebecca said, leaning close to snap a picture of the label.

"Hmm."

Rebecca stood. "Look. I know this'll sound completely off the wall, Matt. You already think I'm a loser. So, okay. But there's something strange here. This room. The air is thick in here."

"It's thick in this whole place."

"I know. But here…something bad happened. I'm no medium. I don't even believe in ghosts. All that spiritual mumbo-jumbo is a waste of time. But I can't deny that something feels different in here."

Matt knew exactly what she meant, although he was loathe to admit it to her. They stared at one another for a time, until Matt went to the window and looked out. "Let's keep moving."

With a heavy sigh, Rebecca repacked, and they continued their climb into the tower.

At the top, nothing had changed. Rebecca took video footage, as she'd already snapped several good stills during her previous, clandestine, visit.

She didn't understand Matt. Why didn't he yell at her? He'd only made the one sarcastic comment, acknowledging her alter-ego, Denise. But nothing more. Why? It made her nervous. She needed to clear the air before leaving town this evening.

Finished with her cameras, Rebecca stashed her pack in the lantern room and returned to the gallery. She grasped the iron railing, running her hands around the length of it, feeling energy from past visitors that had also clung to the icy metal cage. What had it been like for the keepers, the wickies of 1900? 1925? What was it like in 1948, for Darla Foster, Jordan Kent and Stephen Sisco? They stood here, each in turn, during different parts of the film. They climbed those curving steps, peered out the tiny, wood-framed windows. They existed, occupied this space for a moment in time. Left a piece of themselves here.

I'm becoming a loon myself, Rebecca thought, but she wasn't ready to leave. "What happened to the lens?"

"Removed to a museum. Thought you'd know that," Matt said.

"Guess I missed that fact. The owner should at least fix this broken glass," she commented, gingerly touching the many broken panes surrounding the lantern room.

"Vandals would just shoot them out again. High powered rifle practice. In fact, we'd make pretty good targets ourselves."

Rebecca shuddered at the thought. "Okay. I'm done."

They traveled back down the steps, but Rebecca lingered in the galley. Pulling a piece of scratch paper from her pocket, she crumbled it up and tossed it into a trash bin in the corner. As they started to leave the room, she stopped.

"Oh! I just threw away the wrong thing. Hang on," she lied, going back to the half-full can and bending down. *Quick!* She had to commit to memory the items she could see. Empty can of soup; something black and petrified that might have once been a banana peel; a crumbled-up ball of holiday wrap; an empty bottle of champagne...*good*...and another can... She dipped her hand into the trash and quickly flipped it around.

An unopened can of evaporated milk. Beneath that, a bottle of Karo syrup.

"You coming?" Matt called from the stairs.

"Yup. I'm here. I'm coming."

Aside from the copter's spinning blades, the only sound as they returned was that of the pilot conversing with the heliport.

Matt and Rebecca both sat looking out opposite windows. Once on the ground, Matt again carried Rebecca's bag.

"I need to hit the restroom," Rebecca told him. "Watch that, will you?"

Matt nodded, waited in the airport lobby.

Rebecca washed her hands and face, ran fingers through her hair. She took a few extra moments to compose herself. She had second thoughts about talking to Matt. It was probably best to just go home.

"What time is your return flight?" he asked when they were seated in the Jeep.

"There's a bus to San Francisco at 8:00 p.m. I fly out of SFO in the morning."

Matt grimaced. "An all-night bus ride? Are you kidding?"

"Why should you care?" she asked simply, not looking at him.

"Actually, I don't. It just sounds awful, even for you."

"What's that supposed to mean? *Even for me?*"

"You compromise your values, why not compromise your comfort? Anything for the story, right?"

Rebecca felt her face redden. "You know nothing about my values."

"I know enough."

"You can drop me here." She reached for her bag.

"Rebecca, wait."

"No. Stop the car, or I'll get out while it's moving. Could be messy."

Matt pulled over at the next corner. "Have it your way."

"I will. Thanks for the tour. Tell your mysterious, eccentric *client* thank you for me."

Since the night of her mother's death, Rebecca had rarely shed more than a few tears. But tonight, curled onto her balcony chair at her townhouse, the wet stuff flowed from her eyes.

She ached inside. There were so many reasons she could no longer keep track. Matt's refusal to address her dishonesty had shocked her. Wounded by his coldness, Rebecca blamed the fact that she'd treated him so badly. But his retribution had hurt the worst. For when she'd arrived home, wrinkled as an unmade bed, exhausted beyond belief, nauseous from the bumpy flight, she'd discovered his payback: he'd taken the film and memory cards from her cameras.

ANNE CARTER

Twenty-Six

Dragon Rock Lighthouse
Christmas 1948

"You're doing fine, Mrs. Weatherton. The baby's heartbeat is strong, regular. Big for his age, though. You say you're six months along?" The doctor folded his stethoscope and dropped it into his bag. "I would have said seven."

"Yes, doctor. I'm quite sure. *Six*." Darla smiled up at the physician, batted her eyelashes.

"Well then. Your husband says you'll be vacationing here for a few more weeks. Come see me when you get to the mainland. Or, summon me again if you have any serious concerns."

"I will. Thank you, Dr. Stone."

"Merry Christmas."

"Same to you."

Darla hummed to herself as the doctor left the bedroom. She liked that word, *husband*, especially when applied to Jordan, who waited outside the door. She looked from the bed to the dark, mahogany cradle draped with a big, red satin bow and giggled. "Oh, Lana. Look what Daddy's brought for you!" Inside the baby bed was a pink and white blanket and a small pillow. "And just look what he brought for Mama!" From the nightstand she lifted a bottle of champagne. "Yuhhhhmmy!"

Jordan rushed into the room. "Did he tell you anything?" he asked, his face wrinkled in concern.

"Just that we are having the bestest baby ever, that's all!"

Jordan let out a breath. "That's wonderful, dear. I was alarmed at...how much you'd...grown since last time I visited. So, I thought this would be a good time to get you seen. I hope you don't mind the little white lie I told the doctor. It wouldn't be good for him to know who we really are."

"And I'll bet you paid him plenty to take that nasty boat ride out here the day before Christmas Eve."

"A fair amount, sugarplum. Let's just say he'll have a very good holiday this year." He turned to leave the bedroom.

"Jordan! Where are you going?" Darla sat up straight, her voice sharp with angst.

"Nowhere, darling. Just down to the kitchen for glasses. You do want to toast, don't you?"

She fell back against the pillows, sighed in comfort. "Yes. Yes, that sounds delightable."

He returned in seconds with small juice glasses. "Sorry I couldn't get flutes. These will do."

"These will do fineola. Oh, I can't wait to taste it! Oh! Oh! Wait! Go down and put on the music. Put on the Bing Crosby song. We can't celebrate without ol' Bing!"

Jordan smiled and shook his head, then went to do Darla's bidding. She giggled as Crosby's croon filled the lighthouse with romance.

"Okay, now can we toast?" Jordan said, sitting across from her on the bed.

"Yep. You bet. Here's to us, and little Lana, and all the stars in the heavens!"

"Here, here."

They drank most of the bottle, and Darla fell asleep curled against him. Only mildly disappointed, he'd expected they would have sex–had looked forward to it, as Cecelia now slept alone. The moment she'd started to show, Cec's body became off-limits. No look, no touch, no sex. The confrontation with Harrington hadn't helped, either.

Darla's pregnancy merely enhanced her sexuality. Yet she seemed fragile, somehow. The way she'd snapped to attention when he left the room worried him.

Jordan pulled the blankets up over her shoulder and moved in behind her, spoon style, wrapping an arm around her abdomen protectively. Maybe she just looked big because she was such a petite woman. Not to mention the fact that she wore tight sweaters and knit shirts, exaggerating the swell, unlike Cecelia's tent-like, A-line dusters and frocks. He drifted off but became alert when something moved beneath his hand. A smile grew across his lips as he realized he'd just been kicked by his child.

She tried to hide the headache the next morning. Jordan made her pancakes and coffee, and she eagerly poured maple syrup over the flapjacks after downing two aspirin.

"You're a love, Jordie. These are the best."

"Gotta keep the little mother strong, right?" he joked, sitting down at the table with her. "You know I have to go in a bit. A boat's coming for me around ten."

Her face fell, but she lifted her chin. "I know. Let's not talk about it yet."

She dug back into the pancakes with a little less enthusiasm, then brightened. "When are the Oscars this year?"

"We weren't nominated, Darla."

"I know that. I saw the list in the mag. But when is it? In March, right?"

"The twenty-fourth. I hear George Montgomery is scheduled to host."

Darla looked pensive. "If the baby is here by then, I can still go with you, like we planned! Cecelia won't want to go out in public. She'll be as big as a whale by then. Isn't that grand?"

Jordan nodded slowly. "It could happen, I suppose. We'll just have to see." He finished his pancake, took a sip of coffee. "Hollywood's saying Larry will win for *Hamlet*."

"I never got to see it," Darla complained. "Or hardly anything for that matter."

"Movies every weekend when you get home."

Again, she perked up. "I like the sound of that." She reached across the table and patted his hand. "You should have got the nomination for best hero."

"Maybe next time."

He helped her clean up the dishes, then gathered up his small bag. He led her to the bedroom, where they sat on the bed.

"I brought you a little gift, Darla."

"The champagne. I thought–"

"No. This is something better than champagne, darling." He pulled a small box from his pocket and dropped it into her waiting hands.

"What is it? Oh, I do love surprises!"

She opened the hinged box slowly, dragging on the suspense. Finally, she peered inside.

"Oh, Jordie...this is...this...I don't know what to say." She pulled the necklace free of its velvet container and dangled it from her fingers. A stray beam filtered through the red stones, lighting them from within.

"Rubies, dear heart. Red is your color, and these will look stunning on your beautiful neck. Here." He painstakingly latched the necklace behind her and let the tear-shaped rubies fall against her chest.

"My Lord. I'm–I'm speechless. It takes a lot for me to be speechless."

"Merry Christmas, Darla."

She was crying when he left.

"I'm sorry, I don't want you to remember me crying," she said between sobs. "It's just...it's just...I don't know when..."

"I'll be here, love. I'll be back soon. Remember that I can't give you an exact date. In a couple of weeks or so. You know I'll come. In the meantime, you can send me messages with the delivery person. He can call me secretly if you fall ill or need assistance. Understand?"

"Y-yes. Have you been mailing my letters to mother? Like they're from France?"

"Yes, indeed. I have an acquaintance over there, and he's been doing just that. You keep on writing them. Send one to Russell, too, if you don't mind. Tell him about all the wild men you're dating over there!"

She giggled through her tears, then gave him a fierce hug. He kissed her, gave her a lingering look and then pulled away, negotiating the path down to the waiting launch. The water swelled, and he nearly pitched into the rocks while trying to gain his footing in the boat. Darla cringed.

Once again, she watched as his boat became smaller and indiscernible in the distance.

"I love you, Jordan Kent," she whispered, then hurried back into the lighthouse.

It took him all day to get home. It was Christmas Eve, and he hoped the diamond necklace and earrings he bought Cecelia would appease her. Yet he could tell by her face when he walked in the door that all wasn't what he'd hoped.

"The police called. You gotta go down there and bail Russell out. He's in some kind of trouble." Arms akimbo, she stared accusingly at Jordan.

"Wonderful. Do I need money?" he asked, removing his hat and tossing it onto the end of the banister.

"How should I know?"

"Bail money. Did they set bail?"

"Call 'em." She turned her back and walked away. Jordan followed her.

"Look, I'm sorry, darling. I know it's Christmas Eve. I'll take care of this just as quickly as possible. Then we'll have a nice evening." He came up close behind her, embraced her shoulders.

She stiffened. "We'll see about that when you come back."

Jordan sighed. Leaving Darla this morning had taken a toll on him. Having to bail Russell out of jail was the icing on the cake.

They held Russell downtown. Jordan made bail and waited while they brought Russell out. He appeared to be drunk and cantankerous.

"Aw, crap. They shoulda just lef me in there. I don't need you, don' need nobody to take care a me."

"Come on, old man. Let's just get you home."

The officer handed Jordan an envelope containing Russell's wallet.

"C'mere," the policeman murmured, and Jordan accompanied him to the desk. "Guy's been talking to himself all night. Sarge says he's wacko."

"He's drunk."

"More than that. He's talking crazy. About how he's gonna get even with God. How he's special, he's from some other society of super beings or something. Just thought you oughta know."

"Swell. Thank you for your insight." Jordan shook his head and returned to Russell. "Let's go home, pal."

They were in the car and heading for Russell's flat when he started sniffing.

"I smell her."

"You smell her, who?" Jordan asked.

"Darla. It's her perfume. She been in your car?"

"Of course not. I told you before, I haven't seen her since she left town weeks ago. You're imagining it."

"You can't imagine smells. She's been here."

Jordan rubbed his neck unconsciously as he drove. Darla's perfume did cling to him. "Whatever you say."

"I'm gonna find her, Jordan. I'm leaving tomorrow. I got a lead on where she is."

"Oh yeah? What lead?"

"Never you mind. But I'm gonna find her. I got a voice in my head, says she's still here in California. Still in Los Angeles. She's hiding out. The voice is gonna tell me where to look."

"Well, good. Go for it. Here's your stop, brother. You just stay out of trouble, you hear?" He reached across his passenger, opened the door, pushed it out. "And Merry Christmas."

"Merry Christmas. And I'm not your brother."

Cecelia slipped on a white cashmere bed jacket and velvet lounging pants. For the first time in a week, she really wanted a cigarette, so found her pack and lit up. She heard Jordan's car coming up the driveway.

He sagged into the room, leaned against the banister. "He's back home now. He gets crazier every time I see him. The cops said he was rambling on in the cell."

"What else is new?" she asked, got up from where she sat on the couch and approached Jordan. "Look, I'm sorry for how I behaved before you left. You've had a rough day, too. I made you a brandy. Sit with me?"

"I should go and change. I feel like I've been traveling inside the suitcase instead of carrying it."

"Just one little drink before you go upstairs."

He relented, tugged off his coat. "Sounds too good to pass up."

She brought him his drink but held it away when he reached for it. "For a kiss," she said softly, standing close and pressing her lips to his. He wrapped his arms around her, careful not to cause her to spill their glasses, then released her.

"What's that perfume you're wearing? You smell like a two-bit whore."

The words stung for more than one reason. "Oh, on the way to the airport, I shared a cab. This rather obese woman sat next to me, the cab hit a bump, and she fell against me. I about suffocated."

"Hmm. Teach you to share a cab. You can afford your own, you know."

"It happened to be the only one around. I didn't want to wait."

Cecelia handed him his drink and tapped hers against it. "Cheers, handsome," she said, turning to go back to the couch.

"Cheers." He downed the brandy in one gulp, then left the room. "I'll be back down in a moment. I have a little Christmas gift for you."

"You'd better," Cecelia mumbled as Jordan trudged up the stairway.

Twenty-Seven

Los Angeles, California
September

The judge looked down his nose through his bifocals. "I assume the defense is probably going to want to respond, right?"

Matt nodded. "Yes, Your Honor, we would probably wish to respond, if we could."

"Okay. Well, I am trying to get these things resolved as quickly as possible so we can keep to the original trial date. But I want all the information counsel needs to submit to me so I can try and make the best decisions I can. Is there anything the defense has already filed that the plaintiff thinks needs to be responded to?"

The plaintiff's attorney nodded his head. "We're going to sit down this afternoon to discuss it. There is a possibility. If I could ask that *if* we file a response to Mr. Farralone…"

The judge sighed, rubbed his forehead. "I'll give you until Friday to file. This is going to obviously delay a ruling."

Adjourn already! Matt's head pounded. He so preferred a hammer to a gavel.

"Can we have until the *end* of the day on Friday?"

The sidewalk café bustled. Matt pulled a wrought iron chair up to the table and nodded at a waitress who promised to be right over. He pulled his iPhone from his pocket and tossed it onto the table before sitting down.

Today had been a routine, preliminary hearing. No big deal. Yet he'd barely gotten through it, not understanding his own inability to think clearly or stay in control. What was wrong with him?

The vacation. He'd been away too long, had gotten too relaxed. Or maybe–God forbid–law was no longer his thing.

Naw. He enjoyed the courtroom. Dug the research. Ate up the power. As he recalled some of his past successes, he warmed, reliving the glow of a fight well fought, a case ending in victory. No, it was just *now*, just this place in time that he felt a bit off.

Without being told, the waitress brought him a beer in a tall pilsner glass. Matt made a mental note to give her a big tip. He almost didn't answer when his phone rang but checked the screen just in case. Just in case what? Who could possibly be important enough to talk to right now, after 6:00 p.m., with traffic gridlocked, a 72-degree breeze blowing and ice-cold Heineken in front of him?

Jack.

"Are you back in town?" Didn't these guys have anything else to do, Matt thought, a grin spreading across his face.

"We both are. Case is here too. Where are you?"

"At the corner of Wilshire and Blotto, right by my office. Where are you?"

"Looking for a good bar. We're about a mile away."

"See you."

When his friends joined him, they moved to a larger table.

"Here." Case dropped a manila envelope in front of Matt.

"What's this?"

"Your mail. You didn't bother to pick it up when you were there last."

"I was a bit distracted. Anything I need to look at?"

"Maybe one."

Matt took a long draught of beer, dumping the contents of the envelope on the table. "*Occupant*? C'mon."

"Sorry. But there's a letter in there somewhere."

Jack and Case placed their orders, then Jack turned back to Matt. "So, what's up with Denise? Are we getting the money?"

Matt sighed out a groan. "Nope."

"Why not? They didn't like our deal?"

"Well, it's like this: 'they' –ain't."

Case tilted his head. "Am I understanding that the organization doesn't exist? Is that what you're saying?"

"In a word–yes. And Denise Murray doesn't exist, either. It was all a sham."

Jack crinkled up his face in surprise. "I don't get it. Why would she do something like that? What did she have to gain?"

"Access to the lighthouse."

Case's lips twitched into a brief smile. "The photog lady. It was her, right?"

Matt frowned. "Can we talk about something else?"

"Unbelievable! She pulled the polyester right over our eyes," Jack exclaimed.

"It's over; we move on. Just one more reason not to trust chicks who come out of the blue. Stupid."

"But that's diabolical! It's–it's cheating!"

"Jack, just let it go. I'm over it. It's been two weeks, I'm okay, I'm back to work, everything's cool."

Case accepted his beer from the waitress, took a sip. "Or not."

"What's that supposed to mean?" Matt asked. "Look. She pretended to be someone she's not. She had her reasons. She never apologized. I let her know how I felt about it, so I'm done. Closure."

"You'd be surprised how many people aren't who you think they are," Case said softly.

Matt said nothing. He knew Case had a troubled past, more "lives" than most guys he knew. He glanced through the pile of mail on the table. One small envelope caught his eye. Postmarked Phoenix.

He started to stuff it into his pocket when Case again spoke. "Why don't you read it now?"

"Maybe I don't want to."

"Maybe you should. It might affect the quantity of beer you need to order."

Matt flashed a quick grin, then slipped his finger under the envelope's sealed flap. He pulled out the single sheet of flowered stationary, unfolded it.

Dear Matt,
I don't know how to explain what I've done; I only know that I have to try. The story about the grant was a

ruse. My real name is Rebecca Burke, one and the same as the irritating photographer who harassed you about the lighthouse. When you refused to give me my story, I went undercover to try to get you to like me...

Matt huffed out a breath through pursed lips, glanced around, then resumed reading.

...like me well enough to change your mind. I went too far, and I'm deeply sorry for what I did. I don't expect forgiveness. That would be too much to ask. But I cannot go on without at least apologizing for my despicable behavior. It really isn't me. I guess I just wanted to play in the big leagues. I now know it isn't worth it. I didn't expect you to be such a nice guy.

"Well, what does it say?" Jack wanted to know.

Matt read the rest of the letter aloud. "Best of luck to you and your Club. Please know that if I were, in fact, who I said I was, I would be first in line to help out your cause. Best regards, Rebecca Burke--Denise Murray."

"When did she write this?" Case asked.

Matt quickly looked to the date on the letter; three weeks ago. Before the lighthouse tour. Before he'd called her.

"What a schlub I am. Dammit."

I didn't expect you to be such a nice guy.

He knew why she'd said that, too. He hadn't been particularly gracious on the phone when she'd called to ask about the lighthouse.

It really isn't me.

Of course not. That's why it bothered him so much.

...deeply sorry for what I did.

So, he'd mocked her, stolen her film. If only he'd picked up his mail first.

"I have to fix this," he said softly. He checked the envelope for a return address. "Anybody want to ride to Phoenix with me?"

212

"Okay, I've got Christmas in a Castle; it's that Scottish Highlands trip that departs from Edinburgh on Christmas Eve. I've got Christmas, Vegas style, at the Bellagio. Then there's the Rocky Mountain Express Christmas–can't you just see stockings swaying as the train rocks along the track?" Rebecca reviewed her list with Pat, trying unsuccessfully to muster some enthusiasm for the assignment. "Janie is writing up a couple more, uh, something about the North Pole, I think."

"Yeah, yeah, whatever. Okay. Unless you've got something really important to tell me, go away."

Rebecca stood. "Pat. You may think it's your prerogative as my boss to be abrupt. But I'm getting really tired of your rudeness. Being treated like a grunt around here. The least you could do is show some respect." She turned and started out of the office.

"Whoa. Whoa there, missy. Just you turn around and come back over here."

Rebecca paused, considered ignoring his request. If he uttered anything but an apology, she was leaving.

"C'mere. C'mere, *please*."

She took a step forward, crossed her arms.

"What's eatin' you, Burke? This is Pat talking. You know me. I'm an asshole. I have to be an asshole…it's what's got me where I am, I'm sorry to say."

Rebecca stared.

"Look. I'm rough around the edges. If I wasn't, this business would eat me alive, and then where would you be? Waitin' tables?"

"I'd be working for someone else. Someone who listened and cared about what I had to say."

Pat groaned. "I do care, okay?"

Rebecca started to turn.

"Wait. Listen. You are the best God-damned photographer I got and are gonna be a dynamite journalist one day, if you wanna be. We've been the same way to each other for almost three years now. You got a tougher skin than what I'm seein' now. So, what's buggin' you, chickie?"

Rebecca faltered. Maybe she *was* being too sensitive. Pat wasn't acting any differently than he ever did. In fact, he'd been out of character when he'd complimented the car spread.

"You wanna go over to Scotchland and shoot that damned castle? How would that be? Maybe get your mind offa whatever's screwing you up."

"Scotland? Really?"

"See if they'll set up the interior shots for you, and I'm sure they have some stocks of the exterior from last year. Take a week. Relax. Do the hot tub thing, or whatever you kids like to do these days."

"You're serious."

"Yeah, but you gotta go coach."

Fortunately, her passport was in order.

"Are you sure you'll be okay? All of your meds are full, so you shouldn't run out of anything while I'm gone."

"I'll be fine, Bec. I'm just glad you're going. It'll do you good. Britain is a beautiful place. Wasn't so pretty there during the war, but it's got a kind of charm can't be kept down. You'll love being over there." Jeb placed his hand on her back, patted it. "And you might get a chance to take some car pictures!"

"You bet I will. I'm going to do a little on-line research before I leave, see if there are any noteworthy vehicles in the area where I'll be traveling."

"Better do that now if you're leaving in the morning."

Rebecca grinned. Her father, one in a million. She wished he was going, too.

Sky Harbor International Airport wasn't too busy when Rebecca arrived on Tuesday morning. Her father insisted on driving her there, parking and then escorting her all the way to security. She hated to say goodbye.

British Airways provided a comfortable ride into Edinburgh, despite her coach fare seat. She hired a taxi to take her to the tour office, where a dapper young tour guide, Angus Mc-Something-or-other, waited to escort her to Carbisdale Castle, deep in the Scottish Highlands. It took her awhile to adapt her listening to his brogue, but soon, she was laughing and nodding as he described the scenery they passed on the three-hour trip.

"And, a'course we've got William Wallace, our Breveheart. 'Twas filmed out Glencoe wey. Appropriate setting, it was. To yer left there be the Cairngorm Mountains. They'll be havin' a good bit more snow on 'em come Christmas," he explained.

Rebecca smiled, agreed. She still couldn't believe she was halfway around the world from her condo, her father, her car, and...Matt. She shook her head slightly. Why should she include him in any list of things important to her?

The castle, set on a hill, posed an incredible sight. Two huge, stone chess pieces flanked the entrance, and cannons faced them as they entered the driveway. Inside, a multitude of Italian marble statues, elegant furnishings, royal fireplaces and paintings graced the enormous reception and great rooms.

"It's currently a youth hostel, as I'm sure you're aware. So, the Christmas tour helps immensely with the finances," Angus told her.

"I can imagine."

"And before you find out elsewhere, some say we share the castle with five spirits."

Rebecca turned. "Really? I'll be on the lookout, then."

Ghosts. Great.

"I'll show you to your room, then. Will y' be takin' tea with us?"

"If the spirit moves me, yes."

He got no takers. Just as well; he wouldn't have been good company on the drive across the desert. Matt figured on an eight-hour drive to Phoenix, another hour or so to find Rebecca's home in the suburb of Scottsdale. But traffic was heavier than expected; Mondays were truckers' days, and Interstate 10 had more than its share of accidents and bottlenecks on the way. He decided he'd be better off putting up for the night and getting a good night's sleep before tracking down Rebecca in the morning.

Tuesday morning, he got up at dawn, shaved, dressed, and went downstairs for coffee. It was too early by a few hours to call on Rebecca. He didn't know if she actually worked at home, as she'd told him as Denise, or if she went to an office. It occurred to him that he really didn't know the truth from what she created for his benefit. He intended to find out.

215

At ten o'clock he drove up before a modest, one-story stucco house displaying numbers matching those on the envelope's return address. Mustering all his courage, he went to the front door and knocked. He was surprised when an older man answered the door.

"I'm looking for Rebecca Burke. Is she here?"

"Becca? No, not at the moment. You...wanna leave a message or something?"

"When will she be back?"

"Oh, not for some time."

Matt shuffled his feet on the porch. "I've just driven in from Los Angeles to see her. I have her cell number, maybe I should just give her a call."

"I'm afraid that won't work, son. Her plane has already left for Edinburgh."

"Edinburgh? As in, Scotland?" Matt's eyes flew open wide.

"Yep. One and the same. Land o' haggis and kilts and that. She wasn't expecting you, I guess."

Matt's shoulders drooped. "No. No, she wasn't. It was kind of...a surprise visit."

"Well, unless you wanna fly over there, you'll have to wait another week to see her."

"Wow. This is the last thing I expected. Did she go on business?"

"Why don't you just come on in for a cup of coffee. I'm Jebediah Burke. And you are?"

"Matt Farralone. I'm afraid I'm the guy that may have just broken your daughter's heart."

Twenty-Eight

Dragon Rock, California
February 1949

As Darla got out of bed, she pulled the comforter off and wrapped it around her from the neck down. It was colder today, if that was possible.

A small, cracked mirror hung on the kitchen wall, and she imagined the Coast Guardsmen who once manned the lighthouse shaving in front of it. Now, she checked her own appearance. "My hair's too long," she complained. Trailing the quilted coverlet behind her, she shuffled about, making oatmeal with raisins.

The baby had kept her awake during the night. It had grown big enough now to do some intense kicking, and while the movement didn't bother Darla in itself, the excitement did. *It won't be long, now.* She leaned back, stretched. The discomfort of her ballooned size had increased disproportionately in the last two weeks.

As she sat down with her oatmeal, she opened a small diary and picked up her pen. While she'd never been one to set down her thoughts, she had, of late, taken to jotting them in the journal, thinking they might be fun reading one day. Lana, certainly, would get a kick out of reading her mother's crazy thoughts while waiting for her to be born. Someday, decades in the future.

It wasn't all fun stuff, either. She recalled in great detail each terrible storm, unfortunate bird, engine room mishap. The night the lights went out. The aches and pains, the wintry cold, the isolation and loneliness. And because she knew no one else would ever see the words in her lifetime, she poured out her heart, her longing for Jordan and the life she dreamed of with him.

She lifted her pen; thought she heard a noise. Could it be? The note she'd left in the bottle two, no, three days ago included a request for the messenger to knock on the door when he returned. Dropping the pen and the blanket, Darla hurried down the steps into the cavernous engine room and to the outside door.

A boy stood shivering, barely able to hold his footing in the wind.

"Oh, my," Darla breathed. "Who are you?"

"Willie!"

"Well, Willie, come on in out of the wind!"

The boy hesitated only a moment. He looked to be anywhere from 12 to 14. "Would you like some hot chocolate?" Darla asked.

The boy's eyes lit. "Oh, that would be great, ma'am."

She sat him at the table and scurried around making the cocoa. "Have you been the one bringing my groceries?" she asked.

"Yes'm."

"Well, you've been doing a great job. I just wanted a chance to thank you, since we never see each other. Why, I've been very alone for quite a while now, so I thought we could chat just a bit before you go back."

"Okay."

"Did you pick out the movie magazines I got last time?"

"I didn't know which ones you wanted. I just guessed."

"You did great. Can you believe that story about Roy Rogers? Do you like Roy and Trigger?"

The boy nodded vigorously. "Yep. He's my favorite cowboy."

"Mine, too." Darla smiled. "Some people prefer The Lone Ranger. But he doesn't sing. And nobody really knows who he is. I don't like that. I think people should know who other people are. Don't you?"

"Yes'm."

"So, I'm going to tell you my name. I'm Darla, Mr. Willie. How do you do?" She thrust out her hand, and Willie took it.

"Pleased, Ma'am. Darla, I mean."

They sipped cocoa together, Willie politely answering all of Darla's questions.

"Did you see the one where Trigger pulls Roy out of the quicksand?"

Her guest nodded. "It was swell. My favorite is Bullet."

"Roy's dog! Right! He's the best," Darla agreed, licking the cocoa mustache from her upper lip. "Yep, good ol' Bullet."

The boy fidgeted. "You hafta go, huh? Okay. I understand. I have a letter to give you." Darla got up, went to her bedroom, then returned with an envelope addressed to her mother. "You see that the man gets this, will you?"

"What man?"

"The man who hired you to come out here. Whatever his name is. He'll take this. It's very important–" Darla began, then frowned. The baby moved, differently than before. And it felt like she was suddenly peeing down her leg beneath her robe. "Oh, my. Oh, goodness."

Just then, a cramp began, slowly edging its way across her abdomen. "Oh, Jesus. Not now." Quickly she sat down and took a deep breath. "This isn't good."

"Are you alright, Darla, ma'am?" Willie asked, his eyes wide. "Are you havin' a baby right now?"

"Oh, Willie-boy, I just might be. Lordy! I–oh! Lana's sending a message that she's good and ready!"

"Who's Lana?"

"Why, my little-bit daughter, that's who!"

"How do you know it's a girl?"

"Just do. There are some things in this world you just know without seeing, kid. Now, listen. I want you to do me a favor. Get in your boat and head back, and when you get over to the city, you find Dr. Stone and tell him Mrs. Weathering, er, Mrs. Weatherling? Oh, sweet pickles. Weatherington. Whatever. Tell him the crazy lady out in the lighthouse is having her baby now, and he's to come quick. You got it, chappie?"

"Yes'm! I'm going." Willie took the stairs two at a time back down to the caisson door and turned when he reached it. "Thanks for the cocoa, Miss Darla! I'll get the doctor!"

Another contraction tore across her belly.

"I'm tellin' ya, there hasta be foul play involved. My girl wouldn't just leave town and not say goodbye, not write, not call." Russell Harrington spoke into the large, bulbous microphone aimed at his mouth by the reporter from CBS radio. "Something's fishy. She don't just disappear like this."

"But her family has received letters, postmarked Paris, France. What do you say to that?"

"Two letters. November and early December. Then, nothin'. We tried callin' the place where she's supposedly shacked up. They never heard of Darla Foster."

"And do her parents also feel their daughter is actually missing?" the reporter asked, again moving the microphone to catch Russell's words.

"They do now."

"When did you last see Miss Foster?"

"At the premiere for *Cape Seduction*. Right after that, she left town."

"Has anyone seen her since?"

"Not to my knowledge."

The news reporter paused, then asked, "Has anyone filed a missing person report?"

Russell looked up, stood a little straighter. "I did. Today. With the L.A.P.D. And I tol' them where to start looking, too."

"Which would be where, Mr. Harrington?"

"I can't say 'cos it could mess things up. Evidence, you know."

"Well, there you have it, ladies and gentlemen. One of Hollywood's brightest new stars, actress Darla Foster, has been reported missing by her longtime boyfriend, actor Russell Harrington, here in Los Angeles, California. We will continue to check on the progress of this case with the Los Angeles Police Department. Now, for a word from our sponsor, Lux Soap."

Russell cleared his throat and adjusted his worn suit jacket on his shoulders. It seemed to have gotten bigger in the last few months.

"I *will* find her," he muttered.

"Did you say something, Mr. Harrington? We're off the air at the moment."

"No. Nothin'."

The next thing he knew, Russell was driving down Sepulveda Boulevard, heading for Los Angeles Municipal. He pulled over, parked to watch the airplanes coming and going overhead. *The police should be on their way to Jordan's house by now.*

"We're sorry to have troubled you, Mr. Kent. We'll be going now," the police lieutenant said, stepping off the front porch and motioning for his officers to follow.

"Quite all right," Jordan said before closing the front door.

Damned Russell. This was getting out of hand. Now, he'd called the police! He'd have to do something about this. It would drive him crazy and alienate Cecelia even more.

Cecelia. He hoped she hadn't heard the exchange at the front door with the police officers. Jordan climbed the stairs to their bedroom and crept inside.

"I'm awake," she murmured.

"How are you feeling, darling? Is there anything I can get you?"

"No, not now. I'm just tired. Cranky. Just feel like staying in bed."

"That's fine. You rest. I'll be downstairs."

"Okay. But–"

"Yes?"

"You could bring me a nice cup of chamomile tea. With honey. And…" Cecelia considered, making a show of fluffing her bed pillows. "Maybe a candy bar. A chocolate bar."

"Sure, Celia. I'll be right back."

Apparently, she'd not heard the conversation. *Thank God for small favors.*

He went back downstairs, turned on the new television set and started the tea while waiting for the picture tube to warm up. He found the box of chocolate bars in the pantry, selected one, and placed it on a dinner plate. Back in the living room, he tuned the set to Channel 4. "Let's see…" He picked up the program guide from the top of the set, took a quick look, sat down. *Texaco Star Theater* might take his mind off of his troubles.

Just as his interest became piqued, he heard the teakettle beckoning from the kitchen. He hurried back to the kitchen to pour the boiling water over the teabag. Placing the hot tea on the plate beside the candy, he carefully transported the snack up the stairs and into the bedroom.

"I changed my mind."

"What?"

"I want some pistachio ice cream. I'll have the tea, but I need some ice cream."

"I don't think we have pistachio. Maybe some Neapolitan?"

Cecelia turned her head, frowned. "Pistachio. Please, Jordan?" She turned back, a hopeful smile on her face. "For me and the baby?"

Jordan took in a deep breath and put the plate on the nightstand. "Whatever you say, darling. I'll be back in a few minutes, then."

Willie pulled his dinghy ashore and quickly turned it over, barely breaking pace as he continued running toward town. It was nearly dark, but he didn't stop until he came to Dr. Stone's cottage at the Crescent City town limits. He knocked on the door.

"Hello? Dr. Stone? Are you home?" he called when no one answered. "Dr. Stone!" He pounded on the door, then ran around the house to the back windows and peered in. He saw no one.

His heart thumping wildly, Willie leaned against the wall to catch his breath. In his pocket was a note containing the words "emergency only" and the phone number of the man who'd hired him to take the groceries to the heiress in the lighthouse. This, surely, must be just such an emergency.

Willie tried the back door and found it unlocked. He was in luck! He scampered across the sun porch and headed for the kitchen where he found a phone. He lifted the heavy receiver and dialed "0."

After the operator connected the call, the phone rang three times before a woman's voice answered.

"Mr. Weatherton, please?"

Cecelia reached for the candy bar. "Who is this?"

"It's Willie Jacobs. It's about Miz Darla. I mean, Mrs. Weatherton. I can't find Dr. Stone. She–she needs the doc. Mr. Weatherton left this number ina case of emergency. I think the baby is on its way."

"Where is...Mrs. Weatherton right now?" Cecelia asked, sitting upright in bed.

"She was in the kitchen when I seen her last. She asked me to come in. She talked about Roy Rogers, and we had hot chocolate, and she was real nice." Willie paused to catch his breath. "But then, then she got all worried and fearful and like she was hurtin' and she told me to get on back and get Doc Stone. But he isn't around. It took me too long to get back."

"Back from?"

"From the lighthouse. The water's being somethin' fierce right now. Doc Stone probably went out somewheres."

"Yes, he probably did." Cecelia lay back, began winding the telephone cord around her fingers. "You did well, Willie Jacobs. Thank you for calling. I'll see to it Mr. Weatherton gets the message. Everything will be just fine, so don't you worry about poor Mrs. Weatherton. Understand? Just go on home and...do your homework."

"Yes'm. I will. Thank you."

Cecelia replaced the receiver just as Jordan's voice called from the bottom of the stairs.

"Celia? Who's on the phone?"

"Wrong number," she called back. "Did you get my ice cream?"

Twenty-Nine

North Highlands, Scotland
September

The shoot was a success. It went much better, in fact, than Rebecca had thought possible. The tour company worked well with the castle staff, taking great pains to decorate the Great Hall and dining room just as it would look come December, when a group of affluent world travelers would descend upon them in search of the perfect, alternative, holiday.

"Havin' a wee bit of a warm spell," Angus commented, joining Rebecca in the oversized kitchen for coffee with the staff.

"Warm? Are you joking?"

"Must be close to forty-five degrees!" Angus grinned. "Celsius, that is."

"Still! That's like sixty degrees Fahrenheit! We don't call that a warm spell where I come from." Rebecca wrapped her fingers around the warm mug in her hands. "More like a cold snap."

"And what would be the temperature now, at home?"

"At the height of the day, it could be one-eleven. Let's say, around seventy-five degrees 'C.'"

Angus shook his head. "Hottest I've ever been is fifty-five."

"You've never been to the U.S., have you?" Rebecca asked.

"No. I've not had a need to travel. No desire to go."

A woman in the corner rolled out dough on a floured board. She turned, smiled at Angus. "Sic as ye gie, sic wull ye get."

"It's true enough, aye. You get only what you put in. Still, if I sell the cou, I canna sup the milk."

Rebecca rolled her eyes, and Angus laughed. "Hey, I've a good one for y'. *'Muckle wad aye hai mair.'* Means, those who have a lot are always wantin' more."

"I get that. I really do," Rebecca agreed, joining in the laughter. "But you wouldn't have to sell your cow to come to America. You can have your milk and drink it, too."

Angus shrugged. "You know what they say, don' y'? 'Scottish by birth, British by law, a Highlander by the Grace o' God.'"

"Amen," shouted a young man just exiting the kitchen with a large, silver tray.

"Amen," Angus repeated softly. "Can'a get you some more coffee?"

"Please."

It had been a good call, coming to Scotland. Meeting new people, so different from those at home, helped to clear Rebecca's head. While she still thought about Matt, the lighthouse and the visions, the distraction helped.

"Yes, her mother was something else," Jebediah said, reaching into the refrigerator for another soft drink. "An exciting, vibrant, ball of energy. Beautiful, too. Had eyes that always looked knowing. She knew what you were thinking. But always ready for fun, too."

Matt nodded slowly. "You must miss her."

"Every single day. She shouldn't have died so young. Bec was only ten. We waited to have kids, y'know. We wanted to be settled, calmer. Lulu just turned thirty-four, I was thirty-six. Here, if we'd had our daughter like our friends, when we were twenty-four or five, Bec would have been twenty."

"Yeah. That's a tough break. I know Rebecca seems...very unsettled about her death. I mean, not that anyone is ever settled about their parent's death. I can relate. My dad just dropped dead at his desk one day."

"Oh," Jeb acknowledged. "Worked himself to death, did he?"

"Maybe. Didn't take care of himself."

"Happens."

Matt looked around at the homey, well-used kitchen. "You lived here long?"

"Moved here when Bec was a baby. Couldn't bear to leave it after Louise passed. Some folks can't stand to be around where their loved one used to be. I'm just the opposite. I get comfort from being around her things. Like she's still around, a bit. You know?"

"I can understand that. Yeah."

"So," Jeb began, shifting in his chair, "what's this about breaking my girl's heart? Are you the cause of the dark circles under her eyes last week?"

Matt lowered his chin. "It's highly possible. We've had a...rather unusual relationship. We weren't entirely honest with each other."

"Hmph. Can't think Becca would lie to anyone. But then, I'm her father. I'm not one to find fault with my baby."

Matt rubbed the back of his neck. "Let's just say I probably brought out the worst in her, and vice versa."

"And what happens now? You drove out here to apologize or something like that?"

"Something like that, yeah. I probably should just leave her alone. Likely she doesn't ever want to see me again. Problem is...I really like her."

Jeb nodded. "Happens." He took a sip of cola, then stood. "You wanna see a picture of her mother?"

"Sure. That would be nice."

Rebecca's father left the room and returned a few moments later, a framed photo in his hand. "Here she is. My Lulu. Louise."

Matt took the picture and examined the details. "She really was beautiful. Very interesting eyes. Not very tall, was she?"

"Nope. Bec gets her height from me. Louise was a shorty."

"Rebecca mentioned a witness," Matt ventured, gauging the older man's reaction to his statement.

"Yep. A guy standing on the corner in front of the library. Louise had that damned wireless telephone. Talking to me. All aflutter about this man she met. Stepped off the curb. A car come outta nowhere, took her out right there in the crosswalk. Sped off. No license plate, no nothing. Only saw a man behind the wheel."

"Who was the man she met?"

Jeb looked away. "Don't really matter now. Had to do with some of her research. Long forgotten."

"I see."

"So., I reckon you can be in Scotland by Thursday or Friday…that'd give you time to reschedule whatever you do at work." Jeb got up from the table a second time, retrieved a travel brochure from the counter. "Here's the place. Somewhere in the Highlands. She's taking pictures of Christmas trees."

"Christmas in September?"

"It's for the magazine. She's coming back on Tuesday, if you'd rather wait. Just seems to me, if a guy really wants to make it up to a girl, he's gonna do whatever he can to impress her. Unless, of course," he turned a smile Matt's way, dropped the brochure on the table. "Unless he doesn't really care about making amends."

Matt picked up the brochure, turned it over. "Guess I'd better take a coat."

By Friday evening, Rebecca felt relaxed and refreshed. Her return flight on Tuesday seemed too soon; she had mixed emotions about going back. A group of youth travelers had arrived this afternoon, and many guests filtered in and out of the Great Hall as she sat enjoying the fire blazing in the massive fireplace. As immense as Carbisdale Castle seemed, she could hardly imagine there being enough bedrooms for all the young people arriving.

Most of the visitors, young men, arrived with only a small backpack. Some had bicycled. Nearly all were hostel guests and would be doubling up in tiny quarters outfitted with a bunk bed and bureau. She herself had a full bedroom in the staff wing, and she'd yet to see a ghost, she mused. Funny. In California, she'd been visited at least three, maybe four, times. Visited? Was she believing it now? And did that count the second-long glimpse of the infant in the cradle?

Rebecca shook her head, stared into the fire. While she hadn't actually seen anything akin to a spirit, or dare she think, a ghost, while visiting the lighthouse, she'd definitely felt something. Matt felt it, too, she suspected.

Matt. Invading her thoughts, again. She should have let him, and the whole ugly affair, go by now. She shivered; although the castle doors were located across a massive foyer from where she sat, the achingly cold nighttime wind coming off the Highlands found its way across her arms each time they opened. Would they never stop arriving?

Two more entrants hurried in, Rebecca only barely noted from her peripheral vision. She started to turn but was interrupted by a young woman with a drink on a small tray.

"Thought you might be likin' a wee toddy, Miss. To take off the chill."

"Oh, thank you! You must have read my mind."

The hot buttered rum went down very easily, and did, in fact, take the chill off. Rebecca nestled lower in the big, over-stuffed couch and cradled the hot cocktail, relishing the warmth spreading throughout her body. She closed her eyes, let her mind wander, only vaguely aware when one of the men from the registrar's desk approached.

"Mind if I join you?" he asked, standing beside the couch where Rebecca sat.

Rebecca turned her face toward the sound of the voice. Her lips parted softly in surprise, then closed again. She took a swallow of the rum, then shrugged.

"Don't mind if I do," Matt said, pulling a woolen cap off his head and sitting beside her. "Nippy out there!"

"I'm surprised you noticed," Rebecca murmured.

"Ooh, that was low."

"Not low enough."

"And where can I get one of those?" he asked, tugging off his gloves and pointing at her drink.

Again, she shrugged, keeping her eyes focused on the flames.

Almost on cue, the same woman returned with a drink for Matt.

"Now, this is nice," he commented, after taking a sip of the rum cocktail. "So, what do they do for fun around here? Ice hockey in the dining room?"

She tried not to smile, turning her head away lest he see her amusement.

"If it's all the same to management, I'd just as soon sleep right here," Matt added. "Haven't seen my room yet. Are they nice? Honor bar? HD-DVD or Blu-ray?"

"For you, most likely shared bunk beds and a spittoon. My suite has a fireplace."

"Sounds like I'd rather share with you."

Rebecca didn't respond. Inside, she reeled from the fact that he'd turned up in such an incredibly remote locale. Clearly, he wanted something from her.

Neither spoke for a while. The server reappeared, offered refills.

"I think I would like another. Yes," Rebecca said, handing over her empty mug.

"And you, sir?

"Yes. Please." Matt turned on the couch, bent his leg so he could face Rebecca. "I need to talk to you."

"About why you stole my photos?"

"Well, yeah, that, and other stuff. Look, Rebecca, I was really stung. When I realized who you were, I–I felt like a fool. You played me. And yeah, it's not like I haven't been played before. But you, I thought you were...real."

"I wrote you, I tried to explain how–"

"Hear me out. I was being a jerk when you called the first time. I was going through a tough time with my, my ex. I wasn't in the mood to square off with some brassy reporter, which I thought you were. *Mistakenly* thought you were. I was rude."

"It wasn't your fault–"

"Just chill, will you? Shouldn't be too hard in this place. Anyway, when you came to me as Denise, I felt...I had fun for the first time in a while. I know you said you weren't looking, and I respect that. Whether it was true or not. Then, when you talked about how your mother died, I wanted to help you. You seemed so unreconciled. I started doing a little snooping about the accident. That's how I found out who you were. You gave me just a little too much info."

Their new drinks arrived. "Put hers on my tab, will you?" Matt asked.

The waitress giggled. "It's on the 'ouse, sir."

"Thank you. So, the point is, I didn't get your letter until–"

"Until after we went to the lighthouse."

Matt nodded. "Yeah."

Rebecca peered into her mug.

"And it was such a nice letter, too."

"It was the truth."

"There's more." Matt took a mouthful of the toddy, swallowed. "The tour was a scam. I did *not* have permission to take you there. That's the real reason I took your film."

Rebecca looked up, shock registering. "You set up the whole tour thing just to...to hurt me?"

Matt winced. "I was angry. Yeah, I wanted to get you back. I hadn't seen your letter, and you seemed so...callous. So, I tried to be callous back. And it's not me, either."

"Not you," Rebecca muttered, taking a deep breath.

"And I came here to apologize."

Rebecca stared. Really looked at Matt for the first time. Although he'd shaved and wore fresh clothes, he clearly hadn't slept in a while. He had trouble maintaining eye contact, but eventually, he let her look into his eyes long enough to grasp the sincerity of his words.

She wanted to touch his face, feel the texture of his unruly, honeyed hair. Still, she found it hard to speak.

Matt took her mug and placed it on the end table beside his own. He took one of her hands between his own.

"I'm sorry. You're sorry. So, doesn't that kind of cancel out our sins? Can we just sort of start over again? Be friends?"

As the rum massaged her brain, Matt massaged her hand. She didn't have a chance at any possible contradiction, and she was shocked when her own hand decided to squeeze his back.

"I'll take that as a yes. Your dad said you were a reasonable girl."

"My d-ad?" *Oops! Where did that come from?* She pulled her hand away. "You talked to my dad?"

"Am I not allowed? He's quite a guy. We got on well. Don't look so surprised! How do you think I found you all the way the hell up here in no man's freezer locker land?"

"You—you called h-im?" *Damned hiccups!*

"Actually, we had a Coke or two. At the kitchen table." Matt retrieved his drink, clearly enjoying Rebecca's fluster. "Scottsdale is one in-fer-no." He laughed then, reached over and tugged on her chin. "Lake Washington. No wonder you picked someplace cooler."

"I don't want to t-alk about it. In fact, I'm going to b-ed." Rebecca drank down her rum and made an attempt to stand. Matt was quick to brace her when she started to pitch back into the couch.

"I'll see you to your room. Do you remember where it is? Do you have a key or just an ice pick?"

Rebecca frowned but let Matt lead her to her second-floor suite.

Thirty

Dragon Rock
February 1949

She knew in her heart no one was coming. Not Willie, not the doctor and certainly not Jordan. Darla had a powerful urge to use the bathroom, and while entirely ignorant about the birthing process, she knew what was coming out wasn't urine.

"Okay. Okay. Okay. I can do this. I'm up at the plate. I need...oh, God. Oh, God. Oww! Dammit!" She braced herself in the doorway to the bedroom. "A–a–towel. Would be good. A towel." She'd just done laundry. She grabbed a bath towel off the top of the basket and lurched to the bed, quickly spreading the towel and climbing to lie on top of it. "Okay. That's good. We're good now, sweetie girl. Just don't push so hard on Mama, 'kay?"

The wind was singing in the tower, but Darla barely heard the sound over her own heavy breathing. "Now. It will just happen, right? I'll just lay here, and Baby will come by herself. Oh, I wish Mother was here." *Or at least that she'd explained about this stuff!*

"You know, you know, Lana...mommies were having babies a long time ago, before there was even such a thing as doctors and medicines. They just sort of squatted down, and the baby would just pop out. Kinda like...ohh.... oww!" She cried out as the next contraction burned across her abdomen. "Oh, Christ! This is ten times worse than a period! No wonder Mom never told me about this! If you told anyone, they'd never ever have babies again."

She lay still for a minute, panting, squirming. "Oh no! The panties! Oh Lordy, how can I be so dumb!" She wriggled and struggled until she got the now wet panties off. "How could the little love be born with that roadblock!" She tried to giggle, but somehow, the laugh died in her throat. "Jimmy Jeffers, he once saw a movie about the natives in Africa, and, and, they showed

everything, naked girls and even a woman having a baby. He told—
he told me all about it. I remember now. And the baby just came
out, and it was all over."

*I hope. I hope. Oh, Jesus, I can't believe this is happening to
me.* She moaned, and the moan stretched into a cry and then a wail.
And when the contraction had passed, she tried to relax back on the
bed. "That was a loud one! Not like there's anybody listening, right,
Lana?"

Damn Jordan. Damn Cecelia. Damn everyone! "I don't want
to do this! Somebody get me out of here!"

Willie Jacobs sat on the small jetty at Dragon Rock Lookout.
He was used to the cold, the blistering wind. He'd lived with it all
of his twelve years. The lighthouse wasn't visible at night; its bright
beam long extinguished. Yet he knew, from ages of watching it in
the daytime, exactly where it sat in the waters off the Del Norte
coast. He thought of the lady inside it, who might be having a baby
there tonight. Despite what the woman on the phone said, there was
no way anyone could go out there now.

The wind got worse, spraying him with icy sea water. He
stood and found himself walking into town. His father wouldn't be
home from the bar for another hour. Maybe he could find Dr.
Stone.

The streets were quiet. There were two places he could look:
the Pelican's Roost and Redwood Red's. He got lucky at the first
restaurant: Edward Stone's tan Plymouth sedan sat parked at the
curb. He climbed the front steps, pulled open the heavy wooden
door and went inside.

Dr. Stone was eating crab cakes with his wife. When Willie
approached the booth, the doctor frowned.

"Willie Jacobs. Who's sick? Is it your dad again?"

Willie blushed at the memory of his father's infamous mid-
road, face-first pass out of the month before. "No, sir. It's…it's the
lady in the lighthouse."

The doctor turned sharply toward the boy. "There's no one out
there, son. You must be mistaken. No one been out there since
those movie folks left."

"But there is. And she's havin' a baby. Now. Tonight. She needs help," Willie blurted out, wincing at the shock registering on Mrs. Stone's face. "She said to get you."

"How do you know all this?"

"I was there. Today, and we had cocoa and talked about Roy and Trigger. She was hurtin', though, and said to get you. Dr. Stone, she said."

Ed Stone dabbed at his mouth with his napkin. "Okay. I'll–I'll check things out in the morning. Best I can do."

Willie nodded. "Okay. That would be great. Thank you, sir."

"Well, is there something else?" the doctor asked, when Willie remained at the table.

"Just…if you need someone to take you out there, I can do it."

"Fine. Meet me at the dock at 10:00 a.m. If it isn't storming."

Darla turned her head, smeared the sweat from her forehead onto the pillowcase. In all her twenty-one years, she'd never felt anything so painful. So agonizingly raw. Between contractions, she tried hard to visualize a better time, a fun time, when her life was easy and without anguish. But before the thought fully formed, another gut-wrenching spasm would quickly build to a horrific climax, leaving her whimpering and clutching at the sheets.

"Why? Why, why, why!" *Something's not right. This couldn't be right. Someone would have told me about something this bad.*

The urge to push the baby out was suddenly strong and foremost. "Oh, God. This is it." Panting, she gathered what little strength she had and sat up. She bunched up great wads of the sheet in each fist, pulled her knees up and bore down with everything she had left. It wasn't enough, she knew. The contraction subsided, and she reached between her legs. She felt the baby's head only beginning to emerge. It was *something*, and it gave her cause to push harder with the next wave.

Do it, Darla. Get the baby out. You can do this! "I'm splitting apart," she wailed as she pushed once more with exhausted but determined force. She held her breath until she thought her head would burst, focusing all thought on riding the contraction to its ultimate goal. She felt the baby break free of her body, pausing briefly before rushing out in a gush of liquid with one last effort.

Darla sat still, tried to calm her breathing. The urges gone, the pain now a dull ache, the only sound was that of the relentless wind in the tower. Slowly she reached forward, feeling in the dim light for the child that should be lying on the towel.

"Lana?" she murmured, gingerly touching the space between her legs on the bed. "Are you there, Baby?" Oh! Something warm, sticky, plump. "Lana?" she said aloud, again, now leaning forward and scooping the tiny infant into her arms. "Wake up, baby girl. Wake up!"

The baby remained silent. Darla, vaguely aware that they were still attached by way of the umbilical cord, pulled up the clean edge of the towel and wrapped it around the child and hugged her to her chest. Rocked her. Kissed the top of her head. "Oh Lana. C'mon sweetie girl. Wake up now! Now's the time to really kick Mama!" Darla peered into the small face, squinting to see the details. She began stroking the girl's head, pushing back the small tuft of dark hair. Suddenly, the baby gasped and choked.

"Oh! Jesus! What's happening?" Darla watched as the infant turned its head to the side, gagging and choking. "What is it, Baby? Oh, no!" Unsure about what she should do, Darla forced her finger into the baby's mouth and felt around. It seemed to be filled with Jell-O. Quickly she swiped the inside of the mouth, pulling out the thick, mucus-like substance, then turned the baby onto her stomach and patted her back firmly. "Spit it out, girl. That's nasty stuff in there! Good grief."

The baby sputtered and cried, her tiny arms flailing about. Darla began to laugh and cry, hugging the baby to her chest. "You just cry, little bit. You just cry big time. And Mama will cry, too. Ain't nobody gonna hear us, anyway."

Darla settled back into the pillows. She was still cramping, she noticed, but the contractions were mild and inconsequential. It felt like more gobs of gloppy stuff slid from her body, but she didn't care. As carefully as she could, she pulled away her soaked nightgown and placed the moist little bundle against her bare chest, then covered them both with blankets. The baby stopped crying, and Darla closed her eyes. Dawn broke.

She had no idea how long she slept. Lana stirred atop her, and Darla turned onto her side, tucking the baby alongside her.

Although a weak glow shown at the small bedroom window, Darla couldn't discern whether it was morning or afternoon. She could, however, hear the storm that had moved in overnight. There would be water in the stairwell, she knew. She wished for a hot cup of coffee and some soft music, some soothing sound to mask the echo of the wind and rain.

Her breasts ached and felt hot. *At least I think I know what that's about*, she thought smugly. She hadn't given much consideration to how she'd feed the baby. Aside from the cradle, blanket and pillow, she had nothing in the lighthouse to help her care for a child. Of course, she didn't expect Lana to come so soon.

The baby squirmed, twisting her small pink head toward Darla, its tiny hand outstretched and grabbing for air. Darla cracked open one eye, smiled. "I must look like Mae West, to you," she said. Her smile turned to surprise, however, as Lana raised her gaping mouth up to explore her mother's breast.

"Why, I'll be," Darla whispered, watching with fascination the small lips as they sought something to latch onto. "Now this is strange. Well, here goes nothin'." Darla adjusted her position so the baby's mouth aligned with her nipple. After three unsuccessful tries, Lana latched on, and Darla's eyes shot open wide. "Okay, now that's really something else!" Despite the discomfort, tears of joy flooded her eyes as the baby began to nurse.

Dr. Stone and Edna Wyatt stood waiting beside the bait shop. The sun had graced the day with an unusually bright appearance, and the sea was reasonably calm. Willie pulled the small dinghy up to the dock and motioned for the couple to climb in.

"Oh...I'm not very good at this," moaned Edna, as she nearly stumbled into the craft.

"It'll be quick," Dr. Stone assured her, fighting his own misgivings about the trip ahead of them. Willie said nothing as he piloted the boat away and into the surf en route to Dragon Rock.

After several aborted attempts at docking, and amid periodic shrieks from the midwife, Willie finally secured a line to the tiny jetty on the rocks below the lighthouse. At last they reached the door to the caisson. It was unlocked, just as Willie had left it three days before.

"Thank God that storm passed," the doctor said nervously as they climbed the interior steps.

Willie ran ahead and called out to announce their presence.

"Oh! I'm in here! *We're* in here," Darla called back.

She struggled to sit up when the three entered the room. Edna now went headlong into her role and approached Darla. "Let's see how you look," she said, attempting to pull down the blankets covering Darla and the baby.

Darla grasped the covers. "Wait! Just...just a little privacy, please?"

Dr. Stone turned. "I think we could all use a good cup of coffee. I'll be back shortly. C'mon, Mr. Jacobs. Maybe Miss Darla has some more of that hot chocolate you raved about."

The midwife resumed her quest. "You all alone when this happened?"

"Yep. Just little ol' me here. But we did fine, didn't we, Lana?"

"Lana? It's a girl, then?"

"Sure is. Just like I knew. She's a good girl, too."

Edna wrinkled her nose. "The placenta is still attached. You didn't cut the cord?"

"Oh, that? Why that's Lana's handbag, doncha know?" Darla giggled. "No. I couldn't cut the cord. I was too scared to, and anyway, I couldn't get out of bed. You wouldn't want to have trusted me with a knife right then."

"It's just ready to fall off anyway. No harm done. Did you labor long, dear?"

"I lost track. Probably a night and a half a day. Couldn't say. Hurt somethin' mean, though."

"I'm sure it did...looks like it's all here. Let's get a look at the child. Your...daughter. Lana, did you say?"

"After Lana Turner."

"I see. She's been nursing?"

"Like a champ."

"Well, that's good for both of you. Right now. But you won't want to keep that up. It'll make your boobies sag later on. I brought you some things to make some formula for her."

Darla frowned. "Formula? I don't know..."

"And some bottles. You got a big pot to sterilize in?"

"Yes, but–"

"The doctor can give you a shot to dry up your milk. That way it won't hurt so bad when you stop. Okay, my dear, we need to change this bedding. This is a nasty mess. And you need a bath. How in the world do you bathe in this place?"

"Not easy," Darla muttered. "I have a tub, but it takes forever to get warm water."

"No tub for you. We're gonna give you a sponge-over. I'll need a pan of warm water and a washcloth. Some clean sheets and towels. There's no one here to help you at all, ever?"

"Nope. But there's a basket over there with clean stuff in it."

"The baby needs to be cleaned up, too. But let's get the bedding done first." Edna reached for the baby, but Darla held fast to the infant. Edna smiled, pulled back. "It's okay. I've delivered over four hundred babies. You can trust me."

Darla looked down at her sleeping daughter, then reluctantly handed the bundle to Edna. "There's a little bed right over there you could put her in," she offered hopefully.

"Good idea."

After tucking the baby into the cradle, Edna helped Darla from the bed and made quick work of changing the linens. After a minute or two, Darla sagged against the wall and slid to the floor.

"Oh! Dear! Dr. Stone!"

The doctor hurried into the room and lifted Darla back onto the now freshened bed. He took her pulse, looked at her pupils.

"I'm fine, Doc. I'm just a bit weak, that's all. That cocoa just didn't stay with me, did it, Willie?"

Willie watched from the doorway, his eyes wide. "No, Ma'am. Guess not."

"When did you eat last?" the doctor asked. "Has it been since before the boy was out here?"

Darla nodded.

"Oh, good Lord. Mrs. Wyatt, can you make up some lunch for our patient here?"

"Certainly, doctor."

After a brief examination, the doctor declared mother and daughter were doing fine. Darla devoured the sandwich and banana the midwife prepared.

"I didn't realize how hungry I was," she exclaimed happily, sitting up in bed with a plateful of crumbs on her lap. "That was just yummy. It always tastes better when someone else makes it, don't you think?"

Willie, who stood by her bedside while the doctor packed up, nodded.

"I brought you this," he said softly, pulling something from his coat pocket. "It's almost new. My mom, she packed away my baby stuff. I got it out for you." With great purpose, he laid a silver rattle on the bed beside Darla.

"Why, that's just the nicest thing ever. Lana will just love this little be-bop thingy. She can shake it while she dances," Darla said happily, turning the rattle in her hand. "Thank you a lot, Willie."

"Sure."

"And thanks for calling Mr. Weathersberg for me. I don't know what I would have done if he hadn't gotten ahold of Doc Stone."

"Um, it was me that got Dr. Stone, Miss Darla. And he woulda come sooner if it weren't for the storm."

Darla stopped toying with the rattle and stared. "What about Mr. Weatherston?"

"I didn't exactly talk to him. He didn't answer. Some lady talked to me and said she would take care of everything. But I'm the only one talked to Doc Stone. You can ask him."

Darla didn't ask.

Thirty-One

The Scottish Highlands
September

"What was I thinking?" Rebecca stuck her loaded toothbrush into her mouth and attacked her teeth with fury. "Rum!" She nearly gagged herself with the brush, scrubbing the foul taste from her tongue. Angry with herself for getting up late, she realized she'd probably missed breakfast. Yet her chagrin was more about her behavior of the night before than just missing a plate of blood pudding and eggs.

"Stupid," she muttered, then rinsed her mouth and spit the water into the sink. "Stupid, stupid, stupid."

She dressed quickly and left her room, determined to at least get a cup of hot java.

The staff kitchen buzzed with warmth and laughter. It didn't take her but a moment to notice Matt sitting on a barstool beside the butcher block table in the corner, merriment in his eyes.

"Well, look what the wind blew in," he commented, getting off the stool. "You can sit here, if you'd like."

"I can stand, thank you. I just need a cup of coffee."

So complete was her focus on Matt, she didn't notice Angus sitting at the long kitchen table. "Good mornin'," he said, nodding his head politely.

"Oh! Good morning to you, Angus."

"I was just tellin' Mr. McFarralone, here, about some places you might want to be seein' before you go back to the U.S."

"Mr. *Mc*Farralone?" Rebecca turned a questioning eye in Matt's direction, lifting a steaming cup to her lips. "I see."

Matt grinned. "I thought we might take a walk up the road a piece. Maybe take a picnic lunch along."

241

"If ya ask real nice like, you might get a coupla bicycles to borrow, as well," Angus suggested. "Most of our guests are the generous sort."

She wobbled at first, but after a few minutes, Rebecca made good on the adage about never forgetting how to ride a bike. She quickly caught up with Matt and kept pace alongside him as they pedaled north.

The exercise worked like a tonic. The crisp air, startlingly blue sky, and the clean oxygen filling her lungs were just what she needed. By the time they got to their destination, a roadside glen five miles north of the castle, Rebecca felt entirely renewed, the rum and the hiccups forgotten.

Matt spread the blanket and Rebecca opened the basket the kitchen had prepared for them.

"As long as it's not haggis," Matt commented, sitting cross-legged on the blanket.

"Not quite the Scot you profess to be, eh?" Rebecca teased. "But can't say I blame you. I've got a powerful hankering for a taco, myself."

"I could go for some *carne asada*. When we get back, I'll take you to a place in L.A. you will love."

"Yeah? And I would be in Los Angeles because…?"

"Because. Well. My client is turning eighty-eight and throwing a massive birthday party for himself. It's quite an accomplishment, lasting that long. I thought you'd like to go along. Maybe we can talk him into the lighthouse story."

"Do I have to bring him a big gift or something?"

"Your own lovely presence would be enough."

"Is it fancy? He's wealthy, right?"

"Oh, yeah. Yes, and yes. Not a jeans-and-sandals affair."

"Sounds like fun. But I don't need to badger him about the lighthouse. I think I do need to put the whole deal behind me. There's something not quite right about doing that story."

Matt took a bite from his chicken sandwich and frowned. When he'd swallowed, he nodded. "Something's not quite right about the lighthouse itself. Don't know about you, but I got the willies being inside. Especially in the bedroom."

Rebecca looked away, remembering the disquiet she'd felt. "I don't know. Maybe I'm making it all up, but I felt something in there, too." She turned back to Matt, looked him in the eye. "I have to tell you something, Matt. Because you came clean to me last night, I have to be square with you about something I did."

"Worse than the Denise thing?"

"Well, sort of. Before the...Denise thing." Rebecca squirmed, adjusted her position. "I broke into the lighthouse and walked around in there. By myself. In May."

Matt registered surprise but said nothing.

Rebecca held up a hand, as if to stop him from making a judgment. "All I did was walk around and take a few snaps. Nothing different from when we went, except...I don't know whether to tell you about this or not. You'll think I'm crazy."

"Already do." Matt leaned forward, pulled a stray strand of hair away from her lips.

"Fair enough. It happened in the bedroom. I saw that cradle, wanted a photo of it. It seemed so out of place, so new for everything else to be so old. I put my camera up..." she gestured with her hands, as if holding a real camera. "Looked through the viewfinder...and I saw a baby."

Matt stared. "You saw a baby. In the cradle?"

"Yes. When the shutter snapped, there was a baby in the cradle, staring at me, with–with its hand up in the air. I took three pictures in quick succession, then I went to look inside with my own eyes and–" Rebecca again looked away. "The cradle was empty. Later, when I looked at the photos, the cradle was empty there, too." She turned back, leaned closer. "But I saw a real live baby in that bed. I know what I saw."

Matt licked his lips.

"I knew you'd think I was crazy."

"Do you believe in ghosts?" Matt asked suddenly, all traces of humor gone from his face.

"I–I never have. Always thought it was a bunch of malarkey. But...but there's more. I think I was visited," she went on, uncertainty tingeing her voice. "And I think it must have been Darla Foster. The actress in the movie. Her ghost, or her spirit, or whatever. First in my car, then my hotel room...and I saw her on the beach. From the pier. She looked up at me. And–" Rebecca lifted a hand to her forehead. "She blew me a kiss."

"Whew. That's weird. My total experience has been the watching of all three *Ghostbuster* movies, and that flick with Demi Moore and Swayze and Whoopie Goldberg." Matt smiled briefly at her, put his hand on her knee. "But no. I don't think you're crazy. Something strange happened to me, too." He took a moment to describe the bizarre vision he had while watching *Cape Seduction*. "She looked right at me. I mean, it scared me."

"They say she went to France and never came back. That maybe she met with bad luck over there. But she was so young. She had parents in L.A., a boyfriend, a promising career…"

Matt nodded solemnly. "Maybe we should go back."

"To the castle?"

"To the lighthouse."

His words struck a dull chord, and a tingle went up her spine. Yet she nodded. She'd known all along they would go back.

They spent the afternoon bicycling around the area, exploring abandoned ruins and enjoying the last of the purple Scottish heather clinging in patches to the gentle hillsides around them. Matt spoke no more of the lighthouse, but the morbid intrigue stayed with him. He was encouraged, and yet filled with dread, after hearing Rebecca describe her unexplainable encounters with the departed. For surely, whether she met her demise in Europe or California, Darla Foster was dead. Why she would choose them, and now, to haunt the living transcended anything he'd ever thought about. He couldn't quite wrap his mind around that one.

But Rebecca Burke was someone whom he could quite easily wrap himself around. Even now, watching her run from a honeybee, he delighted in just being with her.

"Matt! Help me! I'm gonna get stung!"

"I'll save you," he called, tackling her to the ground and covering her body with his own. "Bring on the bumble bees and hornets! I'll protect you, Maid Rebecca!"

She panted from the run. The proximity of her enticing mouth proved too much for Matt, and he captured her lips in a kiss full of longing and affection. Rebecca's arms slowly climbed across his back and encircled him in a firm embrace. Matt broke off the kiss, then planted a quick buss to her cheek.

"I thought you'd never get around to kissing me again," she said, breathless, allowing her fingers to play with his hair.

"I thought you'd never let me kiss you again. But if you're into kissing, there's more to come."

"I like the sound of more."

They didn't want to go back. They'd come very close to making love in the heather but agreed the pillow top bed in Rebecca's suite would suit them much better, and with that thought in mind, they climbed onto their loaner bicycles and pedaled back to the castle. Anticipation of their growing passion fueled their energy as they rode, stealing glances at one another along the way.

Of course, dinner was about to be served when they arrived, leaving them just enough time for a handful of kisses and longing looks while they washed up. They barely tasted the hearty beef stew and homemade scones, the thick, hand-churned creamery butter and steamed berry pudding.

Angus stopped Matt in the hallway after their meal. "Miss Burke seems a fair bit happier now that you've joined her. Glad I am, for I was thinkin' I might be obliged to ask her to stay awhile. Couldna let her go home from a place as wonderful as this bein' so unhappy."

"She was unhappy?" Matt asked, still reluctant to believe Rebecca cared.

Angus grinned. "Weke up and smell the coffee, m' man." He clapped Matt on the back and went on his way.

The chambermaid had created a toasty blaze in the fireplace. Rebecca played cool at first, making small talk about her flight home and whether or not they'd be flying together. Matt approached where she sat on the footboard bench at the end of the bed.

"You need to know something about me," he said, reaching down and cupping her chin in his hand. "Last Christmas, I broke up with a girl I'd been with for three years. Before that, I dated a few girls, but I'm not a go-around guy."

"A go-around guy? Well I'm not a go-around girl. Whatever that is."

"Good." He bent down, kissed her fully on the mouth, and she seemed to go soft under his touch. Slowly she lowered herself backward onto the bed, all the while managing to stay lip-locked with Matt. She began unbuttoning his shirt.

"Today was my first official 'date' in over two years," she said huskily, now pulling his shirt open.

"I feel honored," he whispered against her lips, his hands hurriedly assisting with the removal of her sweater.

"Wait till you feel this bed," she murmured, rolling to the side and tugging down the thick featherbed duvet. "Mmm. Let me–" she began, undoing the button on her jeans.

"No, let *me*," Matt countered, expertly negotiating her zipper and sliding the pants from her legs before taking care of the rest of his own clothes.

"This *is* nice," he agreed, pulling the fluffy coverlet over them and taking Rebecca into his arms. "I have to admit," he said, grabbing at her bottom lip with his teeth. "You had me at *Denise*, but I like you better as Rebecca. And don't go and stiffen up on me," he added when she did, in fact, harden under his touch. "It's history. It's funny history, now. And you're not a go-around girl, and that suits me just fine."

"Okay," Rebecca said, then reached across Matt to turn off the bedside lamp. In the remaining firelight, she unhooked her bra and pulled it away.

"Ouch! Dammit!' she cried, sitting up and dragging the bra back to her front. "It's caught–the hook is caught in my hair!"

Matt sat up and took the offending lingerie from her, painstakingly untangling the strand of hair wound around the bra hook. "There we go. Matthew McRomance to the rescue."

Rebecca rubbed at her stinging scalp, then let the pout fall away from her lips. She moved closer, pressed her breasts against his chest and threaded her legs around his. "First you saved me from the bee. I kinda like this shining armor thing you got goin' on."

"My pleasure, Madame McSexier-Than-All-Get-Out."

"Me? Sexy? Surely you–" Her words dissolved against his mouth as he again lost control of his desire to kiss her into next Tuesday.

With heartfelt regrets, Rebecca said her goodbyes to Angus and the staff of Carbisdale Castle on Sunday morning. But as much as she wanted to stay, she wanted to return to the United States. But *where* in the U.S.?

Matt remained quiet on the bus ride back to Edinburgh, and she wondered if he contemplated the same thing. Their newfound feelings for each other brought with them the uncertainty of practicality, for while Matt moved easily between Northern and Southern California, adding Phoenix to the mix would be a challenge. And even if Rebecca could work from Los Angeles, she had her father to consider, who would no more think of moving to L.A. than he would Siberia. Could they swing a long-distance romance?

For the time being, they would first return to Los Angeles so they could show up for the gala event Matt was obligated to attend. Then, Rebecca would go back to Phoenix and submit her photos and Christmas story to Pat. After that, they would just have to figure out a way to be together.

Thirty-Two

Los Angeles, California
March 1949

"**W**hy do you have to go now? It's always at the most inopportune time. I don't want to be alone when the baby comes, Jordan. Surely you can understand *that*." Cecelia slammed the car door and started out of the garage. Jordan lifted two bags of groceries from the trunk.

"Look, Cec, the baby isn't due until April or May. The doctor says you're doing fine and are right on schedule. Nothing is going to happen while I'm gone. I just have to go back to Northern California and finish up my mother's property deal. I have to be there for the closing."

Cecelia turned her back, continued walking toward the side door of the house. "Of course, you do. Mother always gets top billing."

"It's not true, and you know it. Look, darling, it's only two days. I'll be in touch by telephone. You should take some time out with your mother. Buy some more baby goods. How about a prom dress? Did you get that yet?" Jordan dangled the keys from his hand while still carrying the bags, and Cecelia took them to unlock the door.

"Very funny. But I was thinking, I didn't get a snowsuit yet. The baby will be old enough to take to Big Bear this winter."

Jordan dropped the bags onto the kitchen table. "Do they even sell such things this late in the season?"

"Not really," Cecelia mumbled. "Promise me you'll call?"

"Of course, I will, darling."

It had been close. He'd already bought his tickets and had been sweating bullets since his conversation with Dr. Stone yesterday afternoon. His daughter had been born; Darla had gone through labor, alone and miserable in that God-forsaken, icy cold lighthouse. As he went about putting away the groceries, he tried not to think about what wrath Darla would bring upon him when he arrived. He hadn't been there in a month.

What would she need? What could he take? Would she demand to be removed from the island, now that the baby had arrived? So jumbled were his thoughts, he barely heard Cecelia's voice as she jabbered on about baby clothes.

"So, we have everything all set up for when the baby arrives, right?" he asked suddenly.

"Why, of course we do."

"Like what things do we have? I'm just…curious, you know. In case we missed anything."

Cecelia raised her eyebrows. "Nice of you to be concerned."

"So, a crib, diapers, pins, powder…"

"You want a list?"

"No. I'm sure you have everything under control."

He went to his room to pack. It didn't take him long.

"I'll call you tomorrow, darling. You take care, don't exert yourself."

"I'll be okay. I can always call Daddy."

No sooner had the cab pulled away from the curb than Cecelia dialed the phone. Impatient, she nearly hung up, but her call was answered on the sixth ring.

"It's Cecelia. You need to straighten up and listen to me. It's important. It's about Darla Foster."

For once, Jordan didn't fret over the airplane ride. He was too wrapped in thought, too worried about how the next two days would unfold to be concerned about air turbulence. He recalled, with sadness, the phone calls he'd made from the airport. The Johnsons, Lester A. and his wife, would be waiting for their new baby girl at the Arcata Airport. She would arrive via helicopter. He could only hope the helicopter pilot wouldn't be early, and his own flight and subsequent bus ride and boat crossing wouldn't be late.

They seemed to be a good couple, with strong values and ethics. The husband had a decent job, married to a wonderful housewife, purportedly a good cook. Childless, but unable to adopt through normal channels due to Lester's police record: he'd stolen a live turkey at eighteen and given it to his starving family for dinner. He'd also run away from home once or twice. Didn't look good on an adoption application.

Jordan looked quickly out the window, trying to dismiss the thought of giving up his newborn daughter to strangers, never to see her again. Darla would be heartbroken; no, devastated. Maybe. But if he could get her to see the value to her career, the roles that waited for her right now in Hollywood...especially after her mysterious absence. Everyone was talking about her. She could be the next Mary Pickford.

He pulled an antacid from his pocket, unwrapped and popped it into his mouth. It would all be over soon, he reminded himself. The baby would be safely placed; Darla would return home, to the great relief of her parents and to any number of new fans who'd fallen for her in *Cape Seduction*. She would get lots of offers...while he, himself, would be welcoming a new son or daughter at home with Cecelia. Jordan felt a twinge of discomfort. Cec had a stranglehold on him now, with the baby coming. He'd likely never spend time with Darla again.

He let his mind drift, back to the summer nights they spent on the beach near Crescent City. Darla's playful games and pouting lips, her appetite for sex and penchant for trouble. She'd bewitched him, and he could hardly bear the thought of not having her in his life. Even when they'd returned to Hollywood, the hours spent in "their" room at the Chateau Marmont had been magical for him. Of course, it was that magic that had gotten him into the mess he was now in.

With a deep sigh, Jordan sank lower into the window seat he occupied. For he wasn't only losing his daughter, he was quite possibly losing the love of his life.

Darla held her nose with one hand and the cloth diaper in the other, carrying it to the bathroom and dumping its contents into the toilet. "Ew-wee! Lana made a stinky one," she called back to her daughter, who lay in the middle of the double bed with pillows around her. "Do you think you could make them a little more solid, sweetie pie? These smeary ones are hard for Mama to clean up!"

251

Darla picked Lana up and cuddled her. "You are just the bestest little girl, you know that? And it's time to eat now, Mama can tell..." She sat down and opened her blouse, settling Lana against her to nurse. "I've been thinkin', sweetie girl. I'm not real sure we actually need a daddy around. I mean, after all, we've done pretty darn good these two weeks. Daddies are good for some things, like a good turn in the sack, but unless they are with you and help you with money and chores, well, what good are they? My dad works real hard, but he's never home to help your Grandma much. He's a riveter. He works on big airplanes in Burbank."

Lana's eyes fixed on her mother's face, and Darla smiled. "Your daddy, your *real* daddy, he's not such a bad guy, I guess. But I'll let you decide for yourself when you're older. Deal? We might even get to pick out a different father for you, if we're lucky."

After a time, she put the baby on her shoulder and patted her until she burped, then switched her to the other breast. "Wait'll you see all the cute little dresses Grandma Helen will make for you! She made some real nice ones for me when I was a little bit like you. She'll be good to you, too, when Mama's away working on pictures. And someday, you'll see me on the big screen, when you're old enough. And you'll say, 'Lookie there! That's my mama up there!'" Darla giggled. "Yeah. That will be one fine day."

Soon, Lana fell asleep, and Darla tucked her into her cradle and covered her with the blanket. She went to the kitchen and poured herself a talk glass of milk, sat down to read January's *Photoplay Magazine*. She turned quickly to the column, "What Should I Do? Your Problems Answered by Claudette Colbert" and read the first reader's question.

"Oh, this is just plain silly. So what if her husband is too serious. Whose fault is that? She needs to make him laugh more." She perused the next question, then turned the page. "So, who made Claudette Colbert a psycholotrist, anyway? I'll bet she couldn't solve my problem. 'Dear Miss Colbert: I am a twenty-one-year-old mother of a new baby, and my boyfriend, who's actually married to the worst bitch in Hollywood, has locked me away in a gray tower in the middle of the ocean. Do you suggest I stay with this lout?'"

Darla giggled, kept turning pages. "'Ronald Reagan...seen at Mocambo with Shirley Ballard.' Can't figure why the heck stupid Jane Wyman let go of that one...Oh! Here he is again with Dorothy Shay. What a guy...'" She lingered over an ad for Helene Curtis Crème Shampoo, which promised billows of foam instantly, even in hard water. It sounded so luxurious.

"Oh! Oh!" She sat upright, poring over a story on Lana Turner by Louella Parsons. "'These days, she is more interested in diapers than diamonds.' Hey, just like me! Wow!"

She started to get sleepy. Lana had been awake during the night, every night, since her birth. Darla thought she might take a little nap while Lana slept. She closed the magazine and stretched, yawned. Then she heard the door to the outside slam shut in the engine room.

She picked up a small iron skillet from the stove and stood at the ready beside the kitchen door. It wasn't Willie, for he always announced himself as he ascended the stairs. So, when Jordan stepped into the room with a large bag slung over his shoulder, she nearly dropped the pan on the floor. Instead, she stared, unable to say anything for the first time in ages.

"Darla! Oh, my sweet, I just got the news! Where is she? Are you all right?"

Darla put down the skillet and gestured toward the bedroom. "She's asleep. I'd appreciate it if you do *not* wake her up."

He tried to hug her, but she made herself wooden. He wasn't getting off easily this time. Not after what she'd been through. She turned away from his hurt expression, folded her arms across her chest.

Jordan went to the bedroom and stood peering into the cradle. Darla watched him from the doorway. "What did you name her?"

"If you'd cared enough to pay attention, you would already know that. Her name is Lana Leigh Foster."

He came back to her. "Darla, I am so sorry. You can't imagine the hell I've been going through with Celia. She's become a monster since the pregnancy."

"Become one? Are you blind, or what? She's always been a Frankenstein to me. When are we leaving? Did you drive yourself over here?"

"We need to talk about that. Sit down."

"You sit down. I'm all packed. Have been for thirteen days. Lana is packed, also."

"Well, that's good because we are going today."

Darla dropped her arms to her sides. "Honest injun? Today?"

"Yes. But please sit down, dear heart. I need to explain some things."

"Okay." Hesitant, wary, Darla sat across from him and automatically flipped open her magazine. "What's the deal? Because I sense there is some kind of deal I'm not going to like, right?"

"Lana will leave first, in a helicopter, that's coming even as we talk. Now, now, before you get all huffed up... it's far too dangerous to take an infant in a dinghy. I've commissioned a private pilot, with a woman to help, and they'll take the baby to the mainland and hold her there until we can... pick her up, you know, anonymously. We can't risk–"

"No. Lana and I go together."

"We can't risk your being seen together. That's the whole point. One person gets the idea you've had a baby, and your career is over, my love. That's really important to you, right? Why, right now, there are offers waiting on the table for you in Hollywood. Everyone's asking, 'When will Darla Foster return?' You will be everywhere, even on those news programs they've started having on television!"

Darla lowered her eyes. What Jordan was saying made a sort of twisted sense. If they could get Lana to her mother's house without anyone knowing, Mother could tell people she adopted a new baby. *Yes, it might work.*

"I don't like it. But I guess it could be okay," Darla murmured, still not looking Jordan in the eye. "And I'll leave with you, in the boat?"

"Yes. Of course, Mrs. Weatherton. Is she–Lana–really all packed up?"

"Nearly. She's just been fed."

"Excellent. I think I hear the helicopter now."

All the antacids on the planet couldn't fix the sick feeling in Jordan's stomach as he watched Darla saying goodbye to Lana.

"Where did you get those supplies?" he asked, as Lana rechecked the pink flowered diaper bag a third time.

"Mr. Willie picked them up for me. But then, you wouldn't know that, since he couldn't get you on the phone."

"The boy tried to call me? When?" Jordan's angst increased tenfold as Darla shrugged.

"Oh, about the time my guts were splitting apart, perhaps? Two weeks ago, give or take a few agonizing minutes?"

"Where did he call me?"

"Lower your voice. You're upsetting your daughter."

The baby began to cry. Darla kissed her one last time, then handed her to the woman who would hold her during the flight. "Don't worry, Lana-bean, Mama will be there soon to get you back." Her eyes reddened, and she looked away, wiping her cheeks on her sleeve. "All her stuff is in the bag. She oughta be fine until we meet up again."

The woman exchanged looks with Jordan, then turned and went out the door onto the catch deck. Darla went to the closest window and looked out at the helicopter.

"It feels bad, Jordie. It feels like something isn't right. I don't like it."

Jordan moved in behind her, embraced her shoulders. "It will all work out fine. Lana will be fine."

"I just feel—" Darla's voice broke over a sob. "Just feel like I might not ever see her again. Oh, Jordie, tell me it isn't so!" She turned, hugged Jordan with a fierceness that scared him. Behind her, the helicopter lifted off the caisson.

"If that ever happened, you would survive, my love. You are a survivor. Look—look what you've done here, for four months!"

Darla pulled back, turned sorrow-filled eyes up to Jordan's face. "It's true, isn't it?" she said softly. "Lana's going away forever, isn't she?"

"Whatever makes you think that?" Jordan lied, now turning away from the unbearably betrayed expression on Darla's face. "Now, let's get your things and get out of here. Oh! I almost forgot!

I brought you a little gift. I thought you might like something new to wear home."

Darla sniffed, wiped her face with her fingers. She took the wrapped paper bundle and untied the string. A red silk dress tumbled out.

She'd nearly finished packing. "I can't wait...I can't wait to see Mother again," she murmured, walking to her bedroom as if in fog.

She took her time changing, collecting her last items, looking at the two rooms where she'd spent most of the last few months alone. The lonely days and nights, the bitter cold, the wet floors... and the last week, spent cuddling in bed with her newborn daughter.

"Oh no," she exclaimed, reaching across the bed for a forgotten item. "Lana's rattle! I almost forgot it!" She picked the silver bauble off the bed and hugged it to her chest.

"Here, give it to me. I'll put it in my pocket."

"Okay, well, I guess that's all. I'm ready."

"Do you want this magazine?"

"No. It will remind me of this wicked place."

As Jordan picked up Darla's suitcase, the sound of the engine room door flying open stopped him in his tracks.

Thirty-Three

Hollywood, California
September

Halfway across the Atlantic, Rebecca changed her mind. When they landed at LAX, Matt helped her get a standby flight to Phoenix, and they parted ways with a long, lingering kiss.

"Call me tonight. Call me when you get home," Matt amended, squeezing her hand as she glanced nervously at the gate. "I know. Go. Be safe. Call me!"

"I will, I will! You be safe, too," she called back, then dashed into the jetway and down the ramp.

She fidgeted on the flight home. So much had changed since she'd left Arizona barely a week before. It wasn't just rectifying things with Matt; a whole new relationship, a potentially serious one, had her head spinning, an exciting prospect where before hid emptiness. It felt good and downright scary.

Her father waited just outside security. She could tell he was bursting with things to say but held his tongue in view of her fatigue and preoccupation. There would soon be enough time to talk.

Later, they lingered over dinner.

"Leaving again tomorrow, you said?"

"Yeah. Matt's got a big important party to go to, and he invited me to go along. Sounds like it will be fun. Glamorous, even."

"Need to get something to wear?"

"Nope," Rebecca said, getting up to clear the table. "I have the dark red taffeta I wore to Jenna's wedding last summer. One reason I came home, to get the dress and stuff. It should be fine."

"You look stunning in that dress. You'll really knock his socks off."

Rebecca paused at the sink, turned. "You really liked him, didn't you, Dad?"

"Yep. He's a pretty okay guy. I guess he made a couple of bad choices, but it sounds like you both got off on the wrong foot with each other. His heart's in the right place."

It better be, Rebecca thought. Because she already knew she was losing hers.

Jack picked her up at the airport the next day.

"Matt's just getting out of a deposition right now. Traffic in West L.A. is an absolute zoo," he told her, as they inched along northbound on the San Diego Freeway.

"Well, thanks again. It's nice to have the back up."

"For Matt, I'd do it even if I didn't owe him."

"You owe him? As in, monetarily? Oh, I'm sorry. Forget I asked."

Jack laughed. "Money wasn't the object. He counselled me when I had to challenge my ex a while back. She tried to take my son away to Zanzibar or something. She broke a court order. I needed some muscle to go after her. Matt stepped in and it was all over."

"So, you've been married before?"

"Not exactly. I use the term 'ex' loosely. We weren't married. We had a kid; we split up. I married Maddie, *we* got custody of Duncan. *She* got visitation rights. Before she could appeal, she had an accident and passed away."

"Wow. Sounds like a mess. I'd like to meet your family sometime."

"It's bound to happen. You been married?"

"Oh, Lord, no. Been the maid of honor a few times, yeah."

"Well, at our wedding, Maddie's *ex's daughter* was the matron of honor. How's that for weirdsville?"

Rebecca liked Jack. Always so upbeat, funny, relaxed. "I hope you and Case weren't too mad at me over my stupid stunt," she blurted out.

Jack chuckled. "We'll find a way to get back at you."

He took her to Matt's house in the canyon and let her in. "He oughta be home within an hour, I'd say. Said to tell you to make yourself at home, make yourself a drink, get naked and wait for him in bed."

Rebecca turned a startled face toward Jack, who couldn't hold a straight expression.

"Okay, so he said the part about making yourself at home. I kind of embellished it a little."

"You *are* bad," Rebecca scolded with a smile. "Would you like something to drink?"

"Naw, I gotta git. You kids have fun at the par-tay. Should be a gas."

Rebecca wandered until she found the guest bedroom and hung up her dress. It hadn't wrinkled much on the trip. Checking the clock, she decided she would go ahead and shower to give herself plenty of time to get ready. She was used to sharing a hot water tank at her dad's and didn't want Matt to run out of the hot stuff when he showered later.

After her shower, she put on a robe she found in the closet and toured the house, delighting at the small effects that made up Matt's home. It wasn't overly cluttered, she noticed. Photos on the wall, the mantle, the piano, all displaying himself with a couple she presumed were his parents, famous clients, various dogs.

No pictures of girls. No dates, prom pictures or candid-but-posed couple snapshots. Miss December must really be out of sight, out of mind, Rebecca thought. *Unless, of course, he removed them all last night.*

She'd no reason to distrust him. In fact, the dust on the piano and mantle hadn't been disturbed in some time. She was staring at a family portrait when he walked in from the garage.

"Hey! You made it in one piece." He crossed the living room and wrapped her in a bear hug, then kissed her soundly. "Jolly Jack pick you up on time? Any trouble at the airport? Gosh it's great to see you...I love the robe."

Rebecca was struck speechless by his attention.

"You didn't shower without me?" He tugged on the cuff of her robe.

She giggled. He smiled. "I'm sorry I wasn't there to pick you up."

"It's okay," she said at last, enjoying his banter. "Jack is a sweetheart."

"That he is. And about the only one of my friends I'd trust with my valuables."

After a fifteen-minute, stand-up necking session, they parted to get ready for the festivity. Rebecca took extra pains to apply her makeup and curl her hair just right. The dyed-to-match pumps looked perfect and nearly new; her matching jewelry, elegant and appropriate for a Hollywood soirée.

He waited in the living room. The black, modern cut tuxedo did justice to the body built by laboring all summer at the construction site. But most attractive of all, Rebecca thought, was the soft sigh that escaped when he saw her.

He tilted his head, shook it slightly. "Words rarely escape a talker like me," he murmured. "But they've all high-tailed it right now." He took her hand, kissed it. "The other ladies there tonight will likely vote you right off the island."

Rebecca felt herself coloring. His praise, unexpected, thrilled her, coming from someone other than her father.

"You clean up pretty nice yourself," she said softly, leaning close for a kiss. They delayed as long as they could, until at last Matt cleared his throat.

"We'd better get going. I can't be late."

"I thought you were a guest?" she asked, grabbing her handbag off the piano.

"I am."

A valet took the Cayenne after helping Rebecca from the car. Matt took her arm and led her into the wide, formal foyer. It was a warm night, so Rebecca wore no wrap. The mansion blazed with festive lighting as hordes of well-to-do partiers sipped, laughed, and gossiped. Matt got them each a glass of wine, then took her through the house and into the back yard where the pool flickered with floating candles. Eighty-eight of them.

"His idea, I'm sure," Matt said, shaking his head. "Oh, here's someone I'd like you to meet." He took Rebecca by the hand and led her to the outdoor bar, where an attractive, mature woman chatted with other guests.

"This is my mother, Eleanor Farralone. Mom, this is Rebecca Burke."

"Why, what a lovely surprise, Mattie. How nice to meet you, Miss Burke." Matt's mother held out a gloved hand.

Immediately self-conscious, Rebecca shook her hand, then subtly pulled her bare hands behind her back. "The pleasure is mine," she said softly.

"What an exquisite gown," Eleanor commented. "Is it vintage? Versace? It looks like one I had years ago. I'd never fit into it now, of course...Have you introduced her to your grandfather, yet?" she asked, turning back to Matt.

"On my way, Mom. Just got here. So, if you'll excuse us..."

But his mother had already caught the eye of another old friend. Rebecca whispered into Matt's ear. "You didn't tell me your family would be here!"

"You didn't ask. Come on. Let's meet the old bastard."

Rebecca didn't have time to register her surprise before Matt whisked her back into the house and to the library, where their host showed off a large-scale painting of his late wife. He turned when the couple entered, the sound of Rebecca's heals on the parquet floor tipping him off.

"Why, Matthew! It's about time you got here." He lifted his cane, pointed it, his expression critical as he eyed Matt and his guest.

"Keep your shirt on, old man. I have someone I'd like you to meet. Rebecca, this is my grandfather, the illustrious, infamous and obscenely wealthy Mr. Jordan Kent. Granddad, this is...Miss Rebecca Burke, my girlfriend."

The fire in the older man's eyes faded, and he put the cane down, leaned against it. "Burke, you say? How...How do you do?" He extended his hand, shook Rebecca's briefly while his eyes examined every aspect of her face. His seemed to grow pale right before their eyes.

"You okay, Jordan?"

"I'm just fine. Just..."

Rebecca felt as if she were under a microscope. Her hand went to her throat, fingered the jeweled necklace which seemed to grow tighter around her neck. She could hardly breathe. "It is a bit warm in here." She turned to Matt. "You should have told me you had such a famous grandfather. I'm a big fan of yours, Mr. Kent."

Jordan seemed to recover a bit of his aplomb. "You aren't old enough to even know I exist," he said, stepping closer to Rebecca. "May I ask a question, my dear? Where did you get that exquisite necklace?"

Rebecca looked down at the rubies held loosely by her fingers. "My mother left it to me. It was given to her by her mother, my grandmother."

"It's stunning on you. But pales in the presence of your beauty," Jordan said, his eyes still fixed on the necklace. "Quite valuable, I would imagine."

"I've never bothered to have it appraised, but I'm told they're real rubies. They don't cut them this way anymore. I've often wondered how a farm girl like my Gramma Clare got her hands on it. But I'll never know," Rebecca finished, wishing she hadn't said quite so much.

"Well, in any case, it's a tantalizing piece."

Matthew shuffled his feet. "It *is* hot in here. It's September, for cryin' out loud. Why do you have the fireplace going?"

"Because this is my house, and I was cold. Now, go mingle. So nice meeting you, Miss Rebecca Burke."

Rebecca nodded at Jordan's slight bow, grasped Matthew's hand and nearly pulled him out of the library.

Once they'd reached a quiet corner, she turned on him. "Your grandfather is your mysterious 'client'? Why didn't you tell me it was Jordan Kent? Jordan Kent! The star of *Cape Seduction!* He owns that damned lighthouse?!"

"Settle down, spitfire. Yeah, he's the guy. I don't tell people, not at first. He doesn't like people to know."

"Your mother, Eleanor, is his daughter?"

"So I hear."

"And you said your grandmother is dead?"

"Last time I looked."

Rebecca blew out a breath, causing her wispy bangs to flutter. "Unbelievable. So, he knew Darla. Darla Foster. The ghost! You're connected to her, Matt. Don't you see? He was connected, and now you're connected to me! That's why, that's why we're all involved in this deal."

Matt stared into Rebecca's eyes. "You might have something there, darlin'. You just might."

"Well I don't know about you, but I could use a refill."

They took their drinks back outside and mingled with other guests around the pool. Rebecca, polite and chatty, enjoyed meeting some of Matt's clients and friends. His mother was particularly friendly and seemed to genuinely like Rebecca. Yet Rebecca couldn't get the image of Jordan Kent's surprised expression out of her mind or the startling revelation that Matthew was somehow connected with Darla.

Just before they were to leave, Jordan sought Matt out and asked him to rejoin him in the library.

"I won't be a minute, Bec. Just hang out with the A-listers while I'm gone." He kissed her cheek, an action that sent a thrill throughout Rebecca's body. As she watched Matt go into the library and close the door behind him, she wondered what Jordan had to say to him.

"Break it off."

"What? You can't be serious."

"I am deadly serious. You cannot have a serious relationship with that girl. Trust me."

"Trust you? On what basis? You don't even know Rebecca. You'd never even heard of her up until a couple of months ago."

"I know enough. You continue this affair, and heartbreak will be on you like a cancer. It will eat you up."

Matt smiled, shook his head. He stuffed his hands into his pants pockets, shuffled around. "I'll take it under advisement. Anything else?"

"That should be enough. I'm serious, Matthew. This woman cannot... Dammit. You can't possibly understand."

"You know, I'm getting pretty sick of your telling me what I can and can't understand. I grew up a long time ago, Pops. I happen to care a lot about Rebecca. In fact, I think I just might be in love with her. If you think for a moment I'm going to walk away based on some superstitious nonsense, you're crazier than you look."

"There are things happening that—"

"Are you going to start with those things-I-don't-know again bullshit? Because if there's something I should know about Rebecca, spit it out now or shut the fuck up!"

Jordan grew still, stared hard at Matt before turning away without a word.

"What did he want to say to you?" Rebecca asked on the way back to Matt's house.

"Nothing. Nothing worth talking about. Just the ramblings of an old man getting ready to check out."

"You think he'll die soon? He seems really spry."

Matt merely grunted. He'd let the old man get to him, and he regretted their confrontation, the angry words. His grandfather was just getting old and senile. That had to be it. He imagined things, things about a woman he didn't know and couldn't possibly have anything against. Rebecca had done nothing to incur Jordan Kent's wrath.

As if he needed to make it up to her, Matt took extra care in loving her that night when she came to his bed. This wasn't some ancient castle in Scotland, where the setting had pumped up the volume on their romance. This was his own bedroom in his comfortable hillside home; his own queen-sized bed with his favorite, worn-soft sheets and Costco candles burning on the nightstand. His grandfather's words had threatened him, threatened the new love growing in his heart, and he was prepared to defend his love. Now, more than ever, he knew he would do all he could to cement his relationship with Rebecca.

Thirty-Four

"So, you're saying, if Jordan should ever father another child, that child would also be entitled to a share of our...assets." Cecelia leaned back in her seat, crossed her ankles in annoyance. She could no longer cross her legs due to the size of her belly.

"That's correct. If he either acknowledged the child, or it was somehow proven to be his offspring," the attorney said. "It could...get untidy."

"I understand." Cecelia stood. "Thank you for your time. You've been a great help."

"My pleasure, Mrs. Kent."

Cecelia drove herself home, pensive, concerned. She knew well where her husband had gone, and why. She hoped Russell had taken her advice and followed Jordan to Northern California. She'd debated telling him Darla had given birth, opting to let him find out for himself. With luck, he'd created considerable trouble for Jordan and his slutty paramour.

Her father waited for her at the house.

"So, where the hell's that husband of yours?"

"On a trip up north. His mother has some business he needs to tend to," Cecelia explained, pouring Harvey Bregman a cup of coffee. "He'll be back in a day or two."

"Any news on the whereabouts of Darla Foster?"

"Who? Oh, her. No, last I heard, she was off in Europe somewhere doing a picture. Probably some nasty film."

"You don't like her, do you?" Harv asked, bringing the coffee cup to his lips.

"No, I don't. She's a user, Daddy. She's not above doing anything to get ahead."

"Name me one big named actress who is."

Cecelia turned away, stirring sugar into her own cup. "June Allyson. Doris Day. There's two."

Harv grunted. "There are always one or two goodies. Darla has talent, pizzazz. I'm hoping to cast her in *Give Me the Moon* when she gets back. *If* she comes back, that is."

"I wouldn't count on it," Cecelia replied, more to herself than her father. "Got a cig?"

Harv pulled a pack out of his pocket, extended it to her. "So, you got a name picked out?"

"Mother likes Lucinda for a girl, Lucy, for short...but I'm leaning toward Eleanor. And for a boy, Harvey, of course."

Her father shrugged, sniffed. "Whatever you think, Princess. But the poor kid's gotta live with it all his life."

"Then he'd better hope he's a girl."

Clare Johnson had bitten her nails down to the quick. Waiting for the helicopter to land was agony. What if the baby wasn't on board? Worse, what if she wasn't as described? She squeezed Lester's arm.

"I'm so nervous, Les. Do you think it'll be okay? I'm so afraid someone will find out."

"No one will find out. It's all handled. Weatherton has fixed it. Besides, when we move into our new house next week, no one will even think twice. You're the mom, I'm the pop, and nobody knows anything different."

"I hope you're right. Oh! Look! It's coming!"

The couple watched through the airport window as the helicopter approached, landed. The pilot got out first, then assisted a middle-aged woman carrying a small bundle. Clare turned excitedly to her husband. "She's here. She's really here."

In only a matter of minutes, Clare held her new daughter in her arms.

"Oh, Lester. Isn't she just the sweetest, most beautiful baby in the world?" she cooed, staring down into the baby's face.

"She sure is. Got great skin. Pretty eyes." Lester gestured to the woman who'd handed over the infant. "This hers?" he asked, holding up a pink flowered diaper bag.

"Yes. There are only a few items inside. That's all she has."

Clare held the baby close in the car. The child woke only briefly, then went back to sleep. Darkness prevailed by the time they reached their house on the outskirts of Santa Rosa, California.

The house was nearly all packed up, as they would be moving to Arizona in a couple of days. But the baby's bassinet waited, along with a mobile, a teddy bear and a small baby doll. Clare put the baby in the small bed, then began unpacking the bag.

"Just a few diapers, some lotion...extra diapers pins...a couple of nightshirts. Baby powder, Vaseline. Wait."

"Wait, what?" Lester called from the hallway.

"There's something in this can of powder." Clare pried the lid off of the baby powder tin and stuck her fingers down inside. "What is this?" The powder wasn't quite all gone, but something rattled inside the can. Finally, her fingers were able to pinch the item and pull it out.

"What the Dickens is that? Some kind of teether?"

"Why, I don't know. It looks like...well, it's all covered with powder, but it looks like a necklace. Some kinda red stones. There's a little piece of paper here, too." Clare unfolded the note and blew the powder off. "Says, 'Dear Lana, please keep this for Mama until we are together again. But don't put it in your mouth, you might choke. Love, Mama.' Well, I'll be."

"As if a baby could read," Lester muttered, holding the necklace up to the light.

"As if they were planning to meet again someday," Clare said softly. "It's very sad, isn't it?"

"We'll make sure she gets the necklace when she's grown. For now, we'd best just put it in a safe place."

Clare nodded and dropped the necklace back into the can of powder.

It grew dark while Helen Foster sat at her kitchen table, but she didn't get up to turn on the lights. She'd done the dishes and wiped the counters down. The oven sat cold, for she hadn't thought to make dinner.

The table was void of all except two small pink envelopes. Both postmarked "Paris, France," they held brief, breezy letters from her only child. The police had handed them back, saying Darla's failure to write since November did not constitute a crime. Nothing found in either letter indicated she had any trouble; to the contrary, she was enjoying Paris as any other young girl might. Post-war France, they said, posed no threat to American travelers.

Helen knew better. She knew her daughter, knew she'd never been so far away from home before. Never went more than a few hours without talking to her mother until she'd turned twenty. Even during her location shooting of *Cape Seduction*, Darla had called her every few days.

Her eyes drifted across the shadowed envelopes. Fear crept into her heart, born of a certain, mother's instinct; something was gravely wrong. She'd kept it inside for weeks, hiding her suspicions, only occasionally mentioning to Ted when another week had passed without word from Darla. But then Russell Harrington showed up with reporters, and her resolve broke. She was no longer alone in her fears.

Now, in the dark of her once comfortable kitchen, Helen wept with quiet grief.

Cecelia sat down on the back porch, watched her father wield his club on the small putting green behind his white-columned Beverly Hills mansion. She wasn't feeling well, despite the sunny March morning. Her back was killing her.

"Am I the best, or what?" her father called, after sinking the four-yard putt.

"You are. But I think I'm going to go inside and lie down."

"What's the matter, sweet pea? Not feeling good?"

"No. I'm achy and just...feeling sick."

"Could it be the baby?" Harv approached, leaned his golf club against the porch wall.

"You know I'm not due for another month." But Cecelia pressed a hand to her basketball shaped abdomen, moaned.

"Get your things. I'm taking you to the hospital. Where's your mother?"

Shirley Bregman sat alone in the waiting room, despite the fact her husband sat beside her. She knew, without doubt, the first person her daughter would ask for would be Harv. Most girls longed for the comfort of their mother's touch; Cecelia barely knew her mother, cared little about her life. Shirley had always thought that when Celia eventually became a mother herself, she would finally begin to need her own. Apparently, she was wrong.

The hospital wasn't particularly busy this afternoon. Cecelia's doctor came in periodically with progress reports, and to look anxiously around for Jordan Kent. Shirley rolled her shoulders, stretched her neck. Her elusive son-in-law had suffered a fate similar to her own; competition with his wife's father seemed an unfair burden put upon the young man, who'd had such charm and dignity when he'd first courted Cecelia.

No wonder he spent so much time away.

The double swinging doors burst open once again and a grinning intern emerged.

"It's a girl," he announced, reaching out to shake Harv's hand. "Congratulations, Grandpa!"

Shirley smiled, looked down at her own idle hands in her lap.

ANNE CARTER

Thirty-Five

Dragon Rock
September

"You're sure you want to do this?" Rebecca called over the sound of the waves hitting the dock as she handed the Igloo cooler to Matt, already in the boat.

"I don't feel like we have any choice. Do you?"

Rebecca shook her head, accepted Matt's hand as she stepped into the boat. "The water's pretty rough today, though."

Matt nodded, steadied her. "We'll take it real easy. I've done this before, many times, as a kid."

"How long has your grandfather owned the lighthouse?"

Matt started the motor, adjusted his seat. "Since forever. He took ownership not long after they made the movie. Kept it shut up all these years."

"Sixty years! There's got to be a reason," Rebecca said, hugging her arms in an attempt to rub off the ocean chill.

"That's where I'm goin', too. I love the old fart, but he's got secrets that might need to be told."

They motored the six miles, fighting the heaving surf the whole way. Rebecca felt nauseous as they neared the reef. Matt zigzagged the dinghy in an attempt to get closer without hitting the rough rocks that only occasionally emerged from the surface.

"Hang on," Matt yelled, and Rebecca could see he was losing control of the boat.

"I am holding on," she screamed back. "Are you okay? Maybe we should go back!"

But Matt couldn't answer as wave after wave tossed the small boat, finally crashing it onto the reef beneath Dragon Rock. The impact sent Rebecca flying over the side of the boat and into the water, her scream drowned out by the seawater instantly filling her mouth.

Matt wasted no time in pitching himself over the side of the remains of the boat, hitting his shoulder on the outcropping of rock. Forcing himself away from the rock, he dove deeper and tried to see through the water, murky with foam and silt.

"Rebecca," he called when he surfaced, looking around in desperation before again diving into the churning waters. He saw her then, thrashing about just beneath the surface not twenty feet away. He made his way through the roiling surf and grasped her around the middle, then struggled toward the rocks.

They dragged themselves onto the islet and lay back, panting. Rebecca coughed up seawater. Matt felt piercing pain in his shoulder. It was some time before either attempted to sit up.

"You okay?" Matt asked at last, gingerly touching the reddening tear in his shirt.

"I think so. But you're hurt!"

"It's okay. We need to grab that cooler before it gets away." Matt got unsteadily to his feet and carefully navigated the rocky surface to where the Igloo floated, caught in a small tide pool. He snagged the cooler, dragging it back closer to where Rebecca sat. "We should get inside."

They found the outside door to the engine room unlocked and carried the cooler together, up the stairs, into the kitchen and dropped it to the floor. Rebecca sat down at one of the two kitchen chairs.

"It feels pretty weird being in here, now."

Matt nodded. "Different than last time, that's for sure."

"I don't remember seeing anything akin to a towel or blanket last time, do you?"

"Actually, yes, I do remember a basket of towels in the first bedroom upstairs. But they've probably been sitting there for sixty years."

"If they're dry, I don't care," Rebecca said, shivering in her soaking wet clothes.

"You've got a point. I'll be right back."

Rebecca fingered one of the magazines still on the table. *Photoplay*, January 1949. *Someone sat here, reading this magazine almost sixty years ago. But who?*

She closed the magazine and opened the ice chest. Fortunately, it had remained tightly sealed against the ocean water.

Matt returned with three small bath towels. "Not too rotten," he commented, tossing one to her. "Bad news, though. My cell is gone."

Rebecca slapped a hand against her jeans pocket. "Got mine!" She stood, tugged the phone out and opened it. "Uh, it's a bit wet. Won't turn on."

"Maybe it'll work after it dries out. I once dropped mine in the sink. It worked again after about two days."

"Two days? Can we last that long?"

"We're supposed to have the boat back tonight by 6:00 p.m. They might consider that we had trouble."

"Might. Yeah."

They shared granola bars and water, then went about their task of looking for evidence of anything unusual that might have occurred in the lighthouse. In the first bedroom, the bed was stripped of its sheet and covers. Only a bare mattress remained. The closet gaped empty, the dresser bare, save for a small, ornate lamp. The cradle was as they remembered it from their prior visits. They continued to the third floor, also a bedroom.

Here, a bed frame leaned against one wall, its mattress missing. An old wooden chair stood in the corner. Otherwise, the room was barren. As they continued on up the tower, they found nothing of interest or any personal note. They returned to the kitchen.

It was nearing sundown.

"Wanna eat our sandwiches now?" Rebecca asked. "I'm starved."

"Okay. I figure if no one picks us up by tomorrow night, I'll light a fire in the lantern room. That would surely get someone's attention.

Rebecca nodded and began unpacking the Igloo.

"You packed a flashlight?"

273

"Yep. It's pretty dark downstairs, and I thought we might need it. Also, a couple of candles in a sealable bag."

"Smart guy." Rebecca set them a table of submarine sandwiches, chips and water. Searching the kitchen cupboards, she found a candle holder and stuffed one of the candles into it. "Might as well make the best of it," she said with an uneasy smile.

"Resourceful woman. I like that."

Their clothes had nearly dried by the time they packed away their leftovers. Rebecca lit the second candle and began opening more cabinets. In the bathroom, she found an Army-issued first aid kit.

"Take off your shirt," she ordered, returning to where Matt now sat on the bed.

His protests proved futile. Rebecca cleaned and dressed the wound in his shoulder, then gave him a spontaneous kiss on the cheek. Before she could pull away, Matt captured her in his arms, pressed his lips to hers for a serious, sensual kiss that heated them both. They lay back on the bed, rolling together in anticipation of an intimate encounter–until Rebecca lifted her head and stiffened.

"What it is?"

"Do you hear it?" she asked, eyes wide in the increasing darkness. "Singing."

Matt too raised his head, then sat upright. A lullaby. A woman's voice. Coming from somewhere inside the lighthouse.

"Matt…" Rebecca began but couldn't finish her thought.

Hush little baby, don't say a word…

"Let's go." Matt pulled on his torn shirt, grabbed the flashlight off the bed and stood. "We both hear it, so it must be real."

"I don't know," Rebecca murmured, holding onto Matt's arm as they stepped out of the bedroom and listened more. "It's coming from down below."

They stopped in the kitchen to get one of the candles, which Rebecca carried. They passed through the utility room, then opened the door to the engine room. The singing became louder.

Mama's gonna buy you a mockingbird…

"Is it okay to be scared?" Rebecca whispered.

"Completely okay. Do you want to go down there with me?"

"No. But I need to."

274

"Okay."

They edged down the stairs, hugging the interior wall of the great caisson. At the bottom, they paused, then walked to the approximate center of the room. The sweet sound of the lullaby grew softer, less clear. Matt shown the flashlight around the room, training it on the huge, sleeping generators, the dead batteries, the air compressors that would never again power the immense foghorn.

Diesel tanks sat dormant. Pieces of what once was the boom derrick lay stacked against one wall. Tool cabinets, their doors hanging on worn out hinges, gaped empty save for nondescript debris. Matt swung the light in a new direction, exposing tall, massive tanks labeled "lubricating oil." Beyond those, a long, low, metal storage bin marked "life preservers."

Matt turned to Rebecca. "The sound is almost gone. But it seems to be coming from over there."

Neither was in a hurry to approach the storage bin, but once before it, Matt knelt, shown the light on the front. The singing had stopped.

"It's padlocked," he muttered, lifting the lock and then letting it drop. He examined the top of the bin, then whistled softly. "The hinges are shot. Rusted through," he told Rebecca. "All I need is a hammer or something."

Rebecca turned, held the candle up. Hanging on the wall beside one of the oil tanks was a huge wrench. She took it off its hook and brought it to Matt.

"Probably used to shut off the valves. I think all I need to do is give these a couple of good..." He swung the wrench as he spoke, slamming the side of the first hinge and shearing it clean off the locker's lid. He did the same with the second hinge.

Matt took a deep breath. "It's probably just full of tools," he said, turning to look at Rebecca, who stood beside him. "Right?"

Rebecca didn't answer. She felt her own anxiety building, filling her with fear and dread. And yet, she had the same profound compulsion to open the bin that Matt obviously felt. Whatever was inside needed to be found.

"Okay?" Matt prompted again, and this time Rebecca nodded, squatting down before the locker. "Okay." Matt reached to the back edge of the lid, lifted it toward them, letting it fall forward to hang from the lock. Rebecca could hear Matt's breathing; he was nearly panting in anticipation.

Matt lifted the flashlight and turned it down to shine into the bin. The first thing visible was the striped white and blue ticking of a thin mattress, rolled up and stuffed into the bin. Rebecca immediately thought of the bare cot in the second bedroom.

"Strange," Matt whispered. "Just a mattress."

"No. There has to be more," Rebecca said. She blew out her candle, dropped it on the floor. Involuntarily, she reached into the locker and tugged at the mattress, pulling until one edge of it came free and unrolled toward them. Rebecca carefully let the mattress hang over the front of the bin, then leaned forward, along with Matt, to peer into the bin again. Matt lifted the flashlight.

There, shrouded within the rolls of small cloth-covered coils, lay a skeleton wrapped in tattered red silk.

"Oh my God," Rebecca cried, bringing the back of her hand to her mouth. "Oh, God...Matt!"

It took the better part of an hour for Rebecca to calm down. Now they sat, side by side, on the floor of the kitchen, a bottle of cabernet between them. She still wept. Matt, too, was filled with despair.

"It's her. I know it's her. She's been here, Matt, for almost sixty years. Her parents are surely dead, her boyfriend–who knows what happened to him–and *he* knew it all the time. Your grandfather. How *could* he?"

Matt squeezed her closer. "We don't know the story yet, babe. Don't get me wrong. I'm not sticking up for him. But I need to get answers. We both do."

"She–she was so pretty. So young. Younger than me, even! She didn't deserve this."

"I know. I know."

"She was calling out to us. She needed us to find her, Matt."

"It would appear so."

"I think she died in the bedroom. That's why it felt so bad in there. I can't go back in there."

276

"We don't have to, Bec. Try to rest. We'll find a way out of here in the morning."

"Oh, God. It hurts so bad."

"I know. Me too."

They might have slept four hours. Matt woke first, a bright beam of sunlight reflecting off the chrome toaster hitting him in the face. He shook Rebecca gently.

She opened her eyes, confused at first. As conscious thought, and memories of the night before, returned, she frowned in pain. "What are we going to do?" she asked.

Matt stood, helped her to her feet. Placing his hands on her shoulders, he looked her in the eye. "I think we need to confront Jordan."

"We can't leave her here."

"No. Absolutely not. She'll have a proper burial, Bec. I promise. But I have to talk to my grandfather first. We'll come back, as soon as feasible, and get her laid to rest."

Rebecca nodded, let herself slide into his arms. "There's more to the story, you know."

"What do you mean?"

"The cradle."

Matt nodded, stroked Rebecca's hair. "Yeah. The cradle."

They both started at the booming sound of a megaphone from outside. "This is the United States Coast Guard. Is anyone there?"

Thirty-Six

Dragon Rock
March 1949

Jordan let Darla's bag drop to the floor.

"What are *you* doing here?" he asked, taking a step between Darla and their surprise visitor.

"Well, well. If it isn't the cozy little love nest. I shouda known. The two a you been shackin' up out here all this time, eh?"

"It's not like that at all, Russ. Darla's been ill. She didn't want anyone to know. She's well now, and as a matter of fact, I just got here to take her home. Surely you can understand—"

"Oh, I understand just perfectly. She was *ill*. That the best you can do? Why don't you just tell me she grew a second head!" Russell sauntered into the room, leaving the door to the engine room stairs open. "Whatsa matter, Darla, cat got your tongue?"

"What's to say, Russell? You caught us. Here we are, out in the middle of the ocean, in this rundown, freezing cold, nasty old lighthouse, and you have to assume the worst. You can't stand it, can you, that I let you go. And for the record, it wasn't for Jordan. I would have left you anyway. I tried to explain that to you—"

"Don't waste your breath, Darla. He's never been anything more than a two-bit bum. We need to get going." Jordan reached for the luggage he'd dropped, but Russell kicked it away before Jordan could get a handle on it. The violence of his action elicited a small cry from Darla.

"Worried about your boyfriend, are you? You should worry. You know, doncha, that Cec's having a baby any time now, and that Papa here will pretty much be tied up for a while. You just might hafta find yourself a new sugar daddy."

Eyes cast down, Darla turned around and walked up the stairs to her bedroom, closing the door behind her.

279

Russell turned to Jordan. "So. You wanna settle this right here? Now?"

"Settle what? Look, I don't have time for this foolery. We need to get back to the mainland. We have a plane to catch."

"That's what *you* think."

"I told Mother you would always be a problem. Now, look at you. You can't get a job; you hang around mooching off of people who work for a living. I'm sick of it, Russell. Sick of bailing you out for the last fifteen years. Ever since middle school. You broke Mom's heart, you know that, don't you?"

Russell stared hard at Jordan. "So, the Golden Boy does remember his humble beginnings. You know what she used to say about you, don't you?"

"I don't need you to tell me what Mother, *my* mother, thinks about anything. She and I have always seen eye to eye. You're the one she's been disappointed in. She worked hard to keep you off the streets, ever since the day you conveniently dropped into our lives. And how did you pay her back? No, you'd never admit it. Always poor Russell, can't get a decent break. Well here's a headline for you. You'd better learn to stand on your own feet because I'm not gonna be there to catch you anymore." Jordan flung the words into Russell's face, leaning toward him in barely restrained fury. "Now, I suggest you get out of my way."

"You ain't goin' nowhere until we have this out. You owe me. Owe me bigtime. If you hadn't moved in on my girl, everything would be different. I woulda got a role in a big picture by now. She'd respect me, not you, you lousy, lyin', two-faced bastard!"

"That's enough! How dare you talk to me like that? Have you lost your mind? You're starting to sound like a bitter old man, Harrington. Bitter and sick. Maybe you need professional help. I might be able to recommend–" Jordan's words were clipped short by Russell's right hook to the jaw. Jordan stumbled backwards, hit the wall. He reached up to touch his smarting face.

"Why, you worthless…" Charging forward, Jordan punched at Russell, meeting only air with his fist as his target darted to the side.

"Too quick for ya, am I? Just keep trying. You haven't had the advantage of the streets, like I have!"

Jordan didn't respond. Gaining his balance, he swung at Russell again, this time making good his contact with Russell's chin. Blood spurted from his lip; fury grew in his eyes.

"I'll kill you for that! You miserable excuse for a human bein'!" Russell rushed Jordan again, fists flying. Jordan reeled backward in surprise, unable to recover between blows. Russell pummeled him again and again, each time forcing Jordan closer to the open door and the engine room below. He paused, stared hard at Jordan's bloody face, then landed one last forceful blow to his cheek, sending Jordan flying back through the opening and tumbling off the side of the stairs into the dark abyss of the engine room.

The silence that followed answered any question Russell had regarding Jordan's ability to continue the fight. He turned and headed up the stairs to Darla's room.

"Did you see it? Did you see the helicopter?" Willie asked the old mariner behind the counter at the bait shop.

"Yer seein' things. Ain't been no heliocopters around here since the war."

"No, really..." Willie paused, thinking again about pushing the issue. Maybe it was a good thing the old man hadn't seen the copter. "Never mind."

But when he finished sweeping up, he made his second trip in two weeks to Doc Stone's house. This time, the doctor was in.

"What's up, boy? Everything okay with the lady at the light?"

"A helicopter just took off from the lighthouse, Dr. Stone. It flew off to the north."

"Yes, I saw it."

"Whaddya think's happening? Did Miss Darla leave?"

Dr. Stone looked away, toward the water, from his front porch. "I heard Mrs. Weatherton and her daughter are moving to Canada for a while."

"Canada! B.C.?"

"Not sure. Not our business, anyway, is it now?"

"No, sir. I guess not. I just thought...I wish I coulda said goodbye."

The doctor grunted. "Sometimes it's better this way."

"I saw two men leaving to go out there today. In two different boats. One went alone, th'other got taken by Mr. Farley. You think they went out there to help Miss–Mrs. Weatherton get ready to go?"

"Separate boats, you say?"

"Yes, sir."

Again, the doctor uttered a throaty note of displeasure. "Like I said. It just isn't any of our concern, Mr. Jacobs. Now I have some work to do. You run along. Give my regards to your father."

"Yes, sir."

Willie wandered back to the dock, sat down. There was a feeling in his gut he didn't like. Kind of like when you knew you were about to be sick and couldn't do anything about it.

Darla stood beside the cradle, wanting badly to cry. To just throw herself across the bed and cry until her eyes swam from their sockets. But the tears wouldn't come. It wouldn't do to have either Russell or Jordan see her weak and pining. And anyway, in just a matter of hours, she'd be home, home with Lana and Mama and, sometimes, her father. The lighthouse, with its moaning winds, weeping walls and inescapable loneliness would be only a foggy memory.

She bumped the cradle with her knee, setting it to gently rocking. She tried to imagine her daughter lying in the little bed, a vision just beginning to form when the door slammed open. Darla spun around to face Russell as he strode into the room.

"C'mon, Darla. Let's go." He beckoned with his fingers. "We'll take the boat."

"I'm not going anywhere with you."

"Yes, you are. Because you are my girl. Always have been. Now, let's be nice and cooperative so nobody else gets hurt."

"What do you mean, nobody *else*? Jordan? *Jordan?*" she called toward the open bedroom door.

"He ain't gonna hear you, dollface. He's too busy examining the basement floor right now. Let's don't waste any more time. C'mon." He reached for her, and she sidestepped, causing him to crash his shins into the cradle.

"What the *hell* is that?" Russell took a step back, squinted in the dim light. "It's a baby bed! A god-damned baby bed!" He turned to Darla. "What does this mean?"

Darla backed farther away, said nothing. Russell advanced.

"I *said*, what is a baby cradle doing in your bedroom?"

"Okay, okay, it was for a baby, all right? Jesus! Stop yelling at me!"

"Whose baby?"

"What?"

"I said, whose baby was in that damned bed?"

Darla turned to look Russell in the eye. She squared her shoulders, straightened her petite frame. "Mine."

"Yours?"

"You got a hearing problem, Russell? Mine. Mine and mine alone."

"You little shrew. So that's why you come up here to disappear. You had a god-damned baby up here!"

"Not that it's any business of yours."

"It sure as hell is my business! You're my girl, and if you got knocked up by some other guy, it sure as hell is my business! So, who's the father? It better be mine!"

Darla sat down on the bed, crossed her legs. "As if I would tell you." She fixed her eyes on his, her bitter gaze unwavering.

Russell's head swelled with red-hot rage. Before either of them knew what was happening, he swung his arm to the side and backhanded Darla across the face. Her cheek flushed red from the blow, but she refused to break her stare.

"Who? Who, dammit!" This time, he slammed her other cheek.

Still, she remained silent.

"It's Jordan, isn't it? The Golden Boy strikes again. God damn stinking son-of-a-bitch!" Russell began to pace quickly, words rushing out of his mouth in a jumbled frenzy.

Darla uncrossed her legs, edged slightly closer to the door. Her eyes never left Russell's face.

"All that time, it was true. All that time, he was bangin' you, up there, and…and…you didn't call…you didn't…oh God…this is crazy, this is…oh, no you don't!"

He caught her making a move for the door. Grabbing her by the shoulders, he tossed her down on the bed. "So where is the little bastard now? Rushed off to some high-priced boarding school? Huh? Where is he!"

"He's dead." Darla proclaimed, slowly moving back to a sitting position. "He died when he was born."

Russell stared hard at her. "You're lying."

"If I'm lying, then where is he? Huh? You stupid louse. You don't have the sense you were born with."

He swung at her again, this time drawing blood from her mouth. "Whore!"

Darla narrowed her eyes. "Yes," she snarled. "I did it with Jordan. And Sisco. And even Harvey Bregman. I did it with all of them. The camera guys, too. And you know what? They were all better than you. Because you are a stupid man, Russell. Only a stupid man would get tied up with Commies! You are one stupid man."

Blind rage drove him now. Leaping onto the bed, he pushed Darla down and straddled her, grasping her around the neck with both hands. "You tramp! Tell me! The truth! Is Jordan Kent the father?"

Despite her terror, Darla smiled. "You'll die never knowing, dear Russell. I'm the only one who knows. But I can tell you, he was a beautiful baby, with crystal blue eyes and gorgeous dark hair...just like his daddy..."

From somewhere deep within him, a primal growl began and built until the sound tore from his throat and echoed throughout the lighthouse. His fingers moved in concert with his scream, squeezing Darla's neck with the fury of a lifetime of unrequited love. As he pressed his thumbs against her throat, she went through several incarnations of all the women in his life who hadn't loved him. He no longer saw sweet-faced Darla Foster writhing beneath him, trying to scream Jordan's name, for the woman fighting for her life was faceless, nameless, loveless. And was also, he eventually came to realize, now dead.

Thirty-Seven

Grogan's Head, California
September

C ase McKenna poured three cups of coffee, carried two of them outside to the front deck of his mountain cabin. He handed one to Matt.

"Double caff," he said. "You look like you need it. Sleep okay?"

"Yes and no. Bec still in the shower?"

"It just shut off. You guys had a rough time. She okay?"

"I can't tell," Matt said softly, looking out at the redwood forest surrounding Case's cabin. "It was pretty traumatic."

"What's next?"

"Well, we have to go talk to my grandfather. It doesn't look good for him."

"You think he killed her?" Case asked.

"He either killed her, or he was an instrument. Whether he did it or not, he hid her death, and that's wrong."

"Will you bring charges?"

Matt leaned forward on his deck chair, hung his head. "I'm in kind of an awkward position. I'm an attorney. I represent the law. But in reality, there's probably nobody left alive that would–"

"I'm alive," Rebecca said from behind them. Her hair was wet, hanging in small waving curls that she shook back from her face. "I'll speak for Darla Foster. I'll see justice is done."

Matt stared at her from his seat, lifted his coffee mug to his lips.

"Can I use your phone?" Rebecca directed her question to Case, who handed her his cell. She went back inside.

"Sounds like she's gonna make a case against Jordan."

"We'll see."

"Don't let this put a wedge between you," Case advised. "She's a good person."

"It won't. I'm a good person, too." Matt leaned down to pet Lucas, who rubbed against his legs.

Case chuckled. "I stand corrected."

"Thanks for taking care of my cat. He seems to like it here," Matt said, lifting Lucas into his lap.

"More mice."

Rebecca returned from inside, her face flushed. She held out the cell phone to Case, turned to Matt.

"I've gotta get to the airport. My dad's in the hospital!"

She barely said a word during the two flights they needed to get to Phoenix but held tightly to Matt's hand.

"He'll be okay, Bec. They said he's stable. That's good news. Only a mild heart attack. He's lucky." He thought of his own father, face down on his desk at work. He never had a chance.

"You're right. I keep telling myself that. I just–I just need to see for myself that he's okay."

"I understand."

And he did. Only too well.

Jeb was sleeping when they arrived, but Rebecca insisted upon sitting with him. Matt went to the cafeteria to wait and grab a snack. Soon, her father woke.

"There you are. I knew you'd be here when I woke up," he said with a smile. "But it would've been okay if you weren't, too."

"I got here as quickly as I could, Daddy. Are you okay?"

"I think so. It was pretty scary at first. I'd crawled under that damned Ford. Had to replace the oil pan after all. Stupid piece of machinery."

Rebecca smiled. Oil pans she understood. Heart attacks, not so much.

"So, while I was in the ER, I was thinkin', what if, what if I didn't get a chance to talk to you again. What if I–"

"Shh. Don't even talk like that."

"No, seriously, Bec. There's things I need to tell you, get off my chest. Truth is, I could've died underneath that old wreck, and you woulda gone on the rest of your life not knowing things you might need to know."

Rebecca's head began to swim. What more could she possibly need to know, now? But she grasped her father's hand and settled in emotionally.

Jeb drew in a deep breath, looked her in the eye. "Your mother. God rest her soul. You know I loved her like no other. We had a marriage made in heaven, girl. She was the kindest, most endearing woman I ever met."

"That's not news, Dad."

"No. But…where do I begin? The night she died. I guess that's as good a place as any. The man she met at the library was her father."

"But Grampa was already dead."

"No, I mean her real father. Your mother was adopted."

Rebecca's mouth dropped open slightly. "Adopted?"

"Yep. Her parents told her when she turned sixteen. Gave her that red necklace you now have. It came, they said, from her real mother. I guess they say 'biological' these days."

Rebecca looked away, envisioning her mother's face. "So he met her at the library. Go on."

"He'd contacted her the week before. Said he wanted to meet her. She was so excited. Got all prettied up, you know, had the hair done and all. We'd just got our first cordless, wireless, whatever they called cell phones back then, and she promised to call me since she was goin' downtown Phoenix to meet this guy. So, she calls me, all flustered and giggling and happy. Says, 'Jeb, you won't believe this. My father is Jordan Kent, the famous movie star from the forties!' So I said, 'Imagine that,' you know, I was happy for her. And her mother, she said, was that gal from the movie you asked me about…Bec? Honey, are you alright? Nurse! Nurse! Get in here!"

The cold water helped. "I'm okay, honest. I just got some really shocking news. I haven't slept much the past few days," she told the nurse. "And I have to get a decent meal in my stomach. But I'm fine."

The nurse patted her shoulder. "Call if you need me."

Jebediah frowned. "I'm sorry, Bec. I didn't realize it would affect you so strongly."

"It's okay. Just finish the story."

"There's nothing else, really. We talked for a few minutes as she walked away from the library."

"Did he say anything to Mom about her mother's disappearance?"

"Just that they'd gone their separate ways, he loved her very much, and she was a beautiful, sweet, loving person that your mom would have been proud of. That he missed her greatly."

Rebecca swallowed the lump in her throat. "Missed her. *Right.*"

"And just after we hung up, she got hit by the car. I had no way of reaching Kent. And really, something told me I didn't want to. I had fears. Unfounded, I'm sure. But I was nervous about you. If someone was out to get your mom, for whatever reason, they might want you, too. A stupid, needless fear, I'm sure."

Rebecca straightened up. "Thanks, Daddy. Thanks for telling me the story. It means a lot to me. I'd rather Matt didn't know about this right now, okay?"

"Matt? No, I won't mention any of it to him." Jeb reached up, stroked Rebecca's cheek. "You like this guy, do you?"

"He came all the way to Scotland to apologize to me."

"You didn't answer my question. I know you're picky about men, Bec. Otherwise you would have been married a long time ago."

"He's nice, Daddy. I like him a lot. We have a few things we have to work out between us. And maybe we'll end up together. Maybe."

"I sorta hope so. I think he's a good egg."

"I have to go back to Los Angeles. It's something that just can't wait. Will you be okay?"

"I got Chuck to come get me when they boot me outta here, sweetie. You go, don't worry, I'll be fine. Chuck's gonna fill in with me at the shop for a while. He needs the work; I need the help."

"Okay. I love you, Daddy."

Rebecca didn't know whether to laugh, cry or throw up. She slipped into the ladies' room to wash up, found herself lingering inside before going to join Matt.

Jordan Kent was her mother's biological father. That made him her grandfather.

Darla Foster was her grandmother. The corpse they'd discovered had been, at one time, her flesh and blood. No wonder it hit her so hard.

It was the reason Darla had stalked her. Darla, she now remembered, had blown her a kiss. Had appeared in her car, in her hotel room, in her dreams. Had sung a lullaby to her baby daughter.

The baby! The baby in the cradle was *Rebecca's mother.*

She sank down onto the fainting couch in the restroom and hung her head.

Matt sensed a change in Rebecca but attributed it to the double traumas of finding the remains of Darla Foster and having her father hospitalized. After a trying day in the courtroom, he couldn't wait to see her. He'd left her sleeping that morning at his house.

She sat on the back deck, staring out at the view, he thought. But on closer examination, he could tell her stare was blank; whatever she saw played inside her head and not beyond his property line. She turned.

"Didn't hear you come in. Wow, you look nice!"

"Work clothes. Can't wait to get into my jeans."

"Well I'm ready when you are."

"Thought we'd grab dinner and then head over to Jordan's."

"Fine."

He didn't want to upset her further, so refrained from telling her about the phone call he'd received this morning. Three days before, his uncle had walked out of the assisted living facility where he'd lived the last fifteen years his life. Still hadn't been found.

He'd deal with that tomorrow. Tonight, he faced his biggest case ever: trying his grandfather for murder in his own home.

Jordan waited for them in the study, a glass of scotch in his hand. He sat behind his massive desk.

"I hope you haven't had much of that yet. I need you to be clear-headed," Matt admonished without hesitation. He knew he had to steel his feelings and not let things slide.

"I'm sharper now than you've ever been," Jordan spat. "What's this all about, anyway?"

"It's about Darla Foster, Grandad."

Jordan put down his glass and clasped his hands. He looked up then but directed his eyes to Rebecca.

"She was a vivacious, talented, exciting woman," he said. "And I was in love with her."

Rebecca squirmed in her seat but kept her mouth closed.

"What else do you want to know?"

Matt licked his lips, leaned forward. "We found her. Her...remains."

Jordan sat stock still. Matt continued.

"We want to know what happened. How she died. And why the hell you hid her all these years!"

The thickness of the air in the room was palpable. Jordan swallowed, stood from his desk, walked to one of the floor-to-ceiling bookcases behind him. He appeared to be looking for something.

"It was an accident," he began, running his hands lightly over the leather spines of the books. "She wasn't supposed to die. I never wanted her to die. I loved her."

"Did you kill her?" Matt asked.

"No. I did not."

"Who did?"

"I can't tell you."

Thirty-Eight

Crescent City, California
March 1949

Jordan smelled diesel fuel and tasted blood. Blood, and dirt. His head thundered with pain; his left leg buckled as he tried to stand. Gaining his wits, he called out, "Darla! I'm coming!"

It took him an excruciatingly long time to make the climb up the steps out of the engine room. The lighthouse was quiet, except for the distant, muffled sound of someone sobbing. As he reached Darla's bedroom, he paused before opening the door; terror squeezed at his heart, for the person quietly crying was not Darla.

He pushed open the door. Darla, in her bright, cherry red Cheongsam, lay motionless across the bed. Jordan rushed to her. "Oh, no. No. You didn't," he murmured, lifting her limp hand, touching her face, staring into her sightless eyes. "Oh, Darla. Darling." He leaned close to her face, gently kissed her still-warm lips and then drew back, holding his hands near her cheeks as if he could not quite touch her flesh. She was gone, really gone, and he needed a picture to imprint upon his memory. His eyes took in all, her tiny curling bangs, the full, pursed red lips. The purple bruises on her neck.

He remembered then, the pitiful weeping coming from the man on the floor in the corner.

Jordan swallowed hard, gently used his fingertips to close Darla's eyes. "Goodbye, my love," he whispered, then stood from the bed. He turned to Russell.

"Are you mad? How could you do this? You...you miserable bastard. You filthy pig! Get up. Get the hell up!"

Russell's face glistened with tears and saliva. He got to his feet, still crying, waited for Jordan's instructions.

"I should kill you for this." Jordan looked around the room, fought to think clearly. "We have work to do. You sweep this room. You make sure nothing is left behind, you understand? There must be no evidence that Darla ever occupied this room. Then, the kitchen. The utility. You check every cabinet, every drawer, every square inch. Because as God is my witness, if you leave anything behind, you will hang for her murder. I'll do what I can because you are obviously incapable of rational thought. But I can only do so much."

Russell, his eyes wide with fear, stared back at Jordan in horror.

"Go," Jordan shouted, pointing accusingly at Russell, who jumped into action.

Jordan left the room, made a quick tour, formed a plan. He waited in the kitchen until Russell appeared.

"I checked everything. I only found this." He held up a package of bobby pins. "In the bathroom." He sniffed, ran a sleeve across his face.

"Okay. We have to hide her body. In the caisson. Downstairs. I'll need your help."

"I loved her! I really did. You–you don't understand..." Russell wailed, his eyes welling with tears. "She used to love me back."

"Stop your blubbering. Hold the door for me," Jordan snapped, limping back up the stairs to Darla's bedroom. "I'll carry her down there. You go upstairs, get that thin mattress off the cot on the third floor."

Despite his injuries, Jordan managed to move Darla's body to the engine room. Russell eventually joined him, lugging the rolled-up mattress. He placed it on the floor. Jordan gently laid her on the mattress, said a silent prayer, then rolled the mattress around her. Russell helped to lift the bundle into a steel floor locker that once held life preservers.

"I'm going to put a lock on here," Jordan said, tucking the mattress in around Darla's body.

"She should be b-buried," Russell moaned. "Proper like."

"One day. Not now. Are you sure you didn't miss anything?"

"I'm sure."

"Okay. We'll take her stuff in the boat and go back. When we get to shore, you say nothing, you got that?"

"I got it. Yeah. Nothing."

"And quit your whining. You killed her. It's over. We can't bring her back. You had a moment–a crime of passion. If you are a good boy and keep your trap shut, no one has to know what happened out here. Got it? Nobody."

"I got it. I got it. You won't tell?"

"I have nothing to gain by exposing your insanity. It would only devastate Mother. She's suffered enough because of you."

The pair endured an arduous, painful trek back to the shore. Jordan turned in the rental, tipping the dock master for his trouble. Russell wandered around the bait house, edgy and feeling morose. A boy of twelve or thirteen hung around, staring at Russell as he paced.

"What're you lookin' at?" Russell demanded.

"Nothing, sir."

"You better be lookin' at nothin'."

"You went out to the lighthouse this morning. I saw you," the boy ventured.

Russell frowned. "You know what's good for you, you won't remember what you saw this mornin', kid."

The boy seemed taken aback, but then lifted his chin. "What's happened to Miss Darla? Did she really go to Canada?"

Russell leaned close to the boy's face, gave him his sternest look. "You keep askin' questions, somethin' real bad is gonna happen. My advice to you is, you better disappear for a while, or someone's gonna get hurt. An' she wouldn't want that, would she?"

The young man's eyes grew round, wary. He shook his head, backed away. Russell turned, began to laugh. His laughter grew until Jordan joined him, grasped him hard by the forearm. "Let's go, brother. Say goodbye to this place once and for all."

Russell stopped laughing, his face now somber. "Okay. I'm ready." They started for the parking lot where Jordan had left a borrowed car. Russell turned, looked over his shoulder at the boy, who still watched, partially hidden behind the bait shop door. Russell sent him a look to reinforce his threat.

During the long and tedious trip back to Los Angeles, Jordan barely slept, and Russell came in and out of lucidity. As Jordan listened to him babble, whine and curse, a thought formed. He had but one choice, he decided. From a phone booth at Los Angeles Municipal, he made several calls while Russell waited.

At last, he had a direction. Beverly Glen Convalescent Hospital would take Russell in immediately for evaluation. Jordan hailed a cab at the curb, and within ninety minutes, left the hospital with his copies of Russell's temporary admittance records. With luck, Russell would become a permanent resident.

Jordan rubbed the back of his neck. He didn't remember when he'd felt so fatigued, so brittle, so emotionally spent. He couldn't think about Darla, or Russell, or anything else. He merely wanted to get home, drink a bottle of scotch and go to bed. Yet when he reached his house, he found a note from his father-in-law: he was to get to St. Joseph's Hospital as soon as he arrived.

He took time to shave and to change his clothes. His car was in the garage, a blessing, and he drove to Burbank in autopilot, thankful for the light, midnight traffic. He arrived at St. Joe's just after 1:00 a.m.

Mrs. Bregman looked more like a ghost than a new grandmother, sitting alone in the waiting room. She barely looked up when Jordan entered. He stood before her, patient, waiting until at last she looked up at him.

"It's a girl," she muttered. "You have a daughter."

Jordan nodded, marveling at the numbness engulfing him. He smiled, not because of his mother-in-law's news, but because he cared so little to hear it. He went to the nurse's station and was told Mrs. Kent wasn't receiving visitors. No, not even her husband.

Unfazed, he wandered down the hall to the draped nursery windows. He tapped on the door, and a nurse appeared.

"I'm Jordan Kent. I'd like to see my daughter, if it's all right. I've just gotten back into town."

The nurse smiled, clearly sympathetic to his request. "I'll open the middle curtain. She's right in the front."

"Thanks," he murmured. He went back to the window, waited. Slowly, the draperies parted. As promised, the bassinet centered in the front row held Baby Girl Kent. "Eleanor," the card above her head read. She was sleeping. Tiny, but healthy. Three weeks early but still five pounds. Very pink, a small shock of wispy, fair hair.

Jordan leaned his forehead against the window glass, his fisted hand beside his cheek. The baby stirred, yawned, stilled. She was beautiful. But as he watched her, a vision came between what he actually saw and his mind's eye. The vision of another baby, being held by her mother, saying goodbye. Lana's bright brown eyes and bow-shaped mouth came into view, then morphed into Darla's sweet, sassy, loving face, staring at him from the bed where she lay in her last moments of life.

His eyes burned. Jordan turned his back on the window, slid to the floor and hung his head. All of his jobs were complete; his responsibilities, for the moment, accomplished. Now, the tears began to flow. Deep sobs wracked his body as his tormented soul gave in to the heart-wrenching grief he'd held in check for so long.

Darla, my love...I'm so sorry...

Thirty-Nine

Hollywood, California
September

Matt became annoyed, and he sensed Rebecca was about to come out of her chair.

"What do you mean, you can't tell us! You realize you could be accused of murder? You really think anyone is that worth protecting?" Matt asked, abruptly standing.

"I made a promise," Jordan said simply, now locating the book he sought. He placed the thick tome on his desk.

"A promise. That doesn't cut it in a court of law."

"And well you should know, Matthew. I didn't put you through law school for nothing."

Rebecca now stood as well. "Mr. Kent, a woman died in that lighthouse! A young, vital, *vibrant* woman. Who are you to stand there and say you can't tell us how she died because of some stupid promise you made!"

Jordan turned toward Rebecca. "You have every right to your anger, my dear. I actually applaud you for your defense. And as painful as Darla's death was for me, I simply cannot, at this time, divulge–"

"Aw, why not. You might as well spill it all."

The words came from the doorway, where an elderly, hunched man stood.

"It ain't gonna matter now, Jordan. I'm half dead, and you're on your way, too. Mattie here, he deserves the truth. As much as I hate to tell him, cuz he's been the only one ever cared a rat's ass about me."

"Uncle Russell," Matt exclaimed, rushing to the old man's side. "What–How did you get here?"

"Walked out, hailed me a cab. Visited some of the old places, you know, the studios. The diner. Nothin's the same, y'know?"

No one said a word, at first. Russell shuffled into the room and sat in Matt's chair. He became serious. "I killed her. I killed Darla. Jordan here, he made it so's no one would find out." He paused, fussed with the buttons on his shirt. "I didn't mean to do it. I was just so mad. She made me mad. All the time. She just wouldn't stop. She called me names. Said I was stupid! Said I–"

"It's okay, Unc. Settle down." Matt put a hand on Russell's shoulder to calm him.

"She called me a Commie. I wasn't no Commie. I never was."

Jordan sat down behind his desk. "Well. There you have it. Mother's health was frail. I was afraid if Russell was arrested for murder, it would kill her."

"Yeah, right. More like, you didn't want Cec to find out about the baby."

Silence settled on the room as each of the others considered Russell's accusation.

"And she woulda, too. She knew everything. She had it all figgered out."

Jordan shot Russell a look but said nothing.

Russell continued, looking up at the massive oil painting of Cecelia on the library wall. "She was some dame. A real smart cookie. She come to see me once. Asked lotsa questions. Wanted to know about Darla's baby and where it went. I told her what I knew…wasn't much. She said it was important cuz that baby could get what was sposta go to her own daughter. She wadn't about to let some bastard child get what was due her own kid, she said."

"This is absurd," Jordan proclaimed, pounding a hand down on his desk. "She didn't know about any baby."

"That's where you're wrong, Jordie-boy. She knew. She went lookin'. Some private eye, our Cec. She told me she was gonna take care of that baby, one way or another. An' I don't mean take care of, like in a good way. She was gonna see to it that baby never got a chance to get any of the family fortune."

Rebecca gasped. "You don't mean…she meant that baby…that person harm? Would she have gone so far as to…"?

"Kill her? Don't underestimate Cecelia Kent, young woman. Once she set her mind to somethin', there was no stoppin' her. She had a lot of connections. People to do her dirty work. And what she couldn't do, she'd get her daddy to do. She never liked Darla."

Rebecca turned abruptly to Matt.

Matt sighed. "This all puts me in an awkward position. You've just admitted to murdering an innocent young woman. Both of you covered it up. You could both be convicted and sent up forever."

Jordan placed his palms down on his desktop. "I suppose you could. But you might not want to drag Rebecca through all that pain."

"Rebecca? What could she possibly have to do with all this?"

Jordan turned to Rebecca. "Do you want to tell him, or should I?"

"Tell him what?" Rebecca asked, sitting back down and crossing her legs.

"Who you are."

Matt frowned. "I know who she is. At least I think I do, now. What does he mean, Bec?"

Rebecca fidgeted. Bit her lip. Swallowed, ran her hands through her hair. "My father just told me that my mother was adopted. That the night–the night she was killed, she met with her biological father, for the first time. That man was you. Jordan Kent."

Incredulous, Matt turned a horror-stricken face from Rebecca to Jordan. "What?"

Russell began to laugh.

"But that would mean...you...the baby was your mother? Darla and Granddad's baby was *your* mother?"

Eyes welling with tears, Rebecca nodded. "He just told me yesterday. I wasn't ready to talk to you about it–yet. But what I am hearing now is that she–" Rebecca pointed an accusing finger at the portrait on the wall "–*she* may have killed my mother! All for greed! Afraid that after finding out who her father was, Mom might come out here and try to get her hands on the Kent money! This whole thing just...sickens me."

"Whoa, whoa–hold on here. We don't know that for sure." Matt came to her side. "Is that true? Did you really go to visit Bec's mother in Phoenix fifteen years ago?" he asked Jordan.

Jordan stared at his grandson, then nodded. "I did. I had an investigator track her down. I guess it's possible Celia discovered my research and beat me to Arizona. Figuratively speaking, that is. Had I known I was endangering Lana's life, I never would have–"

"Louise," Rebecca corrected. "My mother's name was Louise. And just to absolve your own well-deserved guilt, you had to look her up and put her in danger. She'd still be alive today if you hadn't gone to Phoenix. And I have to wonder," she added, tears now streaming down her cheeks, "if your wife killed my grandparents, too."

Enlightenment changed Matt's expression. "That's another issue we might look into."

"What's the point, now? Cec is gone. Darla is gone. Rebecca's dear mother is gone. Soon, I'll be gone, too. There is no point." Jordan exhaled, looked away in despair. "You want to lock Russell up? Seems to me he's spent enough time imprisoned. Me? Take me away. I'm beyond caring."

"Somebody has to care. Somebody has to pay," Rebecca demanded. "You talk about it like it's no big deal, just because it happened sixty years ago! How can you be so callous? And you claim to have loved her!"

For the first time that evening, Jordan looked uncertain. His hands trembled slightly as he ran them over the surface of the book before him, and his skin tone pinkened. "You have little idea of how she changed my life," he said quietly. "She was a gift from God...and a curse from hell. She gave everything, took little, brightened the days and nights of a man locked into a loveless marriage to a self-absorbed woman and her egotist father. And I have been damned, every day of my life since the moment I met her. Cursed with loving that which I could never really have."

He stood, pressed a button on his desk. His personal assistant appeared at the door.

"Esme, see that the green room is made up for Mr. Harrington. Call Beverly Glen in the morning and have them send a car over to collect him by 9:00 a.m. Matthew, I believe you and Miss Burke have some things to discuss. My fate is in your hands."

Rebecca got to her feet. Matt put his arm around her shoulders.

"Oh. This," Jordan added, picking up the book from his desk. "You should have these." His fingers still shaking, Jordan flipped open the cover of the faux book to reveal a cigar-box shaped opening. Inside, a small group of letters bound with a rubber band. "She wrote these to her mother. I couldn't send them on without reading them first. But...I was never able to read them. Her mother's been gone now, ten years maybe. Her father disappeared. These should be yours." He held out the opened, hollowed out book. Rebecca reached in, hesitantly, then plucked the packet of letters out. She said nothing more, turned to go.

She held the letters to her chest all the way home. In the light of the oncoming headlights, Matt could see the tears glistening on her face.

"I can't imagine how you must feel," he said softly. He felt like crying himself, only slightly relieved as he maneuvered the Porsche into the garage at his house. He opened the door for Rebecca, helped her out.

Inside, he heated water for tea. His mother always made an herbal brew when family strife arose, a frequent occurrence when his grandparents both still lived. He brought two steaming cups to the living room where Rebecca sat on the couch.

"That piano is too big for this room," she said.

"Your father never told you Jordan was your grandfather. Unbelievable."

"I knew he had secrets. He suffered so much when Mom died, I never wanted him to relive that pain. I held onto my questions." Rebecca took a sip of the tea.

"I guess that's kinda how I felt about Jordan. Over the years, I saw glimpses of the softer guy he probably once was. I suspected his life with my grandmother had hardened him. She wasn't a nice lady. Oh, she was good to me, her only grandchild. But she treated him horribly."

Rebecca sighed. "This is all just too sad." She put her cup down on the coffee table. "So unfair."

Matt stroked her hair, caressed her cheek. It *was* unfair. No one deserved to be dumped on like they both had been. "Let's just turn in. We can talk tomorrow. I'll clear my calendar. We'll go down to the beach, get breakfast, just talk."

Rebecca shook her head. "I don't think so. There's not much to talk about. Jordan's right. There's no point, now, in doing anything other than making sure Darla is buried. Your uncle will be cared for, Jordan has the means to live out his life in comfort. I guess–I guess he did what he had to to take care of his brother. I give him that."

"Foster brother," Matt murmured. "Story goes, Great Gramma Alice took Russ in when he was a kid on the streets of Santa Rosa. She never formally adopted him, but they grew up like brothers. When Granddad got into show business, Russ wanted in, too. But from what I hear, he was too rough around the edges. He met Darla, and she got him to introduce her to my grandparents."

Rebecca nodded. She picked up the letters, got to her feet. "Nonetheless, I don't think there's much we can do about the future, Matt." She walked toward the great, arched window that displayed a twinkling view of Los Angeles. "Once we get her home, buried, all settled, I need to get back to Phoenix. Back to my life."

Matt stood, confused. He went to her, took her by the arm. "What are you saying?"

"There's no future for us. We can't be together. You do understand, don't you?"

"Don't talk crazy. Don't do this, now. You–we're good, Bec. You and me. Finally, everything is clear and easy between us. I thought you cared...I thought you–"

She turned abruptly to face Matt. "I do care. I do! But don't you see? We're related. We're *blood* related. Jordan is our grandfather. Doesn't that mean anything to you? We shouldn't be...together."

Matt chuckled in surprise. "Incest? You're worried about incest? Jesus, Bec, we're bigger than that! For Christ sakes, I–I love you! For the first time in my life, I'm really in love. Doesn't *that* mean anything to you?"

"Of course it does! And it hurts like hell! Please–don't make this harder."

"Not that we've talked about it, but is it children you're worried about? There are ways around that. There's surrogacy, adoption–"

"No. Not now. I can't talk about this now. It's too–too much."

Matt looked away, scratched at his forehead. "Okay. Tomorrow. We'll talk. Just–just give me a chance, Rebecca. Give *us* a chance. Don't make a decision right now when the whole damned world is out of whack. I'm going to bed. Let's go to bed, okay? Just for tonight, forget about this mess."

Rebecca moistened her lips. "Okay. I'll be there in a little while. Can I just drink my tea and think for a bit?"

Matt came back to her, took her slowly into his arms. He kissed her forehead, her cheek, her lips. Lifted her hair, kissed beneath her ear. "I love you, Rebecca Burke. I need you in my life. I want you in my life, forever. Screwed up DNA or not. Fate's dealt us a blow. But you're worth whatever it takes to keep this thing together."

His words made her weep. A blow *had* been dealt. It was like some great, cruel hoax, each of them part of a hideous curse that began one fateful night sixty years before; the night young and hungry Darla Foster met the lonely, charming Jordan Kent.

She opened all of the letters. There were five. She arranged them in chronological order, for each was carefully dated in the upper right corner. Four were written on pink scalloped-edged stationary.

Rebecca took a deep breath, began reading. Immediately enthralled by the fanciful words, the screwball observations of Darla's supposed life in France, Rebecca smiled. Missing, however, was the description of the making of any sort of film. By the fourth letter, the tone had changed. Loneliness pervaded her words, the longing for home apparent. Anticipation of returning was the only bright thought.

Melancholy, Rebecca picked up the last letter. The handwriting in this one wasn't as letter-perfect as in the previous four; manic, haphazard, written over time with various pens on torn, lined paper. Rebecca frowned.

I'm sorry I didn't tell you about the baby, Mama. I'm also sorry you never told me how hard it was to have one. I feel bad for how you must have suffered having me. But Lana is worth every gut-wrenching pain I had. She is so beautiful, and you will love her to death.

Jordan still hasn't come. There's a boy, a cute boy named Willie who comes every few days to bring me stuff. He even brought me Kotex. And some diapers and stuff for Lana. He's a sweetheart, and we like to talk about the movies. His mother is dead. He is an only child, just like me.

Rebecca paused, took a sip of tea. She remembered the man who'd taken her to the lighthouse the first time, Bill. He'd talked about a boy, a boy who'd died. His friend, he'd said.

Bill. Short for William.

Oh, Mama, if Jordan doesn't come back, I don't know what I'll do. I know Willie could get us off this nasty cold island, but without Jordan, I don't want to do anything. I believe once he sees Lana and me, he'll just know he has to leave that witch he's married to. She makes him so unhappy...

I don't know if Jordan will ever come back. I'm afraid he might have figured out he is not really Lana's father. Although I don't know how he could know. No one knows, but me. And no one will know, if I can help it, that Russell got me pregnant right before I went to Crescent City. No one but you, Mama. I know you'll keep my secret.

Yeah, I was stupid. I let Jordan believe he was the father and for a bit, I tried to make myself believe it, too. I had too. But during these awful weeks and months, I remembered. Certain things. Certain times. Things I did.

Luckily, Lana looks just like me. Luckily because I wouldn't want her to look like her real father. Someone might get nosy.

Rebecca's eyes raced over the words. But now, she stopped and backtracked.

Russell got me pregnant...

Russell Harrington. *Not* Jordan Kent. Slowly, Rebecca put down the letter and lifted her eyes to stare out the window once more. Her heart soared. That crazy old man, the one who'd actually killed her grandmother, was her biological grandfather. Not Jordan Kent.

This, most certainly, was a good reason to wake Matt.

Forty

Hollywood, California
October

Acrowd gathered at the Forest Lawn graveside in anticipation of the services about to begin. Rebecca looked around, surprised to find so many youthful faces in attendance. The obituary in the *L.A. Times* was to blame, Matt told her, for Jordan Kent had many fans that obsessed over his forties and fifties films. He'd become somewhat of a cult figure.

The funeral coordinator directed her to sit in the single row of folding chairs set up before the gleaming, flower-draped, mahogany coffin. Beside her, Matt, and then Eleanor, sat. On Rebecca's other side, Russell was seated in a wheelchair, Esme to his left.

The services were brief. The priest reviewed Jordan's illustrious life, extolled his long-term marriage to a wonderful woman who preceded him in death, credited his amassing a sizable wealth to a sharp business aptitude. Touched on a few philanthropic efforts. He went on to say that Jordan, while giving his last confession, expressed relief that several aspects of unfinished business had been resolved. He was at peace.

All aspects except one, Rebecca thought. Matt's request that they withhold the knowledge of Lana's true parentage may or may not have been the right choice. They would never know.

As they walked from the graveside, they detoured past a newly erected stone mausoleum.

Darla Mae Foster
1927 – 1949

"Do you think getting Darla settled allowed your grandfather to let go of life?" Rebecca asked.

"It's likely. He was a troubled man for most of his life. Seeing her buried must have been very liberating. Do you regret not moving your mother to rest here with Darla?"

"Mom would want to stay in Arizona. She didn't know this mother. She knew Daddy. They planned their burial many years ago. He wouldn't have agreed to it anyway." She pondered a moment, smiled. "At least here, Darla is close to Jordan."

Matt nodded, opened the car door for her. "Are you up to this deal? There'll be an even bigger crowd."

"We really need to be there."

Mourners filled Jordan's Hollywood mansion.

"This is all yours, now," Rebecca said, spreading her arms wide as she stood in the massive living room. "Were you surprised?"

"Yes. I was. He never told me. He handled his will through another attorney. Mom already has some pretty nice digs up the hill, though."

"And he stipulated that my grandfather's care be continued for his lifetime. That was…kind of him."

"I would have done that anyway." Matt shrugged. "He's still my loony great-uncle."

"I guess this means you can finish the Boys and Girls Club in style," Rebecca pointed out.

"Oh, yeah. I have big plans for that. And for finishing our house up there."

"*Our* house?"

Matt lowered his chin, smiled.

They strolled together through the home, greeting visitors. A number of Eleanor's friends and Matt's associates attended, along with a smattering of Hollywood's Golden Age survivors. Stephen Sisco approached them.

"What will happen to the Rock now?" Sisco wanted to know, accepting a glass of champagne from a passing waiter.

"There's a group of preservationists that have been hounding us for years. I think they're finally going to get their wish. They're already organizing a fundraiser. There will be a memorial plaque out there for Miss Foster," Matt told him.

"Send me the details. I'd like to be a part of that."

Because the funeral coordinator thought it a good idea, the screening room projected a restored version of *Cape Seduction*. A dozen or so people watched from plush theatre seats. Rebecca and Matt slipped into the back row, holding hands.

Her heart was calm. Thanks to a simple DNA test to alleviate her fears, her future was finally clear. Rebecca rested her head against Matt's shoulder and watched the sweet and complicated romance play out on the big screen of the Kent family theater.

"Catch me if you can," Darla shouted over her shoulder with a laugh as she hurried up the wooden stairway toward the base of Dragon Rock Lighthouse. Jordan gave chase behind her, charging up the steps in hot pursuit. He caught up with her at the door and swept her into a passionate embrace. The camera closed in for their deep, intimate kiss. Jordan pulled back, peered into her eyes.

"I love you, Darla," he whispered. "More than you'll ever know."

THE END

If you enjoyed this book, now would be a great time to post a review. Scan the code to take you to my Amazon page, and many thanks!

Excerpt from:

Angel's Gate by Anne Carter
Beacon Point Romance – Book Three

Chapter 1

June, 2012 - Los Angeles, California
Nate stood amidst a group of teary-eyed strangers, mourning a man he didn't know. Watching from behind scratched dark glasses, he perused the people surrounding the gravesite, only remotely listening to the words being offered by the minister. Words about a life so foreign to Nate he nearly smiled at the irony.

He bowed his head, his hands lightly clasped before him. He'd already spotted the one he'd really come to see. A man whose own sunglasses failed to hide the grief in his eyes, whose jaw worked as he fought to restrain his emotions. A woman sat beside him, clutching his arm, occasionally turning to check on three children and one teen sitting on her other side.

Nate trained his eyes upon them for a while, wondering about their lives, so different from his own. There was affluence there. While he couldn't name or even know the labels, Nate recognized that the clothing they wore was tailored from fancy materials. Looking down, he brushed a tiny leaf from the borrowed suit coat that hung loosely upon his narrow frame.

Several of the attendees were elderly men. A couple in wheelchairs, some with attendants. Nate grimaced at the sight of a frail man with a tube emerging from his throat, possibly some kind of breathing apparatus. The man wore a military uniform.

311

Perhaps the men were relatives of the deceased. Nate looked back to the younger man, seated in the front row with his family, whose shoulders now shook gently as his wife tried to comfort him. Nate's own throat tightened at the sight. He sucked in his upper lip and bit it lightly, wondering if the trip to L.A. had been a mistake.

At the point where the pall bearers began to lower the ivory, flower-strewn coffin into the ground, Nate slowly backed away and turned to go.

"Too bad Sean couldn't make it." Maddie slipped out of her heels and into a pair of flats.

"My brother is clearly too important to attend his own father's funeral," Jack muttered, hanging up his suit coat. "But why should today be any different?"

"I'm sure he'll be here soon. It was sudden, Jack. Sean's in the middle of that big mess. He *is* the dean of the university..."

"Yeah. Whatever. It's just that whenever Mom and Dad need him, he's in the middle of something. It's always me." Jack sat down on the bed and hung his head. "Never mind. Just feeling sorry for myself."

"You're entitled. By the way, there was a message on your phone from the board and care. Your mom's doing better. The doctor said not to worry about her, nothing will change for now."

"That's at least a relief."

Maddie nodded. "Hey, did you see that guy today?" she asked while helping Claire to untangle her discarded sweater. "Standing in the back?"

"There were a lot of people there, Mad. Who are you talking about?" Jack loosened his tie, slipped it off. "Dad had lots of friends I didn't know."

"He was young. Black hair, sunglasses, black suit..."

"And that describes a lot of the guys there." Jack tried to keep the annoyance he felt from his voice.

"But *young*. Maybe... twenty-five, twenty-seven. He had a scar on his forehead, over his left eyebrow. He walked away during the interment."

Jack shrugged. "Who knows? Maybe he worked for the company."

"Just seemed odd, that's all. I don't think he spoke to anyone else. Like he was a complete stranger."

"We're all strangers."

Maddie went to her husband and embraced him. "You gonna be all right?"

"I will be. After a pint of Guinness."

Nate didn't rush. His bus to Phoenix wouldn't leave for an hour, and he preferred the brisk morning walk to sitting in a dim and aging terminal. There'd be plenty of time to sit.

As he thought about Jack McKenzie and his family, he tried to keep the jealousy at bay. Envy was a liability, not an asset. It solved nothing. And Jack surely wasn't a bad man. Look at the outpouring of love at the funeral! His many friends were a testament to his character.

Yet Nate couldn't help the lingering desire to be a part of that world.

###

Meet Anne Carter

Everyone needs a little romance in their lives," Anne Carter will assure you. "Some need more than others." She should know. A storyteller since 7th grade, Anne and her younger sister would dream up a new chapter to a romantic saga each night before going to bed. Soon, writing became an obsession. Raised in Southern California where she, her husband and three children make their home, Anne interrupts her passion occasionally to run her bookkeeping business and possibly put dinner on the table.

Cape Seduction is the third book (including the prequel) from the Beacon Point Romance series. Anne asks: "What ties these stories of romance and intrigue together? Lighthouses - and mysteries brought upon a group of friends who solve them - while falling in love, of course!"

Ever & Always, the series prequel, details Jack & Maddie's history and courtship. Jack McKenzie goes on to appear as a supporting character in *Point Surrender* and *Cape Seduction*. Finally, Jack gets his own romantic suspense in *Angel's Gate*.

If you enjoyed this book, please consider leaving a review on Amazon or your favorite review site. Thank you!

Visit Anne at http://www.AuthorAnneCarter.com

Also by Anne Carter

Paulie & Kate's Story:

Unmasking Paulie Bingham
For the Love of Katrina Bingham

StarCrossed Romances (Series):

StarCrossed Hearts
A Hero's Promise
The Gypsy in Me

Beacon Point Romances (Series):

Ever & Always (Prequel)
Point Surrender
Cape Seduction
Angel's Gate

Redmond Family Secrets (Series):

The Secrets Within Us
Make Me Tell Lies
My Truth Be Told